MW01115765

THE GIRL IN THE LOVE SONG

EMMA SCOTT

The Girl in the Love Song

Cover Art by Lori Jackson Designs
Interior Formatting by That Formatting Lady
Editing by Rebecca Fairest Reviews

www.emmascottwrites.com

PLAYLIST

I Can't Make You Love Me // Bon Iver (opening credits)
Dissolve //Absofacto
Yellow // Coldplay
Godzilla // Eminem
Dance Monkey // Tones and I
Take Me to Church // Hozier
when the party's over // Billie Eilish
Take What You Want // Post Malone (feat. Ozzie Osbourne)
The Best // Awolnation
Finally/Beautiful Stranger // Halsey
Perfect // Ed Sheeran
The Greatest // Sia (closing credits)

MILLER'S SONGS

All I'll Ever Want // music by Future Ghost Brothers, feat. Rich Trapp and Joshua Lopez, lyrics by Emma Scott

Wait for Me // music by Future Ghost Brothers, feat. Rich Trapp and Joshua Lopez, lyrics by Emma Scott

DEDICATION

For Robin, who saw this book when I couldn't and who helped me get back up every time I fell down. With love.

PART I

i

Dear Diary,

The first thing you should know about me, since we're going to be friends, is that my name is Violet McNamara, and I'm thirteen years old. Today is my birthday and you are one of my presents. Mom gave you to me because I'm on the "cusp of womanhood" —insert major eyeroll—and said I might want to write down my emotions. She says they're bound to get "dramatic" at this age and writing them out can help keep them from burrowing deep and then spewing out later.

That's ironic. Lately, she and Dad have been spewing out their "dramatic emotions," screaming constantly at each other. Maybe they need a diary, too. Maybe that's what I'll get them for their anniversary next month. If they make it that far. I don't know what happened. We were all so happy and then it started to dissolve, piece by piece.

God, they're screaming right now. This house is huge and yet they fill it up with their rage. Where did it come from??? Makes my stomach feel weird and I just want it to stop.

Happy Birthday to me.

I set my pen down and put my headphones on. Absofacto blared in my ears, drowning out Mom and Dad's raised voices. A shattering of glass broke through my music. I flinched, my heart jumping in my chest, and a teardrop smeared the ink on my first diary entry. I carefully dabbed it away, turned up the music, and waited for the storm to pass.

They're done now, but God, one of them smashed something. Mom probably. That's the second time that's happened. Things are getting worse. Just two weeks ago, they were still sleeping in the same bed and now Mom's taken over the bedroom and Dad's in the den.

Maybe it's a phase. Maybe if I work hard enough and make them proud of me, they'll be happy again, and everything can go back to the way it was. I'm going to be a doctor. A surgeon. Someone who puts broken things back together. Maybe I'll start with them, ha ha.

Anyway, I don't want to write more about what's happening to this family. I'll write about something better. Namely, River Whitmore. <3

It's probably every cliché multiplied by a million to fill a diary with thoughts about boys, but I've had a crush on River since forever. But if you saw him, Diary, you'd understand. He's like a thirteen-year-old Henry Cavill, only not British. You can tell he's going to be big and muscular and sexy when he's older. (OMG I can't believe I wrote that!)

ANYWAY, his dad owns Whitmore's Auto Body shop, and River helps out there in the summer. When Dad takes the Jag in for any work, I tag along, even though I always clam up around River. Another cliché: the nerdy girl and the popular jock who doesn't know she exists. He's a star football player who's going to keep playing quarterback all through high school and then in college or maybe he'll go straight to the NFL.

That's what his dad is always saying, anyway.

As for me, UCSC is my dream school. Santa Cruz is so beautiful. I can't imagine living anywhere else. I'll eventually have to leave for med school, of course, which will be hard since specializing in general surgery means years of study. And a crap-ton of student loan debt. But get this: for my last birthday, Mom and Dad said they'd pay for all of it!!!

I was over-the-moon happy when they told me. Grateful beyond words and glad because I could stay close to them. Only now it feels like our happy life was temporary, and it's all falling apart. I don't know what happened to them. Something money-related, I think. (See? Money can really suck)

Anyway, I~

My pen scratched at the paper as a sudden silence jarred me. There was a trellis on the wall outside my second-story bedroom, and a bunch of frogs that lived in the leafy vines had just gone quiet. Sometimes, I'd imagine River Whitmore climbing the trellis to rescue me from my parents and their disintegrating marriage, but it would also make a perfect ladder for an intruder. I snapped off my desk lamp and sank back into the darkness of my room, breath held.

Slowly, the frogs started up again.

I pushed my glasses higher up on my nose and looked out my window, over the darkened Pogonip forest of redwood and oak that bordered our backyard, then leaned over my desk and peered down.

There was a kid. A boy.

He looked about my age, though it was hard to tell only by the light of the moon hanging fatly in the sky. He had longish brown hair, and his shoulders were hunched into a dark jacket. The boy paced a small circle in frustration, as if he'd come to a dead-end—my house—and didn't know where else to go.

I glanced at my clock; it was nearly ten.

Why is he out here? Alone?

The boy slumped against the wall beneath me, next to one of the coiled hoses hanging off its faucet. The frogs went quiet again as he slid down to sit on his butt. He drew his legs up, dangled his wrists off his bent knees and hung his head. I wondered if he was going to sleep like that.

I ran my tongue over my braces, thinking. Should I call Dad? The police? But that would get the boy in trouble, and he looked like he was already having a crappy day.

I lifted my window and warm June air wafted in. Wood scraped wood, and the boy's head shot up. Moonlight fell over his face, and I sucked in a little breath.

He's beautiful.

What a random, silly thought. Boys aren't *beautiful.* None that I knew. Not even River, who was more dashingly handsome. Before I could debate this issue with myself further, the boy scrambled to his feet, ready to run.

"Wait, don't go!" I called in a hissing whisper, shocking him and myself in the process. I don't know what prompted me to stop him or why. It just popped out, like I couldn't help myself. Like it'd be a mistake to let him go.

The boy stopped at the edge of the boundary where the path became forest. I lifted the sash higher, so I could lean over and rest my arms on the sill.

"What are you doing out here?" I whisper-shouted.

"Nothing."

"You came out of the woods?"

"Yeah. So?"

"Well, it's trespassing for one. This is private property. You shouldn't be here."

They were always saying that on TV, sounded good then.

The boy scowled. "You just told me not to go."

"Because I wondered what the heck you were doing. It's late."

"I was just…taking a walk."

"Where do you live?"

"Nowhere. I don't know. Someone's going to hear us."

"Nah. Our neighbors are pretty far." I sucked on my braces again. "But this whispering sucks. I'll come down."

"Why?"

"To talk better," I said and wondered if turning thirteen had magically erased some of my shyness.

Or maybe it's just this boy.

"You don't know me," he said. "I could be dangerous."

"Are you?"

He thought for a second. "Maybe."

I pursed my lips. "Are you going to hurt me if I come down there?"

"*No*," he said, irritated. "But you shouldn't be taking chances."

"Just stay put."

I was in my pajamas—leggings with a slouchy UCSC sweatshirt over them. I grabbed my Converse shoes from the closet of my super-neat room and slipped them over my socks.

I stuck my head out the window again. The boy was still there.

"Be right down."

I sounded as if I climbed down the trellis on the regular. I wasn't the sneaking-out-at-night type of kid, but I was surprising myself right and left that night. I tucked my dark hair out of my way, climbed up onto my desk, and then stuck one foot out onto the ledge.

"Don't," the boy said from below. "You're gonna fall."

"I will not," I said, and carefully found my grip on the inside of the window ledge with my hands while my right foot snaked out for a rung on the trellis.

"How do you know it'll hold?" the boy called up.

I had no idea if it would hold, but I'd already left the safety of the window ledge for the thinner, wooden crisscrosses of the trellis. I brushed vines out of my way and climbed slowly down, making sure to take my time, to find each foothold. Then I plopped to the ground and dusted my hands together.

"See? Stronger than it looks," I said.

The boy glowered. "You could've been hurt."

"Why do you care?"

"I…I don't. Just saying."

He jammed his hands in his jacket pockets and flipped a lock of hair out of his eyes. He had beautiful eyes—blue like topaz. Up close, I could see his jeans had holes in them and not because that was the style. His jacket was worn at the elbows, and his hiking boots were scuffed, the laces held together by knots. A ratty old blue backpack hung off his shoulders.

But he was even better looking than I imagined from that first glimpse, though in a totally different way than River. This boy had a softer face, somehow. Still manly—I imagined he'd grow up to be very handsome. His eyebrows were thick but not too thick and looked perpetually knitted together with worry. He had a nice nose, and his mouth was pretty perfect. I actually had no idea what a "perfect" mouth looked like on a boy, except that this boy had one.

We stood for a few quiet moments, taking each other in. The boy's eyes swept over me and I wondered if he were taking inventory of me the same way I had of him. Normally, I'd have been self-conscious about my glasses, my braces, and my boobs that were growing in faster than I was ready for. I had no feature that anyone would call "perfect," yet somehow, it was okay to be standing there in the dark with him.

"So…I'm Violet."

"Miller."

"Miller is your first name?"

"Yeah. So?"

"It's usually a last name."

"Violet is usually a color."

"It's still a name."

Now that we weren't whispering, I noticed Miller's voice had pretty much already changed. Deepening but without that squeak to it, like poor Benji Pelcher, who sounded like he took hits off helium balloons. Miller had a nice voice. Low and kind of scratchy.

"Well?" Miller asked. "What do you want?"

I cocked my head at him. "You're awfully grouchy."

"Maybe I have a reason to be."

"Which is…?"

"None of your business." He glanced around at the darkened forest behind him. "I should get back."

He said it with a kind of sadness. The giving-up kind. Like he would rather do anything than go back.

So don't let him go.

I softened my tone. "Can you at least tell me what you're doing out here?"

"I told you. Taking a walk."

"In a dark forest at night? Do you live nearby? I've never seen you before."

"We just moved. Me and my mom."

"Cool. Then we're neighbors."

Miller jerked his chin at my house. "I don't live in a house like that."

The bitterness in his voice was so strong, I could practically taste it.

"Won't your mom worry you're out here?"

"She's at work."

"Oh."

I didn't know any parents who worked at night in my neighborhood, unless they were in tech like my dad. He spent late hours at his computer, but I doubted that Miller's mom was working late at InoDyne or one of the other big places near the university.

Most tech kids could afford shoelaces.

A silence fell, and Miller kicked at the dirt with his boot, hands still jammed in his jacket pockets, eyes on the ground, as if waiting for something to happen next. Frogs chirped, and the forest breathed behind him.

"So, you're new here?"

He nodded.

"I go to Coastline Middle."

"I'll go there too."

"Cool. Maybe we'll have some of the same classes."

Maybe we can be friends.

"Maybe." He glanced up at my house, a longing expression on his face.

"Why do you keep staring at my house?"

"I'm not. It's just…big."

"It's all right." I slumped down against the wall like he had earlier.

He smirked and sat beside me. “What’s wrong with it? Not enough butlers?”

“Ha ha. The house is fine. It was perfect, actually.”

“And now it’s not?”

“My parents aren’t happy lately.”

“Whose are?” Miller tossed a pebble into the dark.

“Yeah, but I mean, they’re *a lot* unhappy. Like screaming matches and throwing things…never mind.” My cheeks burned. Why did I say that?

But Miller’s eyes widened in alarm. “They throw things? At you?”

“No, it was just the one time,” I said quickly. “Maybe twice but that’s it. No big deal.” I cleared my throat. “All parents fight, right?”

“I wouldn’t know. My dad died a few months ago,” he said, looking away. “Just me and Mom now.”

“Oh my God, I’m so sorry,” I said softly. “That’s got to be hard.”

“What do you know about it?” Miller asked with sudden tightness in his voice. “At least you can live here. At least if your parents start shouting, you probably have a big cushy room to hide out in, instead of…”

“Instead of what?”

“Nothing.”

Another silence fell. Miller’s stomach growled, and he quickly tried to cover up the sound by scuffing his boots. He started to rise. “I gotta go.”

But I didn’t want him to go.

“Today is my birthday,” I said.

Miller froze and then sat back down. “Yeah?”

“Yeah. I’m thirteen. You?”

“Fourteen in January. You had a big party, I suppose.”

“No. My friend Shiloh and I saw a movie and then my parents bought me a cake. I only ate one piece, and I don’t think Mom and Dad had any. There’s a lot left. Do you want some?”

Miller’s narrow shoulders rose and fell.

“It’s going to go to waste if we don’t eat it,” I said. “And there’s nothing sadder than a birthday cake with only one piece cut out.”

“I can think of a hundred things sadder,” Miller said. “But yeah, I could eat some cake.”

“Great.” I got to my feet and swiped dirt off my butt. “Let’s go”

“Into your house? What about your parents?”

"It's safe in my room. Dad sleeps in the den now. Mom will be in her room, but she never checks on me. Like, ever."

Miller frowned. "You're gonna let me hang out in your bedroom?"

I started to climb back up the trellis. "Yes. I never do anything I'm not supposed to, but today's my birthday and they screamed at each other on my birthday, so here we are." I peered over my shoulder down to him. "Are you coming or not?"

"I guess."

"So, come on."

I climbed back into my room and Miller followed. I moved the lamp to make room for him as he crawled across my desk and gracefully jumped down.

"Now we know the trellis can hold both of us," I said.

Not sure why I felt that was important, except that something told me, even then, that this wasn't going to be the last time Miller came up to my room.

But having him there, up close, and in the light of my desk lamp my insides felt funny. A little bit scared, a little bit nervous, a little bit excited. He was taller than me by a few inches, and his blue eyes looked miles deep. Filled with thoughts and a heaviness I didn't see in any kid I knew, except maybe my best friend, Shiloh.

He saw me watching him and how my hands were clutched together in front of me.

"What?" he asked warily.

"I don't know," I said, pushing my glasses up and fidgeting with a lock of my black hair. "Now that you're up here, it's a little…different."

"I'm not going to steal anything. And I won't hurt you, Violet. I never would. But I'll go if you want."

"I don't want you to go."

Miller's brows unfurrowed for a moment, softening his entire face, and his bunched shoulders loosened.

"Okay," he said roughly. "I'll stay."

My heart squeezed with a little ache at how grateful he sounded. Like he wasn't used to be wanted around, maybe.

He looked away from me—I was probably staring—to take in my impeccably neat room with its queen-sized bed and white, ruffled comforter. Bookshelves took up the wall facing the window, and posters of Michelle Obama, Ruth Bader Ginsberg, and the soccer player, Megan Rapinoe, up on the walls.

"Don't all girls cover their walls with movie or rock stars?"

"Yes, because *all* girls are exactly the same," I said with a grin. "These are my inspirations. Michelle reminds me to stay classy, Ruth keeps me honest, and Megan pushes me to do my best. I play soccer, too."

"Cool." Miller's eyes widened, taking in my en suite bathroom. "You have your own bathroom? Wow. Okay." He gave his head a disbelieving shake. He looked almost mad.

"Okay, so um, hang tight," I said. "I'll go get the cake."

I left Miller in my room and shut the door quietly behind me, then crept along the long hallway, passing guestrooms and bathrooms, toward the staircase. My nervousness tried to creep back in.

It's a little bit crazy to let a perfect stranger into our house. You know that, right?

But I was a straight-A student, and teachers were always telling me how smart I was, how I had a knack for remembering facts. And the fact was, Miller had shown concern for my safety no less than three times in our short conversation. His grouchiness came from suspicion, like he couldn't figure out why I was being nice to him.

Because he's not used to people being nice to him. Or bedrooms with attached bathrooms.

In our huge, granite-and-stainless-steel kitchen, I took the birthday cake box out of the fridge. The sound of Miller's growling stomach echoed in my head, so I filled a Trader Joe's shopping bag with paper plates, a bag of tortilla chips, a jar of salsa, two cans of Coke, forks and napkins. I slung the bag on my shoulder, carried the cake box with both hands, and snuck back upstairs.

I fumbled my bedroom door open. Miller was gone.

"Crap." My shoulders slumped with disappointment that bit harder than I expected. Then I nearly dropped the cake box when Miller appeared from my walk-in closet.

"Wasn't sure if it was you," he said.

"I thought you bailed on me."

"Still here." He eyed my grocery bag, and his voice tightened. "What's all that?"

"Food. I've been studying all night—"

"You study in the summer?"

"Yes. I take high school prep classes. I'm going to be a doctor someday. A surgeon. That takes years of school and training so I'm trying to get ahead."

"Oh. Cool."

"So, I was studying, and it made me hungrier than I realized. It's not much. Just chips and salsa and soda. Plus, birthday cake. Not exactly *Health Food Weekly*'s snacks of choice…"

Miller said nothing, and I sensed that he was too smart to fall for my thinly disguised charity. His hunger must've overcome his pride, though, because he didn't argue but let me set up our small picnic on the floor, shielded by the bed should a parental unit walk in.

I sat against the wall while Miller sat perpendicular to me, against my bed, his long legs in front of him. I laid out the food, and we ate and talked about some of the kids at school he'd meet.

"The captain of the youth football team is the quarterback, River Whitmore," I said and immediately wished I hadn't made him my opener. My face flushed red. "Do you play football?"

"No."

"Um, yeah, so he's the quarterback."

"You said that already." Miller's sharp gaze slid to me then away. "You like him."

"*What?*" I practically shrieked, then lowered my voice. "No, I… Why do you think that?"

"Because of how you said his name. And your face got all red. Is he your boyfriend?"

"Hardly. I mean, look at me."

"I am looking at you."

And he did. His topaz eyes were on me, not just observing but *seeing* me. I felt as if the deepest secrets of my heart were painted all over my face. Warmth swept over my skin and I had to look away.

"You know how it is," I said. "I'm a geek, and he's a football god. He doesn't know I exist. But we've been in school together since kindergarten and I… I don't know. I can't remember a time when I didn't have a crush on him." I smacked both hands to my cheeks. "I can't believe I just told you all that. Please *do not* tell anyone when school starts. I'll be mortified."

Miller looked away, reached for his soda. "I'll forget you even mentioned it."

"Right, so…anyway, you'll also meet Shiloh. She's super smart and sarcastic. And beautiful, too. She looks a lot like Zoë Kravitz. She's my best friend. My *only* friend."

"I got none. You're doing all right."

"Yeah, but you just moved here. I've lived here my whole life." I brushed a lock of hair behind my ear. "But you and me—we're friends now, right? Let's exchange phone numbers! So we can text." I grabbed mine from off the bed. "Holy crap, it'll be so cool to get a text and not automatically know it's Shiloh."

"I don't have a cell phone," Miller said, brushing his hands off on his torn jeans, not looking at me.

"Oh. Wait, really?" I let my phone drop in my lap. "How do you survive?"

"If you have to live without something, you just do."

"I can't imagine it."

He scowled. "I'll bet."

"Hey…"

"Well? Didn't you just say you couldn't imagine it?"

"Yes, but that's not fair to—"

"Fair?" Miller scoffed. "You have no idea about fair."

"Why are you getting mad at me?"

He opened his mouth then snapped it shut. "I'm not."

I let a few seconds go, then glanced up at him. "It's okay. You can tell me stuff. If you want."

"What kind of stuff?"

"Any kind."

Like where you live.

"We just met," Miller said. "And you're a girl."

"So?"

"So. Guys don't talk about stuff with girls. They talk with other guys."

"Friends talk to each other, remember? And besides…" I made a show of looking around and then peeked under the bed. "No guys here."

He snorted a laugh. "God, you're a dork. But kind of brave, too."

"You think I'm brave?"

He nodded.

My cheeks felt warm. "No one's ever called me brave before."

A small smile flickered over his lips as our eyes met. The air between us seemed to soften and grow still. Kind of perfect, just sitting there with this boy on my birthday.

Then my mom threw open her bedroom door from down the hall with a *bang*, and her footsteps thumped down the stairs.

I flinched, and then Miller and I froze. A few minutes later, her voice rose and my father answered, both of them growing louder and louder, until they were in a full-blown shouting match. I could feel Miller watching me, and my face burned. My stomach tightened into knots around all the food I'd just eaten, making me feel sick.

"I can't believe it," Mom screamed from below. *"Another one, Vince? How many more?"*

"Jesus Christ, it's after ten at night. Get off my back, Lynn!"

Their words became indistinct—Mom probably chasing Dad deeper into the house, waving some papers at him like I'd seen her do.

Humiliation burned right through the center of me. I drew my knees up and covered my ears, wishing they'd both drop dead. The green scent of pine needles and the spicy bite of salsa wafted over me.

I peeked one eye open. Miller had moved to sit beside me. He didn't put his arm around me but sat close enough that we were touching. Shoulder to shoulder. Making contact. Letting me know he was there.

I leaned over, tipping into him, and we listened until my parents' blow-up faded out. Mom's footsteps thumped back upstairs. Her door slammed. Below, the den door slammed too, and silence descended.

"They fight a lot?" Miller asked in a quiet voice.

I nodded against the worn material of his jacket. "They used to love each other and now they hate each other. I feel like I was in a simulation of the perfect family, but there's a glitch in the programming."

"Why don't they just get divorced?"

"I think there's some kind of money situation. They don't tell me anything, but I know they can't split up until it's fixed." My eyes stung. "But I keep hoping the money situation will sort itself out and it'll fix them too."

Miller said nothing, but I felt his shoulder press into me a little more.

"We're friends, Violet," he said finally, looking straight ahead.

"What?"

"You asked…and yeah. We're friends."

I peered up at him, and he looked down at me, and happiness filled in the cold spaces left by my parents' new hatred of each other.

I found a smile. "Ready for cake?"

I cut slices of strawberry cake with vanilla icing, and Miller and I ate and talked some more. I nearly made him spew Coke out his nose laughing, telling him about the time one of the skater dudes, Frankie Dowd, tried to jump his board off the lunch table in the cafeteria and fell, sending trays of food flying into people's laps.

"It set off a food fight," I said. "Oh my God, the principal was *pissed* and tried to give the entire seventh grade detention all at once."

Miller laughed harder. I loved his laugh; it sounded good in his scratchy voice and his entire face lit up. That stressed-out tension went away, just for a few minutes, and that made me feel like I'd done something even better than giving him food.

We ate until we were stuffed, and Miller heaved a sigh. "Crap, that was good…" A thought seemed to occur to him, and that damn worry swept right back over him again. "I should go."

"You don't have to—"

"Yeah, I do." He got to his feet and shouldered his backpack. "Thanks for the food. And the cake."

"Thanks for eating it with me, so I don't feel so pathetic."

"You're not pathetic," Miller said fiercely, then jammed his hands in his pockets. "Do you think maybe I can take another piece with me?"

"Take the whole thing. I don't want it."

"No," he said, his voice low. "I'm not taking your birthday cake. Just one piece. For my mom."

"Oh. Of course." I wrapped a piece of cake in napkins and handed it to him. "Miller…?"

"Don't," he said, putting the cake into his backpack.

"How do you know what I was about to say?"

"I know what you're going to ask but don't bother. Tonight was a good night. I don't want to mess it up."

"Telling me where you live would mess it up?"

"Yeah, it would. Trust me. Might mess *us* up."

"Us?"

"Being friends," he said quickly. "You might not want to be friends with me."

"I doubt that, but okay. I won't bother you about it anymore."

For now.

"Thanks. And thanks for the cake."

"Sure," I said. He started toward the window, and I bit my lip. "See you tomorrow?"

"You want me to come back?" His blue eyes lit up for a quick second, then he offered a careless shrug. "Yeah. Maybe."

I rolled my eyes and clasped my hands in front of me. "Oooh, *maybe.* So I'll just wait up all night for you, *hoping* and *praying* and *pining* for you to come back."

He laughed a little. "You're so weird."

"And you're grouchy. We sort of fit. Don't we?"

He nodded, his eyes dark in the dimness. "I'll see you tomorrow." He started to climb out the window.

"Hey, wait!" I said, stopping him. "I didn't ask your last name. Is it a *first* name? Ted? John…? Oh! Is your name Miller Henry?"

He smirked. "It's Stratton."

"Mine is McNamara. Nice to meet you, Miller Stratton."

He smiled but turned his head away before I could see all of it. "Happy Birthday, Violet."

Oh my God, Diary, that was nuts!!! I just snuck a boy in my room! We talked and ate and laughed, and I feel like I've known him forever. I don't know how else to explain it. Like when I met Shiloh, and we were friends right away. Miller's not like any other boy at school, who makes dumb sex jokes and plays video games all day. He's deep. No, that sounds cheesy. He has depth.

His grouchiness doesn't bother me either, and he didn't mind—too much—that I asked a million questions. Even so, he's still kind of a mystery. Like it could take years to get to know all of him, I think. He wouldn't tell me where he lived. I get the feeling he and his mom are poor since he was so hungry, and his clothes are in bad shape. But all the houses around here are huge. He can't have walked very far to get here.

I invited him back tomorrow. I hope he comes. I want to give him some more food without making it look like he's my charity case. But mostly, I want to talk to him more. I want to get to know him and let him get to know me. I mean, how often does that happen? Getting to know a brand-new person...that's kind of like opening a birthday present.

Speaking of which, I now have two friends.

Happy Birthday to me!

ii

Miller came back that night and the night after that, and for the next two months solid, as the summer came closer to its end. My first friend, Shiloh, lived with her Grandma but spent every summer in Louisiana visiting relatives, so Miller slipped into her vacancy perfectly.

We hung out in my room at night, eating snacks—Miller was always hungry. I studied and he wrote in an old, bent notebook. He never showed me what he was writing, and I never snooped. But once I caught a flash of a page and saw what looked like poetry.

Most days, we walked to downtown, or we went to the Boardwalk and played video games in the arcade before walking along the beach. Other times, Miller was busy doing odd jobs around town to make money to help his mom. He said she worked at the diner on 5th but he never brought me over there to meet her.

I introduced him to my parents, and by my secret request, Dad hired Miller to do yard work once a week, even though we already had a gardener.

"He paid me fifty bucks," Miller had told me later after his first day on the job. He glared at me accusingly. "That's too much."

"We have a huge lawn," I'd replied innocently.

He wanted to argue but I think he needed the money more.

One late August night, Miller sat with a notebook on his knees, scribbling at something while I studied.

I shut my algebra workbook and took my glasses off to rub my eyes. "Done. One less class I have to worry about in high school."

"You're going to be like that old show, *Doogie Howser*," Miller said, finishing off the ham and cheese sandwich I'd made him. "You'll be in college when you're sixteen."

"Nah. I'm not that good."

"You're damn smart, Vi," he said.

That was another thing. He started calling me Vi. Which I sort of loved.

"Are you ever going to tell me what you're writing?" I asked.

"My college master's thesis." He tucked the notebook in his backpack. "Thought I'd get a jump on it."

"Ha ha." I shrugged my shoulders up and down and stretched my legs in front of me. "I'm nervous."

"Why?"

"You're meeting Shiloh tomorrow."

She was back from New Orleans, and I thought it was overdue for Friend One to meet Friend Two.

"That makes you nervous?"

I toyed with my pen. "You might like her more than me."

"Then I won't meet her."

"That's…dumb."

"Yeah, it is," he said, watching me with the intent way he had. Like he was absorbing me somehow, in all my geeky glory. "Because there's no way I'm going to like her more than you."

"How do you know?"

"I just know." Miller's eyes darkened. "Besides, what do you care? You like River What's His Name."

"True, but that's just a pipe dream. I may as well have a crush on Justin Trudeau since it's *never going to happen.* And anyway, I'm not worried about you *liking* Shiloh. She says she'll never date a boy ever, though she won't tell me why. I'm worried you guys will hit it off and be BFFs." I shrugged a shoulder. "I don't want to be left out."

"I won't ever leave you out."

Irritation scratched at me for being so self-conscious. "Ugh, forget it. I was friends with her first and I was friends with you first, so why am I the one worried about being left out?"

"Because you overthink everything." Miller gave me one of his rare smiles. "I don't even want to meet her. I hate her already."

I smirked. "You're not allowed to hate her. Just ignore me. I'm being silly."

"Paranoid, maybe…" he teased and then yawned.

Dark circles ringed his eyes lately, and his face was pale in the light of my desk lamp. Miller always seemed kind of sad, but the sadness had worsened over the last few days. Sunken into him deeper, somehow. I'd tried to ask him about it several times—about being tired and the headaches he seemed to have a lot. But he always shut me down and assured me he was fine.

But it's obvious, he's not fine.

I bit my lip. "Can I be honest?"

"When are you not?"

"You don't look so good. Are you okay? Don't mess around. Tell me for real."

"I'm fine."

"You look like you've lost weight—"

"I'm fine, Doctor McNamara. It's just a headache."

"You keep saying that but you're not getting better. Is it because school is almost starting? Are you nervous about that?"

Miller said nothing. I moved from my desk chair to sit beside him, but he jumped to his feet. "I need to use your bathroom."

He went and closed the door. I heard him pee and then run the faucet.

"That's another thing," I said when he came back out. "You're always thirsty, always peeing."

"Jesus, Vi."

"It's true. So, it makes me wonder." I swallowed hard. "Do you not have…plumbing at your house? Running water?"

"Leave it alone."

"You can tell me, Miller. You know you can."

"I can't."

"You can, and I—"

"Forget it. You wouldn't look at me the same way." He slung his ratty backpack on his shoulder. "I gotta go."

"Fine," I said, pretending to be mad. "I'll see you tomorrow."

"Vi…don't be like that," he said tiredly. "There's not anything you can do, so don't worry about it."

"I said *fine*. You don't want to talk about it, so I won't." I made a big show of stretching and yawning. "I'm going to bed."

He studied me a moment longer, then nodded. "Okay. See you tomorrow."

"Yep."

Miller climbed out the window. When he was below my line of vision, I threw on my shoes and grabbed my sweatshirt, then peeked over the ledge. He had just reached the ground and was heading back to the woods. I counted to ten in my head, then climbed out as quietly as I could and ducked into the woods after him.

He was a dark, indistinct shape moving in the shadows, weaving between the looming trees, blocking out the moonlight. It was so dark, I could hardly see where to put my feet. I nearly had to give up and turn around. Then Miller turned on the mini flashlight he kept strapped to his backpack, and I followed his light deeper into the woods.

He took the access road that the park rangers had probably used a long time ago. It was overgrown now with greenery and potholes. Miller kept to the edge, heading northwest, deeper into the forest. I wondered if there were cabins this far in. The Golf Club was on the other side of the Pogonip. Maybe his mom worked there at night and they had housing for their employees…?

Wrong. So, so wrong.

Just off the old access road sat a station wagon. Old, olive green with wood panels. Rusted. Dented. T-shirts were tucked into the windows to make curtains. A woman's T-shirt lay rumpled on the dash, along with fast food wrappers and empty drink cups. The car was sunken into the ground, like it hadn't moved in so long, it was becoming part of the forest. My heart clenched as if I'd been punched in the chest. There was no destination this car would take them to. It *was* the destination.

I peeked from behind a tree as Miller unlocked the back hatch on the station wagon. He dragged a cooler out onto the ground, opened it, grabbed a water bottle. He sank on the closed cooler and drank the entire bottle down, then his shoulders slumped. Defeated.

My eyes filled with tears. I stepped out of the woods and onto the access road where the moonlight shone brightest.

"Hi."

His head shot up in alarm, then he hung his head again.

"Hello, Vi," he said dully.

"You're not surprised to see me?"

"I'm more surprised you haven't followed me sooner. Have you?"

"No," I said. I was in front of him now, the two of us standing in the dark and my voice cracking. "Miller…"

"Don't do that," he said, jabbing a finger at me. "Don't fucking cry for me, Vi. Don't feel sorry for me."

"I can't help it. I care about you. And you never said… You never told me…"

"Why would I?"

"For help. You never asked for help."

"There is no help. What can you do?"

I shook my head helplessly. "I don't know. Something. Anything."

"You give me food. That's enough. It's too much."

"No…" I glanced around, trying to comprehend how two people's lives could fit in one car. How they had to cram their entire selves into that small space.

How could Miller fit when he's so much?

"Where…?" I swallowed, tried again. "Where do you shower?"

"Friendship Park, at the clubhouse."

"That's for members only."

"I sneak in. You don't want to hear this, Vi."

"Yes. Yes, I do."

Tears were streaming now.

He's so brave.

I didn't know what I meant by that, but it felt true. Brave that he lived this way, never complaining, never stealing. Doing odd jobs to help his mom out.

"It's not because of drugs, if that's what you're thinking," Miller said, darkly. "My dad left and took all the money."

"You said he died."

"Because I wish he were dead. But he left and we were evicted from our apartment in Los Banos. My mom thought we'd get a fresh start here. Lots of jobs. But it's too expensive and the car fucking broke down, so we can't leave. But she got a job at a café, and at night…"

He shook his head, his blue eyes glittering in the dark. I waited, my breath held.

"Sometimes does stuff with men for money. How's that? Heard enough yet? Want to know what it's like to wash your hair in a Costco bathroom? Or listen to your mom come back to this fucking car, smelling like strange men and smiling at you with smeared lipstick, telling you everything's going to be okay?"

I sucked in a shaking breath. "Where is she now?"

"Where do you think?"

"Will she be back tonight?"

"I don't know. Sometimes they let her stay over at the motel to shower and stuff. If they do, she stays and sleeps in a real bed. I don't blame her. Then she'll go right to her job at the café in the morning."

I wiped my nose. “Leave her a note and get your stuff.”

“Where am I going?”

“With me, Miller. You’re coming with me.”

He looked too tired, too damn defeated to argue. He put the cooler away and grabbed his ratty old backpack.

“You have laundry?”

He nodded.

“Get it.”

I waited a respectful distance away while he reemerged from the back of the station wagon with a trash bag, half-full. We walked in silence back to my house, Miller leading, since he knew the way best. Instead of going around the back, up the trellis, I took us through the side door to the garage and led us straight into the laundry room.

“Your parents?”

“If they see us, I’ll say you got grass stains working on the garden. You’re here because your mom’s working late, and you got locked out of your…house.” My throat tightened. “You have to spend the night.”

Miller nodded listlessly.

I opened the lid, and he poured his clothes—and a few items of his mom’s—into the huge washer. Then I took him by the hand and led him through the house, upstairs to my bedroom, stopping at the linen closet on the way. I grabbed a towel, and inside my room, pointed him toward the bathroom.

“Take a shower if you want. Or a bath. Take as long as you want but toss your clothes out, and I’ll add them to the wash.”

“You want me to give you my underwear?”

“Wrap them in the jeans. I don’t care. I won’t look anyway.”

Miller did as he was told, and I took the bundle of his clothes downstairs. They didn’t smell bad. They smelled of the forest and leathery car interior and him.

When the washing machine was churning, I headed to the kitchen and grabbed a shopping bag. I took two bottles of Mom’s favorite water and dumped them in.

No running water. No toilet. No sink. No shower.

Tears filled my eyes again, but I blinked them away and grabbed two more water bottles. I was determined to change Miller’s reality somehow, but the guilt that I hadn’t followed him sooner was hot and sharp in my chest.

Mom must've gone to the grocery store that day; the fridge and pantry were stocked. I made two ham and cheese sandwiches and wrapped them in tinfoil, then grabbed a bag of Doritos and a package of chocolate chip cookies and headed upstairs.

Miller was just turning off the shower when I arrived back in my room. I set the bag down and rummaged through my drawers for the least girly things I owned: a pair of black and white plaid flannel pants and a white UCSC sweatshirt with the yellow banana slug mascot on the front.

The bathroom door cracked open, steam seeping out.

"Uh, Vi…?"

"Here." I put the clothes in his hand.

He came out of the bathroom a few minutes later. The flannels were too short for him but fit around his narrow waist. He eyed the grocery bag.

"You can eat now or take it with you," I said.

"I'm tired."

"Then sleep."

In a real bed.

I pulled back the covers and climbed into bed. Miller hesitated, then climbed in beside me. We lay on our sides, facing each other. His head sunk into the pillow and he sighed with relief so deep I nearly cried.

"How long?" I asked.

"Eleven weeks, three days, twenty-one hours."

I bit the inside of my cheek. "You can't stay there anymore."

"I know. When school starts…I don't know what the hell to do. They'll crucify me."

"They don't have to know. But you have to get out. To a shelter, at least."

Miller shook his head against the pillow. "Mom refuses. She says they'll take me away from her. She says that at least the car is something that's still ours. And everyone would find out for sure. No one sees me hiding in the woods. I have a shot."

"And if a ranger kicks you out?"

"Mom's getting the money together for a deposit and I'm helping."

"How long will that take? You both should move in here. We have more than enough room."

"No, Vi."

"Why not? Don't you think your mom would want to…not do what she does?"

"Yes," he said through gritted teeth. "But she doesn't trust anyone. And neither do I."

"You can trust me, Miller."

His hard expression softened, and he started to answer, but the timer on my phone went off.

"That's the wash. Be right back."

I hurried downstairs, past the den where I could hear the TV droning and see its blue-ish light spill out from under the door. Dad, still exiled out of the master bedroom to the foldout couch, while Mom was ensconced in their king-sized bed.

I stopped outside the den door. I could ask my dad for help. For advice.

Then I thought about him waking Mom because Miller was in my room—my *bed*. They'd freak out, humiliating us both.

In the morning then.

In the laundry room, I switched the clothes to the dryer, and when I came back up, Miller looked to be asleep.

I propped my desk chair under the doorknob just in case my parents remembered I existed and turned out the light. I lay down beside him and pulled the covers up around us. My head nestled against my pillow and he opened his eyes.

"Vi…" he whispered.

"I'm here."

"What am I going to do?" His voice was thick, and my heart felt like it was cracking into a thousand little pieces.

"Sleep," I said, trying to sound brave. Like he told me I was. "We'll figure it out."

He shook his head. "I don't know. We've been in that car for weeks, but it feels like I was born there. Sometimes, I just want the earth to open and swallow me up."

"I won't let it. I need you."

"You can't tell anyone. Swear to me you won't."

"Miller…"

"Swear it, or I'll leave right now and never come back."

He seemed too exhausted to move, but I knew he'd haul himself up and crawl out my window if I didn't promise. I squeezed my eyes shut, hot tears leaking out.

"I swear."

"Thank you, Vi."

I bit back a sob and snuggled up close to him and put my arms around him. He smelled so clean and warm, but thin. Too thin.

He's lost weight since we met. It's making him sick, living in a car

Miller stiffened for a second and then pulled me in close, and I tucked my head under his chin, and we fit together so perfectly. Like puzzle pieces.

His chest pushed against my cheek in a deep sigh, and I listened to his heartbeat—a little too fast, I thought. If I were a doctor already, I'd be able to help him instead of feeling so helpless. The beats were like seconds, counting down to something, though I didn't know what. Something bad, maybe. I drifted to sleep, the fear sinking down with me.

The next day, we walked downtown Santa Cruz, along tree-lined sidewalks, past cute little shops, restaurants, and art galleries. We were headed to the Brewery Café to meet Shiloh. I watched Miller closely, noting how his face still looked pale. I'd found two empty water bottles in my bedroom trash when I woke up, and he'd complained of being tired, even after sleeping in my bed.

"I hardly remember a real bed," he'd said that morning. "I forgot what it felt like."

My stomach tightened. "You can sleep in it every night."

I'd said it like an offer, but it was a command. If his mom got to sleep at motels, then I'd make him sleep in my bed and drink all the water he needed. I watched Miller walking beside me, stoic and uncomplaining. We took so much for granted every day: heat, toilets, water at the touch of a tap. Privacy, space, a bed. Miller had none of that and yet he'd kept it all inside, faced it alone.

On the sidewalk outside a pawnshop, Miller stopped and peered in. A beautiful acoustic guitar sat front and center on a stand. Scratches marred its pale wood but the deeper brown on the neck was rich and gleaming.

"That's beautiful," I said.

"It's mine," Miller said softly, to himself.

I swiveled to look at him. "What?"

His eyes widened and then he scowled. "Shit, nothing, never mind." He started walking fast down the sidewalk, and I hurried to catch up.

"It's yours? I didn't know you played."

"There's a lot you don't know about me."

"I guess so," I said, trying to keep the hurt out of my voice. "Are you good? Have you been playing a long time?"

"Since I was ten. I taught myself how to play watching YouTube when we had a computer."

"Can you sing?"

He nodded. "Mostly covers, but I write my own stuff too."

I blinked at this new facet of himself unfolding in front of me. "Why didn't you tell me? Is that what you've been doing in your notebook every night? Writing songs? You could've played for me—"

Miller stopped and whirled on me. "Well, it's too late for that, isn't it? Jesus, Vi. Do you ever stop asking questions and helping and…meddling in my shit?"

I recoiled as if slapped. "I don't…I thought…"

He carved a hand through his hair. "I shouldn't have told you about the guitar."

"Why not?"

"Because now you're just going to go take your rich-girl allowance and buy it back for me. You've helped enough. You've done *enough.* I can't take anymore."

I stared at the intensity in his eyes that were miles deep and sucking me into him, where the pain was deep and dark. Where *want* and *sacrifice* and *going without* lived. Things that sleeping in a real bed after a hot shower and a meal had woken in him.

"I won't buy it back," I said.

"Promise me."

I bit my lip, shuffled my feet.

Miller set his jaw. "It's something I have to do for myself. Promise me, Violet."

"I will if you answer one question. Is not having your guitar what's made you sad lately?"

"I'm not *sad…*"

"It was a week ago, right? That you sold it?"

He nodded reluctantly. "But I didn't sell it, I pawned it. There's a difference. If it's sold, it's gone for good. If it's pawned, I can get it back."

"What if someone else buys it?"

Miller's eyes widened, fear burning in them at the thought.

"We have to get it back," I said. "Because you haven't been yourself. Like a piece of you is missing, and I just think—"

"Don't think, Violet," he said, suddenly out of breath. His face turned ruddy, as if he'd just run a sprint. "Don't *do* anything. Just leave it alone. *Promise.*"

"Okay, okay, I promise," I said in a low voice, mostly because this conversation was making him upset.

"I'm sorry I got angry at you," he said. "You've been…really good to me. Hell, you've made life bearable." His hand came up as if he wanted to brush the hair that had come loose from my ponytail, then jammed it in his pocket. "You're the best thing to happen to me in a really long time. I'm just not used to…*having* things. A long shower. A bed. And it just makes me miss what I don't have even more."

"I want you to keep having those things," I said softly. "At my house. Any time. And your mom too. Whatever you need."

I touched my fingertips to his wrist and then slipped my palm against his. To my shock, Miller's eyes filled with tears as he glanced down at our touching hands. His rough fingers twined with mine and held on so tight…

Then he quickly let go and turned away. We continued down the street in silence. After a block, Miller's steps grew uneven. Weaving slightly, he had to push off the wall of a restaurant or shop when he veered too close.

"Hey." I grabbed his arm. "What's going on?"

"I don't know. Nothing. Just thirsty. I need…water."

He crossed the street toward the 7-Eleven on the opposite corner in shuffling steps and without looking for traffic. A pick-up truck hit the brakes, horns blaring, but Miller paid no attention.

I hurried to catch up. "Miller, hey. You're scaring me."

He ignored me, his gaze fixed on the 7-Eleven. Inside the convenience store, he headed for the drink refrigerators and grabbed the largest Gatorade they had.

"You want anything?" he asked, his voice sounding tight, as he fished in the front pocket of his jeans for a fiver tucked there.

"No, thanks." Warmth infiltrated my worry for him because he was trying to take care of me, even when he'd had to pawn the most valuable thing he owned.

Miller paid for the drink, and we rounded the corner to the side of the building. He slid down against the wall and chugged the neon yellow liquid. I watched him down half the bottle in a few huge gulps and then close his eyes in relief.

"Better?" I asked, crouching beside him. *Please tell me you're better.*

He nodded but then drank the other half, draining the bottle.

I stared. "That was thirty-two ounces. Miller…"

"I'm *fine*, doc," he said, tiredly. "I should get back."

He started to haul himself to his feet, but I held him back. "No. You need help. Your face is flushed, and your eyes are kind of glassy."

"I'm fine. I promise. Go meet your friend without me." He smiled wanly. "I'll see you at school on Monday. Christ, won't that be fun? First day of school. Can't fucking wait."

I studied him closer, again wishing I could read these symptoms, and that I had the clout to make him listen to me. But he pushed off the ground and went down the way we had come, the empty Gatorade bottle still in his hand. But he was walking steadily, like normal.

He's okay, I thought.

Because he had to be.

It made sense, I told myself as I headed for the café. The fact that Miller was living out of a car with his mom was going to take a toll on him. Stress. Hunger. Cold. He was probably coming down with a fever from inadequate shelter. One night in my house clearly wasn't enough.

That has to stop. They need help.

But Miller had sworn me to secrecy. Demanded it. He'd never speak to me again if I tried to get him help—not that I even knew how to do that. If word got out he lived in a car, it'd kill him. There were poor kids in our district, but that wasn't the same as being *homeless*.

There has to be a way, I thought. *I can borrow money from Dad. Or earn it fast. Maybe take it out of my college fund. Enough for a deposit and first month's rent on an apartment.*

My thoughts hit a brick wall.

And if they can't pay the rent every month after that?

Shiloh waved at me from inside the Brewery Café, her many silver and coppery bracelets glinting over her arms. I replaced my worried frown with a smile. She couldn't know about Miller's situation either, even though I was dying to tell her. She'd say I had to tell someone else, immediately. But I'd promised Miller, and I always tried to keep my promises.

But sometimes keeping a promise wasn't good or right. Sometimes, it was the worst thing you could do.

That night, I left my bedroom window open to hear Miller in case he showed up. All was quiet until nine or so, and then it sounded like someone crashing through the woods. I looked down to see him stumbling and mumbling to himself. Like he was drunk.

"Miller?"

He turned his face up and a gasp stuck in my throat at how pale he was. Ghostly white. Confused. Like he didn't know who I was.

Oh God, this is bad. So very bad...

He mumbled something and fell to his knees. I climbed down the trellis as fast as I could, slipping once. My palms scraped the wood, then I hit the ground just as Miller turned on the faucet to our garden hose. He drank from it as if he were dying of thirst. As if he'd been in a desert for months. The scent of urine—his pants were dark with it—hit me, mingled with a fruity smell that didn't belong there.

"Miller, wait... Please, stop."

I reached to take the hose away from him. The way he *needed* it was terrifying—like a rabid animal, water flooding his mouth, choking him, spilling all over his face and shirt. He shoved me aside and kept at it until his eyes rolled up in his head to show the whites. Then his body went limp, and he collapsed to the ground, hard. Not moving.

A strangled cry tore out of me. My heart crashed against my ribs. I tossed the hose aside and crawled to put my ear on Miller's chest, damp with water. He was still breathing, his heart still pumping but faintly.

"Someone help!"

The night was dark and swallowed my scream. I rocked in helpless desperation, feeling around my pockets for a cell phone I was sure I'd left upstairs.

It was in my back pocket.

"Oh, thank God." My hands trembled as I dialed 9-1-1. "Hold on, Miller. Please. Hold on..."

They say your entire life flashes before your eyes when you're about to die, but they don't tell you that it also flashes when someone you truly

care about might die, too. Like a movie on fast forward, I saw Miller's funeral, the first day of school and me crying all day, sitting in my room alone...

It's now two in the morning and I just got back from the hospital.

Yesterday, Miller drank a huge Gatorade like a frat boy chugging beer on a dare.

Tonight, he passed out in my yard while sucking down water from our garden hose as if he were trying to drown himself in it.

I called 9-1-1, and then Mom was screeching down at me from my bedroom window, and Dad was running around from the backyard. The firetrucks showed up, EMTs, and everyone was asking me what was going on. All the while, Miller lay in my lap, hardly breathing, not moving, his face pale as death.

They wouldn't let me go in the ambulance with him, and since I had no way to contact his mom, he rode alone. He was all alone. On the way to the hospital, my parents grilled me about why Miller was outside my bedroom window late at night, and did this happen frequently, and just what the hell was going on?

And because my parents were my parents, they started screaming at each other that no one had been paying attention so now the "lawn boy" was sneaking into my room every night.

Good. Let them fight like assholes, because at least then they weren't asking me about Miller.

But at the hospital, the cops asked. The doctors, a social worker... They all wanted to know about him so they could contact his parents while he was rushed into the ICU for who-knew-what treatment. Did he have a stroke? An aneurism? No one would tell me anything.

Crying until I could hardly see straight, I told them what I knew. That Miller's mom, Lois Stratton, worked at the 24-hour diner on 5th during the day. I said she worked nights too, but Miller hadn't told me where. That was mostly true, at least.

Where did he live? Address?

I cried harder as I told them he didn't have one. I didn't want to break my promise, but a part of me was relieved. Like maybe now, someone would help them.

I held a little bit of hope we could keep the kids at school from hearing about it, but one of the police officers was Mitch Dowd, Frankie's dad. He would tell Frankie, and Frankie would blab it everywhere, riding around on his skateboard like he was Paul Revere.

In the waiting room, I silently told Miller I was sorry, but he could be mad at me all he wanted if only he'd wake up and be okay.

After what felt like years of terrified waiting, they finally told us. Type 1 or juvenile diabetes. Miller's blood sugar levels nearly topped six hundred milligrams, and the term 'diabetic hyperosmolar syndrome' was floated by one of the doctors. I'd heard of diabetes, of course, but had no idea what the rest meant, except that he'd nearly died.

The doctors said Miller was stable. The police said they'd find his mom. There was nothing left to do but go home.

In the car, my parents were too tired to do more than snipe at one another, and they sent me to bed with the promise that "We'll talk about this in the morning."

But no sooner had I shut the door than they started up again, blaming each other for not knowing what was going on under their own roof.

I hate them.

I love Miller.

I'm saying it now for the first time, writing it down in black and white, because it's absolutely true. I've never felt like this before. Like my body and all my senses are lit up, but I'm scared too. I'm sure he doesn't feel the same. Why would he? I'm the geeky, annoying girl who meddles in his business. He's always saying so. But we're friends. He's my best friend. My soulmate, if a soulmate is the person you can't live without. The person you'd do anything to keep safe and happy.

That's what I know for sure. I can't lose him again, and the more pressure you add to two people, the more crushed they became under the weight. Just look at my parents. They were best friends once too.

I'm not going to mess things up by adding more to us. But I can take care of him and make sure he's safe.

That's how I'll keep him forever.

iv

That's when I knew I'd love her forever.

The doctors left. They explained my diagnosis, and the weight of it sank into me, pressing me down. For the rest of my life, I'd have to watch what I ate and drink as if I were on Weight Watchers, constantly measuring and counting carbs and grams of sugar to keep my numbers stable. Exercise is good, they said, but I have to be careful about exerting myself or I could go blind, lose a foot, or fall into a coma and die like Julia Roberts did in Mom's favorite movie. A ball and chain of rules and diets and restrictions, needles and pills that I'd have to carry across a tightrope without a net, for the rest of my life.

Then Violet stepped into my hospital room, dressed in a yellow T-shirt and jean shorts. Her shiny black hair is in a messy ponytail and her dark blue eyes behind her glasses are filled with worry and care. For me.

And in her hand was my guitar.

My body weighed a thousand pounds, but in that moment, a heavy burden lifted off of my soul.

"You promised…" I croaked.

"I don't know what you're talking about," she said, trying to smile around shaky, watery words. She laid the guitar on my lap. "Do you even like guitars? I had no idea. This is a get-well present. I saw it in a window and decided you had to have it."

A dam broke and sobs shook her shoulders. I couldn't lift my arms to hold her as she buried her face against my side.

"I'm sorry. I'm so sorry," she cried. "I should've…done more. I want to be a doctor for God's sake, and I didn't know. I didn't see the signs."

"You saved me."

Violet abruptly sat up and took off her glasses to wipe her eyes. "No. I called 9-1-1. But it wouldn't have gotten that far if I'd done something sooner."

I shook my head against the pillow. My fingers reached for the guitar, feeling its smooth wood, and the weight of it on my lap. Dad gave it to me when I was ten years old, in the good times. The first time I held it, I'd felt as if some part of me that I hadn't even known was missing, had been restored.

Violet had been right—pawning the guitar had been like tearing off a limb and handing it over to that sweaty guy behind the counter. I didn't think I'd ever hold it again.

And now it was back. Now I could play for her all the songs I'd been writing in her room, with her sitting not a foot from me, oblivious to how perfect she was…

"But I'm never going to be so ignorant again," Violet said, putting her glasses back on and sitting straight. "Type 1 diabetes means insulin shots and monitoring your glucose and keeping track of your diet. I'm going to study up on it. I'll learn how to do the shots and the finger pricks and how to read the monitors and make sure that you stay level. And I'm going to make sure you do it, too. That you take care of yourself so that you don't… You don't ever…"

Hiccupping sobs took over and the tears came again.

"Vi, don't…"

"I was so scared, Miller," she whispered.

"I'm sorry."

"It's not your fault."

Guilt that she had to see me like that ripped through me, even as hope bloomed in my chest. Her tears, her anguish… They can only mean one thing.

She loves me too…

Then a nurse came to do a fingerstick and showed me how to gather the drop of blood into a reader that measures the sugar levels. Vi watched closely, mentally taking notes.

"Can I see it?" Vi asked when the nurse was done. "I'm going to be a doctor someday."

"Throw it in the bin when you're finished." The nurse gave her the fingerstick and left the room. Violet waited until she was gone and then punctured her own finger.

"What are you doing?"

She took my hand, pressed the ruby red drop of blood on her fingertip to mine.

"Promise me," she said. "Promise me, we'll always be friends. I can't lose you again. Not ever…"

Always be friends.

I wanted to laugh and tell her how impossible that is. How I crossed a boundary the night we met. How all the broken pieces of my life come together when I'm with her, even for a little while. How we'd been hanging out for months and every minute I tried to find the courage to tell her that this poor homeless kid with nothing to offer would die for her.

I swallowed hard, swallowed down what I want to say, because I'm thirteen and I'm not supposed to love a girl like this. So soon. So completely.

"I promise…"

PART II

four years later

CHAPTER ONE

MILLER

"I promise..."

The bus hit a pothole, jostling my forehead off the window and jarring me from my thoughts. From the memory of that morning in the hospital that was the best and the worst, because the day I knew I loved Violet was also the day I let her go.

"Stupid fucking promise."

I glanced around at the mostly empty seats; it was dark, and no one seemed to have heard me. Or cared if they did. My guitar case sat on my lap, and I gripped it tighter, nerves lit up.

We now lived at opposite ends of the school district. Turns out, my hospitalization and diagnosis four years ago had an upside. A charity program worked with the hospital for kids like me and their families to help get us on our feet so that I wouldn't die in the back of the station wagon trying to inject my insulin. They moved us out of the car and into low-income housing in a shady neighborhood on the rocky cliffs overlooking Lighthouse Beach.

I took the bus to see Violet instead of hiking through the dark woods at night, but I still saw her as much as I could. As much as she had time for, which felt like less and less with every passing year.

She's slipping away because you're a jackass with no backbone.

After Violet brought my guitar back, she asked me to play for her every night that I snuck into her room. I'd never played in front of anyone before. She was my first. Sitting in her room at night, we'd study or talk, and then she'd ask me to sing. So I did. Instead of telling her how I felt, I sang and played, and she never knew. Never suspected.

She thought she was too nerdy for a guy to actually like her and I was too chickenshit to tell her how wrong she was.

I hid behind other people's songs, too. Like "Yellow" by Coldplay. That was her favorite. It became "our song." She thought I'd chosen it because it sounds good on an acoustic guitar. She never suspected that every lyric was a dedication to her. And she always cried, saying over and over again how talented I was. Gifted. Destined for greatness.

I didn't believe her, but I knew I wanted to make music for the rest of my life. Violet showed me the way and I loved her for it. I loved her in a thousand ways, but she cherished our friendship above all else and so I gritted my teeth and respected that.

I let her feed herself lies about how terrible love was and how it ruined everything.

I let her listen to her parents argue and think that's what happened to everyone.

And I'd promised to be her friend. Sealed it in blood.

To plunge the knife deeper, she still carried a torch for that bastard, River Whitmore. I suspected she kept her crush going because it was safe. Violet carried her shit close to her heart too, just in a different way from me.

But I couldn't do it anymore. Tomorrow was the first day of school. I was about to face down another year—our senior year of high school—with Violet never knowing how I felt. I had to tell her before it was too late. Convince her to set aside her fear and see how right we were together. How fucking perfect.

How we just fit.

Violet must've been waiting for me, since the window flew open the second I came around the side of her house.

"Get in here, quick!"

She waved me up, a white, rectangular envelope flapping in her hands. Her parents didn't care if I came in the front door or not. But every night I visited her, I climbed up the trellis like Romeo does in the play. Except in this version, Juliet friend-zoned Romeo. Hard.

I pushed my guitar case through the window first, and Vi carefully set it aside while I crawled in and hopped down from the desk, like I always did. Also, like usual, I took a breath to drink her in.

Violet McNamara had been a self-proclaimed geek when I first met her, but over the last four years, she'd morphed from a warm, fuzzy caterpillar into a butterfly—deep blue eyes, shiny black hair, and a body kept fit with soccer but rounded everywhere that mattered to guys.

To me, she'd already been perfect.

I loved how she used to run her tongue over her braces when she was thinking hard, or how she'd polish her glasses on the front of her shirt like a college professor, serious and smart.

So fucking smart.

Two years ago, she got her braces off. Shortly after that, she'd gotten whacked in the face playing soccer. I guessed her new contact lenses were a shitty prescription since she still couldn't see how beautiful she was. Or maybe she did, though she'd never say so. But her confidence grew with her looks. She stopped hanging around with just Shiloh and me all the time and started hanging around study group friends, girls on her soccer team; she joined debate and the Math & Science club. Everyone loved her, including the popular kids.

Kids like River fucking Whitmore.

I coughed and diverted my attention to the envelope in her hand. "You got it?"

"I did!" she said, then narrowed her eyes at me. "How are your numbers?"

"I—what? They're fine."

"When did you last eat?"

I rolled my eyes, but her concern made me feel warm all over. "After work. Before I got on the bus."

Violet's large, impossibly dark blue eyes narrowed, studying me the same way I imagine she'd size up her future patients.

"Can I…?"

I smirked as she grabbed my wrist to look at the numbers on the smartwatch that was connected to my Continuous Glucose Monitor. The small CGM device was attached to my stomach with a sensor imbedded with a needle under my skin. It continuously monitored my glucose levels and sent the numbers to my watch. If they got too high or low, the watch made an alarm. A gift, courtesy of the State of California, since we were too poor to afford it on our own.

"Okay," Violet said slowly, releasing my arm. "The numbers are okay, but if you need a snack or something, tell me."

"Quit wasting time and *tell me*. Are you in or not?"

"I haven't opened it. Waiting for you." She started to tear open the envelope that had UCSC Medical Center's logo embossed on the front, then stopped. "What if they don't want me?"

"How could they not want you?"

How could anyone?

"The Patience Care Volunteer program is super competitive," she began, but I waved her off.

"Your GPA is a four-point-a-million and you aced the interview. Not to mention, you were born for this. So open the envelope already and get your assignment."

"Right. Okay."

Violet opened the envelope. The smile that broke over her face was going straight into my next song.

"Holy shit," she breathed and covered her mouth with her hand. Her eyes scanned the first page. "I'm in. I'm in!"

She threw her arms around my neck. Her excitement hummed through her body and I held her as tightly as I dared. I inhaled her scent—flowery and clean—and let my hand briefly touch the silk of her hair. Her breasts pressed against my chest and had to fight to keep my hands from sliding down the slim contours of her sides, down to her wide hips and rounded ass. She wasn't just beautiful, she was luscious…as my seventeen-year-old body liked to remind me of, frequently.

I pulled away from her before my dick took it upon itself to broadcast to Violet those exact thoughts. I wanted her, badly, but she needed to know how much I loved her first.

She clutched the paper with both hands. "I can't believe it. The PCV is, like, *the* program I need for my transcripts. The icing on the cake for my med school prospects."

I smirked. "You've mentioned that once or twice."

"Smartass." She gave me a friendly punch on the arm, then flipped to the second page. "Let's see who I'm assigned to. I hope it's you."

I leaned my ass against her desk, casual, not letting it show on my face how much I hoped it was me too.

I didn't want a Patient Care Volunteer unless it was Violet, but my endocrinologist recommended it for me. Managing my diabetes was difficult, more difficult than most. If the universe were being benevolent, it would be my name and address that Violet read. She'd come to my place twice a week, helping me manage my glucose, insulin, needle care and replacement, and making sure my fridge was stocked with food that my meal plan required. Violet did most of that stuff already, whether I asked her to or not, but if she were officially assigned to me, she'd have to leave her endless studying and her new popular friends two afternoons a week. I'd have her all to myself.

But not only was the universe distinctly *un*-benevolent, it was downright cruel.

"Oh my God," Violet breathed, sinking onto her bed. She looked up at me with those dark blue eyes that were now lit up with fear.

"Well? Who is it?"

"Maybe I shouldn't tell you. Patient privacy."

"Come on, Vi. It's me. You know I'm not going to say a word."

Violet bit her lip. "Swear to me you won't tell. Because it's serious. More serious than I expected."

"I swear."

She lowered her voice. "I've been assigned to Nancy Whitmore. River's mom."

River fucking Whitmore. Of course.

I cleared my throat. "She's sick?"

Violet nodded. "It doesn't give details here, but just the other day, Dad took his car to the Whitmore Auto Body shop. When he came back, he and my mom were talking in low voices. I heard the word 'cancer' more than once." Her hand dropped to her side. "Jesus, poor River. That's probably why he hasn't been hanging out with us this summer."

Us was relative, but I let it slide. I never hung out with Vi and her popular friends, but I had been selfishly celebrating that Violet's summer had been relatively River-free. And it was because his mom was sick.

The universe is a straight-up asshole.

I felt like one too.

She looked up at me fearfully. "God, what if it's bad?"

"What do they expect you to do?" I asked, the urge to protect her rising in me. "Not heavy-duty shit?"

"No, no, simple things like changing bedding, bringing her food, reading to her, making her comfortable."

I scowled. "Sounds like end-of-life stuff to me."

"It does, doesn't it?"

"Are you up for that?"

Violet nodded and sat straighter, her trademark stubborn, determined look painted over her features. “I can do it. I want to help. And if I’m going to be a doctor, this is part of it, right? The good and the bad?”

“I guess so.” Making sure a seventeen-year-old diabetic ate his vegetables wasn’t in the same ballpark as taking care of a dying woman.

Violet waved her hand. “But it might not be as serious as we think. She could be in treatment and recovering. We shouldn’t jump to the worst-case scenario.”

I said nothing. In my experience, the only way to prepare for anything was to assume the worst. That night, I should have taken my own advice.

“Just be careful,” I said. “If it’s too much, tell them.”

Violet smiled. “I will.”

You won’t.

If River’s mom was terminal, Violet would stick with her to the end, no matter how much of a mental toll it took. And the bitch of it all was that she’d be in River’s house twice a week. I hated that jealousy gnawed at my guts when the poor guy’s mom might be dying, but I knew what would happen. Violet would Florence Nightingale her way into being more enamored with River Whitmore, and he’d fall in love with her compassion and bravery. How could he not?

It’s what I did.

Violet caught my dark expression. “I’m sorry I wasn’t assigned to you, but I’m glad you’ll have someone helping. Don’t give your PCV a hard time, okay?”

“Who, me?”

“I’m serious. I worry about you.”

“Don’t.”

Violet rolled her eyes. “Like that’s possible.” She tilted her head and stood up, took a step closer. I could smell her perfume and the soap she used in the shower. “You look a little pale, right now actually. Are you feeling low? Do you need a snack?”

“*I don’t need a snack*,” I practically shouted, making her flinch.

The song I’d come to sing for her felt stupid and incredibly selfish after the severity of her assignment. And how could I tell her what I felt while her thoughts were entirely filled with River?

My hands clenched the side of the desk until my knuckles ached. Anger at the Whitmores for ruining my plan simultaneously battled with feeling like shit for the tragedy unfolding in their lives.

So, I did the mature thing and took it out on Violet.

"Miller…?"

"I'm fine," I bit out. "I'm always the same. You're the one who's different. What the hell is going on with you, anyway?"

"Me?" Violet sank back down on the bed. "What do you mean?"

"You've been distant."

She blinked. *"When?"*

"Last week. This summer. All last year. Ever since you started hanging around Ri—Evelyn Gonzalez and her friends. Is that how it's going to be this year? We're not cool enough for you anymore?"

Jesus, my petulant bullshit had become a runaway train I couldn't stop.

"You know that's not true," Violet said. "And who is *we*? Has Shiloh said something? I just hung out with her yesterday—"

"No."

"And you? We're literally hanging out *right now*." Her face turned down in concern. "You really think I ignored you at school last year? That's not true."

"I'm not a fucking pity case, Vi. I'm just telling you what I—we—notice. Something's different and has been for a while."

"I have new friends. That doesn't mean I don't care about my old friends."

"Uh huh. How are things with River?" I gritted out.

"Aside from his mom maybe *dying*? There are no 'things.' I've told you a hundred times. He hardly says a word to me. We're not dating or anything."

"Yet."

She crossed her arms. "Jealous, are we?"

I swallowed hard. Here it was. Now or never. Confess or wallow in misery forever.

But in the silence that stretched between us, Violet began to stare at me fearfully, scared that I might be on the verge of imploding our friendship. Of breaking our blood vow.

My jaw worked as I wrestled with myself until downstairs, raised voices—one low, one higher pitched—rose up from the floor like a seismic eruption. As always, it shook Violet's foundation, eroded her happiness. She tore her gaze from me and stared at the floor, then flinched as the sound of breaking glass from below. Footsteps thundered up the stairs. We both froze as her parents' voices grew louder.

"No, you are not going to do this, Lynn," her dad shouted. *"Do not do this to her."*

"Don't tell me what I can and can't do," her mom spat. *"This concerns all of us."*

I instinctively moved in front of Violet as the door flew open and her parents crowded the doorway, her mom stopping short at seeing me. She smoothed a flyaway lock of dark hair from her mad dash down the hall and stood straight. Vi's dad was a boxy guy who'd played football in college. He looked it—a former linebacker in a rumpled dress shirt, unbuttoned at the collar. They both looked worn out.

"What are you doing here this late?" Lynn McNamara demanded.

"Lynn…" Vince rolled his eyes and fixed me with a tired smile. "Hey, Miller."

I lifted my chin. "Hey."

Lynn pinned Violet with a hard look. "It's nearly eleven. You have school tomorrow."

"I know, Mom—"

"And honestly, Miller, our front door works, you know. I don't even want to think about the damage to my trellis."

"You haven't planted anything on it in years," Violet said.

"Of course not," Lynn replied. "Why would I, if it's just going to get trampled every night?" She swiveled to me. "Is it *every* night, young man? Just what are you doing in my daughter's bedroom?"

Violet flushed pink. "*Mom.* I've told you a million times, Miller is just a friend. My best friend." She looked to me, pleading. "Isn't that right?"

My heart cracked, and I felt my head nod, my throat thick. "Yeah. That's right."

Her eyes were soft with gratitude, then hardened as she turned to her parents. "And what are you doing here, anyway? You can't just barge in like this."

"Sorry, sweetheart," Vince said, frowning at his wife. "You're absolutely right."

Lynn scoffed but was calmer now. "We'll talk about it in the morning." Her gaze shot to me. "We'll talk about *everything* in the morning."

She stormed out, and Vince followed, offering a weary smile. "Not too late, Vi. Goodnight, Miller."

The door shut, and Vi sagged against me. I put my arms around her, held her close.

"I'm sorry," she whispered against my chest. "God, it's so humiliating."

"It's okay, Vi."

"It used to not be like this. We used to sit at the table and laugh. Talk. They loved each other so much. Mom told me once she was lucky she married her best friend. We were so…happy."

I inhaled, I had to try. Gently. "Not every couple ends up like them."

I wouldn't let it happen to us. Ever.

She hugged me tighter and lifted her tear-streaked face. "Tell me the truth, Miller. Are we…okay?"

Her brave tone couldn't mask the fear in her eyes. The agonizing bottom line was that she needed me to be her friend. In the last few years, her family had been on shaky ground, forcing Violet to grab on to any steady thing she could.

Like our friendship. Even if it tears my heart to shreds.

I swallowed hard. Swallowed down everything I'd come to say and sing to her. I even managed a weak-ass smile. For her.

"Yeah, of course we're okay. I told you. It's no big deal." I shouldered my backpack. "I gotta go."

Violet didn't protest and that was almost worse.

Her own smile widened tentatively, hopefully. She wiped the tears from her eyes. "See you at school tomorrow. First day of senior year. I think it'll be our best yet."

"Yep," I said, taking up my guitar case and moving toward the window. "See you, Vi."

"Miller?"

"Yeah?"

"Thank you."

God, she was so beautiful in her pajama shorts and t-shirt, her eyes shining and full of gratitude. Athletic from soccer but rounded with curves, intelligence in her eyes, and a smile that could tear down a guy's defenses in a heartbeat and leave him naked and raw and wanting…

I smiled with knives in my chest. "Always."

The bus ride back to my neighborhood felt darker. The bus was emptier, and the streets outside the window were black and deserted. My guitar case sat on my lap, full and heavy. A thousand unheard notes bursting to get out.

She doesn't love you like that. Get over it.

I mustered every broken piece of my pride, sealed up the cracks in my heart. Lesson learned: loving someone wasn't enough to keep them. Didn't work for my dad. Or with Violet.

I didn't know why I kept expecting anything else.

CHAPTER TWO

MILLER

I got off the bus a few blocks from home—near the cliffs overlooking the ocean—and nearly tripped coming down the steps. The ground tilted beneath me, and my hands trembled as I clutched my guitar case. The bus hissed and rumbled off into the night, just as my watch sounded the alarm. I peered down at the number. 69 and sinking.

"Shit."

I sat down hard on the curb and fished around in my backpack for the glucose gummies my doctor had prescribed. Orange juice worked faster, but I wasn't going to make it the two blocks to my apartment for that, and I'd stupidly forgotten to bring a bottle.

I chewed three gummies and waited for my watch to give me a better number. A few minutes later, it registered a 74 and my limbs felt stronger and less watery. I hauled myself up and trudged along the darkened streets.

Shitty apartment complexes, much like the shitty apartment complex Mom and I lived in, rose up around me: peeling paint, concrete stairs, and rusted metal railings. They all had names like Ocean Front, Beachside, and The Coves, as if they were luxury condos with the ocean for a backyard, instead of rundown housing where the nearest "beach" was a rocky, unforgiving shoreline.

It was after eleven when I climbed up an exterior set of cement steps to 2C at the Lighthouse Apartments. Our new home, after my escapade with Violet's garden hose. It was a small, two-bedroom, one-bathroom, with a heater that worked only when it felt like it and a shower that had shitty water pressure. Roaches scuttled in and out of cabinets and across counter tops when the light came on.

But it *had* a shower. A toilet. A sink. It had *rooms.* It had a stove and even a tiny little patio off the shoebox living area. I had a bed and so did Mom. She cried when we moved in.

I wanted to cry too but reminded myself of the truth: nothing good lasted and everything could be taken away at any second.

Or it could turn to shit at the drop of a hat.

I turned the key into our place and found my mother sitting on the couch when she wasn't due to be home from her second job at the diner until midnight. Instead of her yellow uniform shirt, she was in sweats, and her dark hair was tied up in a loose ponytail. Her house uniform. I suspected she hadn't gone to work at all. The yellow light of our shabby floor lamp cast a warm, homey glow over the beer bottles, overflowing ashtrays, and fast food wrappers on the coffee table.

A middle-aged guy I'd never seen before sat next to her. Warily, I shut the door, set my guitar case down.

"Hey," I said flatly. "I don't believe we've met."

"Jesus, Miller," Mom said with a tired laugh. She was only forty-one—she and Dad had me young—but she looked a decade older and was always tired. "This is Chet Hyland. Chet, this is my son, Miller."

Chet stared me down from across the small room, a meaty hand holding a beer, resting on the belly of his mostly white wife-beater. I'd stopped thinking of the tank as a "wife-beater" but it fit Chet. Unshaven, dark hair unwashed, and jeans stained with grease or dirt, he watched me with beady eyes. He set off every internal alarm I had; the hair on the back of my neck stood up.

Then a friendly smile burst over his face. "Good to meet you, Miller. Beer?"

"No, thanks."

My hands were shaking again, and my watch was showing a 70. Still too low. I went to the kitchen, my skin breaking out in a cold sweat.

"You're home late," Mom called from the couch.

"I went to Vi's after work."

"Miller works at the Boardwalk," Mom said, and I heard the flick of a lighter and an inhale off a cigarette.

"Ah, a carny, eh?" Chet chuckled.

"He works at one of the biggest arcades down there," Mom said, managing a smile for me. "Just promoted to assistant manager."

I opened the fridge, my trembling hands reaching for an orange juice. My meal plan required I keep a stockpile of certain foods and drinks at all times, and we had to do it on a threadbare budget. I wasn't as good as Vi about keeping my shit in order, but there were five bottles of juice this morning before work and now there were only three.

I plucked one from the shelf and shut the door. "What the hell?"

Mom frowned. "What the hell, what?"

I held up the juice "I'm short two."

"I might've had a couple today," Chet said, his eyes never leaving mine. "Didn't know you were keeping count."

I gave Mom a *What the fuck?* glare.

"Miller has to count everything," she explained. "He has diabetes."

"Yeah, I do. I'd have thought she might've mentioned that to you, *Chet*."

Like, immediately, so you don't eat and drink all the shit I need to live.

"My bad, buddy. Won't happen again."

He smiled at Mom, and she smiled back. It'd been a long time since I'd seen that smile—almost happy. The kind of happy that comes from not being alone anymore and no other reason.

I swigged my juice, one hand planted on the fridge door to keep me steady.

"Feeling okay? Your CGM went off a while ago." Mom tapped her fingers on a smartphone—an old model, several generations behind the newest—from amid the crap on the coffee table.

"I'm aware," I said, trying—and failing—to take the bite out of my words.

Before I had the CGM, I needed to fingerstick every two hours, twenty-four hours a day. Mom being *my mom* was supposed to set her alarm and check on me at night. Two trips to the ER in three months, I learned to set my own alarm. Mom was sleeping through hers and shutting them off in a half-sleep.

I couldn't blame her. She worked two jobs to keep us afloat, and my diagnosis required more time and energy than she had to spare since my pancreas had decided to close up shop: *Out of insulin. Come back never.*

I'd learned pretty damn quick that when it came to taking care of my diabetes, I was on my own.

Except for Violet. The hospital could've sent her to me...

But they didn't and that's life.

I drank half of the juice and tucked the bottle in my backpack and slung it and my guitar case over my shoulder.

"Where are you going?" Mom called as I headed for the door.

"Out."

"It's late, and you have school tomorrow."

"Does he give you trouble?" Chet asked Mom in a low, warning voice.

"No, he—"

"Hey. Boy."

I froze with my hand on the doorknob. My head turned on a stiff neck to meet Chet's dark, hard gaze.

"You give your mom a hard time, son?"

His words, casually threatening, slid icily down my spine. I tilted my chin and somehow managed not to blink. "I'm not your son."

A short silence fell where I could only hear the beat of my heart crashing against my chest.

Mom waved the smoke away as if she could dissipate the tension between us. "Nah, he's good. He's a good kid."

Chet's eyes never moved from mine as he said to me and only me, "He'd better be."

"Fucking hell," I muttered, hands jammed in my pockets as I walked down the silent, darkened streets that wound down toward the beach. Over the last four years, Mom had guys come and go in various shades of loser-ness, but Chet felt like King Loser and permanently fixed to our couch.

That day was a shit day, and I wanted nothing more but to sleep. But now that Mom was having a sleepover with Chet fucking Hyland, I took a walk instead.

Even after Mom and I moved out of the car and to the apartment, I didn't stop roaming at night. Walking to be alone. To escape. Sometimes I had the urge to walk all night and not stop. But without my meds, I'd wind up dead somewhere, and they wouldn't find me until the seagulls had picked my bones clean.

"Cheery thought," I muttered, the wind whipping my words away.

That night, I wandered the remote stretch of rocky beach fronted by high cliffs. I hunched deeper into my jacket. It was technically summer, but the Northern California coast didn't get the memo.

Black waves, bearded in white foam, crashed against the rocky sand, clawing at it and then retreating, over and over. To the west, the glittering colored lights of the Boardwalk looked garish and wild. Even a mile away, I could hear the last roller coaster of the night rattle up the track, followed by the happy screams of the riders as it plummeted. The Ferris Wheel turned silently and slowly behind it.

I turned my back on the color and light and trudged deeper amid the craggy, porous rocks that were black and jagged under the meager moonlight. The high tide forced me to stay close to the boulders, and soon enough, I was climbing more than walking. To my right, the cliffs loomed. On my left, the ocean reached for me in angry grabs, spraying me with cold water with every attempt. I'd never come this far before.

Only when I stumbled, scraping my palm on a rough, salt-beaten rock to catch my balance, did I surrender. The water was starting to squelch around my boots, and if this stupid foray damaged my guitar, I'd never forgive myself.

I'd started to turn around and pick a path back amid the rocks and dampening sand, when I heard it. Distant but clear, between the roar of the waves. A creak followed by a slam. Like a wooden door on a busted hinge, opening and shutting with every gust of wind.

Against all good sense, I kept going, and my curiosity paid off when the boulders thinned slightly. I was able to pick a precarious path over smaller, rounded stones. The shoreline curved up, away from the water, and the waves couldn't touch me any longer. The way grew easier. The sound—*creak-slam!*—grew louder.

Finally, I came around a huge cluster of boulders. Ahead, the cliffs had slid toward the ocean, and there was no more beach.

Dead end.

Then I heard it again. Behind me.

I turned and there was the door. It hung on loose hinges, and every time the wind blew it open, it revealed a rectangle of pitch black. It took me a second in the dark of the night to make it out, but I realized I was staring at a square wooden shack built against a collection of high boulders.

I should have left it alone and gone home: first day of school and all. But what was at home? A stranger in our small space. And school was nothing but another year of being bullied for the unforgiveable crime of being poor. And thanks to my colossal failure tonight with Vi, I'd spend it watching her get closer and closer to River until I lost her forever.

I fished my cell phone from the back pocket of my jeans and flipped on the flashlight function.

"This is how teenagers die in horror movies," I muttered into the wind. The creaking door slammed, making me flinch.

I held up the meager light and peered in, using my guitar case to prop open the door.

"Hello?"

Jesus, I sounded like a scared dope. But if someone—or two or ten someones—lived here, I didn't want to be rude.

Or murdered.

The shack was empty. And bigger than I thought. My light wasn't strong enough; I had to illuminate parts of it at a time. Moonlight filtered in through cracks in the roof and through the one glass-less window cut into the side, drifts of sand piled against it.

I guessed the shack was about two hundred square feet. Rickety, uneven wood planks made up the flooring. A tangle of poles still wound with fishing line—like white witch's hair—stood in one corner. A bucket. A bench. Even a small table with a rusted scaling knife resting on it.

I'd found a fisherman's shack, weather-beaten, salt-rusted. Out of sight and forgotten and unused in months, if not years. It had its own small stretch of beach, and the ocean crashed a few hundred yards away, too far away to threaten.

Mine.

I sank down on the splintered but sturdy wooden bench. Suddenly, I was so fucking tired. I pillowed my head on my arm on the table, smelling wood and salt. My eyes fell shut at once.

When my CGM's alarm went off, dawn's first light was filtering in the shack's lone window and streaming in from gaps in the planks like slivers of gold. I knew immediately where I was, as if I'd been coming here for years.

Treasure. I found buried treasure.

Just as I had four years ago, the night I'd stumbled out of the forest to see Violet McNamara's face peering down at me from her bedroom window.

I popped a few gummies and finished off the bottle of orange juice. When I felt steadier, I stretched the cricks out of my bones for sleeping hunched over a table and grabbed my guitar case.

Outside, the sun was just cresting the horizon to the east. My eyes stung with tears—probably just the cold wind—as I watched the light spill over the ocean that was no longer angry but calm. Serene.

In front of my shack, I found a flat rock and sat facing the water. I took my guitar from its case, looped the strap around my neck. The fingers of my right hand found their home on the frets, and the left went to the strings.

The sun rose, and I played Violet's song. My voice—rough and scratchy, like old wood—sang the words that had been trapped in my heart for years. I sang them louder, strummed the guitar harder. Fueled by fruitless, hopeless longing, the words rose up and up…

Until they were caught by the wind and torn to shreds.

All I'll Ever Want

Pretend I'm doing fine on my own
a lost soul with nowhere to go
I got holes in my shoes walking away from you
there's living and then there's life
don't tell me it'll be all right
this nomad needs a home a home
So maybe fall in love with me tonight

You're right there but so far away
A thousand words in my mouth
And I got nothing to say
put you in my love song, hiding in plain sight
Don't make me say it again
Guess I'll have to play it again
And make you fall in love with me tonight

Feels so good and feels so weak

This love cuts until I bleed
Don't touch me, baby, don't look at my scars,
Until you want to know which ones are yours
All I'll ever want
All I'll ever want
Is you and me

Don't know how lost you are
Until you're found
you can't see the road, when the rain's comin' down
You call me home
I'll take you to bed
Turn off the light and I'll pretend that you said
I fell in love with you tonight

Feels so good and feels so weak
This love cuts until I bleed
Don't touch me, baby, don't look at my scars,
Until you want to know which ones are yours
All I'll ever want
All I'll ever want
Is you to fall in love with me tonight

CHAPTER THREE

VIOLET

The first day of senior year. I'd have plenty of first days of classes to come—years' worth in undergrad and med school—but this was the last year of high school. Shiloh was fond of pointing out how ridiculously excited I got about the first day of school when everyone else was bemoaning the end of summer.

"Like a rite of passage," I murmured, as I dressed in skinny jeans and an off-the-shoulder, waist-length sweatshirt.

I studied myself in the mirror. The jeans highlighted my curves more than I was used to but otherwise seemed plain. But in choosing my outfit for the day, Evelyn had warned me not to make it look like I was trying too hard.

"You're naturally stunning, you bitch," she'd told me, laughing, while we shopped at the King's Village Shopping Center the week before. "Just show off that ass of yours, and no one will give a crap what else you're wearing."

I turned in front of the mirror that morning in my bedroom, lips pursed. Two years ago, Evelyn Gonzalez and her crew of popular friends hadn't paid me a second glance. But a friend from my soccer team took me to a beach party last year. Somehow, I ended up in the sandy-floored bathroom, comforting a crying Evelyn who'd just broken up with Chance Blaylock, her boyfriend of six months.

"You're really sweet," she'd said, dabbing her eyes. "Most girls at school would be thrilled to see me like this. Weak and pathetic."

"You're not either," I said gently. "You're human."

Something in those words must've touched the Queen Bee because suddenly she was looping her arm in mine and introducing me to her friends. Which included River Whitmore. I still hadn't the guts to talk to him, but whenever I hung out with them that summer, we exchanged smiles and once he bought me a shake at the Burger Barn. True, he'd been buying everyone a shake, but it felt nice to be included. A high school experience a bookish girl like me would never have imagined.

But then River stopped hanging out with us and now I knew why.

I grabbed the envelope that held my Patient Care Volunteer assignment from the UCSC Medical Center and tucked it into my backpack, then headed downstairs.

My parents were having breakfast in the spacious, sunlit kitchen, sitting as far apart from each other as possible—Dad at the gray marble counter, sipping coffee and reading the paper. Mom at the table, spreading jelly on a slice of wheat toast.

No fighting. No tension. Yet. I felt like I was in one of those movies where the spy has to cross a room without tripping the red lasers that crisscrossed all over. I had to move carefully, slowly, not to set them off.

"Morning," I said brightly.

Mom didn't look up from her toast. "Good morning, honey."

"Morning, pumpkin," Dad said with a tired smile.

Shiloh liked to say the universe took my parents' best features and gave them to me. I got Mom's thick, almost black hair and Dad's dark blue eyes. After that, I looked nothing like them. Mom was tall, slender, with pale blue eyes, while Dad was sandy-haired and stockier.

"Are you excited for your first day of senior year?" Dad asked.

"Definitely. I'm going to be pretty busy, what with soccer, debate, and now this." I sat next to Mom and pulled out my Patient Care Volunteer acceptance letter and placed it on the table.

"You got in?" Mom beamed and reached to give my arm a squeeze. "I knew you would."

Dad brought his coffee over and pecked me on the top of the head. "Proud of you, pumpkin." He sat down so that I was between him and Mom. "And do you know who your assignment is?"

"Is it that Miller?" Mom said, focusing on her toast and being careful to keep her tone casual.

Four years later and my best friend was still *that* Miller to her: the boy who'd lived in a car and nearly died in her backyard.

"No, not Miller," I said tightly, clinging to my smile. "Nancy Whitmore."

Glances were exchanged between my parents.

Dad shifted in his chair. "I visited the Whitmore Auto Body last week."

"I know. It's cancer, isn't it?"

"I'm afraid so. Liver cancer. And it doesn't look good."

"She's terminal," Mom cut in, her voice stiff. "Let's be honest with Violet, *for a change.*"

Dad's lips made a thin line, but he turned to me. "You going to be okay with that, sweetheart?"

"I'm going to be a doctor. Like I told Miller, the hard stuff is part of the deal."

Mom set down her toast. "You told Miller before you told us? When? Last night?"

"Lynn…"

"Yes," I said. "Last night."

Before you burst into my room like a pair of crazy people.

"I can't understand why he's still climbing up my trellis," Mom said, fuming. "If you're not trying to hide him, Violet, then he can come through the front door like everyone else."

"Lynn, we've been through this," Dad said. "They're friends. That's how they do things. Right, pumpkin?"

"*Yes*," I said, not adding that the few times I'd had Miller come to the front door, Mom and Dad had either been in a rage or a cold front. Humiliating for me and awkward for him.

"And anyway," I said, "he has the same concerns you do about me working with Mrs. Whitmore. Because he's a good person. The best."

Mom let it drop, but the thoughts behind her eyes told me talk of "that Miller" wasn't over.

"When do you start?" Dad asked.

"This week. Tuesdays and Fridays."

"That's fast. Well, I'm proud of you," Dad said. "You're going to make an excellent doctor, and this program will be the perfect finish to your college applications."

"Thank you, Daddy."

"And on that note…" Mom smoothed her napkin on her lap. "Seeing as that process is going to begin soon, it might be a good idea to look into a few scholarship opportunities."

"For God's sake, Lynn…"

"What? She's top of her class. A shoo-in for Valedictorian. Why shouldn't she be rewarded for all her hard work?"

I glanced between them. "Do I need to apply for scholarships?"

"No," Dad said firmly while Mom started to speak, then snapped her mouth shut.

My stomach felt like it had suddenly turned to stone. My parents offering to pay for my entire college tuition, even through med school, had been the greatest, most precious gift of my life. Not only for the money but because it meant that they believed in me.

"Is everything okay?" I asked.

"Everything is fine," Dad said, glaring at Mom. "There is no need for you to apply for any scholarship. We promised we'd cover it, and we will. Isn't that right, Lynn?"

Mom met his gaze steadily. "If you say so, Vince."

"I do say so. And I'm going to be late for work. Have a great first day, honey." He brushed his finger over the tip of my nose and left without another word.

I turned to my mom, afraid to ask and afraid of the answer. "Mom…?"

She stirred her coffee. "Don't ask me, ask your father."

"He won't tell me. You guys never tell me anything. You just shout at each other. In front of my friends now, too."

Mom sipped from her mug.

My hands twisted under the table. "Mom, please. I want to be a surgeon. Even with the college credits I've earned already, that's still ten years of school, minimum. If it's too much, I get it. Things change. If there's an issue with my tuition, you can tell me."

Tell me you and Dad are going to be okay.

"We'll talk about it later," Mom said, rising from her chair. "You'll be late for school." Her fingers trailed over the envelope of my PCV assignment. "You've been quite friendly with River Whitmore, haven't you? I hear you talking about him more and more. Even more so than that Miller, which is why I was surprised to see him in your room last night. I thought he was out of the picture."

I blinked at the abrupt change in topic. "Miller will never be out of the picture. Because we're best friends."

"I thought Shiloh was your best friend."

"She is. They both are."

"And River? You've had a crush on him for ages and now you're hanging out with his crew."

"Yes, but—"

"I've made an appointment for you to see Dr. Crandle next Thursday."

"The gynecologist."

"Yes. Since it's become clear to me that I can't keep track of which boys come to your room at night, better safe than sorry."

"Good idea," I said, my face burning. "I might lose track, myself."

Mom sighed. "I'm just being realistic. You're seventeen now, and I know how the world works." She pursed her lips. "Should I have done it sooner?"

God, I wanted to sink into the floor. "Uh, no, Mom. I haven't even been kissed. Going on birth control is overkill, don't you think?"

"Oh, honey," she said, regret swimming in her eyes. "You work so hard, and I know we haven't been around as much as we should. Not like we used to." She cupped my chin in her hand. "I'm just trying to do the mom-thing and take care of you. Okay?"

I mustered a smile. "Okay. Thanks."

She smiled back with pained amusement. "You were supposed to say, 'No need, Mother dear, I'm saving myself until marriage.'"

"Seeing as how I'll never get married, that's a little too long to wait."

"I hope that's not true, though God knows we haven't set the best example."

I swallowed hard. "You used to. You and Dad used to be…so happy."

She stiffened. "Yes, well. Things have come up."

"Mom…?"

She blinked and patted my hand. "I'll make that appointment. Have a great first day."

Shiloh and I didn't have any classes together until History that afternoon. I met her on the expanse of grass in front of the shaded cafeteria tables at Santa Cruz Central High School at lunch. My friend wore a loose bohemian-style dress over her slender frame, and her dark hair was box braided in hundreds of tiny braids, the ends flowing loose and wavy over the light brown skin of her shoulders. Chunky bracelets, necklaces and rings—most of which she made herself—completed her look that I called Earth Goddess Chic.

Everyone couldn't stop telling me how I'd "blossomed" in recent years, but Shiloh Barrera was a natural beauty largely because, like everything else, it came so naturally to her. I'd never met anyone as confident as Shiloh. Comfortable in her own skin.

"Hey, you," I said, flopping next to her. We hugged, and I smelled sweet perfume that she made herself out of flowers from her grandma's garden.

"What's with you?" she asked, studying me. "You don't look like your usual First Day of School self."

"Mom's putting me on birth control, and I'm beginning to suspect there's no money for my college. How was your morning?"

It took a lot to shock Shiloh. Now her eyes widened. "Sorry…*what*?"

"It's more of my parents' drama. Forget it. How was Louisiana?"

"Hot," she said. "And *do not* go changing the subject after dropping little gems like birth control and… Really? No college fund? I thought that was a done deal."

"So did I. Dad denies it, but Mom suggested I look into scholarships. But what if it's worse than that? What if they're broke?"

"Your dad still has his job, right? Your mom still drives the Jag?" She gave my arm a squeeze. "It's probably not as bad as you think."

"Maybe. But God, I wish they'd just be honest with me. I'm going to apply for merit-based scholarships anyway. They're competitive as hell, but I can't sit around and do nothing. And if there is a situation they're not telling me about, I should help out." I inhaled and exhaled easier. Making plans and following a course of action always made me feel better. "I'll do what I have to do."

"Of course, you will," Shiloh said. "Now let us revisit the Birth Control Situation. What gave your mom the idea that you needed to get on the pill, you hussy?"

"My parents busted into my room last night, and I had Miller over."

"Did you two…?"

"*No*," I said, ignoring how Shiloh looked almost disappointed. "You know the deal with us. My mom's paranoid because Miller comes over all the time and because I was assigned to the Whitmores as a Patient Care Volunteer." I lowered my voice. "River's mom is sick."

"I heard." She brushed her hands off on her lap. "Okay, tell me the real deal. You and Miller. You and River. What's going on with…all of you?"

"Miller and I are—"

"Just friends. Uh huh. Does *he* know that?"

My head whipped to her. "Of course, he does. Why? Has he mentioned something to you?"

Shiloh looked at me for a long moment, then said, "No. He hasn't."

I eased a small sigh of relief. "Good."

Shiloh rolled her eyes. "Because you're afraid of messing things up and you don't believe in real love anyway."

"I believe in love, but yes, I'd be afraid of messing things up with Miller. He's too…special to just date or whatever and then have things go south. It'd ruin us." I shook my head. "I nearly lost him once, Shi. I can't do it again."

"So Miller lives permanently in the friend zone but River gets a free pass?"

"I've had a crush on River since always, you know that. But he's the most popular guy in school, in his senior year, and on his way to a storied career in the NFL. I'm completely busy studying and prepping for college. Neither one of us have time for anything serious. I mean, he's barely spoken to me, but yeah…we could date. That would be nice."

"You mean safe."

"Well, yes. I don't want to get to college with zero experiences, but if it turns out there's no college money, I'll have to work even harder than I am now."

"So, you want to date River and have what kind of experiences? The kind that require birth control?"

"Maybe."

Shiloh's brown eyes widened. "You'd let him punch your V-card?"

"What? You think because I'm a dork who spends all her time in the library that I don't have the same sex drive as everyone else? I'm a geek, Shi, not a nun. And God, I haven't even been kissed yet. I'm ridiculously behind."

"It's not a race," Shiloh said. "And anyway, you're not a geek anymore. You're going to be in the Homecoming Court and probably Prom Queen. *Especially* if you start dating the future Prom King."

"No way. Evelyn's got Prom Queen locked up."

"I wouldn't be so sure." Shiloh leaned back in the grass on her elbows. "What if you fall in love with River, despite your best attempts to remain a casual slut? What if he falls in love with *you*?"

I laughed. "If something happened with us—and that's a pretty big *if*—we'd be practical about it. I'm going to UCSC, which doesn't have a football team. River has to go somewhere else, like Alabama or Georgia. It would be stupid to get serious and then go our separate ways."

"Wow, you have it all figured out, don't you?"

"I have big plans, Shi. Trashing my heart isn't one of them."

"We don't always have a say in what our hearts want," she said in a quiet tone I'd rarely heard her use. "You know that, right? Didn't you tell me you loved Miller?"

My stomach inexplicably fluttered to hear her say that out loud. "I do. You know he's like…a brother to me."

The words tasted sour in my mouth, but I didn't take them back.

"Have you *seen* your brother lately? You're not the only one who's matured into a stone-cold hottie." She arched a brow at me. "You haven't noticed?"

"No. I mean, *yes*. But I don't think of him…in that way."

Shiloh stared at me a moment more and then shrugged. "If you say so."

More words to protest rose up, but she was right. I had noticed that Miller was no longer the skinny, underfed thirteen-year-old he'd been when we met. He'd grown taller, bigger, his shoulders broadening, his muscles defined. His handsome features had become more chiseled, more masculine, his jaw and cheekbones more angular. A shadow of stubble and his longish hair—paired with his usual flannel shirt and knit beanies—gave him a scruffy, alternative rocker vibe.

It was very easy to picture him on stage at a festival, thousands of fans—girls—clamoring for him as he sang in that rough, soulful voice of his…

"Hey." Shiloh nudged me gently from my thoughts, her voice uncharacteristically soft. "I get it. You're protecting something precious."

I nodded. "I've seen what love gone rotten looks like. My parents were once best friends, too."

She put her arm around me and gave me a hug. "I know."

A short silence fell, and then I sucked in a breath. "Are we okay?"

"Of course. Why?"

"I don't know. Miller said some things last night. That I've been distant lately. Hanging out with new friends instead of you two."

"You're moving up the social food chain. Scratch that. You're casting a wider net. Everyone loves you."

"I don't know about that."

"I do. You're kind to everyone. And it resonates."

"I guess. Evelyn said there's a party at Chance Blaylock's this Saturday—"

"Nope. Not my people."

"Why not? You'll know me, and I'll get Miller to come—"

"I doubt that." She gave me an arch look. "Do you have the political capital to invite me to a party you're not throwing?"

"It's a rager. No one knows how anyone gets there."

"You, Dr. Violet McNamara, are going to a rager?"

"It's an experience." I smiled and looked away, watching other students milling around the grass or talking and eating at the tables. "Evelyn said River specifically asked if I was coming."

"Then I guess your master plan is working." She shielded her eyes with one hand and jerked her chin across the crowded cafeteria. "Hey, check it. Fresh blood."

I followed her line of sight to a devastatingly handsome guy with hair that was probably blond under the silver dye. He leaned his tall frame against a cement column at the edge of the cafeteria, surveying the scene with casual detachment.

"That's Holden Parish," I said. "Evelyn told me about him this morning."

"Evelyn is the TMZ of this school. She should have her own channel."

I smirked, though she wasn't wrong. "She said he moved here from Seattle, and he's mega rich."

"You're mega rich."

I inwardly flinched. *I'm not so sure about that.*

"Holden is *millionaire* rich," I said. "Maybe billions."

"He certainly dresses the part."

Holden leaned against the pole, hands tucked into a expensive-looking black pea coat. An emerald green and gold-patterned scarf was wrapped round his neck and tied in an elegant knot. His jeans were perfectly tailored to fit his lean physique, and thanks to endless hours hanging out with Evelyn Gonzalez, who had her own popular fashion YouTube channel, I knew a Balenciaga boot when I saw one.

"Holden Parish," Evelyn said, materializing beside me as if I'd conjured her. She stood over us, hands on the hips of her short denim skirt. A skin-tight black tank hugged her slender torso, highlighted her small, perfect boobs. Her huge hoop earrings glinted gold in the afternoon, as did her warm light brown skin. "He is so hot."

Shiloh smirked. "I'm sure he is. It's seventy-five degrees out, and he's in a coat and scarf."

Evelyn rolled her eyes. "He's got impeccable style, and he looks as cool as a cucumber. I'll bet he's hung like one, too. Time to introduce myself." She held her hand to me. "Let's go."

I let Evelyn pull me up, then looked to Shiloh. "Coming?"

She waved us away. "Go. See you in History."

"What is her problem, anyway?" Evelyn asked as we crossed the outdoor cafeteria. "I've been nothing but nice to her."

"She does her own thing."

"Well, she doesn't have to be a bitch about it."

I started to defend Shiloh, but we'd arrived at Holden Parish. He watched us approach, casually pulling a sleek package of cigarettes out of the pocket of his pea coat with *Djarum Black* embossed on the front in gold.

Evelyn flashed him her best smile and tossed her Ariana Grande ponytail over her shoulder. "I'm Evelyn, this is Violet. We thought we'd come over and say hi, since you're new and all."

"Am I?" Holden heaved a sigh. "It's only noon, and it feels like I've been here for ages."

He tucked a cigarette between his lips while his eyes—a stunning peridot green, clear and light—took us in from under sandy blond eyebrows. He flipped the lid on a gold Zippo and those brilliant eyes narrowed as he inhaled deep and blew it out; the air between us was filled with the pungent scent of cloves and tobacco before wafting away in the afternoon breeze.

Evelyn gave him an appreciative glance. "This is California, not Paris. There's no smoking allowed at school."

Holden crossed his arms, the black cigarette held elegantly in his slender hands with ink-stained fingers. "I'm sure there isn't," he said and took another drag.

"There's a spot under the bleachers on the north end of the football field," Evelyn said, her smile turning coy. "Good place to smoke or do *other things* you don't want anyone to see." She cocked her head, her lip gloss shimmering in the sunlight. "Care for a tour?"

Holden eyed her up and down, a smirk on his lips and cunning intelligence in his eyes. But they were heavy too. Shadowed. He hunched against the pole, as if taking shelter from a cold wind only he could feel.

An old soul maybe, I thought.

"As enticing as that sounds, I'll pass. Raincheck, princess?"

Evelyn Gonzalez—two-time homecoming queen and designated 'Hottest Girl in School,' who usually had guys eating out of her hand, took the rejection in stride.

"Definitely. There's a party Saturday night at Chance Blaylock's house. A back-to-school thing. Should be pretty epic."

Holden's green gaze flickered to me. "What do you think, Violet?"

"I think smoking is bad for your health and those around you."

His eyes widened, pleasantly surprised. "So it is."

Evelyn elbowed me in the side. "Don't mind her. Violet is going to be a doctor, so she's anal about stuff like that."

Holden shot me a wink. "So am I."

After a short moment of awkward, Evelyn turned her smile up another watt. "Anyway, if you want to come to the party, give me your number and I'll text you the address."

I had to hand it to Evelyn—when she wanted something, or someone—she didn't waste time.

Holden smiled a lazy smile. "Oh, I think I can find my way."

"Cool. But if you change your mind about a tour, I'm around."

"Yes, you get around," said a voice from behind us. Chance and River Whitmore approached with Frankie Dowd tailing after the football players like a scrawny puppy tagging along with the alpha dogs.

"Fuck off, Frankie." Evelyn punched the lanky red-headed guy in the shoulder.

River's glance flickered to me, and he smiled before turning to Holden. I watched the guys size each other up. If Holden was intimidated by the two jocks and a skater punk surrounding him, he didn't show it.

"I was just inviting our new friend to your party, Chance," Evelyn said, recovering her poise. "Guys, this is Holden."

"Good to meet you, man," River said, offering his hand.

"Likewise," Holden said, not taking it.

The two locked gazes for a moment and then River broke with a laugh. "Okay, whatever."

"Holden is from Seattle," Evelyn said. "Isn't that right…?"

Her words trailed as Holden, wearing that strange, faint smile of his, languidly rolled his shoulders along the curve of the pole until he was on the other side and then walked away.

"He's dressed like it's winter," Frankie muttered. "What a fucking weirdo."'

"Do you ever stop being a jackass?" I shot at him.

He laughed and pretended to be scared. "Ooooh. Someone's on the rag."

My face reddened. Frankie Dowd and a couple of his skater friends bullied Miller all through middle and high school. Miller always told me to stay out of it, and I knew he could take care of himself, but I hated it. Chance and River were never among the bullies; they barely tolerated Frankie, but we'd all gone to school together since forever. Like one big dysfunctional family.

River's gaze lingered where Holden had gone, then he loomed over Frankie. "Get lost, asshole."

Frankie chuckled. "Touchy, touchy, Whitmore. Later, my dudes." He flashed a peace sign and walked away backwards, as if the choice to leave had been his.

River pulled his gaze to me. "You're coming to the party, right, Vi?"

I nodded. God, he was cute. Tall, dark hair, blue eyes. Built like the quarterback that he was, his shirt clung to the muscles that packed his arm and torso. My heart skipped a beat, and it never did that with Miller.

Except that wasn't exactly true.

My heart beat for Miller in a completely different way than it did with anyone else: when his numbers were off and he got sick. When I remembered that awful night when he'd nearly died in my arms. When

I hugged him goodbye after hanging out, and I could feel his own heart beat in his chest, like it was talking to mine.

I realized River was waiting for me to answer his question while I stood there like a dope, lost in thought over another guy.

"Uh yes, I'll be there."

"Great. I'll see you then," he said and strode off with his friend.

"Yep. See you then."

Evelyn was glaring at me, hands on her hips.

"What?"

"Do you have to be such a goody-two shoes? You chased Holden off."

"Me? Hardly. And anyway, I get the feeling it would take a lot more than someone lecturing him about secondhand smoke to scare him."

"True. He looks like he's seen some shit. I wonder what his story is." She ran her tongue over her lower lip. "That's my kind of challenge."

We crossed the grass again, and I spotted Miller sitting on a boulder just outside the crowd of cafeteria tables. He wore torn jeans, boots, and a faded vintage Sonic Youth T-shirt. A sack lunch sat in his lap and he was rummaging in his backpack, probably for his insulin case.

Evelyn followed my line of sight and sighed. "You're going to tell him about Chance's party, aren't you?"

"Of course, I am. Why? Do you think Frankie and those guys are still going to give him a hard time?"

Evelyn shrugged. "Frankie's a moron with nothing better to do. But Miller looks like he can handle himself. Your little boy is all grown up, isn't he? Too bad."

"Too bad, what?" I asked, anger flaring. "Too bad he's poor? Why does that even matter?"

"It's not that he's *poor*. It's the whole picture. He lived in a car. His mom *prostituted* herself. The whole thing puts a...something around him. A cloud?"

"An aura?" I said, crossing my arms.

"Aura, yes! It radiates off of him like a bad smell."

"Evelyn, that's a horrible thing to say."

He used to smell like the forest and now he smells like the beach.

"Don't get your panties in a twist. I know he's your friend. Or your pet project, with his diabetes stuff."

"Yes, he's my friend and you can't talk about him like that. Ever."

"Okay, okay, I'm sorry. Forgive me?" She gave me a quick hug. "Go. Invite him to the party if you want and I'll call you later." She air-kissed my cheek and bounced away, ponytail swinging.

I looked to where Miller sat.

He's not my pet project or a lost cause. He's brilliant.

I only wished everyone at school could see what I saw when I looked at him. I saw the kid who'd lived in a car too, but it'd made him more in my eyes, not less. More beautiful, stronger, braver. And he never complained but instead channeled himself through his music.

And it was high time that everyone at school knew it.

CHAPTER FOUR

MILLER

"Hi, you."

I looked up to see Violet approach. My heart thudded dully, each beat like poking an old bruise. She was so beautiful, drenched in the late summer sun. It glinted in her black hair, pulling out threads of blue. Dark blue, like her eyes that were heavier today, despite the bright smile she put on for me.

Something's wrong.

She plopped down on the grass beside the rock I sat on.

"Hey," I said, my insulin injection pen in hand. "Just about to shoot up. Figure I'd give the new kids something to talk about. First day of school and all."

Vi smiled wanly. She knew I'd endured my share of stupid taunts: that I was a junkie who brazenly shot up in broad day light. Fuck the assholes if they thought I'd hide out in a bathroom to take the medicine that was keeping me alive.

I had to rotate injections all over my body so that no parts were oversaturated. Today, I rolled up the short sleeve of my T-shirt.

"Wait, let me guess your dosage," Violet said. "For practice."

She peered into my bag lunch: ham sandwich, a few strawberries, bag of popcorn, bottle of water.

"Looks like forty grams of carbs so…four units of insulin."

"Correct, Dr. M," I said and injected myself with the pen.

The pain stung, then mellowed into an ache, as I pushed the meds under my skin. When I'd returned the pen to its case, Violet handed me my lunch, though I didn't dig in; I had to wait a few minutes for the insulin to get to work.

"How's your first day going?" Vi asked. She narrowed her eyes at me, taking in my dark circles. "What's wrong? Are you okay?"

"Fine. Rough night, that's all." I fixed her with a stern look that told her not to push it. I wasn't in the mood to talk about Mom's new boyfriend. "I was going to ask the same of you."

"What do you mean?"

"Come on, Vi. It's me."

She smiled sadly. "You must be psychic."

"I can read your face," I said. *I have you memorized.* "Your parents?"

She nodded. "I'm sorry about last night."

"They're the ones who should be sorry," I said darkly. "They tell you what all the screeching was about?"

"Not really, but I have my suspicions. I think my college fund is drying up. Or maybe it's already gone."

My eyes widened. "Oh, shit. You sure?"

"I'm not sure of anything." She waved a hand. "It's fine. If it's true, I'll deal with it. I'll apply for scholarships and make the best of it."

"Don't try to gloss over it, Vi. It's a big fucking deal. To go from home-free to two hundred K in debt? More, since you're going to be a surgeon. Be mad if you're mad."

"I can't be mad at them for that," she said. "That feels tacky and what good does it do? I said I'll apply for loans—"

"You'll have to apply for every loan under the sun to cover med school, but the low-interest kind are for poor schlubs like me."

"You're not helping, Miller," she said, tears building in the corners of her eyes. "I don't even know if it's true, so no point in dwelling on it."

I bit my tongue. Violet faced everything with hope and a smile and even more hard work. I admired that about her. Hell, I envied it. But it made the desire to protect her from anything that would hurt her even stronger.

I'll pay for her college. Every damn penny.

After a moment, she asked brightly, "Have you thought about what you'll do after you graduate?"

I shrugged as if I hadn't been thinking of *exactly* what I'd do after high school. "I'm going to get the hell out of here and make my music."

Her smile faltered the way it always did when I mentioned leaving Santa Cruz. "You realize you have to play for actual people before you can make it as a musician?"

"I will. When I feel like it."

"How does this Saturday sound? Chance Blaylock's party?"

I set down my food and gave her a look. "You want me to be the douchebag asshat who brings his guitar to a party he's not technically invited to? Solid plan."

She laughed and nudged my knee. "Shut up. People will flip their shit to hear you. You're a diamond in the rough! They'll never see you coming!"

I grinned, took a pull from my water. "Uh huh. Next, you'll suggest I wear a fedora and announce my presence with a loud, pretentious cover of 'Wonderwall.' That should solidify my stellar reputation."

Vi's laughter rose and then her voice turned soft. "If you let them hear you play…if they hear your voice, they'll love you. How could they not?"

I don't know, Vi. Why don't you tell me?

I stiffened with sudden bitterness and looked away. "I don't owe them anything."

Violet started to protest, but the bell rang, ending lunch. Students began pouring out of the cafeteria area.

She got up and brushed the grass off her butt. "Walk with me to class?"

"You go head," I said. "I gotta finish my food or else my CGM will go off in Calculus."

"Okay. And I know you hate this stuff, but promise me you'll at least think about coming to the party? Even if you don't play, I want you to be there."

No chance.

"I'll think about it."

She beamed. "Great. See you later. Or tonight? Are you coming over?"

No chance of that either.

"I have to work tonight."

"Oh. Okay." She smiled faintly. Sadly. "Well…don't be a stranger."

"Nope."

She walked away, almost reluctantly. I wanted to follow her. I wanted to spend every fucking second of my day with her. But after last night, everything changed. The hopelessness of us…

It's already too hard.

The next few days of the new school year were blessedly uneventful. So far. I'd gotten into fights at least once a month since middle school. The rumors and whispers had been waiting for me when I got out of the hospital.

Frankie Dowd and his gang of assholes had been waiting for me.

Violet felt terrible that everyone knew I'd been living in a car. "But what was the alternative?" she'd said. "Let you die in my arms?"

That didn't seem so terrible to me.

The first time I came home with a split lip and swollen eye, Mom looked up from watching TV on her short break between her job at the dry cleaners and her job at the 24-hour diner up the street and then went back to the TV again.

"Fight back, Miller. Fight back, or I don't want to hear about it again."

So, I fought back, even though I risked smashing my fingers and losing the dexterity I needed to play the guitar—my ticket out of this shit life.

A life that had, thanks to Chet fucking Hyland, just gotten shittier.

As I feared, he'd become a permanent fixture on our couch and in Mom's bed; I had to sleep with a pillow crammed over my head to block out the squeaking bedsprings.

Worse, Mom seemed to have ditched her second job to hang out with Chet, who was a drain on our already delicate household economy and contributed nothing. Despite his promise, he didn't stop pilfering from my meal plan, and Mom seemed helpless about how to replace it all. Beer became the top import in our apartment, with cigarettes a close second.

"How long's he going to be here?" I whispered to Mom on the morning of the fourth day of school. I'd snuck into her room as she got ready for her dry-cleaning job while Chet watched *The Price is Right* in the living room.

"As long as I want him to be," she said. "Don't give him a hard time, Miller."

"Jesus, Mom, he's a fucking leech. Does he even have a job? Does he—?"

Mom moved in close, her brown eyes hard as they bore into mine. *"Don't give him a hard time, Miller,"* she repeated, her smoky breath hissing and wavering. "Do you hear? Don't do it."

"But Mom…"

"I'm tired, honey. Just so tired." She smiled wanly and gave my arm a squeeze. "You'll be late for school."

I went out without another word. In the living room, Chet watched me prepare my food and meds for the day.

"Off to school, son?" he asked with a hard smile. He threw that word out to bait me. Casting a line to see if I would bite.

I tilted my chin up. "Yeah. And then to my job. You know what a job is, right? One of those places you go to earn money, which is then used to do things like pay bills and buy food."

"Smart guy, aren't you? You got a smart mouth on you." He smirked. "What happened? Your daddy didn't teach you any manners before he took off?"

I felt something in me—that human internal mechanism that kept driving us onward, despite everything—begin to crack and falter. Rage and humiliation flooded me. I thought about what Violet had said, about our senior year being our best yet.

Bullshit. It's all bullshit.

Chet chuckled darkly. "I can see why he left."

"Fuck you."

I heard a gasp from the hallway. Mom, staring and shaking her head at me. I stared back, silently begging her to get rid of this guy before he imbedded himself any deeper—like a thorn that burrowed too far beneath the surface to tear out.

Mom's mouth open and then shut. I went for the door.

"You better watch that smart mouth of yours, son," Chet called after me, his voice chasing me into the early morning fog. "Yes, indeed. Better watch it."

I usually took the bus to school, but I walked through the gray morning, letting the chilly air cool my skin. The sun was out by the time I made it to the front entry of Santa Cruz Central, the bell ringing as I hit the first step.

Vice Principal Chouder stood in front of the administration building, hands in the pockets of his gray suit. "Hustle, hustle, Mr. Stratton. You'll be late."

I kept my head down and continued down the walk, past banks of lockers and classroom doors. My first class, English, was at the end of the open campus on a grassy hill overlooking the band and science rooms.

Class had already begun. Ms. Sanders gave me a stern look but didn't cease her lecture on *The Great Gatsby,* which we'd been expected to read over the summer. The only available desk was next to Frankie Dowd.

Because of course it is.

The lanky guy had his legs stretched out, scabbed knees visible from under his long shorts that were perpetually halfway down his ass. He flipped his head to get a lock of russet hair out of his eyes and smirked at me.

"Why're you late, Stratton?" he whispered. "*Car* wouldn't start?"

"Fuck off."

He laughed with his tongue poking out, like a deranged hyena. I made an easy fist, no pain or bruises. I figured by the end of this shitty fucking day, that wouldn't be possible.

"Frankie," Ms. Sanders called. "Since you're so chatty, perhaps you can answer something for me. Fitzgerald makes numerous references to dust in this novel. 'Ash-grey' men and dust coating everything from cars to actual characters. What do you think it symbolizes?"

"Uh…I think it means stuff is old or…whatever."

A few students laughed, and Frankie triumphantly fist-bumped a friend.

Ms. Sanders pursed her lips. "Let's try a little bit harder next time, eh?" She looked to me. "Miller? Care to give it a shot?"

Some heads in the class turned to look at me with curiosity. Frankie with derision. I've never fit in here. Not in four years. I was still the kid who'd lived in a car and nearly died after pissing his pants in the McNamara's backyard.

"He writes that dust settles over everything," I said. "Because it does. It settles over the whole fucking town. The school. It even gets in your home. You can't get rid of it."

Ms. Sanders nodded, ignoring my f-bomb and the snickers that had followed it. "And what do you think it means?"

"That there's no hope."

They cornered me during P.E., on the way to my locker.

Despite all my calculations and precautions, my numbers were low after running laps. I was still wearing my gym clothes—white t-shirt and yellow shorts, like a dork. My locker was ten feet away when Frankie and two of his buddies rounded the corner.

"Goddamn everything," I muttered, my hands shaking and my watch beeping furiously.

"Well, what do we have here? Does Coach Mason know you're ditching P.E. to go shoot up, Stratton?" Frankie asked, moving in front of me to block the path. His two friends, Mikey Grimaldi and Tad Brenner, hung behind me.

"Fuck off, Dowd," I said and started to push past him.

He shoved me back, and I stumbled.

"Your mom still turning tricks?" Frankie asked, and snickering laughter came at me from all sides.

"I don't know," I seethed, my heart now crashing and my hands shaking so badly I had to tuck them into my arms. "Why don't you ask your dad?"

Frankie's eyes flared for a moment, then he laughed. "You're right. He'd know, since part of his job is to get hookers off the street."

My vision clouded red but now I was swaying on my feet.

"You don't look so good, Stratton. Gonna piss yourself again?"

My watch beeped incessantly, and my leg muscles were starting to feel like sand. I tried to push past him once more, knowing it was futile. Usually, in a fight with Frankie Dowd, I gave as good as I got, but right now, I could hardly stand.

"Get the fuck out of my way."

"I'm good right here," Frankie said, crossing his arms. "Kinda curious about what's going to happen next."

His friends shifted and glanced around.

"Hey, Frankie, he really doesn't look so good," Mikey said.

Tad nodded. "Yeah, and he's got that alarm…"

"Nah, he's alright, aren't you, Stratton?" Frankie clamped a hand around my neck. "You still wearing that little machine stuck in your guts? What would happen if someone took it out? Just to get a better look?"

"*Dude*," Mikey said.

"That's sick, man," Tad added, though neither moved to help me.

I mustered what strength I could, balled my hand into a fist, and swung it upward, striking Frankie under his chin. His jaw snapped shut with a *clack,* and he fell away from me, sputtering and cursing.

"You fu-ther!" He spat a wad of red. "I fu-thing bit my thung."

He came at me a second later, readying a blow I didn't have the strength to dodge. Suddenly, a rough hand shoved me aside and a fist struck out, whacking Frankie full in the nose with an audible crunch of bone and cartilage.

Except for Frankie, who was gasping and cursing, the group went silent, staring at the big, dark-haired guy who'd appeared out of nowhere. He wore torn jeans, scuffed combat boots, and towered over all of us by a good three inches. His faded T-shirt revealed tattoos inking his biceps and one forearm. He looked like an escaped convict, instead of a high school student.

Maybe he is. One of Frankie's dad's arrests is here for some payback.

But I could see the youth in the guy, buried under muscle, tats, and the flat, gray eyes that stared coldly at Frankie. Power coiled and hummed in him, ready to rumble.

Vice Principle Chouder had a sixth sense about trouble on his campus; he materialized like a ghost behind us.

"What's all this?"

"Fu-ther broke my nose," Frankie said, his voice nasally and muffled behind his hand.

Chouder pursed his lips disdainfully at the blood seeping through Frankie's fingers. "Go see the nurse, Dowd." He fixed his gaze on the new guy. "Mr. Wentz. My office. The rest of you get back to class."

My beeping watch finally drew his attention. He sized me up and down.

"Are you all right?"

"Oh sure. Never better."

I pushed myself off the pole I'd been sagging against and managed to make it to my locker and raise my blood sugar before falling into a fucking diabetic coma, wondering where in the hell that guy came from.

I didn't have to wonder long. Gossip spread quickly that a new kid had clocked Frankie in the face. By the end of the day, I'd learned that Ronan Wentz moved here from Wisconsin two weeks ago. He had ditched the first few days of school and was now suspended.

I ditched the rest of my classes, too, to wait for him to get out of Chouder's office.

"You didn't have to do that for me," I said, falling in step beside him as he headed down the front walk of the school.

"I didn't do it for you," Ronan replied. His voice was low and deep, his gaze on the road in front of him.

"Then why?"

He shrugged in his worn-out jean jacket with the fake lamb's wool on the inside. He dressed like me—in distressed clothes—because they were in *distress* and not ripped on purpose like the current fashion. I didn't understand why rich kids wanted to dress like poor kids if they were just going to bag on poor kids for being poor. But that's high school for you.

We continued down the street together; he was headed toward my neighborhood that I guessed might be his neighborhood, too.

Ronan's glance flicked to me and back. "Is it true you lived in a car?"

My skin burned, and I looked away. "You've been on campus for all of ten minutes, and you heard that already? A new record. Yes. A long time ago. No one seems to be able to forget it."

"Then make them forget."

"How?"

He shrugged again.

"The guy you punched? His dad's a cop."

Ronan's lips curled in a smile that was mostly a snarl. "Fuck them both."

"What do you have against cops?"

He said nothing, and we kept walking.

We arrived in my neighborhood of rundown cement boxes with rusted wrought iron over every window. Ronan stopped and stared at one corner apartment on the second floor. A TV could be heard blaring through the torn screen.

"That you?"

He nodded.

"I'm a block down."

He didn't move, and I had a feeling come over me. A strange, out-of-body kind of reaction, one usually reserved for when a song lyric falls into place so fucking perfectly it was as if it didn't come from me but from somewhere else.

Show him the shack.

"You need to get home?" I asked him.

"Home." He snorted the word. "No."

I nodded. Understanding passed between us like telepathy.

"Follow me."

"Found it four days ago," I said. "Been coming here every night, since. After work."

"Yeah?" Ronan turned in a circle. His bulk practically filled the entire fisherman's shack. "Where's work?"

"The arcade, down at the Boardwalk."

Ronan nodded and sat on the bench. "You can see the ocean," he said, his words almost soft, coming out on a gruff voice.

"Yeah, it's nice. A good place to just…"

"Get the fuck away from everyone?"

"Precisely."

"You looked sick earlier." He jerked his head at my wrist. "What's with the watch? That part of it?"

"It's an alarm. My blood sugars were low." I lifted my shirt to show him the CGM. "I have diabetes."

Ronan nodded, and then a sudden smile spread over his lips that he covered with his hand.

"Something funny?" I asked, ignoring the pang in my heart that maybe I had Ronan judged all wrong. *Just another asshole...*

He shook his head. "I knew a girl when I was a kid...five years old." Laughter started shaking his shoulders, coming over him like a fit of coughing—uncontrollable and seeming to take him by surprise. As if it'd been ages—years even—since he'd last laughed. "Her aunt had diabetes. The kid called it dia-ba-titties."

I stared for a second and then his laughter infected me until we were both bent over, chortling like idiots.

"No one...corrected her?" I wheezed.

Ronan shook his head. "Would you?"

"Hell no."

Another round of laughter roared through the shack like a storm, then subsided with gasping breaths and chuckles.

"Shit, hadn't thought of that in years," Ronan said after a minute.

"That's a winner," I said, wiping my eyes. "Dia-ba-titties. Sounds like something my mom's new boyfriend would call it. On purpose."

Even the casual mention of Chet killed the remnants of laughter.

Ronan glanced up. "He's one of those?"

"Yeah. One of those."

He nodded. "They won't fuck with you anymore."

I blinked in confusion until I realized he meant Frankie Dowd and Company. I raised a brow. "You going to be my bodyguard or something? Forget it. I can take care of myself."

Because you made such a convincing case that afternoon?

Ronan said nothing, waiting.

Christ, I needed my hands to play. To make something of my music. To earn a shit-ton of money, so I could give the world a healthy middle finger for being so fucking merciless.

Violet was always telling me I was good at reading people. What I saw lurking under the flat, gray depths of Ronan Wentz's eyes made me sad. Pain. Danger. Violence. The world had been merciless to him too. Something in him was broken. I could be his friend by letting him fight when he needed to fight.

"Okay," I said into the quiet, though I doubted he'd wait for my permission, anyway.

But Ronan seemed satisfied and turned his gaze back to the water.

I shouldered my backpack. "I gotta get to work. Stay as long as you want," I added, but I didn't need to.

It was Ronan's place now too.

CHAPTER FIVE

VIOLET

Friday morning, I dressed for school in flower-patterned leggings and a long white blouse and slipped out of an empty house. Both my parents had gone to work earlier—Dad to his job at the tech giant, InoDyne, Mom to her job as a communication manager for the city. They were both putting more hours in, either to avoid each other or because our financial situation—whatever that might be—required it.

Or both.

At school, a table had been set up on the central quad. A paper tablecloth was draped over it with VOTE FOR YOUR HOMECOMING COURT! in gold and blue paint. Balloons in the same colors were tied to weights and flanked the sides.

Evelyn, Caitlin Walls and Julia Howard surrounded me as I headed to my locker.

"Uh oh," I said with a laugh. "Am I in trouble? Was today the day we were all supposed to wear pink?"

Caitlin and Julia laughed while Evelyn rolled her eyes. "I swear you have that whole movie memorized."

"Memorized? I'm living it," I said with a grin. "Except you guys are sweet." I leaned in to peer at a necklace Caitlin was wearing—a little gold locket in the shape of a heart. "That's beautiful, Cait."

She put her hand to the charm, touched. "Oh, thank you. My grandmother gave it to me—"

"We have ten minutes until the bell," Evelyn interjected with a nod at the quad. "Time to vote."

We veered from the lockers to the table. Two students, sitting between the balloon clusters, took our names to ensure we only voted once and handed us clipboards.

The ballot listed nominees for King, Queen, Prince and Princess, and their accomplishments and contributions to the school. Evelyn was a nominee; her fashion vlog—with more than 25K subscribers—was lauded for her "entrepreneurial spirit."

Julia and Caitlin were nominated too, and—to my shock—so was I, over a fat paragraph of all my extracurriculars and accomplishments.

"Holy crap," I said, a strange little thrill shooting through me. "How did this happen?"

Julia smiled at me. "No idea."

"Me neither," said Caitlin.

"Make sure you all vote yourself in for Princess," Evelyn said, who knew she had Homecoming Queen locked up. "I want at least one of you in that parade with me."

Julia and Caitlin exchanged glances and turned their backs to fill in their ballots, then folded them and stuffed them in the slot.

"I'm not voting for myself," I said. "That feels…weird. It's an honor just to be nominated." I laughed. "Isn't that what they say? But I'll happily vote for you guys."

I bubbled in Evelyn for Queen and River Whitmore for King. Easy. Anyone else was a waste of a vote. For Princess, I filled in both Caitlin and Julia, letting fate decide. For Prince, I wanted to write in Miller, but I knew he'd think it was a joke or that I was making fun of him.

"There," I said and stuffed it in the slot. "I've done my civic duty. Am I free now?"

"Slow down," Evelyn said. "Just hang here until the bell."

"Why?"

"It's good visibility to linger at the voting table," Julia said, tapping her temple. "Strategy."

I smirked. "Puts us in the mind of the electorate?"

"Exactly."

The little zing of being nominated lingered, but hanging around the table felt like trying too hard.

"Oh shit, I almost forgot," Evelyn said. "Did you guys hear? We have another new guy in senior class. Ronan Wentz."

I knew that name. My history teacher had called roll yesterday, but he'd been a no-show.

"Apparently, Ronan is a juvenile delinquent. In and out of jail…"

"Really?"

"I heard he killed his parents and fled the state."

"Get serious, Cait…"

I liked my new friends. They each had beautiful qualities if you got to know them outside the high school ecosystem, but my quota of gossip hit max capacity. I tuned them out, and my gaze wandered until it caught sight of Miller. He was crossing the quad, gaze cast down, shoulders bent as if his backpack weighed a thousand pounds.

"Speaking of the new guy," Evelyn said, nudging me. "Your BFF and Frankie got in a fight after P.E. yesterday."

I grit my teeth as a rush of anger flushed me. "What happened?"

"I heard Frankie was kicking Miller's ass—or Miller was sick or something—until Ronan showed up and beat the hell out of Frankie. Broke his nose and cut off a piece of his tongue."

Caitlin and Julia gasped and murmured while I shouldered my bag and hurried toward Miller, ignoring Evelyn calling me back. I caught up and fell in step beside him.

"Hi."

"Hey," he said dully.

I scanned him for any sign of the fight with Frankie, but his knuckles looked good, and his face was as handsome as ever.

Maybe Evelyn heard wrong.

I glanced up from my scrutiny to see Miller's blue-eyed gaze taking in every part of my face, and then he looked away. He jerked his thumb at the voting table. "You did your civic duty?"

"Ha, that's exactly what I called it." I tried for a smile. He didn't smile back. "I mean, it's silly but kind of fun."

"What a waste," Miller muttered darkly.

"Why do you say that?"

"I can think of a hundred programs that could use the money the school spends renting convertibles for jocks and princesses to tool around the track for twenty minutes after the football game."

"It's tradition. And Homecoming is fundraised like anything else. It's not taking money away from—"

"Right," Miller spat. "Mr. Hodges has to have a bake sale every year to keep the music department running and barely keeps his job. But by all means, let's fund a popularity contest, *for tradition.*"

I stopped walking and put my hand on his arm. "Hey. I know you hate this stuff, but—"

"But you don't."

I shrugged a shoulder. "I'm nominated, which is totally nuts—"

"Ah. Now it all makes sense."

"Hey, that's not fair."

"A year ago, you wouldn't have been caught dead voting for that shit. Guess it's different if you're in the running, eh?"

I flinched, crossed my arms. "You're being a real dick right now."

He fumed, frustrated. "Aren't you supposed to start with Nancy Whitmore today?"

"Yeah? So?"

"Isn't that a million times more important?"

"Of course, it is. But that…" I waved my hand at the Homecoming table. "That's just fun. It's high school. It's experiences, and I want them. I *need* them. My every waking hour is taken up with studying and extracurriculars…my home life is imploding. And if Nancy's really sick—like terminal—I'll take any distraction I can that isn't complete shit. Okay?"

"Fine. Whatever."

We stood in a terrible, tense silence that broke my heart because it wasn't us. So much stress was etched into Miller's handsome face, and I saw new worry suffused in his eyes that already held their fair share.

"I heard about what happened with Frankie yesterday," I ventured.

"I'm sure you did."

"Are you okay?"

"I'm fine. Made a new friend."

"That new guy, Ronan? I have him in History. In theory. He hasn't shown up—"

"He's suspended," Miller said.

"I heard he broke Frankie's nose."

"You heard right. I wasn't feeling up to the job."

My hand on his arm tightened. "Were your numbers low? Again? Maybe you should talk to your endocrinologist. Or what about your PCV? How is that working out?"

"It's not."

"What does that mean?"

He gently extracted his arm from my grip. "Stop worrying about me, Vi. Please. Just…stop."

"I can't. I can never stop caring about you. You're my best friend."

The bell rang, and he stared at me through it, then looked away. "I gotta get to class."

"Miller, talk to me. Please."

The fight went out of him; his shoulders dropped. His deep, gravelly voice sounded even rougher. "My mom has a new boyfriend."

"Oh." My heart sank at the subtext imbedded in those words. "Is he…bad?"

"Remains to be seen how bad, but yeah. The PCV, Marco, came over the other day. Chet made a complete ass of himself. It was fucking humiliating. So I told the guy not to come back."

"Miller, no. You need the help."

"I'll be fine. And I don't want to talk about it, Vi."

I nodded reluctantly. "Okay. I'm sorry you have to put up with that. Him."

His eyes met mine and the hard walls came down a little, like they only did for me. He sighed, ran a hand through his longish brown hair. "I'm sorry for being a dick, but it's just what I've been dealing with."

Wordlessly, I hugged him tight. He leaned into me, let me hold him, but his hands were light on my back as if it burned him to touch me.

"Mr. Stratton? Miss McNamara?" Over Miller's shoulder, Vice Principal Chouder was tapping his watch. "You're both late."

Miller pulled back, shouldered his bag, his gaze anywhere but on me.

"See you later?" I asked.

I wanted to ask if he'd come over that night, like I had a thousand times in four years. But it felt wrong. Everything between us now felt all wrong.

"Yeah, see you, Vi," he said and quickly walked away.

In History class that day, I sat next to Shiloh as usual. Mr. Baskin called roll.

"Watson?"

"Here."

"Wentz?" A silence followed, and then Baskin, a heavyset guy with a graying beard, muttered to himself. "Oh, that's right. Suspended."

He made a check in his roll book, then restarted the movie on the whiteboard that we'd begun last class: a documentary on the Russian revolution.

When the classroom was dark and the documentary rolling, Shiloh leaned into me, whispering, "Okay, Miss Friends-with-TMZ. Who is this new guy who keeps not showing up?"

"Ronan Wentz," I whispered back. "He's suspended for punching Frankie Dowd. Broke his nose."

"My hero," Shiloh muttered. "That shithead had it coming."

I nodded. "He was giving Miller a hard time. Again."

Shiloh scowled and tossed a cluster of small braids over her shoulder. "Frankie's psychotic. Gets it from his dad, I'm sure."

"The police officer?"

"Yep. You're not the only one with gossip. Bibi's friends with one of the detectives at the precinct near our house."

I smiled. "Bibi is friends with everyone."

Shiloh's grandmother was pushing eighty, almost totally blind, and active in nearly every rotary, city, and social club in town.

"Bibi said her detective friend warned her about Officer Dowd. He's had a few disciplinary issues lately."

"Evelyn said this Ronan guy looked like a criminal himself. Not that she was there…"

"He'd better watch his ass then," Shiloh said, facing forward. "If he broke Frankie's nose, his dad is going to be out for blood."

I was quiet for a minute and then leaned back at Shiloh. "Did Miller mention to you about his mom having a new boyfriend?"

"No. He's been pretty quiet lately. Why?"

"I think he's not a good guy. Miller won't tell me much and I don't think he's coming over anymore. I think…"

"What?"

But I couldn't say it. Just thinking that something was wrong between Miller and me made me sick to my stomach. Too much felt on the verge of collapsing all around me.

I smiled. "Nothing."

After school, I drove my white Rav-4 to the UCSC Medical Center. I parked and made my way through the ground floor, waving at receptionists and nurses I'd become friendly with over the course of my three-week Patient Care Volunteer training this summer.

The director waved me in to her office. Dr. Alice Johnson was in her mid-fifties, though she looked younger. Her sleek black hair was style in a side-cut bob, and her red lipstick set off the warm tones in her brown skin as she smiled at me.

"Violet. How are you? Ready?"

"I think so. I *hope* so. I'd also hoped to be paired with Miller Stratton."

"I know you did, but I assigned you to Nancy Whitmore because of all our PCVs, I think you're the most qualified. And the most compassionate. But if it's too much realness, don't hesitate to tell me."

I inhaled. "Is she dying?"

Dr. Johnson nodded. "I'm afraid so. Her oncologist estimates six months at best. Nancy's a lovely lady. Positive, like you. And positivity can make things easier." She studied me from across her desk. "Have you chosen what area of medicine you'd like to specialize in? General surgery, wasn't it?"

A note of doubt touched her words.

"You don't think I'm cut out for it?"

"I think you'd make a fine surgeon. You have one of the brightest minds I've seen come through the program. But is surgery truly where your greatest strengths lie? Doctors are, at their most basic essence, people trained to care for other people. How you choose to care for them speaks to who you are as a person. So it's not a matter of being cut out for it but more a matter of what specialty allows you to utilize all of your gifts. Does that make sense?"

I smiled faintly. "You're saying I'm too soft to be wielding a scalpel?"

"I'm saying that studying as hard as you do and mastering the science of being a doctor is only one half of the equation. Which is why I picked you for Nancy Whitmore. I want you to experience the human side of our profession before you decide your specialty. Your 'softness' is the reason you're the only student here I'd trust with this assignment."

"Okay," I said, bolstered by her faith in me. "Thank you."

Dr. Johnson gave me a final rundown of my duties and handed me a list of things Mrs. Whitmore enjoyed: Earl Grey tea, knitting, classic literature, Hot Pockets…

I looked up from the list. "Hot Pockets?"

Dr. Johnson shrugged with a grin. "We all have our guilty pleasures. I can eat an entire bag of Smarties candy if I'm not careful."

I grinned. "Same. Smarties are life. Thank you, Dr. Johnson."

"Good luck."

I left the Medical Center and drove through Santa Cruz with its little shops, cafes, and greenery. My hometown was smack in the middle of a forest, at the edge of the coast, and butted up against a mountain range. It had all its geographical bases covered and was, in my eyes, the most beautiful place on earth.

The Whitmores lived near my neighborhood on Quarry Lane. I pulled into the drive of a house that was smaller than mine but new. Two stories with a two-car garage and another garage that looked added on at the side. The door was open and the skeleton of a car and various parts were strewn all over. I guessed Mr. Whitmore liked to take his work from his auto body shop home with him.

There was no sign of River's Chevy Silverado.

At the front door, I rang the bell. It chimed inside, and after a few moments, a dark-haired woman about my mom's age answered. She threw open the door with gusto and a wide smile.

"Are you from the hospital?"

I nodded. "Violet McNamara. And you are…?"

"Dazia Horvat," she said, eyeing me up and down. "Nance's best friend. Look at you. Doe eyes. Sweet face. Thank you for being here. Come in, come in."

I followed Dazia into the house, the woman chatting in a faint accent I couldn't place about one of the nurses she didn't like, how nice the weather had been, and how Nancy loved tea but couldn't have it too hot.

I listened while taking in my surroundings. Photos lined the wall up the stairs—River as a baby, as a toddler, playing pee-wee football and looking almost buried under the gear. Family portraits, one taken for every year: Mr. Whitmore, big, dark hair, smiling brightly. River, like a younger version of his dad. His little sister Amelia, three years younger, gap-toothed and smiling as a toddler, beautiful as a teenager. And Nancy…

My throat caught. Bright, vibrant. Blue eyes and dark blond hair and a smile that shown with happiness.

Outside the master bedroom, I inhaled deeply.

Dazia knocked on the door. "You decent?" She shot me a wink, then led me inside.

The Nancy lying in bed did not resemble the woman from the photos. This woman was thin, frail, with a scarf around her head. No eyebrows or lashes, but her eyes…

She's still there. She's all there.

"Hi, Violet," Nancy said. "So nice to meet you."

"You too," I said and fought back sudden tears. Not because I pitied her but because of the sudden, strange desire I had to be with this woman and take care of her in these last, sacred moments of her life. But I pulled myself together, determined not to fall apart on the first day—the first minute—of my job.

"You know my son, River?"

"Yes. Not well, but…yes."

"He speaks highly of you."

"He does?" I lowered my voice. "I mean…that's nice. I think highly of him too."

Oh my God, shoot me now.

But Nancy was gracious enough to pretend not to notice I'd turned pink to my roots.

"He's so busy with football practice and games these days. I don't see him much."

Sadness infiltrated the room like a fog.

Dazia pulled the blanket higher over her friend and patted her leg. "He's a popular kid. That's all. Busy, busy, busy. Isn't that right, Violet?"

"He is. Everyone loves him."

Nancy smiled kindly. Tiredly. "Thank you for saying so. I'm afraid I don't have much for you today. Dazia is in town for a few days and has been hovering over me like a mother hen."

"I stole your job, didn't I?" Dazia flounced into a chair beside the bed and took up a pile of yarn. Nancy was knitting a scarf in blue and purple.

"It's fine," I said. "I can make myself useful. Can I bring you anything? A cup of tea?"

"That would be lovely."

"Dazia?"

"Make it two. You're a peach."

"No problem." I left the room and pressed my back to the door, and this time I didn't fight the tears.

Yes, I was soft. But that didn't mean weak. Being a doctor wasn't about having zero emotions. It was about channeling them toward the patient to give the best care possible. I wasn't giving up on being a surgeon, but in those first few moments with Nancy, I felt a little of what Dr. Johnson must've seen in me. I let a few tears fall for her. And Dazia, Amelia, Mr. Whitmore and River. Especially River.

And then I wiped them away and got to work.

CHAPTER SIX

MILLER

Saturday, I worked from ten a.m. until four p.m. at the arcade. It was the largest on the Boardwalk, a short walk to the rides, coaster, and Ferris wheel that loomed over the beach.

As I walked home, the sounds of explosions, gunshots, and tokens dropping into slots rang in my head. Sometimes, the *wakka wakka* sounds of Pac-Man kept me up at night, conjuring flashes of the little yellow disk endlessly running from ghosts that grew faster and faster, inevitably cornering him.

I hated that fucking game.

Outside my apartment complex, I stopped, inhaled, and mustered the will to climb the cement stairs. Inside, Chet was in his usual spot: his ass glued to our couch, his eyes trained on our TV, his mouth crammed with our food. Cigarette smoke hung heavy in the air. The fact that a diabetic (or anyone, really) shouldn't be living around secondhand smoke didn't seem to faze good old Chet.

"How was the arcade?" he asked. "Making change and trading tickets for plastic shit they're just going to throw out in a day. You're doing God's work, aren't you?"

"It's *work*," I muttered. "Where's Mom?"

"Shopping for groceries."

"We can't afford groceries since she quit the diner."

Chet sneered. "Oh, you think your mom's gotta work two jobs to keep a roof over your head while you play video games all day?"

"I have school and I have a job," I said, gritting my teeth. "And just what the hell do you do?"

"If you must know, Mr. Smartass, I got injured. I get disability and a nice workman's comp check. *That's* why your mom doesn't have to work two jobs. I'm taking care of her. *And* your sorry ass."

Jesus, that was even worse. Not only did Mom want him around, she *needed* him too. Not for the first time, I contemplated dropping out of school to get a better job. My dreams of getting out of this place and playing my music were blackening at the edges. If things got worse, they'd go up in flames altogether.

"The words you're looking for is 'Thank you,'" Chet said, breaking me out of my thoughts.

I ignored him and went to my room—a tiny square that had space enough for a twin-sized bed, dresser, and a small table and chair shoved under the one small window. It was a mess of clothes all over the floor and papers all over the desk, but I'd always kept my guitar safely stowed under my bed in its case.

The case was now on top of my bed's dark green plaid bedspread, open and empty. Disemboweled but for a few pages of scribbled songs spewing out like innards. I hurried back to the living room, stomach twisted in knots.

"What the hell…?"

My words trailed as Chet reached to his feet, retrieved my guitar from the floor behind the coffee table, and sat it on his knees.

In two strides, I was looming over him, the table between us. "What do you think you're doing?"

Chet hefted the neck with one hand, a cigarette clutched between his fingers. His other meaty fingers strumming the strings. "Nice instrument. Your daddy give this to you?"

"Give it to me," I said, my hand outstretched, shaking.

Unperturbed, he played a discordant note. Ash tumbled along the guitar face and into the sound hole. "Nice. Too nice, maybe."

"Give…it…to me," I said, spitting the words between my teeth.

Chet met my gaze while he slowly held the guitar outstretched.

I snatched it back by the neck. "Stay the fuck out of my room."

He chuckled. "Touchy, touchy."

I strode back to my bedroom, returned my guitar to its case, and carried it back out. I had to make a pit stop at the refrigerator where I jammed a few snacks and a bottle of juice into my backpack. Chet's lazy gaze was on me the entire time, like ants crawling over my skin.

"You write a lot of flowery shit, don't you?" Chet observed.

I slammed the fridge door. "What did you say?"

"I read your songs, Bobby Dylan. You think you're in *love*?" He snorted. "This girl you write for… You think she's going to fall for you once she sees all this…" He gestured at the shabby apartment, then chuckled again. "It'd have to be one helluva song."

Rage boiled in me, a red haze that clouded my vision. Then it burned out just as fast, leaving me hollowed out. He was right. Violet's care for me had never wavered, not even when—*especially* not when—I'd been living in a fucking car. But it was one thing to be friends with a charity case. Another to kiss and fuck and walk around the school holding hands with one.

Chet muttered something else, but I barely heard it. I went out, shutting the door behind me, my feet taking me to the beach. To the Shack.

Ronan was already there. He'd gathered up driftwood and charred bits of other people's bonfires to build his own in the small stretch of beach in front of the Shack. He set the last log, creating a wooden teepee, straightened, and whipped a lock of dark hair out of his eyes.

He jerked his chin at my guitar case. "You play?"

I nodded and sat down on a small boulder, resting the case across my knees. "I caught Chet fucking with it. I'll have to bring it everywhere from now on. Here. To school… Fucking asshole."

Ronan opened a small banged-up cooler and pulled out two bottles of beer. He handed me one and sat on another low rock.

"Thanks," I said and scanned the label.

"It's just beer," Ronan said. "Water, barley, hops."

"I need to know the carb count. For my dia-ba-titties."

"Oh, right," Ronan said, taking a pull off his. "That sucks."

"Tell me about it." I made some mental calculations. "Cut me off at two."

"What happens if you have more than two?"

"Depends. Two could spike my sugars. More than that might drop them."

Ronan's dark eyes widened. "Are you saying you can never get drunk?"

"I can." I lifted the bottle to my lips with a smirk. "But it's not doctor recommended."

He blew air out his cheeks. "Fuck."

"Yep."

A silence fell. I'd only had to hang out with him for two nights to know that Ronan wasn't a big talker. I didn't mind. The quiet between us was comfortable. I could think and breathe around him without any bullshit.

The sun wouldn't set for hours, but Ronan reached into his ratty backpack for a bottle of lighter fluid and a box of matches. As he did, I counted at least four tattoos on his forearms and biceps.

"How old are you?" I asked.

"Eighteen," he said, spraying a shit-ton of lighter fluid on the wood. "Nineteen in March. I got held back in Manitowoc."

Eighteen. Dude looked like he was twenty-four, at least. As if life were beating down like a fist, forcing out everything that was young about him.

"Did you get all that ink in one year, or did your parents give you permission?"

"No," he said and struck a match. He tossed it on the wood, which flared into a roaring fire immediately.

I leaned back, shielding my eyes with my beer. "Jesus…"

Ronan stared into the flames, watching the wood burn. When the inferno subsided to a normal campfire level, he sat back down.

"No…what?" I asked. "No permission or—"

"No parents," Ronan said. He took a long pull off his beer. "Mom died when I was a kid. Dad died in prison."

"Shit," I breathed. "Sorry, man. Why was your dad in jail?"

Ronan turned his dark eyes to me, gray and flat, like the rounded stones at our feet. "For killing my mom."

"Holy fuck…" I took a sip of beer since my throat had gone dry. "Who do you live with now?"

"Uncle."

Before I could say another word, Ronan aimed the lighter fluid at the fire. It arched like piss, and the fire flared, hot and bright. Soon, there wouldn't be any wood left to burn.

Another silence fell, this one completely fucking uncomfortable since I had no idea what I should say. But that feeling came over me again—the voiceless knowing that had bonded me to Ronan in the first place. He didn't need or want me to say anything, so I didn't. Pretty soon, the silence felt good again.

The sun began to sink into the ocean, setting it on fire, while the sky turned as deep a blue as Violet's eyes. When Ronan went foraging for more wood, I got out my guitar and plucked a few chords.

Ronan came back with his arms full of kindling. "It's about time."

Self-consciously, I messed with the frets, tuning it. "I don't play much for people."

"Why not?"

I shrugged. "Don't know. Besides, you don't want to hear the shit I've been writing."

"How the fuck do you know that?"

"What kind of music do you listen to?"

"Heavy stuff. Melvins. Tool."

"Yeah, what I play is not that. Mostly, I've been writing songs for a girl."

"A girl." Ronan popped another beer and handed it to me. "Now I really feel bad that you can't get drunk."

"Amen."

We clinked beer bottles.

"What's the story?"

I peered suspiciously at him. "You'll just call me a pussy, tell me to fuck someone else and get over it."

"Yeah, maybe I will," he said with a faint grin.

I laughed, then shook my head. "It's hopeless, is what it is. She's perfect and rich, and I'm a poor bastard without a working pancreas."

I gave Ronan a brief rundown of my relationship with Violet. After a time, he nodded. "Yep. You need to fuck someone else and get over it."

We shared a laugh, watching the flames, then Ronan's voice grew low.

"Nah, that's bullshit," he said. "You need to tell her."

"She's hellbent on us being friends. She thinks it'd ruin us if we tried to be more."

"So? Tell her anyway."

"I can't. She'd shoot me down, and things would never be the same. Though, I guess they're pretty fucked already."

Ronan nodded. "So don't talk to her. Just…I don't know. Kiss her."

"No way."

"Why the hell not?"

"Uh, fucking *boundaries,* for one thing. She's told me how she feels, explicitly. Friends. I have to honor that."

Ronan snorted and drained his beer.

I leaned forward over my knees. "What can I do? I told you, we swore a blood oath."

"When you were *kids*. Does she suspect you like her?"

I don't like her. I love her with every goddamn piece of my soul.

Ronan's thick eyebrows went up, waiting.

"Not exactly," I admitted.

"Where is she now?"

"I don't know." I gave the sand at my feet a little kick. "There's a party tonight. She'll be there."

"So, go to the party and tell her."

"I just said—"

"You gotta fight, man," Ronan said, his deep voice rising, his eyes flared in anger. "You fight because if you don't, it'll be too late. And too late is fucking *death.*"

He looked away quickly, his hands balling into fists, memories that had nothing to do with me coursing through him like blood.

I waited until they let him go, then said into the twilight, "She needs me to be her friend. She needs…me."

"So you're her pack mule. You carry all her shit and try to make life easier on her because you care about her. What about you?"

Ronan swung his head my way, his eyes asking the question beneath the question: *Do you want to be needed or do you want to be loved?*

Maybe the beer was making me tipsy, or maybe it was just the plain simple truth of it all. Violet's home life might be crumbling beneath her, but mine was fucking on fire. If I didn't salvage something good, there'd be nothing left.

I stood up, brushed the sand from my ass, and took up my guitar case.

"You want to come?" I asked. "I mean, it's probably going to be a bunch of drunk jocks playing beer pong to shitty house music."

Ronan got to his feet too and kicked sand over the fire. "I'm coming. I told you. I got your back."

I started to smile as something like happiness tried to fill in my cracks. Suspicion got there first. "Why?"

"You don't annoy the living shit out of me. Good enough?" His tone was harsh, but I saw a tinge of warmth in his slate gray eyes.

The happiness came back. "Good enough."

CHAPTER SEVEN

VIOLET

Chance Blaylock's huge two-story on Ocean Avenue was blaring Eminem's "Godzilla" over a hundred laughing conversations. I felt the base even out on the street as Evelyn and I headed up the walk, muttering a curse. I was at war with my tight minidress; a constant push and pull between tugging it down and hauling it up to better cover my boobs.

"Will you relax?" Evelyn said, looking stunning in black leggings and a black bustier-style top. "You are *fire.* River is going to lose his shit when he sees you."

"I feel half-naked."

She smirked. "Exactly."

In my past life, I'd never worn more than jeans and sweatshirts to social events. This was my first house party, and I felt like an imposter. Or a spy from the "other side" come to see how the cool kids do it.

They're going to see right through me.

Then I chastised myself for being silly and remembered what David Foster Wallace once said: *You'll worry less about what people think about you when you realize how seldom they do.*

Inside, the house was dark with only small lamps lit here and there and a string of lights over a sound system. Bodies filled the rooms, talking, dancing, making out. Most with a red solo cup in hand. The music and people filled every corner of the house, upstairs and down.

Evelyn took hold of my hand. "Kitchen. We need to get our *drank* on."

We squeezed through the crowd and arrived in a spacious, brightly lit kitchen that seemed blinding after the dark of the rest of the house.

The kitchen overlooked the expansive backyard where the party had spilled out onto the patio around the pool. More colored lights were strung in garlands, and people huddled in groups on lounge chairs, the glowing ember of joints passing from hand to hand.

A bunch of football players had set up camp around the keg next to a huge island of gray marble that was covered in bottles, empty solos, and a salad bowl filled with cherry red punch. River was among them.

"Hey, boys. This is Violet's first house party." Evelyn pressed a solo cup of beer in my hand and looked meaningfully at River. "Be gentle."

I rolled my eyes as my face flushed red. "Thanks for that."

"Shh, here he comes."

Evelyn side-stepped away as River came around the island in jeans, a white T-shirt, and a plaid button-down, open and rolled up at the sleeves. The shirt revealed every cut line of his chest, but his forearms were downright mesmerizing.

"Hey," he said.

My gaze shot up to a chiseled face that looked cut from granite, a light shadow over his square jaw. "Hi."

River's faint smile had just the right amount of casual amusement and confidence I expected from the captain of the football team—a guy who was probably going to end up winning the Heisman and being drafted to the NFL in a few short years. But his eyes darted here and there, as if he was aware we had an audience. Or nervous to be talking to me.

Hello, ego. That's impossible.

"So…this really your first party?"

"Is it that obvious?"

"Nah, you're doing all right."

"Any pointers?"

He laughed. "Yeah. If Chance offers you a cup of his 'world-famous' party punch, say *no.* That shit is like gasoline."

I laughed too and felt a loosening in my chest. River Whitmore, who I'd built up into this mythical figure—an Olympian god who wouldn't dare talk to mere mortals like me—was just a guy who needed a conversation icebreaker like anyone else.

River moved a tiny bit closer; I could smell his cologne—woodsy and clean, mixed with a faint scent of motor oil. His voice grew low. Private. "So listen…"

I swallowed. "Yes?

"My mom said it was awesome meeting you."

"Oh. Right."

"You made her happy and that's a big deal to me. So, thanks for that."

"Of course. She's wonderful."

"Yeah, she is." His eyes shone, and he quickly took a pull from his solo cup. Chance and a couple of guys called to him from the next room, pulling their king to the beer pong table. "So…maybe we can talk more later?" he asked. Almost shyly.

"Sure. Yes. I'd like that."

He gave me a final smile. "Don't drink the punch."

My heart ached for him; he seemed a little bit like an imposter too. The most popular guy having to pretend to have a good time at a party while there was fear and pain waiting for him at home.

The party ebbed and flowed around me. I finished my beer, and someone gave me another. I finished that too, and the ground tipped under my feet a little as Evelyn took me by the hand to make the rounds. She was effortlessly popular, confident, perfectly flirty—everything I was not.

Outside, by the pool, I pulled her aside. "I have to ask. How come you and River…?"

"Never hooked up?" She shrugged. "It makes sense, doesn't it? But I don't know. There's something about him I can't figure out. We're not on the same wavelength."

I wondered if that was code for, *I tried but he shot me down.* But I'd grown close to Evelyn; she bullshitted so much, she was easier to read when she wasn't.

"But hey, my loss is your gain," she said. "You guys looked pretty cozy in the kitchen earlier."

"He's sweet."

"Sweet. Uh huh. Did he ask you to Homecoming yet?"

"No. But he's going through some heavy stuff."

"Truth. The poor boy needs a distraction, don't you think? And a little nudge?"

"What's that mean?"

"Leave it to me." Her mischievous smile collapsed as she spied something over my shoulder. "God. Your lost boy is here."

I swung around to see Miller sitting on a lounger, his guitar case at his feet, talking with a big, dark-haired guy who sat on a deck chair beside him.

"Ooh, it looks like he brought his bodyguard," Evelyn said. "That's Ronan, I'll bet. The guy who broke Frankie's nose." She took in the new guy appreciatively. "God, look at those arms. Yummy. Loving the ink, too, but…not my scene. He looks like he just broke out of jail."

Miller met my eye, and I waved. He didn't wave back but said something to Ronan, who nodded. Then Miller left his guitar and approached.

"Uh oh," Evelyn said. "Now is *not* the time to let River see you with another guy."

"That's silly. It's just Miller."

The words tasted funny in my mouth. It's *just* Miller. Like saying it's *just* air; always there but essential to live.

"Hey," he said, giving Evelyn a nod.

"I'm so glad you came," I said, hugging him.

His scent was so different from River's—cigarette smoke he carried from home mixed with the cleaner scents of bonfire smoke and the salt of the ocean. Tension hummed in him, vibrating in his body like a current.

I stepped back. "Are you okay?"

"I…yeah, fine. Would you like something to drink?" He took in my skimpy dress for the first time and scowled. "Or a coat, maybe?"

I scoffed. "Yes to a drink. You can keep the lecture."

"No lecture. I just didn't realize this was a costume party."

"What's that supposed to mean?

"It means you never needed to dress like this before."

"I don't *need* to dress like this now," I shot back. "I *choose* to. And why do you care what I wear, anyway?"

"I don't, that's the point." He carved a hand through his longish hair, frustrated. "Shit, sorry, never mind. Can we go somewhere quiet? I need to talk to you."

"I could use that drink first. Just water. I'm a bit wobbly."

We pushed our way back through the crowds to the kitchen. Curious stares followed us, but no one gave Miller a hard time. He poured me a cup of water from a Britta on the counter, then got himself a beer from the keg.

He downed the whole thing, then sucked in a steadying breath.

"Is everything okay?" I asked. "Did Shiloh come with you?"

"Just Ronan. Listen—"

At that moment, the beer pong game broke up and the guys flooded back into the kitchen, a gaggle of girls following after, Evelyn, Julia and Caitlin among them. More curious glances landed on Miller, but River's eyes—and smile—were only for me. I smiled back, then looked away, acutely conscious of Miller standing beside me.

Evelyn smiled like the Cheshire Cat. "Oh goody, everyone's here…" The snap of a Zippo lighter caught her attention. "I take it back," she purred. "*Now* everyone is here."

The scent of clove cigarettes suddenly permeated the kitchen, and we all turned to see Holden Parish leaning in the corner between the hooded stove and the stainless-steel dishwasher. His sudden appearance was so startling, it was as if he'd been conjured in a puff of his own smoke.

He was dressed all in black—a silk button-down shirt, dark jeans and sleek black Oxfords. Despite the late summer night, he wore a black pea coat—unbuttoned—the collar turned up. A blood red scarf was slung around his neck and dripped down either side of his torso. Tall, slender, elegant, with his striking eyes and silver hair, Holden reminded me a little of Spike from *Buffy the Vampire Slayer.*

"Vampires have to be invited in," I whispered to Miller with a beer-induced giggle. "If he starts feeding on us, blame Evelyn."

She sidled up to Holden, linked her arm in his. Taking possession. "Everyone, you remember Holden Parish."

Chance, his face flushed with beer, frowned. "Smoking's outside, dude."

A lazy smile spread over Holden's lips. "You sure about that? Your living room smells like a Snoop Dog concert." He tucked the clove cigarette into the corner of his mouth, squinting against the smoke, and handed Chance a small paper bag. "A token of gratitude for having me at your little shindig."

Chance pulled out a bottle of Patrón Silver and a grin split his face. "*Dude.* Thanks."

"Perfect," Evelyn said, still attached to Holden as if he were her own personal party favor. "Line up the shots, boys, because it's time to play Seven Minutes in Heaven."

Cheers and *woots* went around and the shitty, cheap vodka punch was replaced with the expensive tequila. Holden poured the first two shots.

"To our host," he said and handed one to Chance.

The guys clinked glasses and tossed the liquor back. Chance shook his head, blowing air out his cheeks, eyes watering. Holden took his smoothly, as if it were water. But the booze seemed to animate him, instantly warming up his cold front. He took command of the kitchen like a circus ringmaster.

"Step right up, ladies and gents, and let's make some beautiful memories."

"I need to talk to you," Miller said in my ear, under another round of cheers.

"She's busy," Evelyn said. She'd detached herself from Holden long enough to press a solo cup with an inch of tequila into my hand. "And it's a party. Drink now, talk later. *After* we play."

"She doesn't need to drink that," Miller said.

"And she can speak for herself," I said, glaring at him. "What has gotten into you, tonight?"

"You just said you needed water."

"Maybe I changed my mind."

"Maybe I don't want you to get date raped by a jock in a closet."

My eyes flared.

Evelyn gaped. "The hell…? Are you for real?"

But Miller ignored her, his blue topaz eyes boring into mine. I'd never seen this side of him. He'd always been intense but never toward me. Not like this. Protective. Possessive, even.

"I-I can take care of myself," I stammered.

Miller said nothing but took the cup out of my hand. His gaze never leaving mine, he tossed back the shot, chucked the empty on the floor, then turned and walked out of the kitchen.

I started after him. "Miller, wait—"

"Let him go," Evelyn said, pulling me back. "He's totally out of line. River is a good guy."

"I know, but Miller can't be drinking like that."

She rolled her eyes. "He can take care of himself. River's going to play my game. Do you see where I'm going with this? You. Him. A dark closet for seven minutes?"

I looked after where Miller had returned to the backyard, and then Evelyn's words sank in to my beer-dampened thoughts.

My first kiss. It might happen. Tonight.

My heart stuttered, and my cheeks felt warm. Evelyn watched my face.

"Ah, now she gets it." She offered me her tequila. "Drink."

I pushed the shot away. "That'll make me sick. And if I'm going to kiss River tonight, I don't want to be drunk for it. I want to be present in the moment. To remember it and savor it."

"Oh my God, you're like Snow White. Pure as the driven snow or some shit. It'll happen. Trust me."

I nodded. Because Miller was wrong about River.

Just because he mistrusts everyone doesn't mean I have to.

"How are you going to make sure that River and I end up in the closet together?"

Evelyn smiled. "Because I make stuff happen."

A bunch of us, five guys and five girls, cleared space in the living room. Music still blared over the sound system, but the dancing had subsided, and we had a small audience. I sat in a circle between Evelyn and Caitlin. River, Chance, Holden—who was everyone's new favorite person—sat across from us. Two other football players, Donte Weatherly and Isaiah Martin, rounded out the guys, while Julia and another girl I barely knew made up the rest.

Miller had taken a seat with Ronan and a small group of people in the corner of the living room by the front window. He had his guitar on his lap and was watching me, an unreadable expression on his face.

But his eyes. They look almost...sad.

Then he looked away, turning his attention to Amber Blake. A pretty girl with long blonde hair. Evelyn called her a granola girl—her nickname for environmentalist, pot smoking vegans she thought made up a good percentage of Santa Cruz's young people.

Amber and Miller's heads were so close together, they were nearly touching. Maybe only to be heard over the music.

Maybe not.

I guess he's not so sad after all.

"Yes, this game is old and cheesy but not the way I run it," Evelyn said, tearing strips of paper lengthwise. "If your name is picked, you go in. Then we pick someone who joins you in the dark." She grinned slyly. "I'll leave it up to you to decide how to figure out who. When time's up, you leave, but that person stays in the closet, and another name is picked. You get it? Like a chain. If you're not picked to go in, you drink!"

The group voiced their approval.

"This is a *woke* version of Seven Minutes in Heaven," Evelyn continued, writing our names on the strips of paper. "That means I don't give a fuck if you're a guy and get paired with another guy, or girl with a girl. You go in and get to know each other." She grinned again. "How well you get to know each other is up to you. Someone have a timer?"

"Yes, my queen," Holden said and jerked his arm from his sleeve to reveal a Philip Patek watch. I recognized the crazy-expensive brand since my dad had one too.

Evelyn unfolded a piece of paper. "Up first…Violet McNamara." She leaned into me. "I got you, girl."

I sucked in a breath and let it out slowly. Out of the corner of my eye, I found Miller watching me again, his expression stony, his mouth a grim line. Suddenly, I felt as if I was getting up in front of a firing squad. Guilt assailed me, and I froze for a second, trying to sort through a strange tangle of emotion.

Then Evelyn nudged me, and I headed to the closet.

Inside, I felt my way along a wall of Mr. and Mrs. Blaylock's collection of spare towels, sheets, and fabric softener, and sat down on the carpet. A few tense, nerve-wracking moments later, the door opened and a huge shape filled the dimness. The scent of woodsy cologne filled the space as River shut the door, cutting the party noise in half.

"Violet?"

"I'm over here."

"It's dark as shit…" River's bulky shadow made its way across from me, and he sat against the opposite wall. A silence fell.

"This is a crazy party, huh?" I said as our seven minutes began to tick down. "That Holden is a strange guy."

"Uh. Yeah." River coughed. "He's fucking weird. Reminds me of that vampire, Lestat."

"Oh my God, I said almost the exact same thing, different vampire. I didn't know you read Anne Rice."

"I don't. Saw the movie. I mean…my mom watched it once. I remember some of it, I guess."

"Okay."

Another silence fell, and the awkwardness between us grew. I wanted to ask how he was holding up with his mom being ill, but he probably needed the party to escape for a little bit, so I defaulted to sports.

"How are football practices going?"

"Good. Long. You play a sport too, right?"

"Soccer. We don't start until spring."

"Cool."

More silence. This conversation was like an engine that wouldn't turn over.

"So, Violet."

"So, River."

"Homecoming dance is in a few weeks."

My heart took off. *Finally.* "Yes."

"Are you going with anyone?"

"Nope!" I blurted and then pinched myself on the arm, marveling that after months of hanging out with Evelyn, not one of her flirting skills had rubbed off on me.

"Cool. So…would you like to go with me?"

"Yeah. Yes. I'd like that. Thank you."

My skin burned so hot with a mixture of happiness and embarrassment, I thought I must be glowing in the dark.

"Great. We can work out the details later," River said.

"Sure."

Another silence and then someone pounded on the door, making me jump.

"Time's up! Come on out, Violet. River, stay put."

"That's my cue."

I started to get to my feet when River's heavy, strong hand found mine. I felt him lean in; the dark between us shifted, and my space was filled with him. I closed my eyes. Heart pounding. Lips parted.

This is it. My first kiss…

"Thank you, Violet," River said, and his breath—tinged with beer and the stronger tones of tequila—wafted over my cheek a split second before his lips landed there.

A thrill skimmed down my neck, making my skin shiver pleasantly…until I realized that kiss on the cheek wasn't an appetizer. It was the main course.

He sat back against the wall and let go of my hand. "You'd better get out of here before Evelyn starts screeching."

"Oh. Right." I got up while wrestling my skirt back down. "Okay…uh. Bye."

I hurried out, a forced smile on my lips, ignoring the group's cat calls and demands for details.

"Well?" Evelyn hissed when I resumed my seat beside her. "What happened?"

"That felt like Seven Years of Awkward," I said through a smile. "God, that was bad. I didn't say *anything* worthwhile or witty. I just clammed up like a dork."

"You weren't supposed to *talk*," Evelyn said, frowning.

"He asked me to Homecoming…"

"Yes! I knew it!"

"I know but… We had no chemistry. Zilch. I just wasn't myself."

And he wasn't exactly all charm and swoon either.

"You got nervous because he's a hot guy, and you like him. Give it time. Going to the dance with him is just the beginning."

"You're right. I'm overthinking it."

My fake smile turned genuine, and I eased a sigh…until I caught sight of Miller watching me. He quickly turned away, back to his conversation with Amber.

That's…good, right? Maybe he'll ask her to the dance. Maybe we can all go together.

For some reason, the thought made me want to laugh. Or cry. Or both. I'd probably had too much to drink.

The crowd was getting impatient, so Evelyn drew another name from the pile to join River. "Holden Parish."

The crowd, guys especially, *ooohed* and nudged each other.

"None of that Neanderthal bullshit," Evelyn scolded. "It's the twenty-first century, for fuck's sake."

Holden tossed back a shot and climbed to his feet, swaying slightly. "If I'm not back in seven minutes…wait longer."

The group laughed as he strode to the closet and disappeared.

"Oh, grow up," Evelyn said to the guys who were still snickering. "My game. My rules."

Everyone took a drink but me, and the seven minutes—timed by Isaiah—ticked down. Two minutes in, the closet door slammed open, and River strode out.

"Fucking asshole," he muttered and stormed to the kitchen like a charging bull.

The guys looked ready to follow, but Evelyn wasn't having it. "The game isn't over." She snatched a name from the pile. "Ooh. It's me!"

"Bullshit," Chance said. "Someone's thirsty for the new guy…"

She gave her ex the finger, adjusted her bustier-style top, and vanished inside the closet. But without Evelyn holding it together, the game was over. The guys got up to join their quarterback in the kitchen. Julia and Caitlin wanted to wait for Evelyn, but Miller was still ten feet away, talking to Amber. Intimately.

I suddenly needed to get outside and get some air.

What's wrong with you? River asked you out. This is what you wanted.

Still feeling as I were on a boat tipping over mild swells, I carefully made my way to a lounger near the pool. Evelyn, Caitlin and Julia found me a few minutes later.

"Well, that was a waste of my time," Evelyn said, fuming. "River's right. That Holden is a fucking asshole. A psycho."

"What happened?" I asked, alarmed. "Did he try something?"

She looked at me as if I were stupid. "*No.* That was the whole point. Instead, he just sat there, singing."

"*Singing?*"

"Yes, Violet. He's super drunk and—" The other girls began to giggle, and Evelyn shot them dirty looks. "Oh, shut up. *I* need to get super drunk."

She flounced off, and Julia and Caitlin burst out laughing. "Vi, you missed it. Evvie stormed out of the closet and Holden went down on one knee in front of everyone, serenading her with that Shawn and Camila song, 'Señorita.'"

I frowned. "But that's a sexy song."

Caitlin shook her head. "She didn't find it sexy that *he* sang to *her*, 'I love it when you call me señorita.' It was pretty epic. That guy is crazy."

Julia nodded. “Rich but crazy. A pity.”

I managed a smile and stood up. “Will you tell Evelyn I left? I think I’m done. I’m calling an Uber.”

“Already? It’s only ten o’clock.”

“Yeah, I’m—”

From inside the house, shouts could be heard, and the sudden smashing of glass. The house music suddenly went silent, and Holden Parish’s voice rang out loud and clear.

“*Everyone shut the fuck up.*”

And that’s when I heard it. The faint strains of a guitar.

I hurried back into the house. The Blaylock’s dining room overlooked the living room. Holden was standing on top of the dining room table. The smashed remains of the Patrón bottle lay strewn at his feet, shards glittering and scratching the polished mahogany. He barked at anyone still talking to shut up, lording over a room that had grew silent under his command.

For Miller.

My best friend was playing his guitar and singing “Yellow.”

Our song…

Others rushed in from the kitchen behind me, Chance demanding to know what the fuck happened to the dining room table. I hardly noticed. Neither did anyone else. Miller’s voice, scratchy and low and perfect, filled the darkened room, the understated strains of his guitar moving under it. His tone and pitch were haunting, melodic. Everything on display. The talent he’d kept to himself for so long, now free and touching everyone who listened.

Including Amber Blake.

She sat cross-legged in front of him, a dreamy smile on her lips. Miller’s eyes were closed; he wasn’t staring longingly at her, but my heart told me he may as well have been.

What do you care? You like River. He asked you to the dance!

But Miller was singing for the first time in public, with Amber. *For* Amber, maybe. And he’d chosen our song. My heart flooded with both joy and pain—like being feverish and chilled at the same time.

The room was rapt. Some sparked up their lighters; others turned on the flashlight function on their phones so that the darkness turned ghostly and starlit. It was so easy to reimagine the living room as a dim concert venue in which Miller and his guitar sat under the spotlight.

I tore my gaze from him to see the looming shadow of Ronan leaning against the wall casually, arms crossed but watching over Miller. Protectively. I looked back to Miller who was now watching me.

Our eyes met, and he held on to my gaze mercilessly while he sang.

"For you I'd bleed myself dry."

I must've drunk too much because suddenly, I felt sick. I couldn't move. My stomach had twisted in knots so tight, I could hardly breathe.

What is wrong with me?

The song ended and quiet descended, until Holden, still on the dining room table, dropped two words into the stunned silence, "Holy. Shit."

The rest of the party erupted into cheers and applause, and that's when I broke free of my stasis. I clapped too. I clapped so hard, my palms stung. My smile was so wide, it hurt my cheeks. Joy filled my heart, and yet, tears were streaming.

Miller witnessed my reaction. His expression softened, and he started to rise, but I pushed through the crowd, out of the front door and into the night.

CHAPTER EIGHT

MILLER

I lost her.

My heart had already shattered into a million pieces watching River follow Violet into that closet. It cracked again when she ran away.

Follow her. Tell her. Now.

I got to my feet to follow Violet out the door when Frankie Dowd and this friends, Mikey and Tad, came in, crowding me and pushing me back.

"Well, lookit who crashed this party. Where you running off to, Stratton?" Frankie said, giving me a shove. His nose was bandaged under white gauze and tape; dark circles ringed both eyes.

"Back off, asshole," I snarled.

Amber's hand was on my arm, and she murmured soft words to come back and sit with her. I shook her off.

Frankie sneered. "Or what? You going to have your convict bodyguard cold-cock me again?"

Ronan loomed behind me, arms crossed, boots planted.

Frankie's eyes widened in fear to see Ronan, then he snarled. "You're fucking dead, dude. You have no idea who I am."

"I know who you are." Ronan's voice sounded like it was coming from the ground. "I know exactly who you are."

Tension tied the five of us together in tight bands that were ready to snap. And Violet was getting farther away…

"Dude! What the fuck are you doing?"

The party noise flattened as all eyes turned to the dining room table. Holden was tap dancing on the mahogany, amid the shattered glass, and barreling through a watery version of "Singing in the Rain." He was drunk off his rocker but managed to keep out of Chance's reach as the big guy tried to get him down. The room was lit, cheering and laughing, cell phones out.

"My parents are going to fucking kill me," Chance raged. "Someone get over here and help me get this prick off the table."

Holden laughed and danced out of the way of Chance's swiping hand. River emerged from the kitchen.

"Show's over," he said, his voice cool and low. "Get the fuck off."

Holden crouched and reached out a hand to River, crooning, "*What a glorious feeling, I'm happy again.*"

River snarled and smacked his hand away. He made a grab for him, but Holden sprang off the table with shocking agility. Both he and Chance chased him the short distance to the living room, where Holden hurdled the back of the couch, landing between two people, then jumped onto the coffee table. Beer cans scattered, a bottle shattered and the glass ground under Holden's shoes.

"Just singin' and dancin' in the raaaaain…"

Like everyone else, I'd been so riveted by the surreal scene in front of me that I'd been ignoring the scene behind me.

"You're dead, fucker," Frankie snarled at Ronan, and I turned in time to see the crazy bastard pull a police-issue Taser from the back pocket of his falling-down boardshorts.

"Whoa, hey…" I began, then ducked as Frankie lunged for Ronan.

Ronan, who'd been like a stone statue all night, quickly feinted right and knocked Frankie's arm up and out. The Taser went flying, and Ronan gripped Frankie by the front of his shirt and drove him a few steps toward Holden and the coffee table. The crowd scrambled out of the way as the guys went down in a heap on the carpet, fists flying and hands grasping and tearing at each other.

River and Chance rushed over to haul them apart, but Frankie—red blood roses blooming on the white bandages on his nose—spat and fought like a rabid dog.

"*Fuck this guy*," he screamed, wrestling out of Chance's grasp. "*You are so dead*." He grabbed the broken beer bottle off the coffee table at Holden's feet and brandished the jagged end at Ronan. "I'm going to kill you, motherfucker!"

More shouts from River and Chance, but Frankie swung the bottle to ward them off. Amber gripped my arm, and I shielded her from the chaos as best I could while I tried to pull Ronan back, but he was as immovable as stone.

The crowd hushed as Frankie took a few swipes at Ronan, and we all gasped as one of them drew blood across his forearm.

Ronan glanced down at the red line opened on his skin, then back to Frankie. "That was a mistake."

His hands balled into fists, and I felt the tension in him coil. Ready to spring. He was going to get cut worse, maybe even stabbed, but not until he beat the shit out of Frankie.

Or kill him.

Then Holden jumped down from the coffee table into the middle of the fray. He stepped between the two guys, ripped his shirt open from under his coat and bared the left side of his chest to Frankie.

"Right here," he seethed, his voice low and cold and empty. He tapped his chest, over his heart. "Put it right here. Go on. Do it. *Do it.*"

The crowd hushed. Everyone stared. No one moved. Frankie breathed through his nose like a bull, eyes wide with shock. The bottle in his hand trembled.

Slowly, I pushed forward and took hold of Holden's arm. "Hey, man. Come on. Hey…"

Holden backed up while River took the bottle out of Frankie's hand. A moment of eased tension and then Holden jerked out of my grasp, pulled his coat together, drew a clove cigarette from his pocket and said jovially, "Anyone got a light?"

Chance's bleary eyes widened. "What the…? Get out. You three." He waved his finger between Holden, Ronan and me. "Get the fuck out of my house."

Holden turned to me with a mock expression of shock. "*Rude*, right?"

An incredulous laugh escaped me and then another, until a full-fledged outburst was building in me. The tequila I'd stupidly drunk did me no favors—I didn't need to look at my watch to know my numbers were sinking, making me feel underwater.

Or maybe it's just this crazy-ass night.

"*Get out!*" Chance bellowed.

He lunged, and Holden and I, laughing like loons, made a run for it. We turned at the door to see Ronan level Frankie with a final glare, and then he strode in long-legged paces after us.

"You're dead, Wentz," Frankie screamed after us. "You're fucking dead!"

We tore down the front steps and onto the expansive front lawn. I tripped—or maybe my strength was failing me—but I hit the grass hard, gasping for breath but still laughing.

Holden went down beside me, and we lay on our backs, staring at the night sky.

"I don't believe we've officially met. Holden Parish."

"Miller Stratton."

We shook hands and Holden jerked his chin at Ronan looming over us. "And who's the Brute Squad?"

I laughed harder. "R-Ronan Wentz."

Holden jerked his hand straight up. "A pleasure."

Ronan crossed his arms. "Crazy bastards."

Another round of laughter rolled through us.

"How did you do that?" Holden asked me, wiping his eyes.

"Do what?"

"Play and sing like you did. Like…a fucking miracle."

Warmth bloomed in my chest. "Nah. Everyone's heard that song. It's a million years old."

Holden shrugged, staring at the sky. "They've heard the song, but you put your heart and soul out there. That's not something people hear every day."

He was wrong. I didn't put my heart on a slab for them but for Violet. And then I shoved it in her face. The tears in her eyes…

It was our song and I gave it away.

The front door banged open. "I said, get the fuck off my property!"

Chance stormed down the walk. River—the fucking asshole who probably gave Violet her first kiss in the closet that night—followed after, his expression dark and solemn. Calm and sober compared to Chance's enraged drunk.

Fuck you.

My laughter died, and I hauled myself off the lawn. Holden scrambled to his feet and drew Chance's attention by climbing onto a Range Rover parked in the drive. The car alarm blared down the darkened street, lights flashing. Amber hurried out of the house, my guitar case in her hand.

"Here," she said, handing it to me. Her eyes were cornflower blue. Light, where Violet's were dark. Her hair was the sun, when Violet's was jet black. Her lips thin, while Violet's were full and ripe to be kissed…

River got her kiss. He'll get all her firsts…

"Miller?"

"Oh, hey," I said, taking the case from her. "Strange fucking night."

"You played beautifully. Just…incredible."

"Yeah, thanks." I hadn't the first clue what to say to her. It wasn't her I wanted to be talking to.

Holden raced passed me, laughing. "Time to go."

"Time to go," I repeated to Amber, the laughter starting to creep back in. "Um…see you later?"

She smiled. "I hope so."

The sound of police sirens wailed in the distance as Holden led Ronan and me toward a black sedan parked across the street. A uniformed driver sat in the front seat.

"Good evening, James," Holden said as we climbed in the back. "Would you be so kind as to remove my friends and me from the immediate area?"

James nodded, and the car sped down the darkened avenue. "Home, sir?"

"Fuck no," Holden said. He looked to us. "Thoughts, gentlemen?"

I exchanged glances with Ronan who nodded once.

"My place," I said and told James the address.

At the Lighthouse Apartments, James parked the sedan in a visitor spot, and we climbed out.

"Cozy," Holden said, eyeing the complex. "After-party at Chez Stratton?"

"Not quite." I nodded at James in the sedan. "How long will he wait?"

"As long as I need him to." Holden lit a clove cigarette and waved away the smoke and our curious stares. "Fear not, James is being well-compensated for his time."

"Okay. Let's go."

Ronan and I led the way down the beach, over the roughest rock and lashing surf. If Holden was upset that his expensive clothes were getting wet and caked with sand, he didn't complain.

At the fisherman's shack, he glanced around, peering in the darkened space.

"Not bad. Could use a few upgrades."

In front of the Shack, Ronan lit a bonfire. The vast black ocean touched the shore in white foam thirty yards away while a million stars wheeled above.

I sat down heavily on my rock and pulled out a few gummies.

"CBD?" Holden said. "Sharing is caring, Stratton."

"Not CBD. Glucose. I have diabetes."

A genuine look of concern flashed over his green eyes. "You okay?"

"Yeah. Thanks." I glanced at him sideways. "What did you do to piss off River Whitmore?"

"I pissed off a lot of people tonight. You'll have to be more specific."

"The quarterback. When you were playing that Seven Minutes game."

"Ah, yes." Holden cleared his throat, then shrugged, his eyes on the ocean. "Don't remember."

"You sure?"

"You sound disappointed."

"I was hoping you kicked him in the nuts."

"Do tell?"

The weight of the night and all that had happened—and not happened—weighed on me, pressing me down. Making me tired. "Not tonight."

"Fair enough."

Ronan offered us beers from the cooler he'd stashed in the shack. Holden took one, I waved it off.

"Still feeling low," I said and pulled an OJ out of my backpack.

"It's nice here," Holden said after a minute. "Really fucking nice. Like I can just…breathe."

I nodded. "Same."

"Same," Ronan said.

"Do you guys hang out here a lot?" Holden asked, and I saw vulnerability in his eyes. The shields came down a little. I'd only seen him on two speeds so far: cool and collected or wildly drunk. For the first time, he seemed more like a seventeen-year-old guy without any costume on.

"Most days," I took a pull from my juice. I checked in with Ronan, who nodded. "You're welcome to come here too. Any time. Mi casa es su casa. Except it's not a house. How do you say, *our shitty shack is your shitty shack* in Spanish?"

"Nuestra casucha es su casucha," Holden replied, immediately, in a flawless Spanish accent.

Ronan and I exchanged glances.

"You speak Spanish?"

"And French. Italian. A little Portuguese and some Greek."

"You some kind of genius?" Ronan asked.

"So they say," Holden said, his gaze on the ocean. "My IQ is 153."

I gave a low whistle.

Holden nodded. "Sounds as if it could be helpful, right?"

"Helpful?" I snorted. "That's like having the answer key to life."

He scoffed. "If only. As far as I can tell, it just means the nonstop thoughts in my head are more cunning and can torment me in multiple languages."

I waited until the tension eased a little, then casually asked, "So, do I email you all my homework assignments directly or do you prefer hardcopy?"

Holden rolled his eyes, laughing, and the dark shadow that had fallen over him seemed to lift. "No chance, Stratton."

I grinned. "Worth a shot."

A more comfortable silence fell. "Yeah, it's pretty damn perfect, right here," Holden said. "Like we're at the edge of the world and no one can touch us."

"Yep," I said, and Ronan nodded.

Holden inhaled and then exhaled. "I'm gay," he said. "I just want to get that out there. In case it wasn't obvious. Is that going to be a problem?"

I frowned. "No. Why would it?"

"Ask my father." He looked to Ronan. "How about you?"

Ronan took a pull off his beer. "No, I'm not gay."

A beat passed and then the laughter came roaring back. My sides ached and tears built in the corners of my eyes. Even Ronan chuckled and spewed more lighter fluid on the fire. Any tension that might've existed between the three of us burned up in the flames, and I felt like I had when I first met Ronan. That Holden Parish belonged here too. With us.

"You're a crazy motherfucker, you know that?"

He wiped his eyes. "So I'm told."

"You could have been in with them, you know? The popular kids."

"Why would I do that when fucking with them is so much more fun?"

"Fun," Ronan said, his voice flat, cutting into the laughter like a cold knife. "Is that what that shit with Frankie was about? *Fun?*"

Holden's smile fled, and a cold shadow seemed to drop over him. "I did it to throw him off guard. That's all."

That wasn't all. Not by a longshot. But we all had secrets and dark shit in our pasts. What made Ronan stick around was that I didn't pry, and neither of us was about to start now with Holden. But as the night deepened, he told us a little about himself. How he'd moved here from Seattle and that he lived with his aunt and uncle in Seabright, the wealthiest neighborhood in Santa Cruz. The mansions even dwarfed Violet's house.

"You had only one more year of high school," I said. "Why leave?"

"Not up to me. After my sophomore year, my father arranged for me to take a little detour into the wilderness."

"You mean like a camp?"

"Sure," he said sourly, hunching into his coat, despite the fire and the warm summer night. "A *camp.* And that camp necessitated that I spend a year in Switzerland. At the Sanitarium du lac Léman," he said in a French accent as flawless as his Spanish. "That's Lake Geneva, to you and me."

"Sanitarium…?"

"Loony bin. Crazy house. Mental institution. Take your pick."

I faced forward. "Jesus."

"There was no Jesus as far as I could see," Holden said, smiling sadly. "Believe me. I looked."

A short silence fell and then Ronan arched another stream of lighter fluid on the fire. "That must've been one helluva wilderness camp."

I held my breath while Holden stared. Then he threw back his head and laughed. "Is this guy for real?"

"One hundred fucking percent." I clinked my juice to Holden's beer bottle. "To you for surviving the camp. And Switzerland."

Holden swallowed, trying not to show how those words touched him. "To Ronan, you magnificent bastard." He reached across me to toast with the big guy. "For being one hundred percent fucking real."

Ronan dug into his jacket pocket and pulled out a small yellow device. "To Frankie, the stupid fucker who didn't notice I swiped his police Taser."

The earth stood still for a split second and then we laughed. All three of us. We laughed so fucking hard that for a few hours, I forgot that my heart was broken.

CHAPTER NINE

VIOLET

The gym was loud with the sounds of cheers, stamping feet, and music. The cheerleaders, Evelyn leading, performed a routine in their blue and yellow skirts and sleeveless sweaters. Metallic gold pom-poms rustled and glinted in the sun streaming in from the huge windows behind the basketball hoops.

The crowd gasped as two male cheerleaders tossed Evelyn high into the air, where she pulled off an intricate gymnastic flip and landed in the cradle of their arms.

I sat with some friends from my study group—guys and girls who were working toward their own med school or MIT dreams—and Shiloh, who had earphones in, eyes closed, tuning out the pep rally as if she were meditating in a forest.

I scanned the crowd and found Miller sitting high up in a corner of the gym with Ronan and Holden. Videos captured on cell phones had circulated in the few weeks since Chance's party. Holden's tap dance on the Blaylock dining room table was a hit, but his confrontation with Frankie had freaked people out.

"He's so hot," Evelyn had lamented a few days after the party. "I don't get it. He's got charisma to spare but also, apparently, a death wish. Not to mention, he burned all his bridges with River and Chance, so now he's relegated to hanging out with your boy and the criminal."

But Holden seemed perfectly happy with Miller and Ronan. That morning, the three were watching the performance, talking and laughing. An odd trio: a grungy musician, a tattooed bad boy, and a billionaire genius who dressed like he was walking the winter runways in Milan every day. None of whom gave a crap what anyone thought of them.

It had been a long time since Miller had hung out with me as freely.

The cheerleaders finished their routine to applause that echoed throughout the cavernous gym of polished wood.

Principal Hayes took a microphone onto center court. "And now, the Homecoming Chair, Layla Calderon, will announce your Homecoming Court."

Layla, a gal with long dark hair in a mini skirt and a tight T-shirt, pushed a small rolling table covered with a black cloth to center court. On it were four crowns: two large and two small. She took the mic from Principal Hayes with the practiced ease of a news anchor.

"The votes have been counted and the results have been tabulated. Put your hands together and welcome your Homecoming Prince…Donte Weatherly!"

The crowd cheered, thunderous in the gym. The football team, sitting in a cluster near the front of the assembly in their letterman jackets, whooped and thumped their star wide receiver on the back as he joined Layla on the court and let her put a plastic, sparkly coronet over his brow.

He tried to walk away, but Layla grabbed his arm. "Not so fast. Every prince needs a princess. This year's Homecoming Princess is…Evelyn Gonzalez!"

A small shockwave went through the crowd that morphed with agonizing slowness into cheers.

I gasped. "Oh shit. Oh no. Poor Evelyn."

Shiloh's eyebrows shot up, and she turned to me. "Queen Vi…?"

"What? *No*. No way. Julia or Caitlin," I said as Evelyn plastered on a tight smile and made her way from the cheerleader bench to accept her coronet.

Shiloh smirked. "I wouldn't be so sure about that."

"And now, your Homecoming King," Layla said and paused for effect.

The football players jostled and teased River, who brushed it all off with lazy amusement.

"River Whitmore!"

The gym erupted in cheers, and I added my voice to the crowd.

"Not a surprise. But I'm still in shock for Evelyn…holy shit."

"Uh huh," Shiloh muttered. "You got your speech ready?"

"Oh, stop."

"And now…" Layla said, quieting the crowd. "It is my pleasure to announce that your Santa Cruz Central Homecoming Queen is…"

The gym went silent, holding its breath. Frankie Dowd shouted into the quiet, "Your mom!"

Laughter followed and a stern shake of Principal Hayes' head. Layla waited until she had our attention again.

"Violet McNamara!"

I sat stunned, while my friends cheered and clapped and urged me to go down and claim my crown.

"This is nuts," I hissed to Shiloh.

She heaved a dramatic sigh. "Being right all the time is *so* exhausting."

A little laugh burst out of me but was smothered when I saw the devastation on Evelyn's face; she wanted it far more than I did. I hadn't truly wanted it at all, I realized, and now that I had it, I had no idea what to do.

I climbed over legs to get to the stairs, then made my way down to the court. River grinned at me, a silly faux red velvet and gold plastic crown on his head. Layla placed a smaller version on mine, while I sent Evelyn an apologetic smile. She quickly looked away, her own smile wide and joyless, as she clapped with the rest of the school.

I leaned into River. "How did this happen?"

"Democracy in action. You got the most votes, plain and simple." His confident smile slipped, and he cleared his throat. "Kind of works out perfect, right? Since we're going to the dance together."

"Right. Except…*are* we still going together?"

"Yeah, sorry I haven't called or anything. Just been busy with practice and games. And…stuff at home."

"No, of course. I'm sorry. I should have thought of that."

"Hey, it's fine," he said quickly, talking under the cover of Layla reading off a list of the Homecoming Court's accomplishments that helped land us up there. "I still should have called you. Or texted."

"I'm not sitting by the phone or anything," I added, then cringed. "God, that came out all wrong. What I mean is, I'm also busy with studying half the time anyway…"

"I haven't even seen you at my place."

"We must be on different schedules."

"Yep."

Like in the closet at Chance's party, conversation with River felt like trudging through mud, getting nowhere.

I cleared my throat. "Tell me, does this royalty gig come with a lot of duties?"

He chuckled. "Aside from sitting in a car and waving? No."

I laughed too with relief. A miniscule step toward being more comfortable around each other. Or maybe it was him. He seemed more nervous around me than I was around him.

The announcements ended, and we were released back to our seats.

"Call you soon," River said. "Promise. Or I'll see you at my house?"

"Definitely." I widened my eyes and put on a scary-wide smile, doing my best impersonation of the Overly Attached Girlfriend meme. "You can't escape me…"

He burst out laughing. "Thanks for the warning." He reached out and awkwardly patted my arm. "See you around."

My smile felt permanent until my gaze went to Miller in the corner of the gym. I gave him a wave and pointed at my crown. "*Crazy, right?*" I mouthed.

He didn't even crack a smile but quickly turned back to his friends. And Amber Blake. The pretty blonde had appeared and was sidled up close to Miller.

A strange ache stabbed my heart. Like any good scientist, I'd clung to logic and facts to untangle the messy emotions that had arisen the night of the crazy party, after Miller had played our song so beautifully. So *powerfully*…with Amber practically sitting in his lap.

1. I drank too much that night, which made me overly emotional.
2. I had a crush on River, and he'd finally asked me to a dance. Achievement: unlocked!
3. Miller was free to date any girl he wanted, and I'd be happy for him.*

Except that mental asterisk wouldn't go away. If he and Amber got together, why wouldn't I be happy for him? Why would it matter that he chose our song to introduce himself to the world as the brilliant musician he was? He was my best friend. Being happy for him was my job.

Except that *my best friend* never called or came over anymore. At school, he'd barely look at me.

Like now.

"Bathroom emergency," Julia said, tugging my arm and breaking me from my thoughts. "It's Evelyn."

I hurried with her and Caitlin to the nearest bathroom, outside the gym. Julia shooed out a freshman who was washing her hands and tapped softly on a closed stall door.

"Evelyn? You okay?"

"I'm fine," came the throaty reply. "I got my period."

Julia looked to me and shook her head. I cleared my throat. "Ev? It's me. You sure you're okay?"

"I said, I'm *fine*. Jesus."

Caitlin shrugged and went to the mirror to redo her lip gloss. "So, tell me, my queen. What's the story with Miller Stratton?"

I flinched and shot a glance at the bathroom stall. "What do you mean?"

"We've been dying to talk to you about him, but you're so busy all the time."

Julia pulled her cell phone from her bag, swiped at it, and then aimed it my way. "She means this."

A video played: Chance's darkened living room but for lit lighters and ghostly phone flashlights falling over Miller as he sang "Yellow."

Julia smiled dreamily. "All this time he was…*this,* and we never knew."

"Yeah, what else are you holding out on us?" Caitlin said with a nudge.

Oh, the irony.

I'd been telling anyone who would listen how talented Miller was for years, but it took visual proof to dispel the aura of poverty and homelessness.

Caitlin peered over my shoulder at the video. "He's got this scruffy, alternative-rocker-hottie vibe going on. You two ever…?"

"No, never," I said, stepping back and leaving the two of them to watch the performance.

"Really? You've been friends for years and never…? Not even a kiss?"

"We almost did. Once. Two years ago."

I leaned against the sink, the memory falling over me. Miller and me in my room, hanging out as usual. He played his guitar and sang for me. Emotion beyond his years pouring out of him. I watched his mouth the entire time, mesmerized by how his full lips moved and the sounds that came from them. And for some reason, at that moment, I started thinking about how neither of us had ever been kissed. No one had kissed that mouth of his and that was crazy.

"What happened?"

"We were fifteen, and neither of us were getting any action," I said. "I told him that we should kiss for practice. So when the moment came, we wouldn't be totally helpless. I told him that it wouldn't count toward a real first kiss or anything. Just research."

"And?" Julia asked, jarring me from my thoughts.

"He refused."

"I'm not kissing you for practice,*" Miller said, the last word coming out sourly. "So that some other guy..." He bit off his words and went back to his guitar, messing with the frets.*

My cheeks burned. "Sorry. Forget I brought it up. Probably better, anyway. It might be weird."

"Yeah," Miller said, still not looking at me. "Weird."

I looked up to see Caitlin and Julia offering cringe-y glances on my behalf. I waved them off, my cheeks flushed again like they had been then.

"No, it's...fine. It just proved what I thought: that we're only friends and that he's not interested in me in that way."

"He seems pretty interested in Amber Blake," Julia said with a sigh and put her phone away. "A pity. Seems like we missed the boat."

My brows wrinkled. "*You're* interested?"

"Maybe. Intrigued, definitely."

"Can't blame her," Caitlin said. "What girl wouldn't want to be sung to like *that*?"

The stall door banged open, and we jumped; we'd all forgotten about Evelyn. She went to the sink and washed her hands. The girls and I waited, tension coiling, and then Evelyn caught our glances in the mirror as she smoothed a stray hair from her ponytail.

"Periods can suck it, am I right?"

Julia and Caitlin smiled with relief as Evelyn turned to me, a sweet smile on her face. She put her arms around me and hugged me close.

"Congratulations, Vi. You deserve it."

"Oh…thank you. It's kind of surreal."

"Did you tell the girls?" Evelyn put her arm around me. "Violet doesn't need anyone's practice kisses. Very soon, she'll be having the real deal with River Whitmore. Homecoming King and Queen are going to the dance together. How perfect is that?"

I searched Evelyn's face for a sign that my coronation bothered her more than she was letting on, but her smile seemed genuine.

The others congratulated me excitedly.

"And not a moment too soon," Evelyn said. "Vi's our sweet little Snow White. Our Drew Barrymore—never been kissed. Girl, you have a lot of catching up to do. *A lot.*"

Caitlin stared. "You've *never* been kissed? Really?"

I shrugged, my eyes on the tile floor. "It just never…happened."

Julia giggled. "You set the bar high by going straight to River."

"Right?" Caitlin said. "Like eating dessert first, without having to choke down the vegetables. God, I remember my first kiss. Thirteen, with Danny Cunningham. *Blech.*"

We exited the bathroom in the bright, mid-morning sunshine, the girls reminiscing about their first kisses, their first everythings. They were all so experienced compared to me, having rounded all the bases with more than one boyfriend, while I'd been sitting on the bench, studying and working and letting those events pass me by.

Maybe Julia was right that I'd been holding out for River. My long-standing crush was finally coming to fruition. Maybe we'd be boyfriend and girlfriend, and we'd make up for everything I'd missed. Then he'd go off to Alabama or Texas for football, and I'd take the first steps toward becoming a doctor. All according to plan.

Except that my grand plan felt dry and hollow lately, and the reason was as stark and simple as a math equation with only one answer: because Miller wasn't in it.

I drove to the Whitmore's after school for my volunteer time with Nancy. River's truck was parked in the drive. Dazia had told me to let myself in from now on, since she was in and out, and Mr. Whitmore worked at the Auto Body shop until late.

I took the stairs up to the second floor, to Nancy's room. The door was ajar and low voices came from inside. River's voice. I started to back off to give them privacy, but something in Nancy's tone—soft but intense—arrested me.

"…more than anything, I just want to see you happy."

"Don't know about that right now, Mom," River said. "There's a lot going on."

"I know. But keep your heart open. That's all I ask. And please don't force anything on my behalf. I was just curious if there might be anyone special."

A short silence fell, and I turned away, ashamed at myself for eavesdropping.

"Violet," River blurted.

I froze, my heart crashing.

"My Violet? Really? She's lovely, but—"

"Yeah, and actually, I have some news. I think I heard her car pull up. Hold on."

Oh shit.

I started down the hall, but it'd be obvious I'd been running away. I turned back around and reached for the door just as River threw it open.

I jumped back with a little cry, my nerves lit up.

"Shit, sorry I scared you," River said. He rubbed the back of his neck, looking just as nervous as me.

"It's fine. I can come back if—"

"No, come in. Please."

I followed River inside. Nancy, looking wan and jaundiced, smiled to see me. A beam of warm light streamed over her from the window.

"Hello, darling."

"Hi, Mrs. Whitmore."

"Nancy, please. Remember?"

"Right. Okay."

To my shock, River took my hand in his large, rough one. I glanced up at him—he towered over my 5'4"—but his gaze was on his mom.

"Violet and I are going to the Homecoming dance together after the game on Friday."

Nancy's eyes widened, though her smile remained the same. "Is that so? How lovely."

"He's the King and there was a glitch in the matrix, so I ended up as Queen," I said with a little laugh. "I think he's contractually obligated."

"Ha, no. I'm happy to." River gave my hand a squeeze and let go. "I gotta get to practice." He went to his mom and kissed her forehead. "Bye, Mom."

"Be safe, Dear."

River flashed me a quick smile. "Call you later?"

"Uh, sure."

That's a first.

"Great." He gave me an awkward peck on the cheek and left, leaving Nancy and me alone in the silence.

"He's really sweet," I said finally.

"He is. You two are growing close?"

"I'd say baby steps. We're both really busy."

Nancy nodded. "Indeed. Might I trouble you for some tea?"

"And a Hot Pocket, maybe?"

She grinned. "You read my mind."

I smiled back and headed down to the kitchen. Nancy rarely had the appetite for more than a few bites of food, but I wanted to get as much nutrition in her as possible without being obvious. Feeding Miller all those years had been good practice for being smooth about it.

I took the stairs down, moving through a current of River's cologne. Faint, but potently masculine.

And he told his mom I'm someone special.

I put the kettle on the stove and put a Chamomile packet in a mug and inhaled, letting a little positivity in. Since the crazy party, life was finally starting to settle down. My parents hadn't had a blow-up in weeks, River and I were going to the dance. If Miller would just talk to me again, things would be perfect…

My phone chimed a text and a little sound of joy erupted out of me to see that it was from him.

I'm sorry I've been such a dick lately. Was thinking about coming over tonight? It's been awhile.

My thumbs flew. **YES! I miss you.**

The rolling dots came and went. Then came back.

Me too.

CHAPTER TEN

MILLER

"Stratton. Let's roll."

I blinked out of the lyrics I'd been messing around with and set down my pen. Ronan and Holden were at the door of the Shack, waiting.

"Yep. Coming."

I glanced over the words once more. Snippets of thoughts. Sketches of feeling. For Violet. Because, of course, it was for Violet. Every note, every tune, every phrase and lyric were born from the same place in me that loved her and always would.

But I have to let her go.

I stashed the notebook with my guitar case in a locked trunk that Holden had bought, so I didn't have to carry the instrument around with me all day. A much-appreciated upgrade.

Twilight was turning the sky outside gold and purple, though it was dim in the Shack. I threw on a plaid flannel button-down over my t-shirt and pulled a knit beanie over my head to keep the hair out of my eyes. I grabbed a juice from the mini fridge, powered by a small lithium battery generator. More of Holden's upgrades. I kept the fridge stocked with food so that I could worry less about Chet pilfering. Ronan stored his beer in it, Holden liked to keep a bottle of his favorite vodka.

Not to be outdone by refrigerators and decent lighting, Ronan and I made valuable contributions to our domicile, too. My boss at the arcade gave me three beach chairs for our nightly bonfires. Ronan brought weights for lifting, an endless supply of lighter fluid, and a ratty but clean-ish futon that Holden refused to sit on.

Instead, His Lordship had brought in a wing-backed chair that barely fit in the door. He sat and smoked his clove cigarettes as if he were an old rich bastard having a cognac in front of the fireplace in his mansion library. The guy threw money around as if the world were coming to an end. That should've pissed me off, but mostly, I was worried about him. He sure as hell drank like there was no tomorrow.

I joined Ronan and Holden, and we made our trek from our hidden spot along the beach up to Cliff Drive and headed east to the glittering lights of the Boardwalk. Holden called it our "nightly prowl." We gathered curious looks and a few murmurs from Central High students that carried back to school.

I didn't give a shit what anyone thought of us, but if I did, I'd have blamed Holden. He dressed in expensive coats and scarves, despite the fact that summer was only just ending. Violet told me Holden reminded her of a vampire. I agreed. An old-world vampire whose skin was pale and cold until he'd had a drink. Booze, not blood, seemed to be the only thing that warmed him up.

As we walked, he sipped from a flask tucked into the pocket of his gray wool herringbone coat that went nearly to the ground, the collar turned up over a black silk shirt and a green and gold paisley scarf.

"Something on your mind?" he asked as we strolled the crowded walk, the scents of cotton candy, funnel cake, and grilled corn in the air. "Preoccupied with greatness since your performance at the party?"

"Hardly."

Preoccupied with how Violet's face looked that night, maybe. Preoccupied with how the tears streamed down her cheeks as she clapped for me and then ran out. Because I'd been cold to her then and ignoring her ever since.

I have to fix this. I miss my friend.

I whipped out my phone.

I'm sorry I've been such a dick lately. Was thinking about coming over tonight? It's been awhile.

A reply came quickly. **YES! I miss you.**

God, those words. I ate them up. Swallowed them down and tried to let them feed me. I was still starving for her. My stupid fucking heart still beat for her. It wouldn't leave her alone.

But it has to.

Me too. I sent back and shoved the phone in my pocket with a sigh.

Holden nudged my arm with his elbow. "What's that all about?"

"I asked Vi if we could hang out tonight."

"And that's cause for dramatic smolder because…?"

"Because he's in love with her but won't tell her," Ronan said.

"I'm not in love with her."

"My ass."

Ronan stopped at the Ball Toss game, his favorite; he liked to smash things.

He hadn't been at school or the Shack for a few days and had finally returned in a darker mood than usual with a bruise over one eye and another peeking out of his T-shirt. I wondered how many more were hiding under his clothes and who gave them to him. But when we'd asked that afternoon, he'd barked at us that it was none of our fucking business.

I worried about him too.

Ronan hurled the ball with tremendous force, and the plastic bottles went tumbling down in a heap.

The carny running the game flinched. "Jesus, take it easy."

Holden grinned. "This game is supposed to be rigged, isn't it?"

"Not when Ronan plays it."

"You can take a small prize now or try your luck again to upgrade," the carny said. "You lose, you get nothing."

Ronan held out his hand. "Ball."

The carny sighed and handed it over.

"Well?" Holden asked me. "Which is it? Are you in love with her or not?"

"He is," Ronan said, taking aim. "He's just trying to talk himself out of it."

He let the ball fly, and another stack of bottles was demolished. One more and he'd take home one of the ginormous teddy bears affixed to the booth's ceiling.

"I'm trying to *talk myself out of it* because she wants to stay friends."

Holden put his flask to his lips. "Unrequited love is the first circle of hell."

"Tell me about it."

Ronan hurled the final ball. It flew so fast and hit so hard, the bottles went flying and tore a hole in the cheap linen tarp behind it.

"*Dude.*" The carny fixed Ronan with a dark look. He spoke into the mic taped to his cheek in a desultory tone, "Winner, winner. See folks? It can be done." He pulled down a huge, cheap, yellow and white teddy bear. "Now, beat it."

"There's something you don't see every day," Holden muttered to me, and I had to laugh at our huge tatted friend in torn jeans and a Tool T-shirt, carrying that stuffed bear down the Boardwalk.

A little girl was standing with her parents, eating ice cream. Ronan handed her the teddy bear without a word—it was nearly as big as she was—and kept walking. He didn't see how her face lit up with joy and surprise, while her parents smiled in begrudging thanks, no doubt wondering just where in the hell they were supposed to put the thing when they got home.

Holden sighed. "He's a teddy bear himself, isn't he?"

"Shut up," Ronan tossed over his shoulder. I guessed he wasn't done breaking stuff, since he stopped at the balloon dart game.

My best friends are a vampire and a criminal, I thought as we fished out a few bucks to play. *What does that make me?*

Violet's text swam in my mind, warming my skin like a shot from Holden's flask. **I miss you.**

Oh, that's right. I'm the pathetic loser.

"Back to the subject at hand," Holden said. "At Chance's party, you were absorbed with that blonde girl. The way you sang to her—"

"I wasn't singing to Amber, I was singing to Violet. But it doesn't matter. She's not interested, and I'm too fucking late, anyway."

"Why?"

"She kissed River in the closet."

Her first kiss. She gave it to someone else...

Holden looked thoughtful. "You sure about that?"

"Isn't that the point of the game?"

He hunched into his coat and didn't answer.

"So you're giving up?" Ronan asked.

"I can't be that pathetic asshole anymore. She's had a crush on River before I came along, and now she's got him. I need to man up and be happy that she's happy. That's all I want. For her to be happy." I tossed a dart and missed. "That's what I'm going to tell her tonight."

"Honorable to a fault," Holden said. "You're the best of us, Miller."

"If that's true, you need to set the bar higher," I muttered. "I just...miss her, you know? I miss hanging out with her. Talking to her. She was my best friend before you guys, and I don't want to lose her."

"And Amber?"

I shrugged. "Something could happen there, but I won't know if I don't cut Violet loose." I swallowed a jagged lump of pain and forced myself to say the words out loud. "She doesn't love me. Not like the way I do. Time to get over it."

"Sounds like a good plan," Holden said. "Except for one tiny detail."

"And that is?"

"You look fucking miserable," Ronan said.

Holden grinned in wide-eyed surprise. "So astute! Our Ronan truly is a big softy under all that brutish muscle and glower."

Ronan flipped him the finger.

"How about this?" Holden slung his arm around my neck. "You and Dr. Phil, here, shoot darts. If Ronan pops more balloons than you, you tell Violet the truth. If you pop more, you can continue to wallow in your honorable misery forever, and we'll leave you alone about it."

"That's dumb. And Ronan is going to win. He always does."

Ronan held out his hand. "Flask."

"Ah yes. A little handicap." Holden turned over his flask, and Ronan tipped it up, downing the entire thing in a matter of seconds.

"That's about four ounces of Ducasse, the Everclear of expensive vodka." Holden chucked Ronan on the back. "How you feeling, champ?"

Ronan's eyes watered, and he blew air out of puffed cheeks. "Better."

Holden smiled, satisfied. "Evened the odds. Right now, our buddy couldn't find his own reflection in a mirror."

Truly, Ronan looked shitfaced, swaying slightly, while Holden produced a wad of cash.

"Six darts, my good man."

The carny laid them out.

"Miller's up first, and no cheating. *Honor* demands you try to win."

"This is ridiculous," I muttered.

I took up my three darts. I missed the first, then hit the second two.

Ronan took his darts and blearily stared at the balloon targets in front of him. Then his eyes suddenly focused, and he shot all three, one after the other, rapid fire. Three balloons popped.

"Fucking hell."

"A deal is a deal," Holden said through loud laughter. "Take your prize… Take this cheap SpongeBob SquarePants key chain to Lady Violet as a token of your love."

I gave my friends the stink eye. Holden grinning. Happy. His eyes clear instead of racing with thoughts or drowning in booze. Ronan wasn't falling-down-drunk like he'd looked a second ago, but was laughing too. Silent chuckles that shook his shoulders.

I bit back my own smile and hurled the plush toy at their heads.

"Assholes."

Game or no game, I wasn't about to confess a damn thing to Violet. I'd been a dick to her, ignoring her and making her feel like shit. I was like that guy in that Christmas movie Mom watched every year—he was in love with Keira Knightly who was fucking *married.* Violet kissing River wasn't quite the same thing, but it may as well have been. I'd been holding out for four years, hoping to be Violet's first…everything.

And someone else got there first.

I took an Uber to the wealthy estates near the Pogonip forest, my thoughts drifting backward over memories. We'd almost kissed. Once. When we were fifteen. Violet wanted to practice, but I'd have rather chewed glass than be her test dummy. A stand-in for the guy she actually *wanted* to kiss. I wanted the real thing.

But she doesn't want me.

I climbed out of the Uber and went around to her backyard. My guitar case banged against my shoulders as I climbed the trellis. Violet had sent me another text that I should bring it.

She was waiting for me, excitement and hesitation dancing in her eyes, lighting her up. Making her pale skin luminous. Her luscious body was hugged by a tight T-shirt and pajama pants. Her breasts were perfectly round and heavy; I ached to fill my hands with them and coax her nipples to stand at attention with my tongue…

Jesus, dude. That's not *what friends are for.*

"Hey," I said, cutting off the heated thoughts before they got me in trouble.

"Hi," she said, breathy and nervous. "I'm so glad you came. It's been awhile."

"Yeah, I'm sorry about that, Vi. I'm sorry I've been cold lately. And I wanted—"

"It's all right," she said, waving her hands. "I know things haven't been great for you since Chet arrived."

"Yeah, he's a fucking barnacle. Don't know how to scrape him off."

"I do," Violet said. "Well, not directly. But I know how you can make a ton of money to take care of your mom and get rid of him forever." She held up her cell phone. "YouTube."

I leaned against her desk. "I know where you're going with this."

"I've been doing my homework. Shawn Mendes is literally a superstar because of his Vine videos. Billie Eilish put a song on SoundCloud and now look where she is. After the reaction to your playing at the party, it's a no-brainer. We put videos of you out there, and the world is going to beg for more."

I smiled, warmed by her confidence in me. "It's just that easy, huh?"

"With your talent? Yes."

"Not that it's going to happen, but I don't want to be famous like Mendes."

"What do you want?"

You.

"To…uh, I don't know. I like performing in front of people. I didn't realize how much until I did it at the party. It felt like all the shit I walk around with all day had an outlet. A safe one, where I don't have to talk about my dad or my past or…"

What I feel for you.

"Or whatever…I can just feel it through the song. And the audience hears and maybe they sort of understand. They understand me." I shrugged. "Make me feel less lonely."

Violet's dark blue eyes were miles deep, so beautiful the way she looked at me, seeing and accepting every flawed and broken piece of me.

The air thickened and turned heavy.

I cleared my throat. "Short answer, I want to make music and earn enough money to live without being so goddamn stressed out all the time. And to help my mom."

Violet smiled softly. "I get that. But with talent like yours, being famous or not might be out of your hands."

I smirked. "I think that's overstating it."

"I don't."

God, her faith in me was total. As if superstardom was a matter of when, not if. But the internet was flooded with wannabe Shawns and Billies. I'd just be another voice shouting into an overcrowded void. On the other hand, my own plan to send unproduced, raw-as-hell demos to record companies wasn't exactly a sure bet either.

"We can try, but—"

"Great! I'm ready when you are."

But I still needed to tell her I was ready to stop being an asshole and be the friend she wanted. To take care of her like she took care of me. Best to do it quick, like tearing off a Band-Aid.

"So, how are things with River?" I asked, unlatching my case.

She sat back on her bed, wary. "Why are you asking?"

"Because you're my friend. And I want you to be happy."

Her shoulders relaxed, and her smile was so goddamn beautiful…

"Thank you. I want that for you too. I've missed you." Her smile faltered. "But River? I'm not sure what's there. If anything."

"No?" My heart stood at attention and my plans instantly wanted to go up in flames. "Why not?"

She shrugged. "He seems interested but then he doesn't. He asked me to Homecoming and then hasn't texted since. It's just weird."

"Oh." I pulled out my guitar and set it on my lap, pretending to mess with the frets. "You looked pretty happy with him at the pep rally."

"That's only because I have to work overtime with my formidable charm and wit just to make the barest of conversation," she teased. "Hell, we played a kissing game, and he didn't even kiss me."

My head shot up, my heart taking off. "He didn't?"

"It's like he's nervous around me, which has to be impossible, right?"

"No. Not impossible at all." My voice had turned gruff. Thick. Violet noticed.

"So…what about you?" she asked, plucking an invisible piece of lint off her pajama pants. "Are you and Amber going to the dance?"

Was it my imagination that she sounded afraid of the answer? But afraid I'd say yes? Or no?

"I haven't asked her yet. Don't know that I'm going, anyway," I added quickly.

Violet tucked a lock of raven black hair behind her ear, her eyes anywhere but on me. "So…shall we?"

I nodded as my every *honorable* intention walked away. The neutral song I'd been thinking about playing followed it out the door as well. "All I'll Ever Want," the song I'd wanted to sing to her on the eve of the first day of school, was now front and center.

"Ready?" she asked.

"What do I do?"

"Introduce yourself and tell us the name of the song you're about to destroy us with."

I sat on the edge of Violet's bed, and she sat beside me, cross-legged, phone held up.

"Five, four, three…"

"So, hey. I'm Miller Stratton," I said, suddenly nervous without the liquid courage of tequila I'd had at the party. The eye of Violet's phone camera stared me down. "Uh, I'm from Santa Cruz, California…"

Suddenly, my knit beanie was itchy as hell. I took it off and scrubbed my hand through my hair. A few locks fell over my brow. Violet's eyes widened and her breath caught. Probably because I was messing this all up. I whipped the hair out of my eyes, cleared my throat, and put my attention safely on my guitar.

"I'm going to play a song called 'All I'll Ever Want.'"

My fingers found the strings and strummed, creating sounds that helped make order out of my chaotic feelings. The emotions and harmonies were like twin currents that carried my voice, and my voice spoke the words—a hundred different ways of saying the same thing. Asking Violet the same thing—to fall in love with me the way I loved her.

At the last chorus, my voice rose up and my heart clenched, squeezing hard and emptying itself, giving everything.

Feels so good and feels so weak
This love cuts until I bleed
Don't touch me, baby, don't look at my scars,
Until you want to know which ones are yours
All I'll ever want
All I'll ever want

Is for you to fall in love with me tonight

The last note wavered then dissipated. Violet held the phone a moment more, then hit stop and dropped her hands in her lap. Her mouth was open, her lush, full lips parted. Her porcelain skin was flushed and her eyes lit up. I saw *me* reflected in her eyes. Someone who just might make it out of this shit life after all with whatever talent God or the universe saw fit to give me.

"Miller, my God…" she breathed. "That was…"

For you. That was for you. You're the girl in every song.

"That was…unreal," she said.

"Yeah?"

Violet put her hand over her heart. "Yeah. *Yes.* Oh my God, Miller…"

She reached across the short distance between us with both arms and hugged me. I slid my guitar away and held her tight, closing my eyes and sinking into the circle of her embrace. Soft, warm…it smelled of her skin, her hair, her sweet breath on my neck.

"You're going to go all the way," she said, her lips against my shoulder. "I can feel it."

And in that moment, bolstered and enveloped by her faith in me, I felt it too.

My head moved a little, led by my mouth that wanted hers. Her smooth cheek brushed against my stubbly one. Another small movement, hesitant, but with my entire heart bared behind it, and my lips brushed the corner of her mouth. She pulled back but only far enough to meet my gaze that was full of naked want. Her lips parted with a breathy little gasp, stripping away any restraint I had left.

With a small, rough sound of pure need, I kissed her.

I kissed my best friend. I altered us forever. No going back nor wanting to. Not wanting anything ever again but this.

My lips claimed hers, gently at first, and then with increasing need when she didn't pull away. I was astounded that she didn't pull away. She kissed me back. Her tongue, soft and warm, shyly sought entry into my mouth. Curious and hesitant. I let her in, taking this kiss and giving it back in waves of heated, wet perfection.

Goddamn, she tasted like apples and sugar, she was warmth and home. She was where I wanted to be, always.

I held her face in both hands, taking and sucking and drinking from her. Breaths came in short rasps through my nose; I needed her more than I needed air. With every passing moment, I grew more shocked—and scared—about how strong that need was. How kissing her was everything and yet nothing I was prepared for.

I couldn't break away or save myself from the depth of my love for her. I thought I'd explored it in my songs. Navigated every twist and turn. Yet touching her like this—*indulging* in her—showed me that I knew nothing. That I'd been wandering a vast cavern for years with only a tiny flashlight. Now the walls were falling away, and the sunlight was pouring in.

Too much. Too good. It can't be real. Can't last. Nothing this good ever does.

And then it stopped.

Cold nothing replaced the warmth and wetness of her mouth as Violet gave a little cry and reared back, pushing my hands away. Her wide eyes searched mine. Her full lips were swollen and still wet from my kiss. Her delicate skin chafed by my stubble. Her nipples, now hard and straining against her shirt, tortured me for want of touching them.

"What are we doing?" she whispered.

I fumbled for something to say. The poetry that lived in my heart for her only came out on paper. In my mouth, it tangled and tripped over my self-doubt. My fears. The voice in my head that said I was a poor nobody, and she was a rich girl who deserved better. The sinister whisper, wearing Chet's voice, that told me she'd wake up someday and realize it too.

Her fingertips flew to the redness on her lips. "Why did you kiss me?"

"I don't… It just happened…"

"I told you River didn't kiss me and your whole face changed," she said, sliding off the bed and backing away, her fingers still on her lips. "You said you were *happy* for me."

"That's not what I said," I told her, my voice hardening. "I said I *wanted* you to be happy. That's all I care about. That's all I've ever cared about."

She shook her head, staring out at nothing, a thousand thoughts in her eyes. The hand on her mouth slipped around to touch the pale skin of her neck which was flushed pink. "You've been ignoring me for weeks, and now you kiss me…"

"And you kissed me back," I said, my jaw clenching.

And it was everything. So much. Too much...

The familiar sounds of her parents blasting each other in muffled but loud voices rumbled up from below. Sudden and unnerving. Like a leaf burning in a beam of light, Violet curled up on herself, hugging her elbows and casting her eyes to the ground.

She said in a small voice. "River and I...we're going to Homecoming."

"So what? You don't like him. That's a story you tell yourself instead of..."

Loving me.

Violet lifted her eyes to me, heavy and shining. "Do you hear them? Is that what happens? It all blackens and rots away?"

Fury raged in me. At her but at myself more, because a part of me was just as fucking scared as she was. Nothing good lasts. Not your health, not the roof over your head...

Not fathers who should stay but don't.

The thought stopped me dead, like a punch in the chest. I never let myself think of him. Ever. I pretended I was okay. I told myself his leaving hadn't cut me to the core, but now I could see my scars were the same as Violet's. Her parents had done *nothing* to guide her, either. We'd both been left out in the cold by the people who should have sheltered us the most.

I inhaled through my nose, a million fiery words burning on my tongue, and tore out of Violet's room. Her footsteps followed behind.

"Miller, wait. What are you—?"

I found them in the kitchen. Mr. and Mrs. McNamara shouting over one another, a broken dish shattered on the floor in front of them.

"What the fuck are you doing?"

They stopped and fell silent, shocked and staring. I felt Violet slip behind me, her hand on my arm, small and trembling.

"Miller, no..." she whispered.

"*Yes*," I shouted, my wrathful glare going between her parents. "Do you know what you're doing to her? Do you care? You just fucking shout and break shit and then pretend like it's all normal? Like she can't hear you? Because she can and *it's fucking tearing her apart*."

The soft sounds of Violet crying behind me. Incredulous stares in front of me.

Mr. McNamara was the first to break free of his shock. "Now, hold on, young man. You can't just—"

"Shut up!" I barked. "Shut up, for once in your lives. Shut up when you think you need to scream at each other. Shut the fuck up and spare one goddamn thought for what you might be doing to your daughter."

I must've been losing it, since all of my own pain bubbled to the surface. Pain I'd tried so hard to keep buried put a red haze over my eyes. I hardly understood the words that were pouring out of my mouth. Or who I was talking to anymore.

"You can't do that to your kid," I raged. "You fucking *can't.* You can't just *leave.* You can't go and leave behind giant fucking black holes in someone's life that suck the light out of everything."

"Miller?"

Violet's hand on my arm gave me a squeeze, grounding me back to reality. I blinked the red haze away, my breath coming hard.

Jesus, what was that?

"How dare you come in here and speak to us like that," Mrs. McNamara said in a seething tone.

"It's about fucking time someone did. Violet won't. She doesn't say anything because she does what she always does. Tries to make things okay. She puts on a smile and keeps going. Working her ass off to stay ahead of whatever fucked up shit you're up to." My throat started to close, and I fought to keep control. "Because of you, she doesn't believe in love. Congratulations. Job well done."

Mr. McNamara raised his head. "That's enough, now, Miller…"

"Yeah, it is," I said, suddenly tired. Adrenaline had run its course and now my watch alarm began to beep. The outburst and turmoil had drained me. I turned and looked to Violet, tears streaming. My own vision blurred. "It's enough, and it's too late."

I walked out of the kitchen. Mrs. McNamara started to shout, but her husband hissed at her to be quiet. Violet's soft footsteps padded after me upstairs.

In her room, I packed up my guitar in its case and started back out the door. "Miller, wait," she said tearfully. "Where are you going?"

"Leaving. Out the front door."

"You can't just go. Not *now.*"

I stopped at her bedroom door. "I'm sorry I kissed you, Violet. It won't happen again," I said and then I left. Left without one more word or thought for the anguish on the face I loved so much, wondering if it'd been the same for my dad.

Just like tearing off a Band-Aid.

CHAPTER ELEVEN

MILLER

Homecoming, senior year: a day of epic fails and poor choices.

Against all better judgement, I went to the football game with Shiloh and watched the Central High Capitals defeat the Soquel Saints 42-16. A gimme game against a lower division designed to make our guys look good. And River, of course, played hero and passed for four touchdowns.

The parade came after. River, still in his game uniform, sat beside Violet above the back seat of a convertible. She was stunning in black velvet, a sparkling tiara on her head and a sash across her dress. She and River smiled and waved at the crowd. They smiled at each other. She looked happy. Radiant, even.

I felt Shiloh's eyes on me. "Why do you do this to yourself?"

"Sorry?"

"Watch her be with someone else."

It should've shocked me that Shiloh could read me like that, but then she'd always had an instinct about people and a zero-bullshit policy. I admired that about her, probably because I wallowed in my own bullshit on the regular. I'd walked out of Violet's room the other night pretending I'd succeeded in letting her go. What a fucking crock. All it took was one sense memory of her lips on mine, our tongues exploring and our hands touching in ways that defied friendship, and I was hopelessly sucked back into miserable want for her.

"I need proof that she's okay with him. That he'll take care of her, or I'll sic Ronan on him."

Shiloh shrugged. "River's unproblematic. At least there's that."

Fuck River, I thought with stupid, possessive pride, knowing that I'd been Violet's first kiss.

And she was mine. Because there could be no one else.

"Speaking of River, did Vi mention that she and I kissed?"

Shiloh's head swiveled to me, braids cascading down her billowy shirt. She tried to corral her shock, but it was too late.

Pain slugged me in the chest. I faced forward. "I'll take that as a no."

"I haven't seen her much lately. But no, she didn't say a word." She nudged my arm. "I'm sorry. I always knew something was going on there."

"Don't be sorry. Just confirms everything she's been telling me for years."

That our kiss hadn't been worth a mention to her best girlfriend. It wasn't still lingering on her lips like it was on mine. It hadn't completely shocked and upheaved her life the way it had mine, throwing the depth of my love for her—and my fears with it—in my face. I'd easily faded from her senses; yet, I could still taste her.

"Is that why you asked Amber to the dance?" Shiloh asked. "To get over her for real?"

To protect myself...

"I have to try. Maybe something could happen with Amber. Maybe if I gave her a chance, I could move on and be the friend Violet wants me to be."

"Uh huh. Amber is a friend of *mine.*" Shiloh pierced me with her strong, dark-eyed gaze. "A real flesh-and-blood human. Not a blowup doll to take your frustrations out on."

"Jesus, I know that."

She released me from her stare. "I know. You're a good guy, too."

"Try telling that to Vi."

"She already knows. That's why she's fighting so hard. In her mind, things are either falling apart or they're standing still. Never becoming something beautiful." She gave me a sad smile. "She's trying to hold the two of you still, so you don't fall apart."

"Where do you think you're going?" Chet bellowed from the living room. Drunk. Again. He usually tossed back a few beers, but lately, he'd started the evening's festivities with rot gut whiskey first.

I stiffened as Mom adjusted my tie in the living room.

"I told you. Miller has a big dance at school." She met my eyes briefly, smiling tiredly. Mom had been pretty before Dad left. Now, it seemed the life was being sucked right out of her. "You look very handsome."

"Thanks. It's just a dumb dance. Don't know why I'm bothering."

"Are your friends going? The two boys?"

"No. Not tonight."

The bastards. Ronan wouldn't be caught dead, and Lord Parish said he had "other plans."

I went back to my room to grab my wallet and phone and to take one last look in the mirror. I'd put on my best—faded—black jeans, a white button-down, tie, and an old gray blazer Mom had found at Goodwill.

Not bad. I was sure River would be dressed in an immaculate rented tux, and Violet would be breathtaking on his arm…

I shoved the thoughts away and headed back out.

"Where's your date?" Chet wondered with a belch. He chuckled. "She coming to pick you up?"

He loved to point out I didn't have a car. Mom still drove the station wagon we'd lived in, but it'd be a cold day in hell before I drove that to *school*. I barely had money for the dance tickets, and when our lights were shut off a week ago, I'd had to work extra shifts to earn the cash to turn them back on, never mind taking Amber to dinner.

"I'm meeting her there." I kissed Mom on the cheek. "Bye."

"Have fun. Don't stay out too late."

Chet snorted. "Late? He doesn't come home most nights at all. Not until the early morning."

I stopped at the door.

"Didn't know I knew that, eh? Yep, comes in before dawn, stinking of beer and smoke. How about that?"

I gripped the doorknob tight. "How about you mind your own fucking business?"

He sat up and leveled a finger at me. "Watch your mouth, son. You'd better just watch it."

Or what? You'll actually get off the couch?

I didn't say it, only because I didn't want to leave Mom with him in a rage. I looked to her, begging her silently to get rid of this asshole before things got worse. She only gave me a final, tired smile, then turned and quietly went back to her room.

I left, letting the screen door bang, and bumped up *Get rid of Chet fucking Hyland* on my mental to-do list. Right after becoming a global musical superstar. Ha, what a joke. As I'd suspected, the video Violet had uploaded of me on YouTube had only a few views and none of them from salivating record execs.

My bitterness flooded me. By the time I got to the school, my mood was thoroughly foul. The Homecoming theme was Hollywood. Standing lights had been set up on the walk leading to the gym, complete with a red carpet. Faculty and photographers—mostly parent volunteers—lined the walk, calling out to attendees like paparazzi.

Amber was waiting for me near the red carpet walk. She looked pretty in a pink bohemian-looking dress, loose and flowing around her ankles. Her long blond hair flowed over her shoulders, and she smiled brightly at me.

"Hi."

"Hey," I said, mustering a smile in return.

She nodded at the small cluster of daisies in my hand I'd picked on the way over. "Are those for me?"

"Oh, yeah," I said, my face heating with embarrassment. "I didn't get you a corsage, but I saw these. Thought you might like them."

"They're perfect." She laced a few in her hair and tucked the largest behind her ear. She was right—they suited her perfectly.

"You look…very nice," I said.

"So do you. Shall we?"

That was something Violet liked to say. I forced a thin smile on my face and put Amber's hand in the crook of my elbow.

I endured the "paparazzi" red carpet walk and stepped inside a dark gym illuminated with follow spotlights that beamed across the ceiling. A papier-mâché Hollywood sign had been erected on one side, and long silver steamers and black and white balloons were everywhere. A DJ spun the latest pop and alternative songs over a crowd of dancing students. Two minutes in, and I already wanted to leave.

"You want something to drink?" I shouted in Amber's ear.

"Sure. I see some friends. Meet me there?"

She pointed. I nodded and left to get us some punch, scanning the crowd for Violet without conscious thought. Shiloh's warning rang in my ears over the base thundering in the gym. She was right. I had to be fair to Amber and not string her along.

At the punch table, Ms. Sanders, my English teacher, guarded the bowl of red liquid like a hawk. She smiled when she saw me.

"Miller! So nice to see you here."

"Thanks. Two please."

"Your final essay on *The Great Gatsby* was pretty brilliant," she said, ladling two cups for me. "I'll return them on Monday, but spoiler alert: you received an A."

"Cool." I took the cups. "And thanks for these."

"Miller, wait." She leaned over the table with both hands. "Your essay was beautiful, poetic, even. But there were…elements to it that frankly made me concerned." She smiled gently. "Is everything okay at home? I mean…now isn't the time or place—"

"No, it's not," I said and then softened my tone. "I'm fine. Thanks for asking."

Translation: things are shit, there's nothing you can do about it, but it's nice that you care.

Ms. Sanders read me loud and clear. "Okay. But my door is always open if you need to talk."

"Thanks."

"And hey, word is getting around that you're quite the musician. Guitar, right?"

"Where'd you hear that?"

"Some kids were passing around a video of you playing at a party. Mr. Hodges has started an instrumental club. Tuesdays and Thursdays." Ms. Sanders smiled encouragingly. "Could be something right up your alley."

I pressed my lips together. "I have to work every Tuesday and Thursday. I have to work every day after school and all day Saturday."

Ms. Sanders' shoulders slumped. "I wish that wasn't the case. Such a failure of our system that lets talented kids like you fall through the cracks so easily."

"I'll be okay. Kids like me have to get shit done on our own." I hefted the cups. "Thanks for the punch, Ms. S."

She smiled sadly. "Take care, Miller."

No sooner had I left the table than three girls I vaguely recognized as new friends of Violet's accosted me.

"Miller, right?" said one. "I'm Julia. This is Caitlin and Evelyn."

I took a step back, mindful I was holding two cups of red punch while wearing a white shirt. "Can I help you?"

"Relax! We just wanted to say that your performance at Chance's party was ah-mazing," Caitlin said.

"Insanely good," Julia said. "You're very talented."

"Yeah, thanks."

"Are you here with someone?" Evelyn asked, glancing at my cups with shrewd, calculating eyes under fake lashes. She was the prettiest of the three.

"Amber Blake. I should get back."

Julia pouted. "I knew it. Too late."

"Too late for what?" But my words were drowned by the DJ dropping a beat and the gym exploding with sound.

"You should have been hired to play this thing," Evelyn shouted in my ear, moving in close. "You would have slayed it. Violet is *always* telling us how talented you are."

My chest tightened at her name. "Thanks. I should go."

"Hold on. Care to spice those up?" She produced two mini bottles of vodka.

I was about to say no but then Julia said, "Oh, I see Violet! God, she looks so freaking pretty."

I gritted my teeth and forced myself not to follow Julia's line of vision. Tradition at Central was that the King and Queen took their spotlight dance together, alone. The entire school would circle around River and Violet to watch them dance like a married couple at their wedding.

I can't. I fucking can't.

Evelyn was watching me with a knowing look.

"Sure, hit me," I said.

She poured one bottle to each cup, leaned in, and planted a lingering kiss on my cheek. "Have a nice night, Miller."

The girls melted into the crowd of writhing bodies, likely to join Violet and River. I downed one cup of punch, the sickly sweetness hitting my tongue first followed by the bite of vodka in the back of my throat. It warmed me from the inside out, and without thinking about the sugar intake or my numbers, I downed the second one.

The night mellowed and smoothed out. Turned liquid and murky in my vision. Somehow, I made it back to Amber.

"No drinks?" She laughed and took my hand. "Come on. Let's dance."

The DJ played "Dance Monkey," and Amber bounced along to it, both my hands in hers.

"I don't dance," I shouted blearily.

"You're so cute."

She twirled herself in my arms but I pulled out of her grasp. I was already having trouble keeping myself upright. The room spun, and I could feel my numbers dropping.

"I gotta stop. Need air."

Amber moved in close. "Good idea. Let's go be alone."

She took my hand and led me out of the gym and into the cool night air. Around a corner and into a deserted hallway, I slumped against the wall. Amber pressed her body to me and kissed me hard, her hands roaming.

"I've wanted to do this for weeks," Amber said between kisses, her voice sounding like it came from miles away. "The way you sang at the party? It was like you were singing right at me. Right into my soul."

God, I'm such an asshole.

I should have pushed her away and told her nothing could happen between us. But her mouth was insistent and hot. Her kiss nothing like Violet's, but then, that was the point, wasn't it? To get over her and move on?

Becoming a global musical superstar felt more realistic.

I struggled to keep my head, but it swam in vodka. I was submerged under the sensations of Amber's body and hands and tongue, watching images swim by: Violet smiling at River, Chet's snarl, Ms. Sanders' pitying look…lights shutting off in my life, one by one.

Amber dropped to her knees, her hands on the fly of my jeans.

"Amber, wait." After what was coming next, there'd be no going back.

She looked up. "What's wrong?"

Inside the gym, the muffled sound of the MC calling the King and Queen to the floor for their dance, followed by raucous cheers.

Violet in River's arms, gazing up at him adoringly…

"Nothing."

My head fell back against the wall as Amber freed me from my jeans. I moaned softly, shut my eyes and let the world spin out from under me.

CHAPTER TWELVE

VIOLET

Dear Diary,

It's been a long time since I've written in here. Years, even. The last entry was the night I told Miller we should kiss. For practice. So that when the real deal came along, we wouldn't be so unprepared.

But I had my first real kiss and nothing could have prepared me.

Miller sang for me so I could put him on YouTube and make him a star. And God, even before he sang a note, my body was humming. He took off his beanie and ruffled his hair... I'd never seen anything sexier in my life. So sexy because he had no idea the effect he was creating in me. I could hardly take it myself.

Then he began to sing and I could hardly hold the phone still. His voice—rough and low and so masculine—went right through me. My heart and soul, and God even between my legs. I felt it—him—everywhere. Like the best fever.

And then he kissed me.

I was completely unprepared. Not only because it was my first, but I was shocked at how thoroughly he took my breath away. How he smelled and sounded and tasted so good. How perfect it felt. How right. It did everything a first kiss was supposed to do; it swept me off my feet and made me want more.

It made me want him. My body now feels awake. Alive.

Miller told me he was okay with us being friends, but that was a lie. No boy kisses a girl like that unless he cares about her more than she could ever have guessed. I felt everything in Miller from his kiss. How he felt about me; how he'd probably been feeling about me for

God knows how long. Maybe he's loved me for as long as I've loved him…which feels like always.

And that scares me.

I've spent years doing exactly what he accused me of, holding him at arm's length for the sheer, simple fact I love him too much. I love him so much my heart feels like it'll burst. I love him so much I'd rather keep him in my life as a friend than ruin us. I know that sounds crazy, but good and precious things like Miller Stratton only come along once in a lifetime. To have him and lose him…?

I can't even write it. It nearly happened four years ago, and that night scarred me for life.

But he kissed me and now everything's different. I feel different. And angry. He shouldn't have done it. But he did, and now, I can't go back.

And the worst part is, I don't want to.

I shut my diary on those words—my confession—and exhaled a shaky breath. If I didn't hurry, I'd be late to the school where River Whitmore would be waiting for me. After the parade, we'd gone our separate ways so I could change for Homecoming while he had a victory dinner with his team. He suggested we meet at the dance in case his dinner ran late. Not exactly romantic but okay.

And I realized it didn't bother me anyway. My crush on River had begun long before I met Miller, but now I felt like I was clinging to it as a safety net. Miller's kiss cut the wires, and now, I was falling…

I wished Shiloh were there to slap some sense into me, but she wasn't going to the dance either. She had other plans. Evelyn had been acting cool toward me, and I was in too much emotional turmoil to call anyone else.

I got dressed alone, donning a white ice-skating style halter dress with lace at the hem, waist, and under the arms. Mom had taken me to a salon earlier that day, and they'd piled my hair onto my head in an elegant but messy bun with little daisy pins stuck here and there and tendrils curling down around my ears.

I examined myself in the mirror. Homecoming Queen. Nothing felt special or exciting. I was as lonely as I'd ever been on a Saturday night. And Miller wasn't going to come climbing through my window to sing for me.

He'll be at the dance with Amber.

Shiloh had told me. That had hurt but was no less than I expected.

"Or deserved," I said softly to my reflection.

I'd hurt him, which was precisely what I wanted to avoid all along. But that's what love does. It hurts.

And yet kissing Miller felt so good.

I put another coat of lip gloss on, but it didn't help. It'd been four days, and I could still taste him.

I waited out in front of the school for River at seven as planned, but there was no sign of him. I texted him, and there was no answer. Minutes passed and I grew tired of waving sheepishly at students going by in couples or groups, many giving me curious stares.

Maybe River's in the gym already and can't hear his phone.

Walking the red carpet alone was more than slightly embarrassing, and inside, there was still no sign of River. I spied his teammates and their dates. No quarterback.

Embarrassment warred with worry. Maybe something had happened to him. Or to his mom.

"Have you seen River?" I shouted at Donte Weatherly, the star wide receiver.

"Yeah, he was at dinner with us. I thought he was coming straight here."

"Me too."

"He's probably just running late." He flashed me his perfect white teeth, contrasting brightly with his warm brown skin. "I'll text him for you, my queen, and let you know when he answers."

I smiled. "Thank you," I said and wandered away, through a morass of dancing bodies. I scanned the crowd but realized it wasn't River I was searching for.

Evelyn, Caitlin, and Julia found me. They all looked beautiful: Caitlin in red, Julia in blue, and Evelyn in black with red roses clipped to her long black hair.

"Where's River?" Julia asked.

My cheeks burned. "Good question."

Caitlin's eyebrows shot up, while Evelyn wore a strange smile.

"He's not here?" she asked.

"I'm getting a little worried, actually," I said to combat the actual fear that I was being stood up.

"We just saw one of the Lost Boys," Evelyn said. Lost Boys was her new nickname for Miller, Ronan and Holden. Outcasts who were seen roaming the Boardwalk almost every night. Given the connection between Santa Cruz and the classic vampire movie set here, the name had spread like fire.

She smiled sweetly. "Your Miller."

My stupid heart fluttered, though I made my voice hard. "He's not mine."

"I suppose that's true," she said as the DJ started "Dance Monkey." She pointed through the crowd. "He's here with Amber."

I followed her gaze. Amber looked beautiful in pink, real daisies twined in her long blond hair that swayed and flowed as she laughingly tried to get Miller to dance.

My eyes drank him up. He wore a suit coat and his hair was damp from the shower but for a stray lock that fell over his brow. Stubble still shadowed his angular cheeks, highlighting his full mouth and those lips that kissed me so perfectly…

As I watched him, something in my heart unfurled. Like a tight fist finally letting go, warmth and lightness expanded in my chest. I sucked in a breath.

He is mine. He's always been mine.

Tears sprung to my eyes, but I willed them back. It wasn't fair of me to ruin anything between him and Amber, but if we could have a real talk before a spark caught fire between them, we might have a chance. If he hadn't already given up on me. If it wasn't too late.

I took a step toward him and then Caitlin grabbed my arm, bouncing excitedly.

"It's starting! Your dance with River."

Evelyn's smile could have cut glass, her eyes boring into me. I turned away to seek Miller again, but he and Amber were gone.

"Oh no…" I stood on tiptoe in my heels, searching.

"And now," the DJ intoned, "it's time for your Homecoming King and Queen to come up here for their official coronation dance. Please help me first welcome your king, River Whitmore!"

The crowd cheered and heads turned to look.

The DJ tried again. "Your king, River Whitmore!"

My cheeks burned as a room full of eyes now were turning to me in pity and curiosity. Some snickering and whispering. My phone vibrated a text within my clutch purse. Conscious that the entire school was watching me while the DJ stalled for time with dumb jokes, I pulled it out and read the text from River.

I can't make it. I'm sorry.

Worry that something had happened to him or his mom evaporated, and humiliation flooded in. It carried with it a strange lightness. As if a burden had been lifted.

"He's not coming," I murmured.

My phone slipped out of my trembling hand and hit the gym floor. I glanced up to a sea of eyes still watching me. Julia and Caitlin gave me pitying stares, while Evelyn couldn't conceal the triumph in her smirk. Someone told the DJ to play another song, and music filled the gym, covering the murmurs and talk.

None of it mattered. I had to find Miller. *He* mattered, and it had taken me long enough to realize it.

I ran out of the gym and rounded the corner, the chilly night air cooling my burning cheeks, and stopped short. My breath caught.

Twenty or so yards away, just outside a cone of light, Miller sagged against a wall while Amber knelt in front of him, her back to me, her hands on his hips, her head bobbing. His eyes were closed, his handsome face twisted in a grimace. Of pain or pleasure, I couldn't tell.

I swung back around the corner, my bare shoulder blades crashing against the rough cement. I clapped a hand to my mouth before any sound could escape. My breath rasped in my nose and my legs went weak.

"Stupid," I whispered behind my hand, tears streaming. "I'm so stupid."

And too late. Four years and a few minutes too late.

After a few ragged moments, the first sharp pain passed. The fist in my chest closed up tight again and sank to my stomach like a heavy lead ball. I sucked in deep breaths and dried my tears, leaving mascara smudges on the heels of my hands.

Then I pushed off the wall and went home.

PART III

CHAPTER THIRTEEN

MILLER

March

Are we hanging out today or not??

I read the text from Amber and sighed.

"Uh oh," Holden said, walking to my left. Ronan was on my right as we crossed the grassy expanse leading into school on a sun-filled morning. "Girl trouble. Again. You could always switch to my team, you know. Less drama."

I shot him a look. "*Less* drama."

"Okay fine, *I'm* a handful, but if you told Amber you were gay, you could finally break up with her and put all of us out of our misery."

"Word," Ronan concurred.

I didn't say anything. They didn't get it. Yes, I stuck with Amber because—like an asshole—I'd let her go down on me at Homecoming. Other guys might have ghosted her by now, but I wasn't like that. Amber was a human being who deserved to not be treated as if she were disposable.

Moreover, I'd talked myself into wanting to date her. She was sweet, smart, and beautiful—like an unpolished Cara Delevingne, with long blond hair and thick eyebrows. I hung out with her because I kept thinking *this* night, or *this* date would be the one where the spark ignited and caught fire, and I could finally get over Violet.

But the spark never caught, physically or emotionally. My stubborn heart refused to let go of Violet. I knew it never would.

"You're right," I admitted. "I just..." I stopped, glancing around. Students were huddled in their usual clusters before first bell, but now they were all watching us, talking behind their hands, and smiling. Girls offered flirty little waves. Guys tilted their head in greeting.

"What the hell is this?" I looked to Ronan. "You?"

He shrugged. "I just got off another suspension."

His fourth. Ronan and Vice Principal Chouder had a relationship modeled after Bender and Mr. Vernon from *The Breakfast Club.* Ronan spent more time in detention or suspended than he did in a classroom.

"You spray-painted *rapist* on Mikey Grimaldi's brand-new Jeep Rubicon," I said. "Most girls consider you a hero. This could be for you."

"They don't know that I did it," Ronan said, "and that's not what I got suspended for."

Holden shot me a commiserating glance. "I know, I can't keep up with his vigilantism either." He gestured at the crowd with a flourish. "This, my friend, is for you. Your performance at the winter Talent Show, perhaps?"

Holden and Amber had pestered me to enter the school's annual talent show so relentlessly that I did it more to shut them up than anything. Plus, I figured I needed the practice of performing in front of a crowd. I thought I'd be scared shitless, but it was easy. Perfect. The stage was where I wanted to be. It felt like home. Safer than the one I actually had.

"That was months ago," I said. "This is some new shit."

We crossed the quad and took a seat on the cement wall that separated the lower level of the school with the upper. Stares, waves, and murmurs followed.

"Quite the mystery," Holden said, leaning casually against the wall, one hand in the pocket of his long tweed coat, despite the fact that spring was rapidly approaching.

Ronan put one booted foot up onto the ledge and rested his elbow on his knee. "Maybe Miller finally fucked Amber, and she's told the school about his magical, giant dick."

Holden's eyes widened. "How do you know his dick is magical *and-or* giant? Are you two holding out on me?"

"Can you both stop talking about my dick?" I snapped. "And no, that's not it. We haven't… Never mind."

Holden sighed. "Still stuck on aggressive cuddling, are we? What are you waiting for?"

"Violet," Ronan said.

I didn't bother to argue. "Amber's getting fed up with me. Can't blame her."

"You tried," Holden said. "You served your blowjob-mandated sentence, but I hereby grant you early release for good behavior."

"Dump her," Ronan said.

"Or what he said."

I snorted a laugh at my friends as Evelyn Gonzalez approached. She wore a short, tight skirt, breast-hugging T-shirt, and her long black hair flowed in waves over her small, lithe stature. I took inventory of her assets with the same enthusiasm I used to take inventory of the prizes at the arcade. She was another beautiful girl in a school of beautiful girls that my heart—and aforementioned "magical" dick—didn't give a crap about.

Including my own girlfriend.

"Ah ha! Answers," Holden said as Evelyn joined us. "Miss TMZ, do you know why the entire school is making eyes at our Miller?"

"Maybe," she said, a mischievous glint in her dark eyes under cat-eye liner. "Now shoo. I need to talk to *my* Miller, alone."

"This is our spot," Ronan intoned.

"Fine. Miller, can we go somewhere private?"

"Sure," I said and hopped down off the wall.

"Did you hear about his magical dick too?" Holden called after. "How am I the last to know?"

I gave him the finger behind my back as Evelyn led me to a bench under a huge oak tree. For all her confident calm, she was practically bouncing in her skin as she took a Mac Air out of her stylish leather backpack.

"Getting some attention this morning, are you?" she said, powering it up.

"Do you know why?"

"I do." She turned her Mac screen to face me. "This is my fashion vlog. You'll note the subscriber count is well over fifty thousand."

"Congrats?"

"Don't be an ass. As of last week, I had half that. But thanks to you..."

She hit play on one of her highly produced videos. After she gave a brief intro about me, the screen flashed to a compilation of my performances: Chance's party, Violet's YouTube video, and the Winter Talent Show.

"That's why everyone's staring at you."

I frowned. "That was Violet's YouTube video. Which she deleted."

Out of morbid curiosity, I had gone on YouTube to see if the video of me performing "All I'll Ever Want" had gained traction or was only a breeding ground for snarky comments, but it was gone.

"I deleted it," Evelyn said.

"Uh…why? How?"

"When River stood her up on Homecoming night, Violet dropped her phone and ran out."

I clenched my jaw. It wasn't news to me what that bastard had done, but it still pissed me off that he'd humiliated her like that in front of the entire school.

"Anyway, her phone was in my possession for more than twenty-four hours, and I'm a *very* curious person by nature. I found the video—"

"You snooped in her phone?"

"Relax. Girls share everything. Anyway, I found the video of you playing, and it was…wow. Just fucking wow."

For a second, Evelyn's carefully crafted and stylized artifice came down, and she looked truly moved. Then she shook her head.

"On a hunch," she continued, "I googled your name to see if that video, or any others from Chance's party, were up. That's when I found Violet's sad little YouTube channel. She was already logged in from her phone, so it was easy enough to go in and delete it."

"Why?"

"Because you can't just throw your commodities onto the internet for free."

"But you can put it on your vlog? You fucking stole it—"

"I repurposed it. It's worth too much. I put it where it would bring me some ad revenue and help you get exposure."

"Jesus, how long have you been planning this?"

"Since Homecoming. Chance's party performance was great, but I needed one more ace. Proof that you could rock a crowd. The Winter Talent Show fit that bill quite nicely. But then we went to Barbados for Christmas and the whole thing took some time to produce…" She rolled her hand in lazy circles. "Long story short, this weekend, you were the subject of my vlog's first ever musical spotlight. My subscribers got a taste of your talent, and as of this morning, the video of you singing 'All I'll Ever Want' has been reblogged and shared on

Twitter and TikTok *thousands of times* and counting." She smiled triumphantly. "Oh, I forgot to mention, I have huge TikTok and Twitter followings too."

I tried to absorb the fact my performances had reached a shit-ton of people. "Do they…like it?"

Again, Evelyn's face softened. "Oh honey, of course they do. They love it. They love you. You should read the comments. Here, let me give you a sample."

I waved my hands. "No, no. I…" I couldn't feel this way. This hopeful. It wouldn't stick.

Nothing did. "Why would you do this? Just to promote yourself?"

She rolled her eyes. "Duh. But also to promote *you*. I'm your ticket to stardom. But we have some work to do. For starters, we need more video. Preferably of you doing covers like that amazeballs, 'Yellow.' Your own song is beautiful, but if someone wants an original Miller Stratton EP, then they need to pay for it. Plus, people love it when someone slays a song they know and recognize. It forms a connection—"

"Wait, hold on. What are you saying? You want to put me on your vlog and hope it goes viral?"

"Honey, you're already viral. Why do you think half the student body—especially the female half—has been drooling over you from afar all morning?"

"So, what's the upshot? We make more videos?"

"After we give you a little makeover of course."

"No fucking way."

"Do you want to have a career in music or not?"

I sat back against the bench. I wanted to make music--and enough cash to take care of Mom, get rid of Chet, and never again have to choose between groceries or keeping the lights on. Or see an eviction notice on our door. My memories shuffled through months of washing my hair in gas station bathrooms, and cramming my long legs into the back seat of the station wagon while the forest night was thick and breathing outside the window, and Mom was out trying to bring home a few bucks…

"Yes," I blurted. "I do."

Evelyn smiled. "Then this is how we do it. *Trust.* We shoot a few more songs, build a bigger following, and the world is going to stand up and take notice. You'll be whisked off to LA and the rest is history."

I sincerely doubted it would be that easy, but what did I have to lose?

"And what do you get out of it?" I asked, my suspicions swooping back in. "I know you're not doing this out of the kindness of your heart. I'm that dirty kid who lived in a car, remember?"

She shrugged, not put off by my accusation. "A diamond in the rough can only shine if someone scrapes off the dirt. And of course, I'm not doing this for free. I have my demands."

"Which are?"

She shouldered her backpack as the first bell rang. "I'll let you know when the time comes, but you have to swear to uphold your end."

"How can I do that if I don't know what your demands are?" I shot her a look. "I'm not killing anyone for you."

She laughed. "I promise it's not something illegal." She offered her long, lacquer-nailed hand. "Deal?"

My eternal pessimism told me this was fucking crazy, but where had listening to that voice gotten me?

I took her hand. "Deal."

We sealed it with one shake and then she jumped off the bench. "Great. Meet me at my house after school today."

"Can't. I work. Sunday is my only day."

She heaved a sigh. "Fine. Sunday. I'll text you the address."

"How did you get my phone number?"

"I had Violet's phone for an entire day, remember?" She glanced at my T-shirt under an unbuttoned plaid flannel and tapped her fingernail to her chin. "This adorable scruffy look works but needs accessories…"

"Hell, no," I said. "I'm not dressing up as someone I'm not."

She rolled her eyes. "Of course, you won't. Luckily, this works for us. Rags to riches… Humble beginnings." She touched her finger to the tip of my nose. "Leave it to me. I got you, boo."

Evelyn strode away, leaving me with a weird feeling in my chest. Her plan was nuts. The chances of anything coming of it were slim. Weren't they?

She'd said a diamond in the rough can only shine if someone scrapes off the dirt. The *dust.* And that's when I recognized the feeling in my chest. Hope.

CHAPTER FOURTEEN

VIOLET

I carried the cup of steaming tea into Nancy Whitmore's bedroom. Spring was fast approaching, bringing warmer weather with it. A beam of brilliant afternoon sunlight fell over her, and I beamed with it.

She's getting better.

Somehow, against all medical odds, Nancy's stage IV cancer was on a pause. Not in remission, but her tumor had shrunk and the cocktail of medications she took every day was holding it at bay. Giving her time.

Dazia, her best friend, was in town again, and her smile matched mine.

"Ah yes, she looks radiant, doesn't she?" she said in her faint accent. Over the last few months, I'd learned that Dazia was from Croatia and that she and Nancy had been roommates at Washington University. Friends for life, like Shiloh and me.

"You do look radiant," I said to Nancy and sat on the other side of the bed. "I'm sad that my time as your PCV is ending. But it seems you won't be needing me anyway."

Nancy smiled. Her skin was no longer sallow, and she'd gained a few pounds. "You're sweet to stay with me so long. I'll miss you."

"Me too," I said, my throat thick.

Over the last few months, I'd come to look forward to being with her. Her calm tone and gentle wisdom felt so maternal, especially since my own mom was caught up in her own turmoil with Dad.

"Would you mind giving us a minute, Daz? I'd like to have a word with Violet."

"Uh oh." Dazia grinned. "I feel a Nancy Talk coming on." She pinched my cheek on the way out. "She's a wonderful schoolteacher but missed her calling as a therapist."

"Agree," I said with a smile, though it faded fast. I suspected I knew what Nancy wanted to talk about.

"It's not about River," she said as soon as the door clicked shut behind Dazia.

I laughed. "Am I that transparent?"

"You wear your emotions all over your sweet face." She took my hand in hers. "I know you haven't forgiven him for standing you up at Homecoming. I can imagine that must've been very humiliating."

"A bit. But I have forgiven him. I've told him a hundred times I've forgiven him. I don't understand why he keeps asking to see me."

Nancy pursed her lips. "You'll have to discuss that with him. He knows I'm disappointed in him for what he did to you, but I don't want to pry into his business beyond that. I'd prefer he come to me about personal things when he's ready. But what I wanted to talk to you about was you."

"Me?"

"You seem so sad lately, and I know it's not because of my son." She cocked her scarf-wrapped head. "You know that same policy I have for him extends to you. No pressure to share anything with me. I just want you to know that my door is open."

My fingers plucked the coverlet. "My parents are not happy. They fight a lot and…there's some other stuff going on with them that I don't want to bore you with."

As much as I loved Nancy, there was no way I was going to air my family's suspected financial issues with her.

"Anything else?" Nancy asked gently, in a way that said, *I know there's something else.*

"Yes." I sighed. "But as much as I'd love your advice, I'm not sure it's appropriate to talk to you about another boy."

Nancy patted my hand. "Because I'm River's mom. I get it. How about you tell me what's bothering you and leave out the details? Not the who, what, and where. Just how you feel. But only if you want to."

"I do want to. Desperately. The last time my mom and I had 'girl talk' it consisted of her making an appointment for me to see a gynecologist."

Nancy's lips made a thin line, then she smiled. "I'm here."

I met her clear blue eyes and tears filled mine. "I screwed it up."

"Okay."

"I was so afraid of losing him or having our beautiful friendship fall apart, that I pushed him away. I pushed him to *someone else*, and our friendship is hanging by a thread anyway. Everything I was afraid of happening, happened, but not how I feared it would."

Nancy offered me a tissue from her box. "Reminds me of that old proverb, *A person often meets her destiny on the road she takes to avoid it.*"

"There's a picture of me right next to that quote in a book somewhere." I stared down at the tissue in my hands. "God, I'm such a coward."

"You're not a coward." Nancy's voice was firm. "How many times did you see Mr. Whitmore in here last winter?"

"Not very much. I figured he was working…"

"He was. But he was also scared. River and Amelia, too. They got over it, but it took time. It's very difficult to look at someone you love and see only the day they might leave you." Her voice gentled. "The urge to protect one's heart is the strongest urge of all. But it's also impossible if you want to live a rich, full life."

I thought back to the night Miller almost died in my arms. And seeing him outside the dance with Amber. The pain was knifelike and brutal. There was nothing rich or full about a life without Miller in it. Or watching him be with someone else.

Especially when I was the one who drove him away.

I dried my tears and put on a smile. "Thanks for talking with me."

"But you don't believe me," she said gently.

"I appreciate your advice, but there's nothing I can do."

"Talk to him?"

"He doesn't want to talk to me, and I can't mess up what he has with…her. They've been together for months now. The last thing I want is to cause any more trouble." I smiled grimly. "Another proverb: I made my bed and now I have to lie in it."

Alone.

I got to my feet. "I'll go tell Dazia she's no longer banished."

At the door, Nancy's voice stopped me. "If we were all born perfect and wise, always making the right decisions and never any mistakes, there wouldn't be much point in living, would there?" I turned, and she was smiling knowingly at me. "Life's a journey, not a destination."

I smiled. "I see what you did there. Your proverb game is strong, Mrs. W."

She laughed, full and throaty. And healthy.

"And so are you, Violet. More than you know."

I left Nancy's room, shutting the door behind me, and crashed headlong into River. My nose smarted from meeting the hard planes of his chest. He wore jeans and his letterman jacket over a T-shirt and smelled faintly of motor oil from his dad's shop.

"Oh, hey," I said, rubbing my nose. I looked up. And up. The guy was a mountain and as gorgeous as ever, and yet, my heart didn't so much as flutter to be this close to him.

"Hey," he said. "Do you have a minute? I want to talk to you."

"River, I told you. We're cool."

"I know. But I…" He rubbed the back of his neck and then pulled me away from his mom's room. "I want you to give me a second chance."

"We've been over this. I don't think—"

"I like you, Violet."

I blinked. "You do?"

"Well…yeah. I think we make a good pair."

I scrunched my nose. "We do? We hardly speak to each other."

He huffed in frustration. "Look, I've been crazy-busy all winter and haven't had time to catch my breath. My dad put all kinds of pressure on me to play well and get into an NCAA Top Ten school. Scouts were crawling all over the field every practice and watching every game. It's been insane."

"I get that, but—"

"But football season is over now." He took both my hands in his. Lightly. "I want us to try again. And this time, I won't flake on you, I swear."

"We've never really talked or hung out."

"That's my fault because I've been so busy. You know how it is, right? Getting your college apps together?"

"Yeah, that was nerve-wracking as hell," I said with a laugh. "Worse, I put in for early decision. I should be hearing back any day now."

I'd applied to UC Santa Cruz, of course, and then UCSF, Georgetown, Baylor, and the University of Cincinnati for back-up. Just thinking about getting the letter with UCSC on the envelope made me queasy with excitement.

River misread the light in my eyes. He smiled and a hint of his usual, insouciant charm returned. The casual confidence of the star quarterback who could get any girl he wanted.

So why me?

"Just promise me you'll think about it, okay?"

He bent and kissed my cheek, leaving me in the hallway with the warm feel of his lips and the slight scratch of his stubble on my skin.

I sighed. I had thought about it. About him. But the problem with thinking about River Whitmore these days was that my thoughts immediately pivoted right to Miller Stratton. He'd set up permanent residence in my mind and my heart, and there was no room for anyone else.

Too late. I fell in love with my best friend and I'm too late.

"Hey, you," Shiloh said, falling in step beside me after school the next day. She wore billowy bohemian pants and a sleeveless linen shirt, her braids pulled back from her elegant neck. Earthy metal jewelry of her own creation glinted in the late afternoon sun. "You're a hard person to get a hold of these days."

"Sorry. Busy with school and now soccer practice. First game is coming up." I glanced at her sideways. My friend was always beautiful, but she looked extra radiant lately. "And I could say the same about you. I feel like it's been ages since we hung out. What have you been doing lately?"

And who with?

"Because it *has* been ages," she said, avoiding my question. "But we're here to talk about you. Specifically, you and Miller."

I stopped and shook my head. "There is no 'me and Miller.' Remember Homecoming? Do you need an episode recap?"

"Don't be bitter; it's not your style." Her lips pursed. "Okay, here's the deal. I've been patient with both you and Miller, and Amber is a friend, but enough is enough."

"What's that mean?"

"It means…"

Her words trailed as she spied something over my shoulder. I turned to look, and my throat tightened to see Miller and Amber walking hand-in-hand to the front of the school. A heavy ball smacked my chest and then sunk into my stomach. She was on her phone, and his gaze was out and away. They walked as far apart from each other as possible except for their tethered hands. As if it were the only thing keeping them from floating off in different directions.

Shiloh gave my arm a gentle squeeze, bringing me back around. "You see that body language? Do they look like a happy couple in love?"

I flinched at her choice of words. "That's just one moment in time. Who knows what they're like alone?"

At night. In his bed.

God, my stupid heart had no right to ache at the thought. *Of course* he'd lost his virginity to her by now. Or hell, maybe to someone during any of the years in which I'd kept him locked in the Friend Zone. And he had every right.

He waited for me long enough.

"Hey," Shiloh said, dragging me from my thoughts. "*I* know what they're like alone because they both tell me. In a word, he's miserable. And she's frustrated and on the brink of dumping his ass."

I didn't hear much after *miserable.* "He is? But why stay with her? Why date her in the first place?"

Shiloh's voice softened. "Why do you think? To get over you."

A moment passed as I took this in. I swallowed my tears down. "I don't know what to say, Shi. They're together now and—"

"Trust me. It's not serious."

"Homecoming looked pretty serious to me."

She sighed. "I know. I warned Miller not to get involved with Amber and he did it anyway. Now he's trying his best to be a good guy. I'm sure he even likes her, but I'm not sure he'll ever be over you."

I tried to keep my face neutral and my voice steady. "So why not break up?"

"Because he's doing the honorable thing. Because things went too far that night, and he doesn't want to bail on her. Because he is a good guy, even if he's stubborn as hell." She arched a brow. "You two have that in common."

I shook my head. "What am I supposed to do, Shi? Barge into their relationship and then what? What happens next? It's not like my fears of us being ruined have magically evaporated."

"Uh huh. And how's not even talking to him working out for you? He's miserable but so are you. Neither one of you are capable of being happy without the other. At the very least, you guys need to fix your friendship. Start there and see what happens."

"How do you know all this stuff about him and Amber anyway? From her?"

Shiloh began to walk, and I followed to catch up. "And him. I'm getting it in stereo."

"Does Miller…talk to you a lot?"

"Sort of. I've been hanging out with the so-called Lost Boys at their beach shack under the Lighthouse Cliffs."

Jealousy stabbed me in the gut. "I wasn't aware that they had a shack."

"Because you've been so busy with your college apps and study loads and *not* talking to Miller." She smiled and looked away. "It's nice. Bonfires at night… The guys drink beer and behave like horses' asses most of the time, but it's…nice."

"Miller invited you?"

"No, Ronan."

My eyebrows shot up. "Really? Since when are you two friendly? He sits right next to you in our History class and you *never* talk."

She waved a hand. "He's an asshole. I can barely tolerate him, but it's worth it to sit and watch the ocean, and nothing smells better than a beach bonfire. And I say all this because it's high time you were there too."

"I'm not going anywhere I'm not wanted, Shi," I said. "Being stood up at Homecoming in front of the entire school aside, I still have a shred of dignity."

"On that note, Miller told me Evelyn Gonzalez stole your phone that night, took the video of him singing 'All I'll Ever Want,' and put it on her vlog."

My mouth fell open. "She did what?"

Shiloh pulled out her phone. "I was hoping you gave her permission, but I guess she even didn't tell you."

"She returned it to me the next day but didn't say a word about Miller. She and I haven't been…close lately."

But she and Miller are?

I watched the vlog footage, marveling through my shock at Miller's beautiful voice, his talent, and that sexy-as-hell way he'd taken off his beanie to run his hand through his hair. Moments after that song ended, he'd kissed me…

The video finished. "That explains why everyone's been smiling and being nice to him."

"Oh, you noticed that too?" Shiloh put her phone away. "Yeah, he's suddenly the town famous person."

"They should be nice to him, but they should've been nice to him this entire time. Not just because of this."

"Agreed." Shiloh put her arm around me. "You've always treated him the way he's deserved to be treated. Come to the Shack. You're wanted there. Believe me." She gave me a squeeze. "And not just by me."

A few days later, I worked up the nerve to take Shiloh up on her offer. As the sun set behind the ocean, she led me on a crazy path over jagged, porous boulders, while the tide washed over our ankles.

"You're not taking me out here to murder me, are you?" I asked, tripping over a tangle of seaweed while protectively clutching a paper bag holding the six-pack of beer I'd stolen from Dad—an offering to the Lost Boys for having me at their bonfire. My Converse were drenched, and the rolled-up cuffs of my jeans were damp. "This is getting a little rough, Shi."

"Almost there."

Shiloh wore sandals and another pair of billowy, linen pants. We'd both worn hoodie sweatshirts, as she'd warned the wind could be bitter at night, fire or no fire. I followed her slim shape, her long braids flowing behind her, and was relieved to see the terrain grew easier and farther away from the ocean.

We rounded a huge boulder, and there he was. Miller sat on a worn-out beach chair in front of a roaring fire, his guitar case at his side. Ronan Wentz and Holden Parish sat in similar chairs, and they were all talking shit and laughing. The Shack was a little fisherman's hut built against the rock.

"Hello, boys," Shiloh said, stepping into the ring of light. She looked pointedly at Miller. "You all remember Violet, don't you?"

Miller met my eye, and I swear the smallest flicker of a smile touched his lips, then vanished. Shut down. He was guarding his heart the same way I had been for four years.

We're like a pendulum, swinging back and forth, I thought, wondering when or if we'd ever be unguarded at the same time.

"Miss Violet," Holden said, rising to his feet and offering me his chair—right next to Miller. "Please. Sit." He kicked at Ronan's boot. "Wentz! Mind your manners, for fuck's sake. We have company."

Ronan pulled in his long legs that had been stretched out to the fire so I could cross to the chair.

"I come bearing gifts," I said with a small smile. "An IPA. I hear it's good."

"You're an angel," Holden said, taking the bag from me and dumping it in Ronan's lap. "He's in charge of libations."

Ronan grunted and shot Holden a scowl, then turned his silvery eyes on me. I knew next to nothing about him, except that he was constantly in trouble at school and that Frankie Dowd had made it his life's mission to one day kill him. Judging by Ronan's bulk, his muscled and tatted arms, and the dangerous aura around him, I guessed he had little to fear. He could break scrawny Frankie in half.

But I wasn't prepared for the shrewd intelligence in his gaze that followed me to my seat.

Holden procured two more chairs, one for Shiloh—between Ronan and Miller—and another for himself, between Ronan and me.

"The circle is complete," Holden said, and then his smile slipped at a sudden thought. "Almost."

"Hi," I said to Miller. Shiloh had assured me he knew I was coming, but I still felt like an unwanted guest.

"Hey." He took a pull from his beer. I bit back the urge to ask how he was feeling and how his diabetes management had been going. That was Amber's job now and that of his friends. I wasn't sure if we were even that anymore.

"How have you been?" I asked.

"Good. You?"

"Fine."

Jesus. Making small talk with Miller after years of deep, thoughtful debates and bickering conversations about life was torture.

I met Shiloh's gaze from across the fire. She jerked her head and mouthed the word *Go.*

I cleared my throat and leaned into Miller. He smelled of smoke and salt and whatever made him, him. "Can we talk? Maybe take a walk?"

He stared at the fire, walls up, his eyes hard. But when he turned to answer me with a *no* on his lips, his gaze softened slightly. "Sure."

He stood up and offered me his hand. I took it, my heart pounding. The last time we'd touched was months ago. When he kissed me. His hand was hard and rough in mine, but gentle, and he pulled me to my feet and then let go.

"We'll be right back," he told the group, a slight emphasis on *right back.*

Feeling three pairs of eyes on us, I dusted sand off my butt and followed Miller. The Shack sat in a dead-end where the cliffs had collapsed and slid into the sea. He led us back the way we had come, away from the bonfire, to the relatively smooth patch of sand before the way became trickier again. The full moon provided our light.

Miller was silent, hunched in his plaid flannel, waiting for me to speak. My pulse pounded in my ears like the surf, scared to death that I'd lost him completely and afraid to know for sure. Nancy's words came back to me, that I wasn't a coward.

I drew a breath. "I'm sorry."

Miller frowned, wary. "For what?"

"For what happened between us. For everything."

His shoulders came down a little. "It's not your fault. I shouldn't have kissed you."

The wind blew my hair over my face, hiding the pain that flashed over me. When I could think of nothing else but our kiss, he regretted it. The pendulum had swung to me and wasn't going to budge.

"Whatever happened, happened," I said. "I came here tonight for the simple fact that I miss you. I miss my friend. That's all I wanted to say. That these last months have been really hard without you, and… I just wanted you to know that."

It was silent but for the wind and the ocean crashing on the shore. Miller stopped and half-sat, half-leaned on a boulder, hands in his pockets, his knit beanie keeping the hair from his eyes as they looked up at me.

"A bunch of stuff to say to you popped in my head when you asked me if we could talk," he said gruffly. "Cutting or cold things meant to push you away. Keep you at a safe distance. But I don't want to hurt you. It's really the last fucking thing I want to do."

I shivered, hugged myself in my sweatshirt. "I don't want you to be hurt either. I love seeing you here with your friends. I'm glad you have them. So glad for that."

Miller's jaw clenched, a muscle ticking in his cheek. Finally, he threw up his hands. "Jesus, Vi. You're standing there, looking like you do, saying sweet things and making it impossible…"

"To what?" I breathed.

"Nothing. Never mind. I just…I miss you too. You've always been there for me. Always. And to not have you…" He crossed his arms, as if holding his walls in place. His voice turned ragged with regret. "But I'm seeing someone else and I don't take any commitment lightly."

"I know you don't. I'm not here to interfere, I promise. But if I am, I'll go. I'll leave you alone."

Even if it wrecks me.

He watched me for a second, then gave a short laugh, shaking his head. "You? Leave me alone?"

I frowned, confused. "I don't—"

"Dr. McNamara can't leave a patient alone if she tried. How hard has it been for you to not ask me about my numbers?"

I eased a breath, understanding what he was doing. "Damn near impossible." I crossed my arms and gave him a stern look, even as my heart was bursting with joy and relief. "Well? How are they? How many beers have you had?"

He chuckled and pushed himself off the rock, toward me. "They're fine. I've had one beer, and I'll have one more. That's it." He was standing in front of me now.

"Good," I said, my throat thick. "And if you try for a third, I'll throw sand in it."

"I bet you would."

Miller's smile faded as he looked down at me. Strands of hair were stuck to my cheek by the wind. His hand came up as if he wanted to brush them away, his eyes on my mouth. Then he caught himself and stepped back.

"You're shivering," he said. "We should get back to the fire."

"Okay."

I wanted a hug to seal the deal. I ached to feel his arms around me, to lose myself in the familiarity of him, but I guessed he felt we weren't there yet. I swallowed back my disappointment and contented myself with the fact that we were talking again. He had a girlfriend now, and it wasn't fair—or right—to ask for more.

We returned to the circle of friends. Shiloh immediately read on my face that things were better. Not to where they had been; after the earth-shattering kiss, they probably never would be, but it was a start.

She smiled, and I smiled back.

Holden read the lessening of tension between Miller and me like an emcee reading the room. He was pretty drunk, I noticed, his clear green eyes bleary with whatever he was sipping from his flask.

"They're back. Got it all sorted? Got it all *straight* between you?"

"Shut up, Parish," Ronan intoned.

"Fuck off, Wentz," Holden shot back. "The long winter of our discontent and his moping is finally over. Time to celebrate."

Miller ignored his friends' bickering and looked to me. "You want a blanket or something?"

"Sure, thanks."

I scooted from the chair to sit in the soft sand. Miller and Ronan procured more blankets from the Shack, along with hotdogs, chips, and ingredients to make s'mores.

The five of us talked and laughed and ate, Holden louder than the rest of us, Ronan the quietest. I watched him and Shiloh closely without letting on, but if there was something between them, it didn't show. Their entire conversations that night consisted of trading barbs and sarcasm.

Holden leaned into me. "It's shameless how they flirt, isn't it?"

"Flirt? They hate each other," I whispered back.

"Do they?" He rubbed his narrow chin thoughtfully. "I guess it depends on your perspective."

Before I could ask him what that meant, he turned to Miller. "Hey, superstar. Stop being so stingy. It's against some law to have a perfect night, a beach bonfire but no music. Play."

Shiloh and I clapped our hands and whistled, and then Holden joined in.

"Okay, okay," Miller said. "I didn't want to be *that* asshole."

"Too late," Ronan and Holden said together, and clinked beer bottle to flask.

Miller flipped them the bird and set his guitar on his lap. His fingers took their places on the guitar as if they'd been born there, and he launched into an acoustic cover of "Take Me to Church" by Hozier.

Miller's voice wasn't as deep as Hozier's, but the rough-around-the-edges growl Miller had made the sex-drenched lyrics even sexier. I sat straight, eyes on the fire, even as every molecule in my body wanted to turn to Miller playing beside me. Wanted to crawl into his lap, tear the guitar out of his hands and kiss him hard and deep. I wanted to taste those lyrics on his tongue, drink them down, and drown in Miller's talent, the essence of him that made him so extraordinary.

God what is wrong with me?

When the pendulum swung, it slammed hard. Miller's kiss all those months ago had woken up something deep in me. Changed me. Changed the love I had for him, altering its chemical structure to include my body, my hormones, my *need.* Months apart had only fermented it until it was strong and potent. I wanted Miller, and the fear I had that we'd ruin our friendship had taken a back seat to basic, red-blooded lust.

The song ended, and the small group stared for a moment. Then Shiloh fanned herself. "I said, *goddamn.*"

"If you could bottle that and sell it at sex shops, you'd make a killing," Holden said.

"Not in the plan," Miller said.

"There's a plan?" I asked, risking a glance at him.

"Evelyn is sort of…helping me."

"Oh right. I saw her vlog." I smiled. "*Slightly* better than my little YouTube channel."

"Your video is what started it all," Miller said. "Whatever *it* is."

"*It* is you getting all the recognition you deserve."

He met my eyes, and I sank into them, the rest of the world falling away…until I heard a loud sniff. I glanced up to see the others staring at us, Holden pretending to dab his eyes.

"Shut up," Miller said, "or else the next song I play will be something from Nickelback."

Everyone groaned, and the mood lightened. Miller played a variety of songs, but none of them his own. The tension in the air was blown away by the ocean wind and filled, instead, with his voice.

The night deepened, more beer was drunk, and the others slid from their chairs to huddle under blankets in the sand. Shiloh shivered, and Ronan took off his jean jacket with the faux lamb's wool collar. Wordlessly, he took the blanket off her shoulders, draped his jacket over her, and then tucked the blanket back around her.

"Thank you," she said grudgingly. Softly. I noticed something like a truce pass between them. He sat beside her, and by the time Miller ended his song, her cheek was pillowed against Ronan's arm.

Happiness and sadness warred within me. Happy for Shiloh and sad that I'd grown so far apart from everyone in the last few months. I'd retreated to nurse my bruised heart and had missed so much.

"It's late," Miller said, making to put his guitar away.

A chorus of protests went around.

"One more, kind sir," Holden said, tiredly, his voice tinged with sadness that made me want to put my arms around him too. "One more to close out the night."

Miller nodded, set his guitar on his lap and gave me a look I couldn't decipher. Then he began to hum the soft strains of Billie Eilish's "when the party's over." He sang the first few lyrics acapella, only bringing in his guitar at the first chorus.

The four of us listened, rapt, as Miller's masculine voice turned the soft song into something with a little more edge. More masculine in its painful longing.

"*I'll only hurt you if you let me*," he sang from beside me, the words pouring in my ear. My heart. "*Call me friend but keep me closer…*"

I closed my eyes, sank deeper into my blanket, into my mistakes, as Miller's voice lulled me to sleep.

I woke, blinking, with the sun's first rays peeking over the horizon. The vestiges of sleep cleared from my eyes enough to see blue plaid, a white T-shirt, smooth skin that grew shadowed with stubble at the jaw…

A little gasp escaped me. I was wrapped completely in Miller, both of us under a blanket. He held me tight to him, my head was perfectly tucked under his chin. Our jean-clad legs entwined like vines, and his chest rose and fell against mine.

Moving only my eyes, I peeked around. The bonfire smoldered. The beach was empty. We were alone.

I should've sat up. I should've disentangled myself, grabbed my stuff and left. But my body felt heavy and satisfied. Perfectly content. The restless nights of the last few months were washed away, and I couldn't move and didn't want to.

Just a little longer…

I let my eyes drift closed and dozed.

When I became conscious again, it was in a murky, half-sleep, half-dreamy state. Miller's arms around me tightened, and his nose was in my hair, nuzzling. His lips touched my forehead. A feather light kiss. I tilted my chin up slightly and my mouth brushed his neck. Half awake, unthinking, I put a little kiss there, open-mouthed, tasting the salt of his skin with a flick of my tongue.

He shifted against me again, and I felt the heavy erection pressing against my center. His hands roamed my back, slipped into my hair, pulling just hard enough. My mouth opened wider, and I sucked at his neck lightly, biting, and then running my tongue over his skin.

Miller's hand made a fist in my hair, pulling my head back. Now I trailed kisses up his jaw, feeling the stubble under my soft lips, scraping myself against it, until I found his mouth. With a growl, Miller rolled me to my back and sank his weight against me, his groin digging between my legs, seeking entry through our jeans, just as his mouth crashed to mine, seeking entry there too.

I gave it willingly. Eagerly. Taking his kiss with long sweeps of my tongue that slid against his. God, Miller's kiss… Just like him. Hard, intense, but beautifully considerate too. Biting teeth and soft lips. Rough stubble around a soft mouth. Muttered curses uttered on soft breath.

He propped himself on one forearm, that hand gripping my hair, holding me in his kiss with delicious possession. His other moved down my body, skirting around my breast, knowing I'd never been touched like this before.

I wanted him to touch me. I'd never wanted anything more.

I took his hand and guided it under my hoodie, under my T-shirt, so he could fill his hand with my breast. He caressed and explored, hefted the weight of it. My soft moans and gasps spurred him on, and he went under my bra where he found the nipple, hard and aching. He pinched and tweaked while I moaned into his mouth, my hands sliding down over his broad back and then up again into his thick hair.

His hips crashed and ground into mine. I lifted mine to receive him and wrapped my legs around his waist. There was so much clothing between us; the denim rubbing a sweet ache in me as his hard erection sought my soft heat.

"Miller…"

The name fell out of my lips between kisses. Escaped. Because in that moment, he was my entire world. All I knew was him…and then he was gone.

Cold air swooped in as Miller tore himself off of me with a ragged cry and a vile curse. I felt as if I'd been violently woken from the sweetest dream. I sat up slowly, Miller beside me. He grabbed a handful of sand and hurled it at the smoldering embers, then shot to his feet.

"Fuck," he said, scrubbing both hands through is hair. "*Fuck!*"

I smoothed my rumpled clothing and pulled the blanket tight around me. Regret, remorse, guilt… They all flooded in, dousing the heat we'd built. "I'm so sorry," I whispered, the words torn away by the wind.

"I'm not this guy," he shouted, his beautiful voice now raised in anger. "I never wanted to be this guy. A guy who fucking *cheats*."

"Miller, I'm sorry," I said, tears building but I willed them back. "But sit and talk to me. Please. We need to talk. *Really* talk."

He whirled on me, eyes blazing with pain. "I'm tired of talking. We've been talking for *four* years. Which is why the fucking second you're near me, I have to touch you and kiss you…" He drew his hand down over his mouth as if wiping us away. "But shit, *now*? I'm with someone else."

"I know. I'm sorry."

"It's not all on you," he said. "That's just it. I did this too. I let this happen, and now…"

He fell into a frustrated silence, shaking his head at the ground.

"You care about her," I said softly, remorse making me shudder.

"I don't know. No, I… *Fuck*, I'm such an asshole. Because no matter what, this will hurt her, and I don't want that. I never wanted that. I only went to someone else because I needed to try to move on. Because I thought you and I were impossible. And maybe we are."

I hunched deeper in the blanket, fending off the chill morning air and the cold finality of his words.

He looked up at me, and it tore my heart in two to see his hazel eyes shining. "You were right all along. We can't get this right. It's fucking everything up."

Without another word, he gathered his guitar case, and his jacket.

"Miller, *wait,"* I said. "You can't just run out every time we touch and kiss and feel the depth of it all. I know it's a lot. It's a lot for me too—"

"No?" He laughed bitterly. "That's what people do, Vi. They run away. Even you, eventually."

"What?" I scrambled to my feet. "Why would you say that?"

But he turned his back on me.

"Come on, it's time to go," he said, his voice cold and empty. Unrecognizable. "We're done here."

CHAPTER FIFTEEN

MILLER

I walked the difficult path from the Shack, Violet behind me. I listened for signs that she was struggling over the rocks or had lost a shoe in the sucking sand since we weren't talking. Not a word.

Her car was parked along a side street near the path down. I waited until she was safely inside. Tires screeched as Violet peeled away in her white Rav 4 and left me in a dissipating cloud of gasoline fumes. The last thing I saw was her face through the window. Shut down. Guarded.

What did you expect?

I ruined us the first time I kissed her. I'd demolished our friendship, and now neither one of us knew what to do with each other. *I* didn't know what to do with the rush of feelings that swamped me every time we touched. Every kiss like a door opening to another life that was too fucking good. I'd been wanting her for so long, keeping her in my love songs where I got to say how it turned out.

But every time the fantasy came close to reality, my old fears came roaring back. Since Mom and I were left to fend for ourselves, I'd pulled my hate for my dad around me like a suit of armor, building strength out of the helplessness and fear. I'd promised myself I would always be the one who left before anyone could leave me. Always.

But watching Violet drive away, I didn't feel strong. Watching her go was like waking up from a dream that fades away before you can catch it.

You're running out of chances to make things right.

If I was going to make anything right, I had to start with Amber. I pulled out my phone. **Can we talk? Today?**

I started to walk home, and the reply came a few minutes later. **UR breaking up with me.**

It wasn't a question.

Meet me at the bench after school?

I take that as a 'yes.' Sure. Fine. CU then.

I blew air out my cheeks and tucked my phone away. I had enough time to eat and take my insulin, but it was too late to shower and change. I had to go to school and break up with Amber, smelling like Violet.

My jackassery knows no bounds…

After a day of classes that felt like an eternity, I went to the bench at the periphery of the main quad. The same bench where I'd sat with Violet the day Homecoming votes were cast. Amber was already waiting for me.

"Hey," I said, sitting beside her.

She glanced me up and down. "You look like hell. Is this actually difficult for you? Or were you up all night doing something else? With *someone* else?"

"I had a late night I didn't sleep with anyone, but I—"

"Of course, you didn't," she said bitterly. "I'm surprised you haven't joined a monastery by now. Or come out of the closet."

I scrubbed a hand through my hair. For Amber, one of my many failings in our "relationship" was my refusal to have sex with her. But my heart and body belonged to someone else, and no matter how many days and weeks and months had piled up, that never changed.

Amber threw up her hands. "Hello? You can't even break up with me without zoning out."

"I know, I'm sorry."

"So this is it, huh? I'm shocked," she said in a deadpan voice. "Shocked, I tell you. This is my shocked face."

"Amber…"

"What happened? What was the final straw?"

"What do you mean?"

"Be serious. You always had one foot out the door. Getting you to spend time with me was nearly impossible, and when you did, you never wanted to mess around. You hardly ever kissed me unless you'd had a few beers. So? Why now?"

"I kissed someone else," I said.

Amber's jaw stiffened. "This story just gets better and better. Who?"

"Violet McNamara."

"Just once? Or have you been cheating on me for a while?"

"Just once. Last night."

But that wasn't even true. I'd always been with Violet, since the day we met.

Amber was glaring at me. "You sure move fast, don't you? But not fast enough. You should have broken up with me *before* you kissed another girl."

"You're right. I'm sorry. It just happened. That's no excuse. I put myself in the position…"

Wrapped around Violet. That's my position. And I never want to leave.

"I've been an asshole."

Amber sighed, some of the sharp aggression draining from her voice. "No, you haven't. That's just it. You're actually a good guy trying to do the right thing. But we went too far Homecoming night, and you've been trying to make up for it since. I'm not stupid, you know. I know you felt roped in."

"It wasn't your fault. I wanted to try."

"Try? Try me on for size? Like a girlfriend coat to see if I would fit?"

"No."

Yes. Maybe.

"I liked you, Amber," I said. "I *do* like you. But—"

"You love her."

"Why do you think that?" I asked pathetically.

"I saw Evelyn's vlog. Shiloh told me that Violet took the original video of you singing 'All I'll Ever Want.' The way you looked at her when you sang it… That wasn't for her, right? After Chance's party, you never sang to me again."

I hadn't sung for Amber at Chance's party either, but no sense in making things worse. I felt like shit enough as it was that I let this go on so long. A charade. An act so tedious, even Amber was tired of it.

"I'm sorry, Amber. I really am. For what it's worth, I never meant to hurt you."

"Famous last words." She tossed her long hair over her shoulder. "Okay, so I guess that's it. Just do me one favor."

"Anything."

"Give me some time before you start walking the halls with Violet, okay?"

"I will. Doubt that would happen soon anyway. I have to get my shit together." I smiled thinly. "Don't need to tell you that."

"No, you don't." Amber's stiff face softened. "I thought I'd be more hurt. And I am. I'm not letting you off the hook."

"You shouldn't."

"But when you sent me that text this morning, I felt almost relieved." She shot me a dry look. "Miller Stratton, you're like a gentleman sharing a brain with an asshole."

I laughed a little. "Accurate."

The asshole was born the day my father left. But Amber didn't need to hear any more excuses.

"And I have a confession," she said. "I got a little wrapped up in the idea of you and me. Of you being this famous musician and me being the girl in your love songs. So maybe I hung around a little bit longer than I should have. But that doesn't mean you should've kissed someone else."

"No, it doesn't. I'll always regret that."

I regretted the timing. I could never regret kissing Violet. Even when it blew us apart.

Amber heaved a sigh. "Okay, you look contrite enough. I gotta go." She shouldered her embroidered bag. "When you do get your shit together, make sure you give Violet more of your gentleman and less of your asshole."

I held up a hand. "I will do my best to give her less of my asshole."

She burst out with a laugh. "See you around, Stratton."

"Hey, Amber."

"Yeah?"

"Thanks for being cool."

She smiled thinly, gave a little wave, and walked away.

I slumped on the bench, relief and regret gusting out of me. Relief that I ended it, regret that it took me so long.

A few days later, I was on the same bench, reading *Tender is the Night*, when Evelyn Gonzalez approached.

"Hey, you. What you're doing?" She glanced at the cover of my book. "Fitzgerald. That's not on our assigned list."

"I know. I'm reading it because I want to."

"Aren't you just the perfect, sensitive artist-type."

I sighed. "What do you want, Evelyn?"

"You." She laughed at my dark expression. "Relax. It's purely business. We need to get to work on your next video. The last one was great but I have some fresh ideas that I want to run by you tonight."

"You know I can only do Sundays."

"This Sunday is no good. It has to be tonight."

"I can't. I have work after school at the arcade."

"After, then."

"It'll be late. Like ten o'clock."

"That works." She looked at me from under lowered lashes. "And if you get tired, you're welcome to stay over."

"Evelyn…"

"Oh my God, I'm *kidding*. You're such a grouch." She got up, straightened her tight skirt. "Ten o'clock, Stratton. Don't be late. We have to strike now, while you're hot and getting hotter. Musically, speaking." She blew me a kiss and strode off, ponytail swinging.

I didn't want to go to Evelyn's and make another video. I wanted to go to Violet. I wanted to climb up the trellis like I always did and play for her. Then kiss her and not run out the door but stay. Hold her and sleep with her. No sex, just sleep. Like I did the night four years ago when she found out where I'd been living.

But I'd promised to give Amber some time and I was fairly sure Violet was sick of my shit by now. Running hot and cold, but mostly just running.

After school, I went home and took a quick shower before work. Chet was there, as usual, demanding to know where I go every night and getting pissed when I refused to tell him.

"If you were my son…" he warned.

"I'm not," I shot back, "so mind your own fucking business."

I let the door slam, anger burning my skin. If Dad hadn't left, Mom and I wouldn't have had to deal with Chet fucking Hyland. We wouldn't be living in a shithole apartment after living in a *car*. If he were still around, I wouldn't be such a fucking mess. I could be the guy Violet deserved.

At the arcade, I spent hours watching tourists plunk quarters in machines or play Skee-Ball for shitty plastic prizes. In a sea of noise, the Pac-Man game seemed the loudest. Over and over, the ghosts trapped Pac-Man and then came the down-the-drain sound effect of his demise.

I have to get the fuck out of here.

So I took the bus to Evelyn's large white, two-story house. It loomed ghostly and quiet in the night. As usual, I texted her I was there, and she let me in, guiding me through the house's clean, warm space; smiling family photos hung on every wall.

Her bedroom walls were covered in collages of lips, eyes, and clothes cut out from magazines, and sketches of outfits that I guessed she had done. I didn't give a shit about fashion, but I recognized talent when I saw it.

"You smell like popcorn," Evelyn said, fussing over me.

"Hazard of the job."

"Ha! You're cute." She ran her fingers through my hair.

"Is that necessary?"

"I'm trying to recreate that look you had in the first video. When you took your beanie off and ran your hands through your hair. If I had a dollar for every commenter who told me that maneuver set their panties on fire…" She tapped a nail to her chin. "Come to think of it, I *do* get paid when that happens."

"Yeah, about that," I said, "do I get a cut, or did I go from giving my shit away for free on the internet to giving it away to you?"

"I told you, we'll work all that out later."

"You said you had demands for helping me."

"I do. In due time."

She looped a bone horn necklace with a leather string around my neck.

"Is this necessary too?"

"It goes with the leather man-bracelets you wear on your wrists," she said. "Draws attention to your forearms. Very hot. The necklace will do the same for your chest and neck."

She moved in front of me, bending over to scrutinize me, her hands in my hair again. I was afforded a view of her breasts pushing out of her top. She caught me looking and a slow smile spread over her lips.

"You're looking at me." Her hands slipped down my chest, palms flat. "Do you like what you see?"

"Evelyn, stop…" I caught hold of her wrists and took them off of me.

"What's wrong? I don't see you with Amber anymore. Or any girl for that matter." She smiled and moved in closer, her knee resting on the chair between my legs. "Nothing wrong with having a little fun."

I stood up gently and pushed her away. "Is this what you meant by your demand? The cost for your help?"

Her dark eyes widened, the heat in them turning cold. "What do you take me for, some kind of prostitute? You think I'd trade sex for a favor?"

"No," I said, flustered. "No, of course not. I'm sorry. But what the hell are you doing?"

"What I'm *doing* is helping you get your music out there."

"You know what I mean." My phone chimed a text. "Fuck. Just…hold on."

I moved to the other side of the room. The text was from Shiloh.

I just heard. Violet's at UCSC Medical. Head injury. They won't tell me more.

Every molecule in my body turned to stone. It felt as if the floor had dropped out, sucking my heart down with it.

My fingers trembled as I typed. **On my way.**

Evelyn pouted. "What's wrong?"

Frantically, I threw on my jacket, chucked my guitar into its case, and shouldered the strap. "I gotta go."

"Now? We haven't shot the video. What happened?"

"Violet. Something… I don't know. I gotta go," I said again and raced out, my pulse thundering. Evelyn called after me, but I barely heard her.

There were few buses at this hour, and I couldn't afford to wait one fucking second. My phone said the UCSC Medical Center was one and a half miles away. A thirty-minute walk.

The words **head injury** kept flashing in my head like ambulance sirens, then I began to run.

CHAPTER SIXTEEN

VIOLET

One day earlier…

They had arrived.

My hands trembled slightly as I took four envelopes from the rest of the mail. My eyes scanned the return addresses: Baylor, Georgetown, UCSF, and UC Santa Cruz. Acceptance or rejection letters.

My heart was pounding as I took the mail into the kitchen. It had been several days since the bonfire at the Shack and Miller hadn't contacted me once. Miller's words chased my every waking hour and followed me into my sleep.

Maybe we're impossible.

We're done here.

Maybe we were done before we'd started. The enormity of it stole my breath whenever I thought of it. So, I didn't. When my thoughts went to Miller—which was every other minute—I shut them down. Closed my heart. I had been right all along. Every time Miller and I touched or kissed, we blew apart. Like magnets, drawn together at one polarity, thrusting away at the other.

And maybe his feelings for Amber went deeper than I suspected. Why else wouldn't he have at least called me to tell me what he was thinking?

I could have asked Shiloh but I didn't want a relationship like that 'telephone' game, where everything comes second hand. But uncertainty was maddening. I'd been a fool to break the promises I'd made to myself and now the heartache was too much. I had to outrun it, out-study it, out-prepare it so that when the next phase of my life began—contained in one of the four envelopes on my kitchen counter—I'd be ready for it. Stronger.

Late afternoon sun filled our spacious kitchen. I was dressed in my pajamas, my hair still damp after a shower. I'd had a hard soccer practice where my coach and teammates were shocked at my aggressive play. *Get used to it,* I wanted to tell them. I had to kick and run until the hurt was pummeled and burned out of me, or I'd collapse and cry.

And I'm not going to be that girl anymore.

I sat at the kitchen counter and opened the envelopes one by one. Baylor: accepted.

Georgetown: accepted. UCSF: accepted.

Joy and pride swept through me. None of these universities were easy to get into, so my odds for UCSC were good. Even so, I held my breath as I tore open that last envelope.

If I got in, I could stay in the city I loved, surrounded by forests and ocean…

Dear Miss McNamara,

Our board of professionally-trained Admissions readers have conducted an in-depth review of your academic and personal achievements and feel you have a demonstrated capacity to contribute to the intellectual and cultural life at UCSC. Congratulations! Accept your offer of admission through our online portal no later than the May 1 deadline…

"I did it. Holy shit…"

The paper wafted to the floor, and I clapped a hand to my mouth. For the first time in months, I felt something other than stomach-churning tension and heartache. All of the late nights studying, the college prep units I'd worked so hard to complete, volunteering at the hospital and with Nancy, the SAT and ACT scores I'd stressed over…it had all paid off.

Dad came home looking harried and exhausted: rumpled shirt, tie askew.

"Hey, pumpkin." He kissed the top of my head and managed a smile. His gaze went to the acceptance letters, and his eyes widened. "Get some good news?"

"The best news. UCSC said yes." I waved the envelope. "The others did too, but this is the golden ticket. I can stay here and…" My words trailed as my dad's expression collapsed. "Dad?"

"That's great, Violet." He gave me a short, tense hug. "I'm so proud of you."

"Thank you," I said warily. "So…we need to talk about the next steps."

"Yes, we do. Better get your mother down here." He sounded like he'd ordered his own executioner.

"She's out with some friends from work. She texted to say she'd be home late."

He sighed and loosened his tie as he slid onto a stool beside me. "Maybe that's for the best." He eyed the stack of acceptance letters. "I'm sorry, pumpkin. I tried."

My heart plummeted to my stomach. "What do you mean?"

"The promise we made on your twelfth birthday. I wanted more than anything to uphold it. But…I can't. I'm sorry."

I sat back, absorbing this like a blow. "Okay. How bad is it?"

His eyes—the same dark blue as mine—were heavy and so, so tired. "Not great. I don't want to get into details—"

"I want you to get into details. For so long, I've been nodding my head and going along with your assurances. Dad…" I clutched the sleeve of his jacket. "Just tell me the truth."

"You don't need the nitty-gritty," he said. "But yes, things have been tough lately, and we've had to pull money from various sources, your fund being one. I had a deal that was supposed to cover it, but…it fell through. I'm sorry. I'm so sorry, Sweetheart."

He looked on the verge of tears.

"I knew it," I said. "Somehow I always knew. I applied for scholarships, but the merit-based kind are hard to win and none will cover everything. I'll need financial aid." I glared at him. "*Will* I need financial aid? You never tell me anything. And you said not to worry. I trusted you and Mom…"

God, Miller is right. Trust is such a stupid thing to bank a future on.

"I know you did," Dad said. "But I was so close. The deal felt like such a sure thing—"

"What deal?"

"An app I'd been working on. But there were…patent issues." He waved his hand. "It's not important. What's important is fixing this. I wanted so badly for you to avoid starting your life with massive debt." He brightened with a watery optimism that made my heart crack in two. "But there are other scholarships that I'm sure you qualify for. More than qualify."

"There are," I said slowly. "But the application deadlines on most of them have probably passed or are about to. There's no time."

"For Fall. But you could apply for Spring next year."

My eyes stung as they met his. We both knew I'd been busting my ass for years to get ahead. If I were to be a surgeon, I was going to be in med school for the better part of my young adult life. I wanted to be finished with it and begin a career and have a family as soon as possible.

"It's fine," I said, sitting up and blinking back tears. I gathered my letters and slipped off the stool. "I'll apply for financial aid and see which scholarships are still open."

"Violet, wait," Dad said. "I know I screwed up, but please talk to me."

My heart wanted to break. I'd never seen my big, strong dad so defeated. It scared me to the bone. And I knew there was more he wasn't telling me.

I held up the letters. "This sucks and it's disappointing, but I can deal with it. But you never gave me a chance to prepare because you haven't been honest with me. Not about the money, or about you and Mom."

"I know. But it's…complicated. The last thing we want to do is hurt you."

I wanted to tell him every time they fought, it hurt. Every time they shattered a glass or slammed a door, it hurt. But Miller had shouted at them for me and nothing had changed.

"I'm tired," I said, swallowing my tears. "Soccer practice was long."

"Okay. Goodnight, Violet," he said. "I'm sorry."

Not so long ago, I'd have wanted to rush to him, hug him, cry on his shoulder about all of it. About Miller. Like I used to when I was little. Back when he and Mom had been happy. Before they'd both turned into people I no longer recognized.

But I left without another word and went to my room. I was becoming unrecognizable to myself.

At school the next day, I went through the motions, kept my head down. Despite what I'd told Dad about being tired, I stayed up late applying for financial aid and researching scholarship deadlines for each of the schools I'd been accepted to and then emailed my counselor for an emergency meeting that afternoon.

I was on my way to that meeting and nearly crashed into Evelyn Gonzalez.

"Hey, girl," she said, with a winning—triumphant smile. "Long time, no see. You've been so busy. I feel like it's been *ages* since we hung out."

I met her gaze with a steely one of my own. "Is that what happened? Or were you embarrassed to be seen with the girl who got stood up by the captain of the football team in front of the entire school?" I didn't let her reply. "Speaking of Homecoming, were you ever going to tell me you stole the video of Miller off my phone?"

"Wow, hostile much? What happened to sweet Snow White? And anyway, I didn't steal anything. You posted that video on the internet. It's a free-market economy."

I crossed my arms. "That's not exactly how it works but okay. What about you deleting my YouTube account?"

"It was in the way. What's your problem, anyway? I was doing Miller a favor. In case you haven't noticed, I'm helping to make him a viral sensation. Not that it's hard." She touched her tongue to her lower lip. "He really is a beautiful specimen of a man."

I stiffened and an ugly feeling surged in my blood. "I'm aware of his sudden popularity. I've seen the video *I* took on *your* vlog. Funny how you all treated him so badly right up until you thought you could get something out of him."

"Possessive, are we? How cute. Don't you want him to be a huge smash?"

"Of course, I do. But doing a fashion vlog doesn't feel like his style. Or something he'd want."

"It is now. He didn't tell you?"

I braced myself. "Tell me what?"

"He's been coming over to my house on Sundays. We've been staying up *so* late, working on new cover songs. He's coming over to my house tonight, as a matter of fact. So, maybe you were once the expert on what he wants but…not so much anymore." She twiddled her fingers. "See ya!"

I watched her go—beautiful, smart, and always focused like a laser on getting exactly what she wanted.

It's none of my business, I thought, drawing deeper into myself. *He won't talk to me. He's not mine. We're impossible.*

"The timeline isn't great," my counselor, Ms. Taylor, said, peering over my scholarship research. "And UCSC doesn't offer much unless it's for low-income families, which we're still not entirely sure you qualify for. Have you heard back about any of the merit-based scholarships?"

"Not yet. But I'll make up whatever I need to in financial aid."

Ms. Taylor took off her half-moon glasses and sat back. "This has to be incredibly disappointing for you, Violet."

I gave her a wan smile. "First world problems, right? Mommy and Daddy can't pay for my fancy school."

She frowned. "I don't need to tell you that being burdened with debt is incredibly stressful, no matter who or why. It's the tragic reason why thousands of young people avoid college altogether. You had a free path and now you don't. It's okay to feel upset about that."

"Being upset isn't going to get me through it," I said. "I'll do whatever it takes, but if I want to start school in the fall, I need to stay on track."

"I'll do my best to help you, Violet, but UCSC might not be the school that works for you. You need to be flexible, okay?"

I'd nodded and promised, but I'd been planning my career since I was ten years old. I loved Santa Cruz. I loved my home. My family. Miller. I had no idea where I stood with anything. As if the ground under my feet were trembling and breaking apart, and I didn't know if I'd withstand the rift or fall in.

⟵•⟶

That afternoon, I let myself in to the Whitmore's as usual, but the master bedroom was empty. A sliver of fear lodged into my stomach until I remembered Nancy had scheduled a doctor's appointment.

I turned to leave, to head home and continue to work on scholarship applications until soccer practice. Then River came up the stairs.

He looked handsome as ever, and his eyes lit up to see me. "Hey," he said.

"Hi," I said.

He cocked his head. "You okay? You look a little sad."

"It's been a rough couple of days," I said, my throat thick.

"I hear you. Want to go somewhere and get something to eat? Take your mind off things?"

He was so handsome and kind, smiling at me with genuine compassion. His kindness threatened to undo all of the hard work I'd done to keep my feelings in check. They bubbled to the surface, but God, I was so tired of crying. So sick of feeling like a lump of clay, molded and shaped by outside forces. I had to be harder than this, or I'd never survive.

He grinned. "It's a yes or no question—"

I flew at River. I flung my arms around his neck and kissed him. I kissed his lips, his jaw, his chin, and then his lips again. Urgently. Desperate to erase Miller from my body's sense memory. To do what he did—move on with someone else and take back control of my own life that was unraveling right before my eyes.

River froze in surprise, his lips stiff and unyielding but eventually parting just enough. He kissed me back, lightly and then harder, his eyes squeezed shut and his brow furrowed, as if our kiss was work that had to be done. Our tongues tangled, out of sync, noses bumping, teeth clashing.

He broke away, his breath short. "Violet?"

"Your room."

"You sure?"

"Yes. No more talking."

Talking would lead to thinking and thinking would lead to admitting that this was all wrong.

We stumbled to his room; our mouths still mashed together awkwardly. I pushed his letterman jacket off his shoulders. He fell back on the bed and I climbed on top of him.

"I never expected this from you," he said.

"Neither did I," I said. Except that I wanted to escape from being at the mercy of my feelings for Miller. River was my lifelong crush. This should work…

But it didn't.

Like trying to get a lighter to spark when it's out of fluid, we tried to ignite with half-hearted touches and kisses that grew shallower. He wasn't hard in his jeans. I wasn't desperate to have him. We were like actors with zero chemistry, rehearsing a scene.

With a small cry of despair, I rolled off of him. We lay on our backs, side by side, our gazes on the ceiling.

"I'm sorry," I said.

"Me too. I'm usually better…at that. You just took me by surprise, is all."

"Okay."

"That's why I wasn't…better."

"You said that already," I said, humiliation for what I'd done burning through me. I covered my eyes with a hand, but the hot tears spilled out. "I'm so sorry."

I'm sorry, Miller.

"Hey." River gently pulled my hand away. "It's okay."

"It's not okay. I don't know what's wrong with me."

"Nothing's wrong with you. It's me who's messed up. Believe me."

I shook my head. "No. You didn't deserve that. Everything's been going all wrong. I used to be so organized and on top of things. Now…" I gestured at the ceiling. "Now it's all falling apart. *I'm* falling apart. Doing things I'd never do. Being someone I'm not."

River turned his gaze to the ceiling, his mouth a hard line. "Yeah. I know exactly how that is."

"You do?"

"Definitely."

I wiped my nose on the sleeve of my sweatshirt and rolled on my side to face him.

"How? I mean…seems like everything's going how it should for you."

"That's because I'm really good at making it *look* like everything's going as it should," he said bitterly. He reached over and plucked a tissue from the nightstand and handed it to me.

"Thank you." I dabbed my eyes. "Nancy told me you got into Alabama and Texas A&M."

"I did," he said.

"You don't look happy."

He turned his head on the pillow to face me. "Can I tell you a secret?"

"Of course."

"Swear you won't tell anyone?"

"Cross my heart."

He faced forward again, his Adam's apple bobbing with a heavy swallow. "I don't want to play football anymore."

I propped my head with my elbow. "What? Really?"

"I haven't wanted to…since forever, actually. It's been more my dad's dream than mine. He was a big star in his day and could've gone pro, until a knee injury took him out."

"Wow," I said, absorbing that. "But you're so good at it. Like Tom Brady or Peyton Manning."

He smiled grimly. "It's wasteful, right? To want to throw it all away?"

"Well, no. Not if it makes you unhappy. What do you really want to do?"

"You'll laugh. Or think I'm a huge dork."

I smirked. "As someone who dabbled in *not* being a dork for a short time until Evelyn Gonzalez returned me to the Land of Dorks from whence I came, you have my word."

He laughed, but it faded fast. "I want to stay here. I want to be with my mom until…however long she needs me. I want to work at the family business. I want to live in Santa Cruz and start my own family."

"I know exactly what you mean, River. That all sounds perfect. Can't you tell that to your dad?"

He shook his head. "It'd crush him. He has this *idea* of me. Of who I should be. I've spent my entire life trying to live up to it. When I play football…" He shrugged helplessly. "That's when he's happy. That's when I feel…"

He bit the word off, but I heard it anyway.

Loved.

River's head turned to me again. "Please don't tell anyone. I don't know why I even told you, except that I feel comfortable with you." A small grin touched his lips. "Just not when we're kissing."

I gave a short laugh. "Story of my life."

We lay back to stare at the ceiling, chuckling. A silence fell that felt warm and calm passed and then River shifted beside me.

"So Violet."

"So River."

"Since we're both secretly dorks in disguise, how about we go to Prom together?"

An incredulous laugh burst out of me. "Oh, sure. Why not?" I looked over at him. He arched a brow. "You're serious?"

"As the plague. We'd just go as friends."

"Don't you have a gaggle of girls waiting for you to ask them out?"

"Ha, no. Honestly, I don't even want to go—"

"Way to sell it to me, Whitmore."

He laughed. "Sorry. I mean. I *do* want to go, for my parents' sake. Dad keeps asking which girl I'm bringing…" He cleared his throat. "And Mom loves you. We should go. It's our senior year."

"I seem to remember a certain other dance that you were supposed to take me to and then *didn't.*"

"I know, I'm so sorry. But this is how I make it up to you."

"I suppose," I said, sadness creeping back into my heart.

Miller hated dances. Hated the money spent that could go to other places that needed it more. Hated the silly gimmicks and themes. But I didn't. I wanted all the high school experiences and going with River had been my plan all along.

But after Miller had kissed me, even my fantasies about those experiences had been rearranged. I imagined Miller and me at the base of the stairs at my house. Mom would take a million photos and Dad would joke, but not really, that Miller had better have me home on time and take care of me.

And Miller would, because that's what he did. At the dance, he'd hold me close, and we'd sway to the music. Maybe he'd sing one of his songs in my ear and then kiss me…

I shook myself out of my thoughts with a shiver. Miller wasn't going to ask me to any Prom, I reminded myself. He had a girlfriend.

And he and I are impossible.

"I'll go to the Prom with you," I said to River. "But only as friends."

His face brightened, and though he was a huge, strong guy, something intangible in his eyes broke my heart. Relief, maybe, that he was going to do something that would please his dad.

"Just friends," he said, then grinned and touched a small cut on his lip my teeth had left thanks to our clumsy kisses. "Safer for me that way."

"I'm never going to live this down, am I?"

He smiled and nudged my arm. "It's already forgotten."

I left the Whitmores feeling shockingly calm. Almost optimistic.

I made a new friend.

It felt weird to think of River that way, since we'd known each other for ages. But my clumsy attempt to kiss Miller Stratton out of my system had backfired in the best possible way. I went to soccer practice feeling better than I had in days.

My phone vibrated with a text as I walked to the field. Shiloh.

Amber told me that she and Miller broke up.

My heart seized up all over again. **OK. When?**

A few days ago. Right after the bonfire.

I stared at the text. Days ago. But no word from him since.

She sent another. **Did something happen with u2 that night?**

I hadn't told Shiloh we kissed. She'd be pissed off at both of us and defensive of her friend. And she'd be right on both counts. I had no idea what to say. Or even think. My silence prompted a phone call.

"Hey, Shi."

"You okay?" she asked.

"I've been better."

"Look, I wasn't going to tell you this since I fucking hate gossip, but the way you've been lately, I think you need to hear it. All of it."

My hand clutched the phone. "There's more?"

"Yes." She inhaled. "Amber told me she realized that 'All I'll Ever Want' was written for you."

"For me…"

The words washed over me, and a small breath pushed out of my open mouth. I felt warm all over. Light. The lyrics swam in my mind, their beauty taking on a new meaning. Sinking deeper into my heart.

Because they're for me.

"I think I knew," I murmured. "I think I always knew. But I was so insistent on sticking to my plans…"

"I'd say I told you so," Shiloh said, "but I'm a bigger person than that."

I laughed. Elation filled me like warm air for a few precious seconds, and then reality brought me crashing to the ground.

"Oh my God," I said, my hand over my mouth that still stung from my blundering kisses with River. "We can't get it right. Not ever."

"What's that?" Shiloh asked. "I can't hear you."

"The pendulum goes back and forth. We're never in sync. Ever."

"What are you talking about?"

"I kissed River," I said. "I kissed River, and we're going to the Prom together."

"Oh Christ." Shiloh hissed air out of her nose. "Are you two back on?"

"No, the kiss was a disaster. We're just going as friends."

"Okay. That's not…ideal but talk to Miller. You two are long overdue—Wait. He hasn't called you yet?"

"No."

"Maybe he just needs time. Or wants to give Amber time."

"Maybe. But God, it shouldn't be this complicated, right? It's like we're at opposite ends of a maze, and every time we get close, someone takes a wrong turn."

"Explain to him about River," Shiloh said. "He'll understand. It's not like you cheated on him."

"Feels like it." I sucked in a breath. "But yes, I'll talk to him. We *need* to talk. We've needed to talk since forever."

"No argument from me there."

"I gotta go, Shi," I said. "Practice is about to start."

"Enjoy. Be safe."

"I will."

I dropped my phone back in my duffel and jogged onto the practice field. We ran drills, and I wove in and out of cones with the ball on automatic, my thoughts running ahead of me. The practice scrimmage began, and I couldn't focus. Twice, Coach Brimner pulled me aside for making stupid mistakes.

"You okay?" she asked. "You've been all over the place lately."

"Yeah, sorry. I'll pull myself together."

"You do that, or I'll pull you from Saturday's game."

I sucked in a breath, pissed at myself for being at the mercy of my feelings for Miller, yet again. Angela Marino was dribbling the ball down the field toward me. I charged at her, sliding with one leg out, determined to punch the ball out of her possession and show Coach I wasn't a lost cause. That I was stronger than that.

I slid too hard, too fast. Grass flew. Cleats and shin guards filled my vision. Angela grunted, trying to jump over me.

The last thing I saw was her kneecap driving toward my head and then nothing.

CHAPTER SEVENTEEN

VIOLET

I woke to see the vast white landscape. A bed. Confusion clouded my thoughts; I had no clue where I was, until I spied the hospital wristband on my left arm. Last night came back in bits and pieces. The doctors had huddled with my anxious parents, telling them I'd suffered a concussion. Scans showed no bleeds or swelling, but since I'd been knocked out cold, they wanted to keep me overnight. Finally, close to dawn, they let me sleep.

My head ached and my stomach felt queasy. I started to try to go back to sleep, when a dark blue blur near the window shifted. I blinked the blur into focus. Miller. He was curled sideways in a chair, his long legs tucked up and his head pillowed on his knees. His guitar and backpack on the floor beside him.

Tears sprang to my eyes.

He's here.

"Hi."

My voice was in tatters, but Miller shot awake instantly. He unfolded his tall form and hurried to my bedside, still half asleep.

"Hey." He dropped into the chair beside me. Stubble shadowed his jaw; dark circles ringed his eyes. "How are you? How are you feeling?"

"Hurts a little, but I'm okay. Better now. How long have you been here?"

"All night."

"You've been here all night?" The hospital room was chilled, but I suddenly felt warm all over.

He nodded. "Shiloh was here for a while, but her grandmother called her home. She wanted me to tell you she hopes you get well soon, and if you don't, she'll kick your ass."

"She's sentimental that way."

"Your parents were here late, too, but I told them I'd take the next watch," Miller said. "Your mom wasn't too keen on me hanging around, but I wasn't going anywhere. I fought like hell to try to see you, but they wouldn't let me in until your dad said it was okay."

"I'm so glad you fought like hell."

Miller's jaw clenched. "I should've done it sooner. Years ago. Fought for you."

The tears threatened again, and Miller's cobalt eyes, which were so often steely and cold, were now dark and soft and nowhere but on me.

"Do you need anything?" he asked. "What can I do?"

I smiled and brushed a lock of unruly hair out of his eyes. "Nothing. Just be here."

He caught my hand and held it in his. The energy between us was different than it had been in months. Or ever. Since we were thirteen and he was the one in the hospital bed. The day I knew I'd love him forever.

He bowed his head. "Christ, I'm sorry this happened, Violet."

"Not your fault. I dove straight into the path of Angela Marino's kneecap. Oh shit, I hope she's okay…"

"She is. I heard your parents talking."

"Thank God, though I'm probably going to be cut from the team."

"You shouldn't be playing anyway," Miller said darkly. "Not until you're better. They said it's a concussion. You'll have to be careful for weeks."

"I will."

A short silence fell. He was still holding my hand.

"Miller…"

"I'm sorry, Vi. For a lot of things. I'm sorry I went silent on you. Disappeared. I'm sorry I ran to another girl when I should have told you the truth, that we always felt like more than friends. From the very first day. But I said nothing."

"Not nothing. You put it in your songs," I said with a smile. My hand in his tightened. "I'm sorry about so many things, too. Evelyn calls me Snow White, and I hate it. But I think it's kind of accurate.

I've been poisoning myself by thinking we would turn into my parents. But then you kissed me that first time and I woke up."

"Yeah?" The vulnerability in his eyes was raw and naked.

"Yeah. Your kisses have magical properties, Stratton. The first rearranged my universe. The second at the Shack turned me into a puddle of lust. I'm a little bit scared what will happen with number three."

His small smile faded. "I still haven't told you the rest. About Amber."

"I know. Shiloh told me."

"I would've told you the minute it was over, but she asked me to give her time and so I did. She deserved better than me. Maybe you do too."

I shook my head, then winced. "Don't say things like that and make me shake my head," I said with a small laugh.

Miller wasn't smiling. "It's true." He studied our clasped hands as he spoke, rubbing his thumb back and forth over my skin. "I walk around every day pretending like it doesn't fucking matter what my dad did. I tell people he's dead because if he's dead and gone, so what if he left? But he's not dead. He could come back any time, and he doesn't. And what he did matters."

"Of course, it does," I said softly, surprised. Miller had rarely spoken about his father in the four years I'd known him.

"It matters," he said, "not just because Mom and I had to live in a fucking car. It messed me up too. I lost a lot, real fast. My dad, my house, my school and our neighborhood in Los Banos. My friends. Hell, I nearly lost my life. It's not his fault I have diabetes, but he doesn't know I have it, and he fucking should. I'm his son."

I nodded, listening, wishing I could pull the hurt out of him so he didn't have to carry it anymore.

He raised his eyes to mine. "He took everything so that's what I have left. The fear that anything can be taken away, at any time. When I heard you were hurt, it fucking killed me. Because maybe I'd pushed you away so hard, it turned my fear into a reality."

He leaned close, pressed my hands to his heart. "This is yours. Always. I'll be whatever you want me to be. I'll be your friend if that's what you want. No more bullshit. Or I'll be…more. I'll be nothing. All I want is for you to be happy."

My throat felt thick and my heart full at what he was offering me. "You can never be nothing to me, Miller. Not ever."

The expression that came over his face was heartbreakingly beautiful. Miller bent his head to me, and while I wanted nothing more than his kiss, we weren't done clearing the path for us ahead. I put my hands on his chest.

"Wait. We have to be honest with each other all the time and talk about everything, okay? That's the only way we're going to survive. That's the real lesson my parents have been teaching me."

"Okay," he said slowly.

"There's something I have to tell you."

He sat back in his chair. "What is it?"

Inhale, exhale. "I kissed River."

Miller stared, his hands around mine going still. "When?"

"Yesterday."

"Yesterday," he repeated flatly.

"Yes, and it was a huge mistake. I knew it before I did it, and I knew it while it was happening. We were like two pieces of plywood smacking together. Painful and awkward and just all wrong."

I could see Miller working this over in his mind. And he wasn't happy.

"As far as I knew, you were still with Amber, and I was trying to do what you did. Get you out of my system. But it's not possible."

"No, not for me either," he said. "I guess I can't be pissed, but I just…I don't like it."

"I know. And I didn't like seeing you with Amber. It wasn't revenge, it was just…trying to take control of my feelings. It didn't work."

Miller inhaled deeply through his nose and let it out. "Okay. Well, I'm glad you told me."

"There's more."

"More?"

"He asked me to the Prom, and I said yes."

Now Miller let go of my hands and scrubbed his over his face. "I don't know if I feel like I'm about to cry or laugh like a crazy person."

"We'd only be going as friends. And I do care about him as a friend. We had an amazing talk. I think he's under a lot of pressure from his parents."

"You'll forgive me if I don't have a whole lot of sympathy right now."

"You don't have to, but you do have to trust me. We have to trust each other and tell each other everything."

"Then I'm going to tell you I don't want you to go to Prom with River." I started to speak, but Miller took my hand in his again. "But you already promised him, and I know it means something to keep your word. I trust you, Vi."

Tears welled up in my eyes. "That means everything, Miller. Like we have a shot."

"We do," he said. "Because I don't ever want to lose you."

Miller leaned over me, and my hands made fists in the lapels of his plaid shirt. My heart was pounding. He touched his mouth to mine softly. My lips parted in a breathy little gasp, and he kissed my upper and lower lip. Then he moved in deeper and I moaned softly. My eyes fell shut as that tingling, breath-stealing euphoria filled me and moved down into my stomach to send it fluttering.

Miller moved to sit on the edge of the bed, one hand cupping my cheek as his mouth moved over mine reverently. Exploring softly, touching gently, we sealed promises—spoken and unspoken—to take care of each other's hearts.

The kiss ended naturally, and Miller pulled back, his eyes roaming every part of my face. He brushed his fingertips over the bandage on my right temple.

"Are you really okay?"

I nodded. "They're going to kick me out any minute now."

"Good. I don't ever want to see you in here again."

"Feeling's mutual," I said, stroking his cheek. "But since they're taking their sweet time about it, will you play for me?"

"Anything."

"'All I'll Ever Want.' Shiloh said you wrote it for me."

"They're all for you, Vi. Even the ones I didn't write. Those are for you too."

Miller kissed me gently, then pressed his forehead to mine. "*I came along,*" he sang softly, almost a whisper, "*I wrote a song for you…*"

A little sob escaped me, and I threw my arms around his neck, pulling him in to me. Inhaling the clean, ocean scent of him, straight into my cells, into every molecule in my body. I held on tight, because now I had him, and I never wanted to let go.

CHAPTER EIGHTEEN

MILLER

May

"Where are we going?" I asked, chuckling, as Violet dragged me across the campus. The sun was brilliant and bright, not a cloud in sight.

"I've always wanted to do this," she said. "A high school experience not to be missed."

Hand-in-hand, she led me down from the main campus, toward the football field.

"The make-out spot under the bleachers?" I asked. "Isn't that cheesy as hell?"

She arched a brow at me. "Well, we don't *have* to go—" Her words were cut off with a squeal as I hauled her into the shadowy corner of the bleachers where it met the gym wall. Mercifully unoccupied.

I caged her against the wall, my eyes roaming her face, taking my time.

"You're such a tease," she breathed. Her hands went to my hips and drew me into her.

I gave a short laugh at her boldness. I hadn't expected it from Violet, but over the last few weeks, I'd been getting to know her in a way that our past hesitations and fears hadn't let me before.

All the kissing and making out was pretty fucking great too.

"What are you smiling about?" she asked, tilting her chin up and arching into me so that her breasts brushed against my chest.

"You," I said, moving in, pressing against her. But even before I kissed her, my erection was hard and obvious through my jeans. I started to back off.

She pulled me back in. “Don’t. Just kiss me…”

Our mouths crashed together, and I groaned into our kiss as Violet parted her legs to bring me closer. Goddamn, she felt so good, smelled so good, tasted so good. I couldn’t get enough of her. Her luscious body I’d been agonizing over from afar was now against me, under my hands, offered willingly by the girl I loved so fucking much I could hardly breathe.

I kissed her hard, a tangling of tongues and rasping breaths, while cupping one breast over her T-shirt, my thumb running circles over the nipple. She moaned and slipped her hands into my hair, down my back, and then under my shirt. Her fingers traced my abs, deftly maneuvering around my CGM implant.

“God, Miller,” she whispered between kisses. “You’re so beautiful.”

“That’s my line.”

“You are,” she said, her small warm palm pressed to my abdomen, fingertips trailing over my skin. “I want to explore you…” She kissed me then, slow and deep, while her hand started to slip into my jeans. “Can I?”

I nodded, once. Quickly. Over the past few weeks, I’d been trying to keep things moving slowly, clothes on, so that we didn’t get carried away. Having unlimited access to her bedroom almost every night didn’t help.

“Ah, fuck,” I grunted when she wrapped her fingers around me.

“You’re big,” she said curiously, almost matter of fact. “So big…”

“God, Vi,” I said, breathing hard. “We have to stop before…”

“You take my virginity right here?”

A shocked laugh burst out of me. “Jesus, woman.”

She laughed too and released me, then straightened my T-shirt. “Sorry. Part of me feels like I need to catch up. I’ve never done any of the things we do. But it’s really just you, Miller. I’m not the least bit nervous. Not with you.” She glanced up at me through lowered lashes. “Just the opposite. I can’t wait for my first time.”

“Our first time.”

She stared. “What? You and Amber never…?”

“Never.” I didn’t want to disrespect Amber, so I kept it to myself that while she was pretty and smart, my mind, heart, and dick weren’t interested. “How did you put it? Like two slabs of plywood smacking together.”

Violet didn't smile, but her dark blue eyes, the color of night just after the sun sets, took me in, looking at me in a new light. "You never told me."

"I figured you didn't want to hear anything about Amber and me."

"Maybe not, but…I'm surprised. And touched."

I shrugged. "I was waiting for you."

Violet threw her arms around me and kissed me deep, all tongue and heated wetness that made me dizzy.

"How about no more waiting?" she whispered.

I gave a nervous laugh and disentangled myself from her. "You have to stop saying things like that in public, or I'm going to get suspended." I slung my arm over her shoulder and pulled her close as we walked out from under the bleachers. "I'm eighteen, but you have a few weeks to go. The state of California strongly suggests we wait."

"You looked it up?" Violet teased.

"Hell yes, I did. Your dad would have my nuts."

Her face fell. "I doubt he'd notice if we did it on the dining room table while they ate."

"Interesting visual." I gave her a squeeze. "Any new developments?"

She shook her head against my chest. We'd come to her last class of the day, History.

"They still haven't told me everything, but I've sent in all my scholarship and financial aid applications. The only thing left to do is wait and see how much I'll be on the hook for."

Her brilliant, optimistic smile returned—the one that I loved so much. Mostly because it was the yin to my yang of eternal pessimism.

"I'll make the best of it, so long as I get to stay here." Violet kissed me softly. "Santa Cruz is, after all, only a short flight from Los Angeles where you'll soon be making records."

That pessimism put a smirk on my face. "Doubtful."

I didn't add that I loathed the idea of being apart from her for any length of time. Not to come off like a possessive asshole but being with Vi made me feel whole. Like how I'd felt when she'd bought my guitar back from the pawn shop. A piece of me had been returned and I never wanted to go without again.

"I have no doubts," she said. "Have you heard *you*?"

Her unfailing belief in me warmed my damn heart. And I hoped she was right. If I hit it big, I could pay for her college, and her parents could take their dysfunctional bullshit and shove it.

The bell rang. "I gotta go," Violet said. "Come over tonight?"

"I'll be there. Hey, Ronan's in this class, right?"

"In theory. He hasn't shown up the last few days." She frowned as students filed around us. "Is everything okay?"

"I don't know. I'm worried about him. Holden too. They're both acting weird and not hanging out much at the Shack."

Violet looked around. "Shiloh's not here today either. I'll shoot her a text and see what's what. I'm late and so are you." She kissed my nose and hurried inside the classroom.

Technically, I was late to PE and technically, I didn't give a shit. I meandered in the general direction of the gym, hoping VP Chouder and his sixth sense for sniffing out tardy students wouldn't catch me.

My phone buzzed with a text. I fished it out of the back pocket of my jeans. Evelyn.

How much do you love me?

Not touching that one. Before I could reply, she sent another, and the phone nearly tumbled out of my hands.

The correct answer should be A LOT. Becuz it happened!!! A rep from Gold Line Records emailed me!!!!

My fingers trembled as I typed. **Don't fuck w/ me, E**

Swear to God!

A string of hearts, then excited and wide-eyed emojis followed. My pulse thrashed in my ears.

Where are you? I typed.

Beach. 2 nice 4 school. But since u went viral, I check email religiously and HOLY SHIT BABY!!

Wasn't touching "baby" either; I was too busy about to have a heart attack. I sank down on a bench outside the gym and hit *call,* then held the phone from my ear as Evelyn squealed.

"Slow down," I said. "You're freaking me out. Start from the beginning and tell me everything."

"It was 'Take What You Want from Me,' The Post Malone cover you did. It put you over the edge. Three million views. *Million.*"

"Holy shit is right," I breathed.

"I knew it. I *knew* this would happen," she crowed. "The email came this morning from an executive assistant to some guy named Jack

Villegas. I'm not a complete moron, so I googled him to make sure we weren't being catfished. Sure enough, major player at Gold Line. But I had to be one hundred percent, so I called the phone number and the assistant answered the phone. When I said I was calling for Jack Villegas, she didn't say *Who?* Or *Wrong number.* She said, *He's in a meeting, what is this regarding?* I mean…*Fuck.*"

I ran a hand through my hair. *Is this real? This can't be real.* "What…uh, what happened then?"

"I hung up."

"You did *what*?" The blood drained from my face.

"I know, I panicked, which is *so* unlike me. But it felt so surreal. Like I was making a crank call. But it's okay. I knew without a doubt that Villegas was legit, so I wrote an email back as your assistant. I mean, he's seen the blog; he knows I basically rep you. *An hour later*, he replied. He wants a meeting. With you. In Los Angeles. On June 4th."

More squealing and this time, I did drop the phone. It clattered to the ground, and I sat with my hands in my lap, every muscle in my body going slack.

Evelyn's voice was tinny, shouting for me. "Miller? Miller, hello?"

I picked up the phone again. "I don't…I don't know what to say."

A meeting in Los Angeles. With a major record label. This couldn't be real. The universe was fucking with me, and I wasn't going to fall for it.

"I can't fly to LA," I said. "I can't afford a flight or even a ride from the airport. And where would I stay? I don't know anyone there—"

"Honey, *relax*," Evelyn said in a quieter tone than I'd ever heard her use. "I know this is a lot. Believe me. But it's real. *They* are paying for the flight. *They* are going to send a car from the airport. *They* are going to set you up in a hotel."

I clenched my jaw to keep from either laughing or bursting into tears. "It's real," I croaked.

"It's real," Evelyn said, then brightened. "Now, you need to come over for a strategy session. And do you have a suit? Something nice to wear to the meeting? Never mind, I'll put something together."

She prattled on and on, and I just stared ahead at the road that had opened to me. A possible future away from the grind and anxiety of endless poverty.

"Evelyn," I said, cutting through her talk. "Thank you."

"Thank me later, babe. Oh my God, this is so exciting! Not that I'm surprised. I gotta go. Call me as soon as you're done with school or work or whatever. Shit, Miller, put in your notice at that fucking arcade. This is it!"

I hung up with her and stared at the phone in my hand. I wasn't about to quit my job. It was only a meeting in LA. That didn't mean anything. It was probably an audition. Maybe I'd suck in front of this Jack Villegas guy. Or he'd see right through me. That I was just another poor bastard with a sob story, trying to make it.

"Jesus, stop," I told the runaway train of shit talk as I pocketed my phone. "Can I have a little hope for one fucking minute?"

"Talking to yourself again, Stratton?"

I looked up to see Frankie Dowd standing a few feet away,

"What do you want, Dowd?"

"Who me? I got nothing to say to Evelyn's bitch."

I snorted a laugh. *If only he knew.* I started to push past him, but he stepped in front of me.

"Where you going?"

"None of your fucking business." I balled my hands into fists. "You going to move, or I do I have to move you?"

"How? You gonna sic your rabid dog on me?" He grinned like a loon. "Oh, that's right. Wentz isn't around, is he?"

Something in his knowing tone dripped down my spine like ice. I gripped Frankie by the collar and yanked him to me. "What do you know about it?"

He tore out of my grip and walked backward, hands outstretched. I wanted to punch the shit-eating grin off his face. "Don't know a thing. See you around, bitch."

When he was gone, I pulled out my phone again and shot a text to Ronan as I walked out of the school. Fuck going to gym.

Where U at?

I'd walked halfway home when the reply came.

City Hall picking up my citizenship award.

I gave a short laugh. Ronan was so much fucking smarter than anyone knew. Street smart *and* a smartass. But I recognized his deflections.

For real. U OK?

It was risky, prodding him even that much. He might go radio silent on me as a signal to mind my own business.

Stay out of my shit, Stratton.

Case in point.

But Ronan was being Ronan. I sighed with relief that he was okay, but I needed more assurances, and Evelyn's news was like an electric current, zipping around my nerves and balling in my stomach. I needed to talk it out before I puked. I wanted to sit around a fire at the Shack with my friends. Ronan would give me no end of shit, while Holden would want to throw a party. And both reactions would mean everything to me.

And Violet…Violet would cry and tell me she'd known it all along. Because she'd believed in me since the beginning. I blinked hard until the phone came back into focus.

Shack 2nite? I texted.

I walked another block before the reply came.

Busy. Can you tell Lord P to put the fucking weights back when he's done?

Another deflection. Ronan would never ask for a favor. Ever. Even one disguised as a gripe. I tried another tack.

Haven't heard from H. U?

But I already knew Ronan was done talking.

"Fuck." My concern for him ratcheted back up. I texted Holden, but there was no answer with him either. There wasn't anything to do. My friends would talk when they wanted to talk. I had to respect that; I demanded the same from them.

Since my friends were AWOL and Violet was still in class, the first person to hear my news would be Mom. As I stared up at the roach-infested building with the shitty plumbing, that felt exactly right.

I stepped into our place cautiously, the knot in my stomach tightening into fear.

Coming home shouldn't feel like this.

Because it wasn't home. It was shelter only and not even our own anymore. At least when we'd lived in the car, it was *ours.*

Mom was sitting on the couch watching a game show. The coffee table was littered with garbage, beer cans, and overflowing ashtrays. Mom looked gray, as if the ash in the apartment had settled over her as well.

Not ash, dust.

"Hey, Mom," I said, moving to sit beside her. She was only forty-two years old, but the last five years had aged her a lifetime. Her dark hair streaked with strands of gray, hung limply around her shoulders, and lines gathered at the corners of her eyes. All of it, Dad's fault.

Fuck him and Chet, both.

Mom smiled tiredly. "Hi, baby. How was school? You're home early, aren't you?"

I glanced around. The place was quiet but for the TV, and our lone bathroom door was open, showing it was empty. "Where's Chet?"

"Went fishing in Capitola with some buddies. Won't be back until tomorrow."

"Good." I sat down on the couch and surprised her by taking her hand in mine. "I'm going to get us out of here, Mom."

She gave me an indulgent look. "Is that so?"

"I'm serious. Something happened today. Something big and I…" My words cut off as I spied a bruise on Mom's forearm. Several bruises in the shape of fingers. A man's fingers. "Mom…what the fuck is this?"

She withdrew her hand and pulled down the sleeve of her shirt, even though it was at least eighty-five degrees in our AC-less shithole. "It's nothing. Tell me about this something big."

"Chet did that, didn't he?"

"Let it be, Miller. It's not a big deal—"

"When?" I seethed. "When did he do this?"

"The other night. I don't remember. I told you, it's nothing."

"Has it happened before?"

"No," she said, and her stern tone told me it was the truth. "It was one time."

One time was too many. I ground my teeth. He'd hurt her. He'd hurt her, and I hadn't been there to protect her. I'd been at the Shack or at Violet's. I let this happen.

"I'm sorry, Mom. I'm going to fix it, I promise."

"You're a good boy. But there's nothing to fix."

"There is. We can dump his ass on the street. I'll toss his shit right now—"

Mom grabbed my arm with surprising strength and sat me back down. "No, Miller. You leave it alone. We need his disability. I can't keep on like I have been. My back is getting worse, and I can't go back to working two jobs. I just can't."

"You won't have to." I swallowed hard and inhaled a breath. "A record executive in Los Angeles wants to meet with me. I'm going to make him give me a deal on the spot and an advance. You won't have to worry, okay? You won't need Chet anymore." Tears stung my eyes, and I blinked hard. My voice turned gruff. "I'm going to take care of you, okay?"

She smiled gently. Her hand, rough and calloused from work, touched my cheek. "Okay, baby. I'm tired. Going to take a nap. There's leftover pizza in the fridge if you're hungry. Just make sure you save some for Chet. He'll be hungry when he gets back."

Except I couldn't eat pizza. Too hard to calibrate with my insulin since the carb release lasted hours. Something Mom already knew.

She retreated to her bedroom—their bedroom now—and closed the door. My heart clenched. She was so beat down, she didn't believe a way out was possible, even when she heard it.

I sat for a few minutes in the quiet, but for the TV game show. I had to go to school and to work and eventually this meeting, leaving Mom alone with Chet. I contemplated changing the locks on our door, but it would only enrage him when he came back. And Mom would let him in, anyway.

"Fuck."

I ran my hands through my hair, that goddamn helplessness swooping back in to smother the shred of excitement I'd had.

I need Violet.

I dragged myself to work at the arcade, handing out cheap prizes in exchange for Skee-Ball tickets and freeing tokens that had been jammed in their slots. A drunk asshole kicked the Mortal Kombat console when he got his ass beat.

"But I have a meeting with a record exec," I murmured.

The words were drowned out in a sea of noise and explosions. It didn't sound or feel real, and it wouldn't until Violet heard it. Then maybe I could believe it too.

CHAPTER NINETEEN

VIOLET

A little after nine o'clock, I heard the familiar creak of the trellis outside my bedroom window. Butterflies took flight in my stomach. I sat on my bed, wearing only a sheer tank top and short-shorts, nerves and excitement racing through me in equal parts. Over the last few weeks, Miller had continued his streak of being a perfect gentleman, kissing and touching me without removing any clothing. To take things slow and make sure I was ready for every step we took together. But I'd never felt more sure of anything in my life. I'd never felt more sure of us.

Tonight, I wanted to show him that trust. To show him my body, to feel our skin touch in a hundred places

We don't have to have sex for me to show him that I'm his.

The night was warm and my window already open. Miller crawled through and hopped down off my desk.

"Hi, you," I said, my voice a little breathy.

He froze when he saw me. His blue eyes were liquid and soft, drinking me in. "God, you look so beautiful…" he said and then covered his face with one hand. His shoulders began to shake.

I hurried to him. "Miller? Hey…"

Wordlessly, he folded me into his embrace and pressed his face to my neck. Hot tears were absorbed in my skin as I held him tightly and stroked his hair.

After a while, he pulled back and turned away, wiping his cheeks in the crook of his arm.

"Sorry."

"Don't be sorry," I said softly, my heart bracing itself. "What happened?"

"A record exec wants to meet with me," he said gruffly. "In Los Angeles."

I stared, my jaw falling open. My hands flew to my chest. "Oh my God… Oh my God, Miller, are you serious?"

"Gold Line Records contacted Evelyn through her vlog." He shook his head, disbelieving. "They're even going to pay for the flight and hotel."

God, my heart was breaking for him, even as it soared with joy. He suddenly looked like a little boy, wanting the new life that has been offered to him but not yet letting himself believe it was his.

"Of course, they will," I said, my throat thick. "I knew this would happen for you. I knew it."

"I didn't. I still don't. It doesn't feel real."

I took his face in my hands. His beautiful eyes were a salty storm of hope and fear, searching mine for the truth.

"It's real," I said. "This is the first step. Your big break."

I could see him struggle. "This doesn't happen to guys like me, Vi. I'm going to screw it up. Or they'll take one look at me and realize they've made a mistake."

"They won't," I said as a sharp prick of anger at his father bit me. For leaving his beautiful son and condemning him to a lifetime of uncertainty. "This *doesn't* happen to just anyone. But you have a gift, Miller. They're going to hear you and they're going to love you. Just like everyone else."

Just like I do.

Miller was quiet for a few seconds, then sniffed a laugh. "God, I'm a fucking mess." He looked up at me, a faint smile touching his lips for the first time. "Come here," he said as he pulled me in close again and held me tight. "I knew if I told you, it wouldn't seem so fucking crazy."

"It is crazy," I said, laughter bursting out of me. "It's out-of-this-world-level crazy, but I'm so happy for you. And you can be happy, too. Okay?"

He heaved a steadying breath. "I guess. It's just…a lot. I'm freaking exhausted."

"You look it," I said, brushing the hair out of his eyes. "You want to sleep with me?"

Miller smirked. "That's a loaded question."

I grinned and tugged him to the bed with both hands. "I meant to just sleep. Although I'm flexible on that point."

He laughed tiredly as he kicked off his boots. We lay down face to face, our hands entwined, our gazes roaming and tracing and memorizing.

"Who else knows about this?" I asked. "Did you tell your mom?"

He nodded. "She didn't believe it either. Not really." His eyes darkened. "Chet—that asshole—is hurting her."

"Oh shit," I breathed. "Oh no. God…what can we do?"

"He's gone until tomorrow, but I'm going to have to stay home most nights from now on."

"To protect her."

He nodded.

"God, Miller, please be careful."

"I will. If he tries anything, I'll have his ass arrested since Mom won't. But I'll be in LA for two days and she'll be alone."

"You'll come back with a record contract and kick his ass out for good."

"That's the plan, impossible as it seems." Miller's eyes widened. "Oh, shit. June 4th is your birthday."

"Last I checked," I said, grinning. "And it's Prom too, as a matter of fact. Which reminds me, I know I promised River, but that doesn't mean we can't all go in a group…"

Miller was shaking his head against the pillow. "That's the weekend of that meeting. Damn, I don't want to miss your birthday."

"Neither do I, for *multiple* reasons," I said with what I hoped was a seductive smile. "But you have an excuse. The best excuse. Overkill, really. Most guys would've come up with something less outlandish than a record deal with Gold Line Records."

"I don't have a deal. Not yet. I don't know what's going to come of this, if anything, but I'm going to take care of Mom. And you."

"You don't need to—"

He silenced me with a soft kiss and then rested his head heavily on the pillow. "I will. Don't argue with me, Vi," he mumbled with a smile, his eyes falling shut. "Too tired."

"Sleep, then." I stroked his cheek, tracing the outline of his full lips, down to his chin and along his jaw.

Beautiful. My beautiful, kind, brave Miller.

I kissed him softly, and my eyes started to drift shut too, while a small twinge of unease hatched in my stomach. A little seed of uncertainty. Everything I'd said to Miller about his future was true. This was his big break; I could feel it.

But that meant our paths were about to diverge drastically, and I wondered where they would take us.

Someone had set off a car alarm. Or maybe I'd changed my phone's alarm from birdsong to a high, tinny *beep…*

Then through the haze of sleep, I recognized the sound. I bolted up to sitting, brushing the hair out of my eyes. Miller's watch was flashing the number 195 in red.

"Miller," I said, jostling him. "Wake up."

He came awake slowly, sluggishly, and gripped his forehead with a grimace of pain as he sat up. "What…? Oh, shit."

I shot out of bed and rummaged in his backpack. "You're high. It's dawn phenomena, right? I read about this. Did you eat a bunch of carbs last night?"

"Pasta," he said and started to climb out of bed. "I need water."

Gently, I pushed him back. "I got it." I hurried to bring him a glass of water from the bathroom sink. He downed it in three long gulps while I rushed to his med kit to find the fast-acting insulin.

I murmured to myself as I tore open the bag, recalling what I'd studied since Miller's first hospitalization four years ago. "One unit of insulin per every fifteen milligrams over one-fifty…" I did the math in my head. "Three units."

I clicked his injection pen to distribute three units of insulin and climbed back on the bed. Miller lay heavily against the bedframe, watching me as I pushed up his sleeve to expose his arm. "You're amazing, Vi."

I'm scared shitless.

For months, Miller and I'd been estranged, and I hadn't been around for his highs or lows. I'd forgotten how scary they could be, and the night he nearly died came racing back, sitting at the forefront of my thoughts.

I injected the insulin then sat with his wrist in my grasp, watching the numbers come down.

"What's your fasting level?"

"Between 80 and 120," he said, eyes closed, head tilted up and resting against the headboard.

I bit my lip. "They're coming down."

He reached 110 and leveled off and I slumped against the bedframe too.

"Sorry, Vi," he said after a minute. "I hate doing that to you."

"You're not doing anything to me."

"Scaring you."

I smiled. "How scared I am is directly proportionate to how much I care about you." I kissed his shoulder and left my lips against his skin. "Has it been hard?"

"It's always been hard. But no worse than usual." He opened his eyes and looked to me. "I missed that. You. Mom's got her own stuff to deal with, and needles made Amber queasy. I missed being around someone who gave a shit."

Tears threatened, but I willed them back. "I give a shit. I never stopped. Even when we weren't speaking much or…at all. I never stopped caring."

"I know," he said, his gaze roaming my face, tracing me with his eyes. "Neither did I. I just had a fucking horrible way of showing it."

He pulled me in to kiss him, but before our lips touched, our eyes met. In that instance—the length of a heartbeat—a lifetime passed between us. An understanding that he and I were inevitable. Fated. The boy with diabetes and the girl who was going to be a doctor. The girl with the romantic heart and the boy who wrote love songs.

Our lips came together in a deep kiss that was both heated but gentle, dire but reverent. The sweetness of the juice on our tongues mingled with Miller's own sweetness. For all of his prickly, grouchy and mistrusting ways, he had the purest soul I'd ever known. And his innate goodness was the sexiest thing about him.

Well, that and his face, his body, his voice, his talent…

My giggle broke our kiss.

"Something funny?" Miller said, his hands slipping around my waist.

"No, actually," I said, my pulse thumping as I climbed onto his lap, straddling him. "I'm very serious about how I feel about you."

Miller's smile faded as he took in my heavy breasts, barely covered by a thin scrap of cotton and held up by two spaghetti straps. "Jesus, Vi."

"Touch me, Miller."

I leaned over, affording him a full view. Beneath me, his erection was hard and heavy in his jeans. I rocked my hips over him as his hands came up under the shirt. Both hands kneaded my breast, thumbs circling the nipples.

"Can I…?" he asked, his voice gruff.

"Take it off," I said, my pulse thundering in my ears in anticipation, to have Miller's eyes on my naked flesh for the first time. His hands slid up the sides of my torso, feeling the curves of my waist, and then up, hooking on the tank top as they went. He peeled it off and tossed it away.

"Holy fuck," he whispered, his glance rising to meet mine. "You are so beautiful."

Before I could reply, he moved in, and I gasped when his mouth took one nipple, sending licks of fire down my spine between my legs. One touch, and then he retreated.

"Shit, wait. Your parents?"

"I put a lock on my door after the last time they busted in."

"You're a goddamn genius," Miller muttered and then his mouth descended again.

His tongue was soft and hot and wet, circling my nipple, while his thumb did the same to the other breast. He sucked and pulled, his teeth grazed as I ground against him, breathless at the electric currents that surged through me. I arched my back, pressing myself deeper into his touch. His hands slid to my hips, grinding me on him while his mouth worked me over.

"Need to feel you," I managed.

My hands found the hem of his T-shirt. I lifted it up and off of him, breaking our contact for a moment, then I wrapped my arms around his neck and pulled him in close. Warm skin against warm skin, chest to chest, heart to heart.

So perfect…

Miller kissed my throat, my chin, and then my mouth. My hands roamed his chest and down to his abdomen. I broke away only because I needed to look at him too, naked for me for the first time. His body was so beautiful, smooth over hard muscle. The CGM imbedded in his lower right abdomen was beautiful too. It was keeping him alive.

The realness of the moment—both of us naked from the waist up and me on his lap—struck me, my every sense suddenly tuned up and awake. Every touch, every breath every moment shone in bright clarity, stealing my air and lighting up my nerves. My hands trembled as I unbuttoned his jeans, wanting more but unsure of where *more* would take us.

Miller caught my hand in his. "You okay?"

"Yes, sure. Just…excited. Or nervous, maybe." I swallowed hard. "I want this. I want you."

His eyes searched mine intently. "I want you too, Vi. But I want you the right way."

I nodded, our gaze never breaking as he rolled me onto my back and settled himself over me. He kissed me long and slow, our skin melding together, his hands cradling my face as if I were precious. Everything soft and warm between us but the stiff denim of his jeans. I winced as the button jabbed me.

He slipped out of the jeans, leaving him in his boxers.

"Just this," he whispered, moving over me again, the length of his body aligned with mine. "Okay?"

I nodded again, and warmth flooded me at his consideration, how attuned he was to us, creating harmony between our desire and what I was ready for. I slipped my arms around him, sealing him to me. His erection pressed between my legs, a few scraps of cloth between us. And that felt perfect. Right.

Miller kissed me long and slow, concentrating on my face, my mouth, his hands in my hair, while our lower bodies began to move, seeking more connection. I spread my legs wider, letting him settle deeper against me. His hips lifted and came down in soft, slow grinds. A little moan escaped me at the sensations building where his hardness nestled my softness. My hips lifted in answer, again and again.

"You okay?" he asked, his breath hot against my lips.

"Yes. It's perfect. So perfect…"

Pleasant, needy tension hummed along our bodies, growing more and more potent with each rise and fall. My panties were damp. A spot of wetness darkened his underwear. Our kiss broke in breathy gasps for air; we moved as if he were inside me. Harder. Faster. My hands slid down the curve of his lower back, pressing him into me. A heavy ache of pleasure was building in me, a peak I sought to climb higher and higher. Miller propped himself on his elbows, his hips driving against mine, the clothing between us a maddening obstacle and the perfect friction.

"Vi…?" he breathed.

"I'm going to…" I clutched at him, every part of me tensed and tight, ready to break open.

"Come," Miller managed, his voice tight, his hips relentless. "Come, Vi."

I let out a little cry that I smothered in his neck, biting his warm, salty skin as my first *real* orgasm swept along every nerve-ending, stronger and more powerful than anything I'd imagined. Or that I produced on my own. The shockwave rushed through me, leaving me weak and boneless.

Miller's hips ground a few more times, coaxing the last of my orgasm while driving toward his. With a strangled grunt, he abruptly tore off me and grabbed for a tissue from the box on my nightstand. He sat at the edge of the bed, and I watched the muscles in his back slide and move under his skin as his release shuddered through him. A small sound erupted from his chest, and my only wish was that he'd still be on top of me so that I could feel, see, and hear him come.

Another time, I thought as pure contentment washed over me. *And it will be perfect.*

Miller cleaned himself up and then stretched out beside me again with a tired laugh. "Good?"

"Good? I had an out-of-body experience."

"I think that's what's supposed to happen."

"It was," I said, smiling softly and brushing a lock of hair off his brow. "It was exactly what was supposed to happen."

And he knew it.

He kissed me softly. "I gotta go. *You* gotta go. We'll be late for school. I don't actually give a shit, but you have a stellar citizenship record to maintain."

"I don't want you to go." I curled up into the sheets. "I'm having my first orgasm afterglow. I want to sleep for days. With you."

He grinned. "Me too. But I got to get home to eat and take my insulin, or I'll have an entirely different kind of out-of-body experience."

"Jesus, Miller, don't say that."

"Sorry, bad joke. I've been hanging out with Ronan and Holden for too long." He got up and drew his jeans on, then leaned over the bed to kiss me again, slow and deep. "You're the best thing that's ever happened to me, Vi."

And then he left the same way he came in, through the window.

I watched him go, then flopped back against my pillow. A laugh burst out of me that morphed into a full body shiver. Miller's touch lingered over every part of me, especially the juncture between my legs where I could still feel the low ebb of the wave that had crashed over me.

But it was my heart that was singing the loudest.

You're the best thing that ever happened to me.

So said Miller Stratton in the same twenty-four hours that a record exec from a major label wanted to meet with him. Then he'd slipped out of my room like a prince in a fairytale.

I couldn't stop smiling until reality creeped cold fingers into my sleepy warmth. This princess was going to the ball with someone else, while her prince rode off into a Los Angeles sunset.

And if all went as it should, he wouldn't come back.

At school that day, I made it to lunch break without seeing Shiloh. I wasn't feeling hungry, so I wandered the campus alone, my popularity stock clearly having taken a nosedive since #HomecomingFail. Caitlin and Julia only ever waved at me from afar these days, both looking cowardly and sheepish, as if the matter of being my friend or not was out of their hands. No doubt Evelyn's handiwork.

Miller had texted, saying he was cutting school to stay home with his mom in case Chet came back drunk and belligerent. I was on my own.

I sent Shiloh a text. **Where are you?**

The reply came a few minutes later as I followed the path down toward the gym.

Home. Bibi isn't feeling well.

My heart clenched. Shiloh's grandma was pushing eighty and mostly confined to a wheelchair. **Is she ok?**

I think so. Going to stay home to make sure. A pause, then another text. **I heard Miller's news!!** Followed by the "mind blown" emoji.

I'm so proud of him. I'd wandered down to the bleachers, perhaps drawn by my hormones after this morning. **And OMG we need some girl talk, STAT.**

I was about to hit send on that text when the phone nearly fell out of my hand. Holden Parish emerged from the make-out spot, and River Whitmore followed after.

They both wore dark, almost angry expressions and looked as if they'd been fighting but had called a reluctant truce. Holden smoothed the lapels of his coat and ran a hand through his mussed silvery hair. River jerked the collar of his letterman jacket into place and tucked in his shirt.

They immediately started for separate directions, but their nervous, darting glances landed on me at the same time.

Holden turned his steps in my direction, tipped an imaginary hat to me. "Lady Violet," he said as he passed. He wore a tight smile on his lips that were red and chafed. He smelled of River's cologne.

I stared then swiveled my head to River. He stood stock still staring at me, in a coiled, tensed fight-or-flight stance. Then his shoulders dropped, and he put his hands in his pockets as he strode over to me.

"Hi," I said.

"Hey," he replied, his glance flying everywhere and then finally meeting mine. "So listen. What you saw—"

"Is none of my business."

He jerked back in shock. His eyes softened and that same heartbreaking vulnerability I'd seen the other day was back. Then suspicious anger hardened his glance.

"You and I are going to Prom together. Aren't you pissed? Or the least bit curious?" His eyes widened as a horrifying thought occurred to him. "Did you know already? He's friends with Miller."

"I had no idea," I said. "No one does. But if it's a secret, coming here is a terrible way of keeping it."

The fight went out of him, and his shoulders slumped. There was a bench nearby, and River dropped onto it. His gaze looked for where Holden had gone. "Tell me about it. But I can't fucking stop…" He rested his forearms on his thighs and hung his head. "You won't tell anyone, will you? It'll fucking wreck me."

"I don't think that's true," I said, sitting beside him. "But I won't say a word."

"Not true?" he scoffed.

"It wouldn't wreck you here at school. We're in one of the most progressive corners of one of the most progressive states in the country."

"Forget here," River said. "Name one openly gay NFL player." He seemed to realize what he'd said, and his face paled. "I mean, I'm not...*gay*. I'm not. I'm...fuck, I don't know what I am."

"Is this why you want me to go to the Prom with you? To keep up appearances for your dad's sake?"

He nodded miserably.

"Do you think he'd be upset if he knew?" After spending months with Nancy Whitmore, I couldn't imagine she'd be anything but completely supportive of her son—or marry someone who wouldn't be.

Hell, she probably knew before River did.

"I don't know," River said. "But I do know that the answer to my NFL trivia challenge is *zero*. There are zero pro football players who are out. One guy got drafted and lasted all of one season. And for my dad, anything that might keep me from going all the way to the Super Bowl is a massive negative."

I didn't have any good advice for River, so I just sat with him, let him lean his huge frame against me for a few moments of quiet.

Finally, he spoke in a low tone. "I'll understand if you don't want to go to Prom with me."

"Forget me for a second. Do you want to go with *him*?"

"Not going to happen."

"Is he okay with that? Are you?"

River scowled. "He's an asshole and I'm a *Brokeback Mountain* cliché because I can't stay away. But shit, Vi, you should go with your boyfriend. *He* says you and Miller are official. Why stick with me?"

"Because I want to keep my word. And, as it turns out, Miller can't make it anyway. We talked it out. Even if he could go, I'm sticking with you, if you want me."

"I do," he said, his smile faint and sad. "You're probably my best friend. And definitely the only person I trust to not spread my shit all over the school."

"I never would. And I am your friend, River. Always."

His grateful smile nearly brought tears to my eyes.

"I'll take you to dinner first, unlike last time."

"Last time…" I mused. "Was *he* the reason you didn't make it?"

River nodded. "That fucker is my kryptonite. But I promise that won't happen again."

"I trust you. But River, if things change—"

"They won't."

"But if they do, I'll understand. Just give me a heads up before our dance comes up." I laughed. "Scratch that. Your dance, not ours. I doubt I'll be anywhere near the Prom court this time around."

"Also my fault."

"It's not important. But now that we've established our BFF status, can I suggest something? Talk to your mom and dad before you head off to college, move away from Santa Cruz, and begin a life you don't want."

He shook his head. "The pressure… It's the weight of an ocean. Dad's pinned all his own broken hopes on me. It'd kill him if I walked away. And with Mom being sick, I can't do that to him." He stood up before I could argue and offered me his hand to pull me off the bench. "Come on, BFF. Confession is over."

We walked in companionable silence as the bell rang at the end of lunch. When we reached my locker, I gave him a hug.

"Thank you," he said in my ear. "I mean it."

"Any time. Oh, and River? It's blue."

"What's that?"

"The color of my Prom dress is blue. For my corsage?" I teased, arching a brow at him. "In case you need the reminder."

"I won't," he said heavily. "My dad won't let me."

CHAPTER TWENTY

MILLER

June 3rd arrived. My flight to Los Angeles wasn't until that evening. Violet had a late doctor's appointment for a final check-up after her concussion, so Evelyn was driving me to the airport to give me last-minute advice. In LA, a car would take me to the Fairmont Miramar Hotel. The next morning, I'd meet with Jack Villegas, senior vice president at Gold Line Records.

Holy shit, I thought for the millionth time that day as I packed.

I didn't have much. I put my best dark jeans in a duffel along with my Sonic Youth T-shirt, which was my least faded. Evelyn had advised me to wear the leather necklace with the bone horn she'd found for me to complement my braided leather bracelets.

"And your beanie," she'd said. "For God's sake, wear your beanie."

The clothing felt shabby and too casual, but I had nothing else. Evelyn said it was the "real me."

But what if the real me isn't good enough?

I cursed myself for being this wound up and invested, but I couldn't help it. Hope was sometimes as potent as fear and just as debilitating.

I went to the fridge with my portable med storage bag and took a quick inventory of the snacks I needed to bring, estimated what I'd eat on the trip, and calculated how much insulin to take. I felt Chet's eyes on me as I removed the refrigerated capsules and packed them in the travel bag.

Since hearing the news about my interview, he'd been in a foul mood. Like a simmering pot ready to boil over.

"Hey, hotshot," Chet called from the couch, then muttered into a beer can, "Yeah, thinks he's fucking hot stuff now. Little bitch is what he is."

My pulse quickened. It was only ten in the morning. Everyone—with the possible exception of Ronan—still had school until three. Mom had called in sick from work, and I'd stayed home with her to make sure she was okay.

I'd been staying home from school as often as I could, since the day I found the bruises on her arm, but she'd told me not to. I was truant, for one thing, but instead of protecting her from Chet, she said me being home all the time made things worse. Put Chet more on edge.

"He's never touched me again after that," she'd sworn, and so I went to school.

But that morning, I was too jacked up for school and even more reluctant to leave Mom. I went into her room to check on her.

"He's ready to blow."

"I know," she said. "But you have to go. Please. You'll only make it worse."

"Me? Kick him out, Mom," I hissed. "Call the cops."

She sat against her pillows, tired and worn. "It'll mess up your day. You might miss your flight and that can't happen. Go, honey. I'll be fine."

I gritted my teeth and bent to kiss her forehead. "Call me if you need me. Promise."

"I will."

I dragged myself out of her room and went to mine to get my stuff.

Vi, Shiloh, and the guys were gathering for what Holden called a *Remember Us When You're Famous* party. I figured I'd go to the beach and wander, try to calm myself down.

I slung my duffel over my arm and carried my guitar case out, then I stopped short. Chet blocked the hallway. His jowls were pasty under days' worth of stubble, and he stank of stale beer and smoke.

"You think your little trip is going to change anything?" he said, eyeing me up and down. "They're going to see right through you. A dirty, punk-ass little bitch singing your stupid songs."

My pulse crashed in my ears and my throat went dry. "Back off, asshole."

Chet looked ready to fight, but the bedroom door opened, and Mom came out. "What's happening out here?"

"Nothing," he said and let me go, giving my shoulder a hard knock as I passed, then followed me into the living room. "Nothing's happening," he said louder as I went to the shabby coat stand near the door to grab my jacket. "You hear me? You're a fucking carny pretending to be bigger than you are. But you ain't shit."

I hunched my shoulders against his words, but they sank in anyway.

"Thanks for the pep talk," I muttered and reached for the door. Behind me, Mom gave a cry, and then my guitar case was torn out of my hand. I spun around to see Chet hurl it at the wall behind the couch. It struck hard enough to leave a scuff mark and tumbled onto the cushions.

"What are you—?"

My words—and air—cut off as Chet gripped me around the throat and shoved me against the door. He moved in close, seething, spittle flecking my lips as he spoke.

"For too long, you've been a smartass hotshot walking around here. I keep telling your mom to kick your ass to the curb. You're eighteen now. I think it's time."

Black starbursts were flaring in my vision. Mom was shouting at him to let me go, tugging his arm and begging. I got my hands around his wrist and yanked him off me.

"Fuck you," I cried hoarsely, then hurried to my guitar.

I felt Chet behind me, then his hand gripped my shirt between my shoulder blades. He yanked me back, throwing me off balance, and then shoved me forward. I stumbled and banged my shin on the coffee table, then crashed headfirst onto the couch. The right side of my face scraped against the edge of my guitar case. Pain flared like a burn.

"Stop it!" Mom cried. "Leave him be!"

I scrambled to my feet and gripped my guitar case. On instinct only, I swung it backward without looking and heard it connect with Chet's gut. He made an *ooph* sound and staggered back. I raced for the door, grabbing my mom's arm on the way, dragging her with me.

She tore out of my grasp. "Miller, no."

I stopped. Stared. Sucking in air, my pulse crashing in my ears. "Mom... Let's go. You can't stay here."

From behind her, Chet was breathing heavily, a triumphant smile splitting his thick lips. "She doesn't want to leave with you. She knows better than that."

I jabbed a finger in the air at him. "Go to hell, asshole, I'm calling the police."

He chuckled. "And say what? You think she's going to press charges? You going to press charges, Lynn?"

I stared at her, waiting for her answer. She cast her eyes to the ground, and I felt something in me break off and fall away.

"That's right," Chet said. "It ain't your house. It's hers. This is her home. But you're a grown man, son. I'd say it's about time you got the hell out."

"Mom?"

She lifted her eyes slowly, heavy with pain, and so tired. She kissed me on the cheek that burned.

"Just go," she whispered. "Get to LA. Be amazing."

I stared, first at her, then Chet smiling lazily, leaning against the kitchen counter as if it were his. Because now it was. I looked back to my mom, the words to tell her that her safety was more important. Her happiness. But she'd already turned and headed back down the hallway to her room in shuffling steps.

Chet's beady eyes met mine. "You heard your mother. Go."

So I went.

I opened the door with trembling hands and stepped outside on shaking legs. It closed behind me, and I heard the lock *click.*

In a half-daze, falling off an adrenaline high, I made my way to the Shack like a zombie. My face was on fire where it had scraped against my case, and my throat felt as if I'd swallowed a handful of rocks.

I stepped into the old rickety room. Holden had nailed a small mirror on the back wall. Or maybe it was Shiloh. She'd been hanging out here more, adding artistic touches here and there, making the place feel homey. The Shack was more of a home than my own.

I took a good look at myself in the mirror to examine my wounds. Fingerprints were darkening on my neck, and the area around my right eye was inflamed. Little scrapes of blood dashed my cheekbone. Anxiety jolted my stomach like an electric current.

I can't go to LA looking like this. I can't play for them like this…

Another terrible fear wracked me, lighting up my insides with panic. I quickly knelt in front of my guitar case and threw open the latches. With two hands, I gingerly pulled the guitar out and turned it over, inspecting it. A sigh of relief miles deep eased out of me, as I set it back in its case, whole and undamaged.

But the damage *had* been done. I looked exactly like what Chet had said. A dirt-poor kid who couldn't manage to stay out of trouble long enough to make it through one important meeting.

The strength drained out of me, and I sat down hard on the wooden bench and stared at the ocean through the Shack's lone window. The battle with Chet replayed in flashes, making me wince. But my mom's defeated face scared me more.

The last thing I wanted to do was eat; but I took my insulin and choked down some food, every bite like a rock in my bruised windpipe. Panic lit me up all over again.

Jesus, what if I can't sing?

I hummed a few bars, wincing at the pain. A few lyrics grated out. I cleared my throat and tried again, louder. For a few nerve-wracking minutes, I warmed up my voice until I could sing past the pain and sound like myself.

"Goddamn," I murmured. Chet had almost ruined everything.

Maybe he did. They're not going to want me either.

The last vestiges of adrenaline left me drained, and I laid my head on the table. The scents of salt and old wood and the sound of the ocean crashing and retreating soothed me like Mom's perfume and lullabies used to when I was a kid. A lifetime ago.

A soft hand touched me awake. I opened heavy eyes to see Violet standing over me. She wore jeans and a baggie hoodie, no makeup, her hair in a ponytail.

So beautiful…

She smiled. "Hey, you. Napping before your—?" Her words cut off in a gasp as I sat up and the afternoon sunlight fell over my face. "Miller…My God, what happened?" She touched my chin, turning me toward her to get a better look and then bit back a little cry. "Your neck. Who did this to you? Chet?"

I nodded. "I'm okay. But shit, look at me. I can't go to LA now."

"Of course, you can," she said fiercely, her voice wavering. "You can't let him stop you."

"I'm going to meet a high-level exec looking like this? It's pathetic. I don't want them to feel sorry for me."

"They won't. Not after you sing." She pulled me to her, cradling my head against her soft sweatshirt.

"He kicked me out, Vi," I said into her middle. "He kicked me out of the house."

I was homeless for the second time in my life.

"No," Violet said in a quavering voice. "He can't do that."

"He did. My mom is too scared and beat down to stand up to him. My only chance now is to go to LA, convince them to invest in me, and kick his ass out when I get back."

Saying it out loud made it sound even more implausible.

Violet sat on the bench beside me. "You can do that, and you will," she said, blinking her tears away, determination taking over. She glanced around the Shack. "I thought I saw a first aid kit around here."

"Holden brought one." I pointed at the small medicine box, sitting near the generator softly *whirring* in the corner.

Violet brought it back to the table. I winced as she touched antiseptic wipes to the scrapes on my cheek. "Tomorrow, it won't be so red. It'll look better tomorrow."

I noticed she didn't say anything about the fingerprints on my neck that looked exactly like what they were. No hiding them.

Voices sounded from outside.

"Shit, the others are here," I said. "I don't want them to see me like this. It's fucking humiliating."

Violet touched my cheek. "It's not. It's just what happened. They're your friends, and they care about you."

Holden and Ronan could be heard bickering at each other as they prepped the firepit, Shiloh cutting in to scold them for being jackasses.

Despite everything, I smiled. I'd missed them.

We exited the Shack. Three heads turned, and three pairs of eyes widened at the same time to see my face. I put my hand up before anyone—mainly Holden—could speak.

"I don't want to talk about it. My mom's boyfriend is a dick. Let's leave it at that."

"But fucking hell, Miller," Holden began.

"I said I don't want to talk about it. I'll deal with him when I get back."

Somehow.

Holden reluctantly backed off. Shiloh's face was a mask of concern. But Ronan…Ronan looked ready to kill. While the others were busy setting up the fire and getting the food, he pulled me aside.

"When you get back," he said in a flat tone, his gray eyes hard and flinty, "we're going to handle it. Okay?"

I nodded, teeth clenched to keep the damn tears from my eyes. "Okay."

"Good," he said, then I nearly fell over as he reached out and gripped my shoulder for a short second. Ronan never touched anyone. He gave me a thump and let me go.

He got the fire started while Holden got the conversation going. For a few hours, I was able to put what happened on the back burner. I sat in the sand, Violet in front of me, her back to my chest, my arms wrapped around her, her head nestled in the crook of my shoulder.

We ate hotdogs and potato chips. Holden told an outlandish story about the time he and another patient at the sanitarium in Switzerland attempted a poorly-planned escape and ended up being chased through sprinklers on the front lawn wearing only bathrobes, their bare asses waving in the wind.

Violet laughed with the rest of us, but I noticed she was watching Holden differently, as if seeing him in a new light.

After the food had settled, Shiloh asked me to play the songs I'd prepared for the meeting.

"Not in the mood," I said with finality.

No one pushed it.

Eventually, it was time for me to say my goodbyes.

Holden put both hands on my shoulders, his peridot green eyes staring intently into mine, serious as death. "Listen to me. If you get to this meeting and start to panic or freak the fuck out, I have a sure-fire solution that I use when I get in tough spots."

"What's that?" I asked, preparing myself for something ridiculous.

"I ask myself one question and one question only… What would Jeff Goldblum do?"

Yep.

"Thank you, that's super helpful."

Holden grinned and then it suddenly fell from his face as his gaze landed on my bruises. Wordlessly, he pulled off the scarf he was wearing, despite the warm afternoon, and slung it around my neck. He wound it loosely so that it covered the marks.

"You don't have to explain anything to them, okay?" he said. "Not a goddamn thing."

"Dammit, Parish." My eyes stung as I hugged him tight. "Thanks, man."

He let me go, and Shiloh took a turn, giving me a hug and a kiss on the cheek. "Knock'em dead. I know you will."

Ronan had already said his peace earlier; he gave me a short nod as the three of them left the Shack. Violet and I lingered for a bit before heading out; I knew she had something on her mind. She gathered my medical bag while I shouldered my duffel and picked up my guitar case.

"I wish I could drive you to the airport," she said quietly as we walked along the beach. "I want to."

"You can't skip that appointment, Vi," I said, brushing strands of raven black hair from her temple. "They need to make sure you're okay."

"I know I'm okay." She bit her lip. "But…does it have to be Evelyn?"

"She has some last-minute advice. Probably along the lines of *Don't fuck this up.*"

"But what's in it for her? She never does anything without an agenda"

"Massive amounts of ad revenue for her vlog," I said. I didn't add that Evelyn had said the true purpose for driving me to the airport was to finally tell me the favor she wanted in exchange for helping me. If it was something wildly inappropriate—which I suspected it was—I'd shoot her down and Violet would never have to hear about it and be hurt.

She didn't look happy.

"You trust me, right?"

"Of course, I do. Evelyn? Not so much."

I cleared my throat. "I mean, not to point out the obvious, but you're going to Prom with another guy."

"You definitely have nothing to worry about, there," she said with a funny smile, then met my eye intently. "But I mean it. I trust you, Miller."

"I trust you too, Vi," I said. And I did, but the idea of River touching her, dancing with her, and taking photos like they were a couple was like rubbing salt in a wound after this morning. Violet was the last good thing that was mine, and I didn't want to share her.

You're being a possessive asshole, I told myself. *A Chet. Don't be a Chet.*

"I'm going to miss you," she said as we drove out of the beach area and onto Cliffside Street in her SUV. I'd texted Evelyn to meet me at the Whole Grounds café instead of my apartment to avoid any more shit with Chet.

"You too," I said. "And I'm sorry to miss your birthday."

"You and me both," she said with a sly smile.

Violet parked the car in a spot in front of the coffee shop. She turned to me, kissed me softly. "Break a leg. Call me the second it's over."

"I will." I cupped her cheek and kissed her again. I tried to take a little bit of eternal optimism with me; let her sweetness wash away my bitterness. But my stomach was a tangle of knots and my thoughts filled with doubt and fear.

"I'll call you tomorrow night. And have fun at the Prom. I know you'll be so beautiful."

"I'll be wishing I was with you." She kissed me a final time, and then I got out of her car, taking my bags and guitar case with me.

I was walking into the café when a screech of tires sounded behind me. Violet had backed out of the parking spot, then pulled back in. She threw open her door and ran to me, stood in front of me, breathless, with her eyes alit. The pale porcelain skin of her cheeks was flushed, and her red lips parted.

"I love you," she blurted.

It whacked me so hard in the chest, taking my breath away.

"I started to drive away, and I couldn't do it. I can't let you go to Los Angeles without you knowing that I love you. I've always loved you. Since we were thirteen and stupid and scared. Scared about how much I loved you. How deep it went." She shook her head, deep blue eyes shining. "Because it's so deep, Miller. I can't see the bottom."

I stared as her speech sank into me like warm rain. Each word melting away the anxiety, loosening the fear, filling me with warmth instead.

Violet studied my dazed expression. "You don't have to say it back—"

I silenced her with a kiss, holding her face in both hands, kissing my love into her—four years' worth of unspoken love behind us and a lifetime ahead.

"I love you," I whispered against her lips. "I'm so in love with you. God, Violet. Things were utter shit and then one night, I came out of a dark forest, stumbling and lost, and there you were."

Tears filled her eyes, but her smile was wide and brilliant. "Well," she huffed, teary and breathy. "Glad we got that settled. And for the record, that's the best…birthday…present…ever."

She kissed me again, holding my hands in both of hers, then backed away and headed to her car. She gave a little wave from the window and was gone.

I sank down at a table outside the café, amazed at how a single day could be both the fucking worst and the absolute best at the same time.

A few minutes later, a black Escalade rolled into the parking lot and pulled up parallel to the shop. The passenger window rolled down, and Evelyn lowered her sunglasses at me. "Hey, baby, need a ride?"

I smirked and opened the backseat door to stow my stuff, then climbed in the front.

Evelyn took off her glasses. "Holy shit, what happened to you?"

I stiffened. "It's nothing."

"Nothing?" she screeched. "You're a mess and…*Jesus,* what's that on your neck?"

Holden's scarf had fallen down, and I yanked it off. "Don't worry about it."

"Don't worry…? God, are you okay?"

"I'm fine, but…it looks bad, right? For the interview?"

"It's not ideal," Evelyn said, putting the car in drive and heading out. Her eyes were suddenly full of thoughts. Calculating. After a few minutes she said, "I'll give you some concealer to put on your neck. I use it all the time for that sort of thing."

I whipped my head. "All the time for *what* sort of thing?"

She swallowed hard, gripping the steering wheel with both hands. "Never mind," she said taking us north out of Santa Cruz toward the San Jose Airport. "The time has come."

"Your demands."

"Think of it more as a quid pro quo. I helped get you to where you're going, now I want you to help me in return."

"I haven't signed a contract yet."

"But you will. And when you do, they're going to ask you to move to Los Angeles to cut a record. An EP, probably. They'll want you to shoot some videos, maybe even do a tour as someone's opener. And when all that happens," Evelyn said, "I want to be there, too."

"What does that mean?"

"I want you to take me with you."

I scoffed. "Yeah, that's not gonna happen."

"Miller, listen to me—"

"I'm not taking you to Los Angeles, Evelyn. To live with me? I'm with Violet."

"This has nothing to do with her," Evelyn said. "And I'm not asking you to take me on as one of your damn groupies, for God's sake. Ego, much?"

"Then what do you want?"

"I need a foot in the door. Contacts. You can't make it anywhere in the world without knowing somebody. You're going to be that somebody, and I'm going to be your personal assistant."

I barked a laugh. "A personal assistant? No. I can't do that, Evelyn. I don't have the clout anyway."

"Have you even bothered to watch any of your videos?" she asked, weaving her car through traffic. "Have you read any of the comments? You're going to be huge, Miller. Where you're going tomorrow? It's not a job interview. It's going to be to sign a *record contract*."

I leaned back against the leather seat of her Escalade, contemplating her words. Then shook my head.

Impossible. Isn't it…?

"You're getting way ahead of yourself," I said. "And no. Sorry. I can't do that, Evelyn. I can't do that to Violet."

"I have to get out of here, Miller," Evelyn said, and I was shocked at the sudden tears filling her eyes. "I have to. What happened to you today? It happens to me too."

I stared, my brain trying to comprehend what she was telling me. All the times I'd been in her house, I never got a sense of anything sinister. Happy photos on the walls, joking around with her dad, an indulgent mom who was clearly proud of her.

"Who?" I asked. "I've never seen—"

"So, if you didn't see it, it never happened?" Without taking her eyes off the road, her hand went down to the hem of her mini skirt and pulled it up. A rectangular-shaped bruise, four inches long and two inches wide, ran across the top of her thigh. She pulled her skirt down.

"He hits me there. So it doesn't show."

"Fuck," I breathed. "Who?"

"Doesn't matter."

"It does matter. Jesus, Evelyn, I'm sorry."

"It's okay," she said, waving a hand. "I can take care of myself. And I will, once I get to Los Angeles. Promise me, Miller. Promise you won't say anything. Promise me that when your dreams come true, you'll help me with mine."

Nothing had happened yet, but if by some miracle she was right, and they did offer me everything I could hope for, it was my responsibility to help other people. My duty. I'd lived in a car. I'd been homeless once, and I was homeless again. If the universe was going to take care of me, I had to pay it back.

"I promise," I said, sealing the deal. My word was unbreakable. I just prayed to God that Violet would understand. That it wasn't asking too much of her…

"Thank you, Miller," Evelyn said, letting out a shaky breath. "You're one of the good guys. You know that, right? That's why they love you so much."

"Who?"

"All those girls on my vlog. That's what they all want. Someone like you, looking at them the way you look at Violet. They all want to be the girl in your love song." She glanced at me, her usually sharp eyes soft now. "Gold Line Records knows that. They're going to bottle you up and sell you, Miller. Are you prepared for that?"

I thought of my mom's face, etched in hopelessness. Covered in dust.

"Whatever it takes."

CHAPTER TWENTY-ONE

VIOLET

I finished my check-up at the Medical Center. As I suspected, my head was just fine, no residual effects of the concussion I'd had months ago. But to be safe, I'd sat on the bench for the rest of the soccer season, cheering the team from the sidelines.

I'd just arrived at my car when Ms. Taylor, my counselor, called. "I've got good news and bad news. Which do you want to hear first?"

"The bad," I said, shutting the driver side door and climbing behind wheel. "Then hit me with the good to take the sting out."

"I'm afraid it's a pretty big sting. UC Santa Cruz has awarded you the Joan T. Bergen scholarship in the amount of $5,000."

"That's a good thing. Per year?"

"Total. There was a lot of competition this year, and most scholarships were already awarded. That leaves you needing to cover about $55,000 over four years. Not to mention housing, food, books, et cetera."

I swallowed hard. "Okay. That's not impossible. I can survive the first year with financial aid, then reapply next year for more help."

"Are you sure? That's a lot to take on."

"I can do it. I'll live at home, get a job..." I let out a shaky breath. "Yeah, I can do this."

I could hear Ms. Taylor's smile color her words. "Good for you, Violet. But before you make any decisions, the good news is pretty good. Baylor University was quite impressed with you. They've awarded you the Physicians of the Future scholarship."

My jaw dropped. "That's...huge."

"It is. And accepting it would look incredible on your med school applications when the time comes. They're going to cover your tuition *in full* so long as you maintain a 3.5 grade point average."

"In full? Holy crap!" I bit my lip.

Baylor was in Texas, so far away from friends and family. And Miller. He was already in Los Angeles, probably building a future there. Santa Cruz was a short flight, hardly an hour. But Texas…

"You'd have to cover your own housing," Ms. Taylor continued, "but considering tuition is higher for out-of-state students, this is a huge win."

I nodded. My first years of college, debt free. "It's an enormous opportunity, but UCSC has been my dream since forever. Santa Cruz is my home. I know you said to be flexible but let me talk to my parents before I make a decision. It's a lot to think about."

"Well, let me know what you decide, and I'll help you answer the schools and figure out the details."

"Thank you, Ms. Taylor. For everything."

"Of course. And have fun at the Prom. You're going with River Whitmore?"

My brow wrinkled. "How did you know?"

"He told me. I've been helping him with his college apps. That boy is destined for great things. The NFL, even."

"Oh, he's still pursuing that?" I asked casually.

"I can't give particulars; I'm sure he'll tell you all about it at Prom. But the Big Ten are all clamoring for him."

I smiled thinly. "I'm sure they are."

I hung up with Ms. Taylor, thinking River and I had a lot in common. We both wanted simple things: to stay in the city we loved and build our futures there, but life had its own plans.

I got home to an eerily silent—but not empty—house. It breathed with tension and anxiety. The hairs on the back of my neck stood up as I entered the kitchen, colored in twilight's amber light. Mom and Dad were sitting at the table, papers strewn all over. The logo for the IRS jumped out at me more than once.

"What's going on?" I asked slowly, moved slowly, breathed slowly. The air felt like glass.

Mom sniffed and dabbed a tissue to red eyes. "Sit down, Violet."

On stiff legs, I sat between them at the table and folded my hands. I looked to my dad, and my heart cracked. I'd never seen him so wrecked—unshaven, disheveled, thinner.

"Daddy?"

He smiled weakly. "Hey, pumpkin. We have some bad news."

"I'm sure she gathered that," Mom snapped but without much energy. She waved a hand. "Sorry. I'm sorry. Just tell her already. Or I will."

"Be my guest."

Mom huffed a breath and faced me. "First, let me say this isn't your fault. You're going to think it is, but it's not. It's the result of years' accumulation of bad ideas, compounded by mistakes we made."

"Okay."

Mom heaved another breath. "Your applications for financial aid have triggered an IRS audit of our finances. Under normal circumstances, this wouldn't be a big deal. But…"

"But we're broke," Dad said. "More than broke."

"We're completely screwed." Mom sipped from a coffee cup that I wasn't sure contained only coffee.

I stared between them. "What happened?"

"A few years ago, I got in some trouble," Dad said. "I developed an app. It was supposed to be a smash, but the deal fell through."

"It fell through because your father stole code from another developer working on a similar app," Mom said.

Dad shook his head at her, his lips drawn down in pure malice. "I stole *nothing*," he seethed. "But yes…there was a patent already pending that I foolishly ignored. They sued me, and it took everything we had to keep it quiet or else we'd be ruined."

"That's where my college fund went?" I asked. "To cover the lawsuit?"

"Not just that," Mom said, shifting in her seat. "The lawsuit judgement was more than we could handle. They were set to take our house, the cars. The lifestyle we have would vanish."

"And your mother couldn't handle *that*," Dad said acidly, and I realized with a pang, there was no love left between them. Not one iota.

"And you could?" Mom snapped back at him. "To admit to the world we were ruined? I plugged a hole in the leaky damn."

"How?" I asked, despite having no desire to hear the answer.

"I stopped paying the taxes," Mom said.

I gaped. "You did what?"

"To keep money in the bank. I fired our tax guy and told him we were going with another firm. Your father *assured* me that his next deal would put us back on top. We could pay it all back. But no new magic deal ever materialized. Somehow, we stayed under the IRS's radar until now."

"Until I filed for financial aid." I slumped back in the chair, my gaze going to the papers on the desk. "That's why you couldn't get a divorce."

Dad nodded. "We didn't want to show a judge the true state of our finances."

"What happens now?" My glance darted between them, fear squeezing the breath out of me. "Not paying taxes is a big deal. Are you…going to jail?"

"No, thank God," Dad said. "My friend, Charlie…you remember him? He's an attorney, and he's agreed to help us get out of the mess, pro bono. We have to sell the house, all of our assets, and put it toward the IRS debt."

"Sell the house…"

The house I'd lived in my whole life. My home. I gripped the kitchen table where I'd once sat in a highchair, Mom spooning me food and Dad making silly faces. Where we'd eaten thousands of meals together, laughing and happy, in a time that was growing more faded and distant by the second.

"Where will we live?" I asked.

"Your father and I will separate," Mom said. "I'll be moving back in with Grandma in Portland."

"I'll be staying with Uncle Tony," Dad said.

"In *Ohio*?"

He nodded miserably.

"And…what about me?"

Mom bit her lip and looked away.

Dad tried to smile. "Well, honey, that's up to you."

I stared. "You want me to *choose* between you and Mom?" The idea made me sick, but then I realized my fate was already decided for me. "No, forget it. I'm not going with either one of you. Baylor is going to give me a full ride."

"Baylor?" Dad's eyes widened. "That's a wonderful school. Congratulations, honey."

His tearful pride threatened to wreck me.

"Are they paying for everything?" Mom asked.

"Almost," I said. "I have some savings. I'll find a place. Get a job. I'll be fine."

"We're proud of you, pumpkin," Dad said. "So proud. So much potential…and we failed you—"

"It's okay, Dad," I said abruptly. Nothing was okay, but I needed him to stop talking. His brokenness was too much to take. He was my father. He was supposed to be strong. Protective. Mom was supposed to be strong, too, and nurturing. They'd both been those things, once upon a time.

Mom took my hand, tears pricking her eyes. "Violet…I'm sorry. So sorry. And Jesus, tomorrow is your birthday…"

A sob burst out of her that she immediately covered with her hand. She pushed back from the table and ran from the room. Dad stood up too and patted my shoulder. He bent and kissed my head.

"We'll make it up to you," he said. "Somehow."

He left, and I was alone in the kitchen. The house went silent again, a quiet that felt permanent. Empty. It swallowed the echoes of happier times until there was nothing left.

The next day, Shiloh came over to help me get ready for the Prom. She brought me a white gift box wrapped in gold ribbon. Inside was a ring she had made herself. A beautifully intricate mix of bronze, gold, and silver strands twining together.

"Happy Birthday, Vi."

"It's beautiful," I said, slipping it over the middle finger of my right hand. "Stunning, Shi. You're so damn talented. I can't wait to see you have your own store front downtown someday."

"You and me both. There's also an inscription."

I took it off. Inside, she'd engraved *Vi and Shi* where the metals were welded together. Tears threatened as I hugged my friend tight.

"I'm going to miss you so much."

"Me too."

She quickly released me to move behind and help me button my dress—royal blue with a crystal-embroidered bodice and a long, sweeping chiffon skirt. In the mirror, I watched her braids fall over her slender shoulders as she worked, her eyes shining.

"I hate that you're leaving," she said. "We were supposed to have four more years together before you abandoned me for med school."

"I know. It makes me sick to think about it."

"What about everything else? How are you taking the divorce?"

"It's for the best. At one time in my life, it would have been the worst thing to happen. Now, it's one more torrent in a giant shitstorm."

"That left you in the cold. I'm worried about you striking off for Texas on your own."

"I have a little saved up."

"Will it be enough?"

"It'll have to be. I can't ask them for anything. They don't *have* anything."

The reality of it struck me hard, how fast things had changed. I stood in my room that had been mine since I could remember, and it was already feeling like I didn't belong here anymore.

Shiloh bit her lip and finished the last button. "Have you thought about maybe asking Holden for a loan?" She held up her hands at my appalled look. "I know, I know. I'd hate it too. But he's got more money than God and doesn't seem to give a shit about any of it. He'd give you some start-up cash, easy."

"I don't know him well enough to ask him, and it's too humiliating anyway." I shook my head, examining myself in the mirror. "No, I have to make it on my own. Maybe this is the universe's way of toughening me up before I become a doctor."

"When are you leaving?"

"I think I have to be ready to go when the house is sold."

"Damn, Vi…"

"It's better that way," I said in a small voice. "Then I can get a job and get settled in before school starts in the fall."

In Texas. So far away from her. And Miller. I have to leave Miller.

I hadn't let myself have the thought, but now it was there, bashing around inside my heart. I sank down on the bed, my hand covering my mouth.

"Oh, honey…" Shiloh sat beside me and put her arm around me. "Don't cry, you'll ruin your makeup. You haven't told Miller, have you?"

"Not yet. I can barely face it myself. What am I going to do, Shi?"

"I don't know, hon. But are you sure you're up to this Prom with River? Can't you call in sick and come over to my place? Bibi will bake you something good to celebrate your birthday, and we can eat and binge-watch *Ozark.*"

Nothing sounded better, but I shook my head. "I promised River."

Shiloh frowned. "What gives with you two? Is he blackmailing you?"

"No," I laughed. I stood up quickly and smoothed down the front of my dress. Shiloh had piled half my hair on my head, pinning it in a messy bun and letting the rest flow over my shoulders.

"You look beautiful," she said, standing with me. "Miserable but beautiful."

"I'm going with the wrong boy."

"Have you heard from *your* boy?"

"No. His meeting is today. All day."

"On a Saturday?"

"They worried he would be missing school. He'll be back tomorrow." I turned to her. "And what about you? I wish you were going."

"Not my scene," she said.

"And what is your scene? Ronan Wentz?"

Shiloh looked away. "It's complicated. I know that's a cheesy Facebook cliché, but it's exactly that."

I smiled softly. "You care about him?"

"*No*," she said, fuming. She flopped back on my bed on her back. "Half the time, he drives me fucking crazy, and I want to strangle him. The other times…"

I lay down beside her. "Other times you want to kiss him?"

She scoffed. "You're going to mess up your hair." I made a face at her, and she laughed, then took my hand and gave it a squeeze. "Happy birthday, Violet. I know everything is all fucked up right now, but if you're hellbent on going to this Prom, maybe try to have some fun tonight. Forget everything for a little bit."

"I'll try."

Shiloh stuck around while my parents pretended to be a normal, functioning family. They took a million pictures of Shiloh and me, and when River arrived, they took a million more. Dad made forced jokes about not keeping me out too late and Mom looked like she was holding back tears.

"Can we get a photo of the three of us?" Dad said, handing his phone to River. "It's a special occasion."

She relented, and I stood between them, all of us with smiles plastered on our faces. The last photo that would ever be taken of the three of us in our house again.

River took me back to his place for another round of pictures. The contrast between his parents and mine was stark. Nancy and Jerry Whitmore fawned over us with easy smiles and real laughter. But there was a different tension in the Whitmore house. Jerry shook River's hand and pounded him on the back, as if they'd sealed a business deal.

Nancy gave me a kiss on the cheek. "He tells me you've been a very sweet friend to him."

"He's been a pretty great friend to me, too."

"That's all that matters then. That you two are happy. Have a great time tonight."

I have to say goodbye to her too.

I felt like my smile was scaffolding, holding my emotions in. If I let it fall, everything would come tumbling out.

River took us to dinner at Lillian's Italian Bistro, where we sat across from each other at a little table for two. River was dashingly handsome in a black tux with a royal blue tie and cummerbund that matched my dress, but my mind kept wanting to mentally Photoshop Miller sitting there instead. He'd look ruggedly handsome, scruff over his cheeks, maybe in dark jeans and a sport coat and tie that he wouldn't stop tugging at. Unpolished and perfect.

"You look very beautiful," River said. "And Happy Birthday."

"Thank you."

"But you seem a little down." He toyed with his fork. "I know you'd rather be with someone else."

"Wouldn't you?" I asked with a gentle smile.

He started to shake his head, then nodded. "Yeah, I do. Not at the dance necessarily but just…"

"To be with him."

"Yeah."

"Me too."

A short silence passed and then River laughed. "God, what a pair we are. We gotta perk up or something. Today's your birthday. Eighteen, right? You're an official adult now. Welcome to the club. It's total shit."

I laughed ruefully. "I know it. God it feels like it hit me all at once. In the space of one day, I had to grow up and learn to fend for myself."

"You mean going to college? I thought you were staying here. UCSC."

"No," I said, feeling the scaffolding tremble. "Baylor, in Texas."

"Oh yeah? I got accepted to Alabama University. We'll almost be neighbors."

"You're really leaving, too? To play football?"

"What else am I good for? I wanted to stay and work at Dad's shop, but he won't hear of it. His heart is set on the NFL. Maybe I'll get to take the shop over when he retires. Then I can come back and be…"

"Home," I said.

"Yeah." River said. "Home."

The dinner was delicious, and somehow I managed to not drop one noodle onto my dress. River had just requested the check when my phone in my purse buzzed a text from Miller.

About to board the plane. Long day but they fucking did it. I have a deal. Head's exploding. Tell you everything when I get back. Love you, Vi.

I nearly dropped the phone. Pure joy suffused me, flooding out all of the disappointment and heartache of the last few days.

River raised a brow. "Good news?"

"The best. I…I can't even believe I get to say this out loud, but Miller got a record deal with Gold Line."

"No shit? That's awesome. Is it because of Evelyn's vlog?"

"Yeah," I said, deflating a little. "She gave him a platform. And they found him."

I quickly typed back. **OMFG Congratulations! You deserve everything good because *you* are everything good. I love you!! xoxo**

The text was marked as delivered but not read. The plane must've taken off. I put the phone away.

River held up his glass. "Here's to Miller. Rockstar in the making."

My joy for him mixed with pain in equal measure. "To Miller," I said. The man I'd have to say goodbye to.

CHAPTER TWENTY-TWO

VIOLET

At the Pogonip Country Club, garlands of lights were strung out over the walkway. The warm night was buzzing with insects and the smell of fresh flowers. Inside the ballroom, a DJ played Awolnation's "The Best." Couples in various shades of formalwear were dancing, huddled in groups talking, eating from the table of appetizers, or drinking sparkling cider.

"Hey, there's Chance," River said. "Let's head over."

"Sure," I said and then my stomach tightened. Evelyn Gonzalez was in the group with Chance and a few other football players and their dates. She looked stunning in ruby red.

She gave me a brazen once-over. "Violet. You are on fire!"

"Thanks, so are you," I said and meant it. Her scarlet dress hugged her curves, and her thick black hair tumbled down her back in waves, sparkles catching the light.

"Oh my God, did you hear from Miller?" she said. "He got the deal!"

"Yeah, he texted me." I wondered with a pang if he'd called Evelyn first and tried to corral the jealousy.

"Isn't it incredible?" she crowed. "Not that I'm surprised. I never doubted my boy for a second."

My boy.

I started to ask her not to talk about my boyfriend like that, but she moved in close.

"Listen, Vi. I need to apologize to you."

"For what?" I asked warily.

"For being cold and distant lately. Okay, fine. I've been a raging bitch."

"I thought you were pissed at me for being Homecoming Queen."

"Oh, that." She waved her hand. "That was an eternity ago."

I had a feeling she was being magnanimous because word on the street was that she was going to be Prom Queen and River would be her King.

"But for real," Evelyn said. "I became caught up in handling Miller's career, and I got carried away. But now that I'm set, I don't want any bad blood between us. Do you forgive me?"

Before I could ask her what she meant that she *was set*, Donte Weatherly grabbed her around the waist and whispered something in her ear.

"Such a pig!" she laughed, smacking his arm. She gave me a little wave and then Donte swept her into the crowd of dancers.

River offered me his hand. "Want to dance?"

I forced a smile. "Sure."

We squeezed onto the crowded dancefloor and were engulfed in the energy and music. River leaned in. "How am I doing compared to Homecoming?"

"Well, considering you never showed up for that one…"

He laughed. "I had nowhere to go but up."

I laughed too, and we danced. One song after another, both of us trying to forget what was coming—college, separations, distance between us and what we loved. Over the course of the night, River was a perfect gentleman, bringing me hors d'oeuvres and sparkling water when we needed to refuel.

The DJ then announced it was time to reveal the Prom King and Queen, and we took our seats at one of the dozen large round tables.

I leaned into River. "Do you have your speech planned?"

He shook his head. "I don't think it's gonna be me."

"Who else would it be?"

He shrugged. "Guess we're about to find out."

Vice Principal Chouder took the stage, microphone in hand, and introduced Layla Calderon and her Prom Committee. The nominees for Queen were read—the usual suspects, and my name was unsurprisingly absent. I didn't care except that it was a symptom of the failing friendship between Caitlin, Julia, and me.

Or maybe that was all a figment of my imagination.

Then Layla quieted the crowd. “Your Santa Cruz Central High Prom Queen is…”

The DJ played in electric version of a drum roll.

“Evelyn Gonzalez!”

Applause and cheers went up, and Evelyn took the stage looking radiant and triumphant. And not at all surprised. She and Layla hugged and kissed, and then Layla hung a sash over Evelyn’s dress while another girl placed a tall tiara on her head.

“It’s like a beauty pageant my little sister watches on TLC. *Toddlers and Tiaras*?”

I smothered a laugh with my hand. “Careful now. You’re up next.”

Layla took center stage again. “And now, I am *beyond* excited to announce your Central High Prom King…Miller Stratton!”

The ballroom went wild, a chorus of girls screaming and cheering the loudest.

Shock ripped through me, leaving me dazed. I looked around for Miller with everyone else, wondering if he was going to come striding through the crowd to take his crown.

“Well that’s something,” River said. “Did you know that was going to happen?”

“I had no idea.”

The cheers died down into confused mutterings, everyone still looking for Miller. Evelyn said something to Layla, and Layla handed her the microphone.

“Miller can’t be here tonight to accept his crown, but I assure you he has a *very* good reason.” Evelyn paused for effect. “He just signed a record deal with Gold Line Records!”

The ballroom erupted all over again, girls clasping hands and jumping up and down with excited, knowing smiles. It was irrational—they only knew him from the videos—but there was a familiarity in their reaction that felt as if they were taking something of him away from me. Evelyn especially beamed as if she’d given him to them like a benevolent queen throwing scraps to her subjects.

“Guess I’ll be playing your King’s own jams at the next party,” the DJ chimed in. “Give it up for your King and Queen, Miller Stratton and Evelyn Gonzalez!”

The crowd cheered louder, and Evelyn threw both arms in the air triumphantly.

I felt sick. A few heads turned to look at me curiously. Piteously. Some knew that Miller and I were together, but most did not. My cheeks ached to keep my smile in place as a strange feeling came over me. That Miller belonged to them. To Evelyn. She had taken possession of him, claimed his success for her own. She'd been the one who propelled him to the record deal, but the feeling in my stomach was green and twisty, and I hated it.

"You okay?" River asked.

"Fine. It's just been a crazy couple of days."

To say the least.

"Yeah, no kidding." He studied me closer. "But for real, you look like you need some air. Or maybe a drink?"

"Water would be great."

"On it." River got up and then froze, his gaze snagging on something over my shoulder. His face hardened into a grimace, even as his eyes softened.

I turned around and saw Holden Parish leaning casually against a wall, dashing in a long coat, the collar turned up, with a vest over a button-down shirt. But his shirt was loose at the collar, his hair disheveled. He scanned the scene with dull eyes, sipping from a flask.

Then his gaze landed on River. A strange smile came over his sharply handsome features. He tilted the flask back, drained it, then hurled it at the drink table.

I jumped in my seat and River muttered a curse as the metal flask smashed into a row of sparkling water and apple cider, shattering one bottle and sending bubbly water spewing. Surprised cries rang out, and the faculty started looking around for the culprit. But Holden had already stormed out.

I looked quickly to River. His face was a mask of anguish. And longing.

"I told him I was going to Alabama…" He swallowed hard. "And that he couldn't come with me."

I put my hand on his arm. "Go."

River blinked and stared down at me. "What? No…"

"Go to him."

"That'll make me two-for-two in ditching you at a dance."

I smiled. "Strike three and you're out."

"Violet…"

"I don't feel so well, anyway. I'm going to go."

"Will you be okay? No, fuck that. I can't leave you."

"I'll be fine. *Go*." I took his hand and gave it a gentle squeeze. "Don't lose him, River."

"I think it's too late," he said heavily, his smile sad. "But thank you."

River kissed me on the cheek and strode quickly out the side door where Holden had gone.

I made my way out of the gym, too, stopping to talk to a few friends from the soccer team and the math club. Each conversation felt more and more forced, until finally I was able to slip out and call an Uber. My head rested against the cool glass in the car. I wanted to climb in bed, pull the covers up and get out from under this heavy sadness.

"Which one?" the Uber driver asked.

"That one," I said. "The one with the For Sale sign in the front."

Worst…birthday…ever, I thought and had to laugh so I wouldn't cry.

The house was quiet. Mom was probably in her room and Dad in the den, where I could see the blue light of the TV flickering under the door. I went up to my bedroom and struggled to undo the buttons on my dress. I wiped off my make-up, pulled down my hair, and changed into my sleep shorts and a T-shirt.

For a long time, I lay staring at the ceiling, thinking about what came next. Moving to Texas. Miller moving to Los Angeles to make his record. My parents moving to opposite ends of the country to get away from each other. So many roads that once ran parallel now diverging, and I had no idea where mine would take me. Or how far from Miller.

I'd nearly fallen asleep, when the familiar creak came from outside my bedroom window on the trellis. It was open to let in the summer air, and then Miller was there. He climbed through and hopped off my desk, setting his bags and his guitar case on the floor.

I shot up to sitting, my eyes and heart drinking him in. "You're here."

"I hope it's okay I came. I can't go home."

I scrambled out of bed and rushed to him, threw my arms around him, concealing my turmoil against his neck.

"Hey…" He stroked my hair. "What is it? What's wrong?"

I shook my head against his chest and pulled myself together. "Nothing. God, Miller, I'm so happy for you. Tell me everything."

He pulled back; his beautiful topaz eyes were lit up, and for the first time in a long time, he looked happy. The heavy burden of poverty lifting off of him just a little.

"I can't fucking believe it," he said. "They talked to me for a while and then took me into a studio. They wanted to get something down that day. To test me out, or…I don't know what." He gave his head a disbelieving shake, then his gaze softened. "I sang 'Yellow.' Our song. Because it was the first song I ever performed in front of someone else. For you, Violet. You are the reason this happened for me."

I shook my head. "It was Evelyn. Her vlog—"

"No," he said fiercely, holding my face in his hands. "You believed in me first. You didn't wait for a thousand views or a hundred comments. You've known who I was from the beginning. You accepted me, dirt poor and stinking of the station wagon." He moved in closer, his gaze boring intently into mine. "I'm going to make this album, and every fucking song is going to be for you. Every one."

My eyes fell shut, and I leaned into him, my hands on his waist, letting him prop me up. Feeling the solidity of him. He sensed something deeper was happening in me, as he always did.

"Vi?" He pulled back and his expression fell to see my tears. "I know. It's going to suck being in LA, away from you. But I can jump on a plane and be here in an hour."

"I want you to kiss me, Miller. Please." His concerned frown lingered, so I brought my lips to his and kissed him. Softly, then harder. Seeking entry. Needing to lose myself in him.

My ardor woke his and his mouth took over the kiss, devouring mine. Our tongues slid against one another in perfect tandem, perfect rhythm; our heads moving side to side, breathing in sync. In harmony.

Because we just fit.

He pulled away breathlessly. "Jesus, I almost forgot. Happy Birthday, Vi."

"You know what that means."

"I do," he said, his eyes darkening, his Adam's apple bobbing in his throat. "You sure?"

I wasn't sure of anything anymore except him. He had to know about Baylor, but not yet. We didn't have to do anything but this.

We breathed together, our eyes locked in the thickness of the moment. Our lips touched and retreated; another look from Miller, checking in. And then we kissed long and deep. Like drinking from each other. Slow kisses that left no room for breath, and I poured myself into every one of them. I filled my hands with his hair, his broad shoulders over his T-shirt, down to the small of his back. But still, I felt his hesitation with desire simmering beneath.

"Touch me, Miller," I whispered. "Touch me everywhere."

The certainty in my words set him free. He lifted my shirt over my head, my hair falling around my shoulders. His hooded gaze swept over me, leaving shivers in its wake.

"So beautiful," he said, his hands full of my breasts, his lips hot against the delicate skin of my neck. "I want this so much."

A little sound fell from my lips to hear such nakedly vulnerable words in his rough voice. "Me too."

Then more kissing until we'd come to the end of chaste touches. I lifted his shirt off and drank him in, my hands on him everywhere, down to the CGM implant.

"Will it be safe?"

"I think so," he said. "I don't know, actually. I've never done this before."

"I still can't believe you waited for me."

He shrugged with a small smile. "You waited for me. We waited for each other, because when you push all the bullshit aside, who else is there? There's no one for me but you. There never was."

He kissed me again, our bodies molded together, his body a wall of muscle under warm skin, his hands rough as they slid up and down my back. He'd worked so hard with those hands, carried so much on his shoulders, and pride filled me that I was going to give him this night.

I went to the bed, pulling him with me, and lay back. The weight of him felt so good. So solid and real, anchoring me into the present moment when my thoughts wanted to drift away to a future in which we'd be miles apart.

He kissed me deeply and with such reverence. Our bodies responding to each other without thought. Instinct only. My hips arched up to meet his while his ground down into me, like they did the last time he was here. This time, anticipation of the *more* that was coming electrified every moment. Unexplored sensations and untouched skin, waiting.

He undid the buttons on his jeans while I slipped off my shorts. He kicked off his underwear while I slid my panties down and tossed them aside.

A flash of heat swept through me along with a tinge of nervous anticipation at the sight of his penis, huge and erect, but he quickly moved to lay over me. My heart was pounding, and it seemed I could feel every part of Miller. I could hear his blood pumping in his veins, feel every slight move and vibration of his body: his bones and flesh and sinew. I felt all of it over me, and I wanted him inside me. I wanted that masculine power, the essence of him, moving and taking.

We kissed and touched until our bodies were both on the brink, crossing the line of hesitation into pure want. He sat up and I sat up with him, naked on my bed. I stared at the size of him, shocked at my own calmness. I felt feminine and womanly in the face of his masculinity. I placed my hand over his heart, felt it beating hard, then moved down his chest, to the magnificent, hard length of him. I wrapped my fingers around its girth, and he made a tight sound in his chest. He seemed to grow bigger in my hand as I stroked him hesitantly.

"Does this feel good?"

He nodded wordlessly. "Everything you do feels good."

Miller kissed me while I stroked him, and his hand slipped between my legs, feeling the heat and wetness he'd already created in me.

"Jesus, Vi."

"I want you," I whispered. "Now."

His eyes searched mine again, his breath trembling over his lips.

I nodded. "Yes."

He kissed me softly, then grabbed for a condom out of his wallet and rolled it down. I lay back, taking him with me. He positioned himself at the center of me, his body thrumming and vibrating over me. I brought my knees up, letting him in, my hands gripping his hips as he guided himself into me, one inch at a time.

My breath hitched at the pain.

"I'm hurting you."

"Don't stop. Please, don't stop."

Slowly, he pushed in farther, and I felt myself stretching to contain him, tearing open to take all of him. The pain was grating and rough but beautiful, too, and it subsided quickly.

"God, Vi," he whispered. "I had no idea..."

"Me either," I breathed back. We were utterly safe and private, sharing this experience completely with no one else in the room.

"Does it feel okay?" I asked him tentatively. Tightly.

He nodded against my neck. "Incredible. You feel incredible."

We kissed again, easier now. I was adjusting to the feel of him inside me, my body getting used to the size and heavy hardness of him. Slowly, he pulled out and then pushed back in. Over and over.

I bit my lip at the sensations, the fading pain and a faint ache of pleasure, like a promise waiting to burn brighter another time. His slow, careful thrusts quickly became more. He moved faster, kissing me constantly, holding my face, and asking me if I was all right. He never let me forget that he wasn't losing himself in his own pleasure until finally the words melted away.

I wrapped my legs around Miller's body, anchoring him to me as he moved inside me. My arms clutched his neck and my fingers in his hair that was damp with sweat.

He grunted, jaw clenched. "Vi…"

"Come," I managed. "Come inside me."

My words sent him over. Miller's body shuddered against mine, his face contorted in a pleasure-pain expression. A few final, erratic thrusts, and then he collapsed over me.

Tears gathered in the corners of my eyes and spilled down my cheeks as I wrapped my arms around him, feeling his naked chest expand against mine as we caught our breath. I held onto him, clung to him and this moment, this experience of having him and giving myself to him. He was mine. He'd always been mine since the day we met and maybe even before that.

The sun was going to rise on a new day and take him away from me, but for those delirious moments and the handful of hours that came after, I had him, and it was perfect.

CHAPTER TWENTY-THREE

VIOLET

As the morning light streamed in from the window, I woke up with Miller wrapped around me. My body ached in the best way. I held onto the feeling, relished it. He'd been inside me, and I could still feel him there. My first.

My only.

I shut my eyes and snuggled closer to him, my back to his chest. His arm around me and his breath, deep and even in sleep, against my neck. I started to drift off again when my phone vibrated with a call amongst the pile of our discarded clothes.

Sleepily, I peered down to see Evelyn's name. I started to ignore it, but then, why would she call me? To gloat? Or was it an emergency?

I stretched out of Miller's embrace and grabbed the phone. I curled to the edge of the bed and kept my voice low.

"Hey, Evelyn, what is it?"

A short silence. "Violet?"

"Yes." I frowned. "Did you mean to call someone else?"

"I'm calling Miller. Isn't this his phone?"

"What? No…" I examined the phone I held and realized she was right. "Oh, sorry. I was half asleep."

"Is he there?"

"He is," I said tightly. "Sleeping."

If it shocked or upset Evelyn to know Miller and I were in bed together, she didn't show it. "Okay, don't wake him. Just pass on the message that I'm ready to go whenever he is. Oh, and tell him, thanks again! Ciao!"

The phone went quiet, and I stared at it for a few moments. The screen reverted back to its locked position, but a text notification was there, the start of the message visible. From Evelyn, sent last night.

You did it, baby!! xoxoxoxo…

I set the phone on the nightstand and lay on my back.

Ready to go…where?

Miller slept for another few minutes then slowly came awake. He glanced around confused, sleep still clinging to him, and his gaze landed on me. The smile that came over him to see me was so beautiful and soft…and short-lived.

"What is it? Was last night…? Was it too much?"

"Last night was perfect."

He looked almost shy. "I thought so too. But what's wrong?"

"Evelyn called you," I said, sitting up against the headboard and tucking the sheet around me. "I answered your phone by mistake. She said to tell you she's ready to go whenever you are."

Miller's head fell back, and he rolled his eyes at the ceiling. "Goddamn her."

"What is she talking about?"

He sat up beside me, covering himself to the waist, and ran a hand through his tousled hair. "She's talking about Los Angeles. I promised her that if I signed a contract, I'd take her with me to record the album. As my personal assistant."

My skin went cold all over, while my cheeks burned as if I'd been slapped.

"Why…why would you do that? Do you need a personal assistant?"

"I don't need anything," he said. "It's for her. To get her foot in the door. To make her own connections and then she's gone. I wouldn't have even entertained the idea except she needs…help. I can't tell you more. I promised her I wouldn't." He bit off a curse. "I know how it looks—"

"How does it look, Miller?" I asked, my voice cracking. "Are you going to be *living* with her?"

"No. I don't know where I'm going to live, but… no. There's nothing between us, I swear. And yes, I can hear myself. I sound like a fucking jackass. I was going to tell you first and explain everything."

"Why didn't you tell me before you left? How long have you and she been planning this?"

"Nothing's planned. She made me promise before I left. Literally, on the way to the airport. It sounded crazy and impossible, but, then again, so did getting a record deal in the first place."

I shook my head and climbed out of bed, feeling more naked than I was. I quickly pulled on a T-shirt and my shorts.

"Talk to me, Vi," Miller said. He cleared his throat. "I thought you trusted me."

"I don't trust *her.* She plays the long game, Miller. It took her the entire school year to get back at me for being Homecoming Queen, but she did it. And somehow arranged for you to be Prom King."

He made a face, then snorted. "No way. That's fucking ridiculous."

"It's true. You didn't see it. *Her*. Taking ownership of you in front of the entire school. In front of me. It was humiliating. But more than that…it just hurt."

Miller rummaged on the floor for his underwear, pulled them on, and then came to me.

"I'm sorry, Vi. I don't know what she's doing, except that I wouldn't have a contract if not for her. And right this second, I fucking need it. They gave me money. An advance. I can give it to my mom and get rid of Chet." He tentatively held both my shoulders. "I swear, I belong to you. And I know it feels like a slap in the face. I can see it in your eyes, and I…" He bit off his words, frustration and pain suffusing him. He swallowed hard. "I'm in love with you. Nothing can ever change that."

"She's going to try," I said in a small voice.

"And fail. She's going to fail because I won't even *let* her try."

Jealousy and self-doubt rampaged in me. But I knew Miller. Once he'd made a promise, he kept it. He promised to help Evelyn and I couldn't ask him not to keep it.

"I have to trust you," I said. "Or we have nothing."

Miller pulled me into him, wrapping me in his strong embrace. His voice rumbled in my ear that was pressed to his warm, bare chest. "You can trust me. I'm doing her a favor, that's all. You'll be an hour away. I'll visit you, or you can visit me this summer, before your classes start. And the very fucking second the album's done, I'll come back—"

"I won't be here."

His arms around me stiffened. "What, why?"

"My parents are divorcing and selling the house. There's no money for UCSC, so I'm going to Texas. Baylor's going to pay my tuition."

"Texas," he said, letting me go and slumping to sit on the edge of the bed. "Jesus. When did this happen?"

"I found out yesterday. They're broke. There's nothing left."

He shook his head, eyes on the ground. "I'm sorry, Vi. And UCSC. I know that was your dream."

I sat on the bed next to him. "What are we going to do?"

"I don't know. Gold Line is going to make an EP, and if the timing works out, there's talk of a tour. I'd join Ed Sheeran as an opening act."

"Ed Sheeran? My God… That's huge," I said, wondering how my heart could swell with happiness and break at the same time.

"It's not a sure thing but shit, Vi. I thought that would be the hardest thing to deal with. Being apart from you for that long." His eyes widened at a sudden thought, and he turned to me, taking my hand. "Come with me."

"Where? To Los Angeles?"

"Yes, and if the tour happens, you come with me then too."

"What about my school?"

"Just for a year. Jack Villegas, the guy at Gold Line, he really fucking believes in me, Vi. Just like you do. Maybe I'll make enough money to pay for your college. Next year, you can go to UCSC or UCLA. We can make it work."

He was so full of hope after years of mistrust and doubt. But I shook my head.

"I can't," I said.

His face fell, his eyes hardening. "Because of Evelyn?"

"Not just her, but yes, that's part of it. She'll at least have a job. A purpose. What would I do? Tag along after the two of you? And what about my own plans? Accepting Baylor's offer is going to help my med school applications. Because I still have about ten more years of college ahead of me. I have to stay sharp. I can't take a year off or put it on hold."

His gaze hardened, his jaw tight. "Then I can. I can call up Jack and—"

"Absolutely not," I said. "You have to go and make that album, and I have to pursue my goals. You can't pay for them, and I can't abandon them for a year to follow you around. I'd be miserable."

"Miserable," he stated. "You'd be with me."

Tears filled my eyes. "Miller…"

"No, I get it. It's not enough," he said and I could hear the words he didn't.

I'm not enough. Again.

The thought was loud in his eyes, swimming with memories of another time someone left him.

"Miller, wait," I said as he began throwing on his clothes. "We need to keep talking. Sort this out."

"I can't. I gotta go. Mom's dealt with Chet long enough."

He drew on his boots, shouldered his bag, hefted his guitar case. When he was dressed, he stood in front of me, his tone hard.

"We'll talk later."

He bent and kissed my head, a short peck, and started to turn. I grabbed his hand and stood up, facing him, and waited until he met my unflinching gaze. Immediately, his steely blue eyes softened. He dropped his bags and case and wrapped his arms around me.

Wordlessly, we held each other. At an impasse. Our love for each other melding us together, while circumstance pulled us apart.

After a few moments, he picked up his bags again and left.

I sank back down on my bed, where my blood stained the sheets. Vivid evidence that last night had happened, though it felt like I'd woken to discover it had all been a dream.

CHAPTER TWENTY-FOUR

MILLER

"It's a highly unusual circumstance for us to cut a check to a new artist on the same day we meet him."

Jack Villegas reminded me of Andy Garcia. Tall. Sharp. Authoritative but kind. We sat on opposite sides of the polished desk in his office that had a view of the Hollywood sign. His brown eyes went to the abrasion on my cheek and the fingerprints on my neck. I'd tried to keep them covered, but LA was hot, and I'd left Holden's scarf in the hotel.

"But your situation is a little bit special, isn't it?" He rose to his feet and paced around the desk. Cufflinks glinted in the Los Angeles sun, and his gray suit probably cost more than six months of my rent. "You're a rare talent. A little more angst than Shawn Mendes, a little less than Bon Iver. But you have that intangible quality, that magnetic pull that makes listeners feel connected to you. You have a story to tell, don't you?"

He didn't wait for an answer because he already had it. I heard his words before he spoke them; a reverse echo that felt like a dream until he made it real.

"That's why we're signing you, Miller. And because we like to consider all of our clients part of the family, you're leaving here with some money." He put his hand on my shoulder, like a father might to his son. "We take care of our own."

On the bus from Violet's neighborhood to mine, I could practically feel the check for $20,000 sitting heavy in my wallet. I felt like a thief and imagined the police surrounding the bus and pulling it over, hauling me out and arresting me. Jack Villegas would somehow be there, saying it had all been a huge mistake.

Stupid shit to be thinking about, but it was better than facing the reality of Violet moving to Texas. I needed to keep my mind occupied. The first order of business that morning was to get rid of Chet and sign over that check to Mom.

But Violet saturated my thoughts. Sense memories of sleeping with her for the first time seeped in and pushed out everything else, even the memory of sitting in a record exec's office as he tells me he's going to give me a brand-new life.

The bus rolled and jounced, and in my mind, Violet was under me in her bed. Beautiful and perfect. I'd loved her for so long, fantasized about that night in a hundred different ways. But being naked with her, being inside her, was better than any fevered imagining. She'd created sensations in me a million times more potent than anything I'd ever been able to give myself in all those fruitless years of wanting her.

And now, I was losing her.

Again, I yanked my thoughts away from her.

One shitstorm at a time, thanks.

The bus stopped at Lighthouse Apartments. I got out but kept walking down to the Shack to stow my bag and my guitar. I took my insulin with a meal of an apple, a bag of Fritos, and a bottle of water I'd bought at the airport the night before. Breakfast of Champions.

When I finished, I pulled out my phone and texted Ronan and Holden.

Let's roll.

In front of my apartment door, I sucked in a breath, blew it out on a shaky exhale, then cracked my neck from side to side, like a fighter getting ready for a match. Holden stood pressed against the wall on the left. Ronan on the right. He gave me a nod, his eyes flat and emotionless, but I felt the power emanating off of him like a low heat.

Holden was dressed as impeccably as ever, although his clothes look rumpled and slept in. His eyes were red rimmed and swollen, and he stunk of stale alcohol and bonfire smoke. As if he'd passed out on some beach last night.

"You up to this?" I whispered.

He shot me a tired wink. "Forward my mail, tell my story, I'm not coming back."

Despite the pit of fear gnawing a hole in my stomach, I snorted a laugh, then sucked in another breath. I knocked on the door to my own apartment.

It opened a crack, and Mom peered out. Her eyes widened for a moment with joy and then shut down again with fear. "Miller. You're back."

"Is he here?

"Yeah, he's—"

The door pulled open all the way, and Chet filled the space. "Go lie down, Lynn. I'll handle this."

Mom looked at me uncertainly. I gave her a nearly imperceptible nod, hoping she would do as he said and take shelter from the storm that was coming. She hesitated, then retreated into the darkness of the apartment.

It took everything I had not to glance at Ronan and Holden, standing like sentries on either side of the door frame.

"You need to get out of my house."

"You don't live here anymore, son. You're a grown man now and can't be leeching off your mom. Now go on."

He started to shut the door, and I blocked it with my boot, at the same time Ronan swung around from the wall, throwing the door all the way open with a *bang*. He strode into the house, gripping Chet by the collar of his shirt and driving him backwards as he went. Chet gave a shout of surprise, stumbled, and fell on his ass.

"Who the fuck are you? You can't be in here!"

Ronan stood over him, still and hard as stone, hands balled into fists, his eyes like a snake's before it struck.

"We're your unwelcome wagon," Holden said, leaning casually against the door, examining his nails. "As in, you are no longer welcome here, fuck-nugget."

Chet's panicked glance went between them as he scrambled to his feet. "Get the hell out of my house."

"You good?" I asked Ronan.

"I got this." His gaze hadn't moved from Chet for a second.

I went to go around them in the small space.

"Where do you think you're going?"

Chet's hand shot out to grab me, and Ronan was there. Like a statue come to life, his fist shot out, connecting square with Chet's flabby cheek. Chet snarled, cursed and flew at Ronan, tackling him to the ground. The two became a tangle of arms and legs, grappling and grasping, cursing and grunting.

"We're good." Holden waved his hand. "He'll tag me in if he needs me."

I nodded and hurried down the short hall, nearly crashing into Mom.

"Miller, don't do this. Please."

"Do you love him?"

"N-no," she said in a small voice. Then louder. "No."

"Good." I went past her into their bedroom as the sounds of our coffee table being demolished came from the living room. "This his bag?"

Mom nodded at the dirty red duffel bag in my hand.

I handed it to her. "Pack up his stuff," I said and went back to the living room.

Ronan had Chet pinned to the floor face down, one knee in between Chet's shoulder blades, the other on his elbow. He had a fistful of greasy hair and was pressing his face sideways to the floor.

"I'll fucking kill you," Chet seethed, his face smashed, spittle flying.

"How we doing out here?" I asked.

"Well, it was touch and go for a second," Holden observed from the door, dabbing a handkerchief to his bleeding lip. "Chester, here, had Ronan pinned, which caused me to heroically jump into the fray and take an elbow to the mouth. My mistake. Ronan was going easy on him to prolong the violence. You know our boy. He needs to get it out of his system every now and again."

I shook my head at Ronan who shrugged one shoulder.

Mom emerged from the back bedroom with a duffel bag full of Chet's stuff. I took it from her and joined Ronan in the center of our smashed living room.

"Let him up."

Ronan released Chet, his eyes never leaving him, clearly ready—maybe hoping—for more of a fight. I shoved Chet's bag into his arms.

"I'll say it one more time. Get the fuck out of my house."

He hesitated for a second, which was one second too long for Ronan. He grabbed Chet by the front of his shirt with both hands and drove him toward the door.

Holden opened it smoothly. "Thank you for choosing Ronan Air for all your travel needs. Please watch your step as you exit, as you could be in for a rough landing."

Jesus, Ronan is going to kill him.

But instead of throwing Chet down the cement stairs as I feared, Ronan gripped him by the shirt collar and tipped him backwards over the balcony.

Chet's arms pinwheeled. "Are you fucking crazy?"

"I live less than a block away from here," Ronan said. "I'll be watching you. If you step foot anywhere near this place again, I will end you. Do you hear me? I will fucking end you."

Slowly, he released him, their eyes never breaking contact as the older man jerked his shirt back into place.

He shot me a pained look. "You needed a man in the house. I did my best. That's all."

"*Your best* was sorely lacking, Chester," Holden observed.

Chet's lip curled but he didn't have any more fight in him. He took the stairs down, muttering and cursing impotently.

Ronan stepped back into the apartment. Holden shut the door. A short silence passed, the four of us absorbing what had just happened.

Then Holden clapped his hands together. "Who could go for some pancakes right about now?"

I shook my head, affection and gratitude for both my friends flooding me, calming the adrenaline rush.

"Can you guys give me a minute? Meet me at the Shack."

Ronan nodded and looked to my mom. "Ma'am."

Holden tipped an imaginary cap. "Good day, madam."

When they were gone, I went with Mom to the couch, stepping over the ruined remains of our coffee table. She stared at the mess fearfully, not fully grasping yet that she was free.

"Mom," I said. "Look at me. Gold Line Records gave me a contract. They want me. I don't know how or why…" My throat was suddenly choked with emotion that was finally bubbling to the surface. Elation. Fear. All of it. I swallowed hard, tears stinging my eyes. "Things are going to be different now, okay?"

"Oh, baby," she said, her brown eyes filling too. "I'm so proud of you. I know I haven't been here for you the way I should—"

"It's okay. I can take care of myself, and I'm going to take care of you. But you're right, you haven't been here. You haven't been *you.* I need you to come back, okay? I need… I need you."

I couldn't stop it. I tried to hold my breath, but the sobs came bursting out of me. Mom put her arms around me and hugged me and held me like she used to when I was a kid. Before Dad left and her every waking hour had been about survival.

"You're right," she said, holding me close, stroking my hair. "I'm sorry. It just got too hard. Losing our house in Los Banos. The car. You being sick. I felt like anything could be taken away at any second. Including you."

I raised my head, shocked to hear my own familiar thoughts repeated back to me. "I felt it too. But we can't live that way. We have to keep going."

I have to somehow keep going, without Violet.

I wiped my tears on the sleeve of my shirt.

"I'm going to LA, and I want you to come with me. I'll get you set up in a new place. A better place than this, okay?"

"That sounds good, baby. Real good."

For the first time in a long time, there was a light in her eyes and a little bit of color to her skin where there had only been gray.

It happened all at once.

Two weeks after we threw Chet out on his ass, we all graduated from SC Central—Ronan by the skin of his teeth. Holden with Honors thanks to his IQ and not because he ever studied a day in his life. Violet was class Valedictorian. Her parents sold their house, and the next day, she was going to drive her SUV packed with stuff to Texas. That same day, I was getting on a plane to Los Angeles with Evelyn. She'd wanted to ride with me to the airport, but I insisted on meeting her there.

I had to say my goodbyes.

Ronan, Holden, Violet, and Shiloh all gathered at the Shack. The afternoon was overcast and gray, reflecting our collective mood.

Holden was uncharacteristically subdued and quiet, hardly saying a word. After I heard everything that had happened to him on Prom night, I worried about him the most.

Violet sat in the sand in front of me in our customary position, her back to my chest, my arms wrapped around her. We'd spent the last few days either at her house, so I could help her pack or mine, so she could help me. Not that I had much.

Nights were spent in her bed, her taking me inside her wordlessly, sometimes desperately. Kissing and touching and grasping, as if trying to take a piece of the other with us, as the days grew closer to this one.

The sun began to set over the ocean, and it was time to go. Shiloh gave me a hug and a kiss first. "Be safe. Do good."

Holden gave me a hug that was saturated in expensive vodka. "If you ever need anything and I hear that you didn't ask me first, I will personally hunt you down and kill you."

I smiled and hugged him back. "I don't need anything but for you to take care of yourself, okay?"

"Me?" He scoffed. "I'm a paragon of good life choices."

"My ass." And then I hugged him again, a sudden fear that I'd never see him again, washing over me. "I mean it. Take care."

"Careful, Stratton, or I'll have to assume you're in love with me."

But I was, in a way. Him and Ronan both. Leaving them was nearly as hard as leaving Violet.

Ronan clasped my hand and pulled me in until our elbows touched. "I'll watch your mom's place until you get set up down there."

"Thanks, man. Shouldn't be long."

"However long it takes."

My damn heart ached, and I was perilously close to tears. I had to say something ridiculous, stat.

"Promise me, Ronan. Promise to write to me every day."

Ronan barked a laugh. "Get the fuck out of here." He gave me a shove, though I didn't miss the almost-smile my dumb joke got out of him.

Violet drove me to the airport, up the winding 14 highway, through the forest that led out of Santa Cruz. Before she got to the highway that would take us to the airport terminals in San Jose, she abruptly pulled her SUV into a restaurant parking lot.

"Vi?"

"The police at the airport won't let me stay and hug you and kiss you as much as I need to. So I have to say goodbye here..." She flapped her hand at the restaurant sign. "In a Denny's parking lot, for God's sake. And I don't want to say goodbye at all."

I reached over and pulled her to me and held her for the longest time. Stroking her hair, inhaling her scent, memorizing how she felt in my arms, how good it felt to be held by her.

For the millionth time, the words to beg her to come with me rose to my lips. But I couldn't hear *no* again. And she'd be right. She was going to be a brilliant doctor and had a long road of medical school before she could even begin a career. Mine was taking off like a shotgun, hers was a long runway. I couldn't stand in her way.

Even so, it gnawed at my guts that she wouldn't come with me. Wasn't logical, wasn't fair; I had to be one of the luckiest bastards alive to have a record deal right out of the gate, and yet, in that moment, I was so close to throwing it all away and going with *her* to Texas.

As I held her and kissed her, a different future rolled out in front of me.

We'd get a place together. I'd get a job while she went to class. Hell, I'd get two jobs to help support her, so she wouldn't have to work at all. She could concentrate on being a student and then come home and fall into bed with me. Long lazy Sundays in the Texas heat, sweating between the sheets. I'd make her come so hard, her cries would fill the space of our place that was just hers and mine. I could play small clubs on the weekends and build my career piece by piece, instead of being slingshot into the stratosphere. I never wanted fame. I wanted my mom in a safe place, not one crawling with roaches and no AC. I wanted a little piece of security, and I wanted Violet.

Part of me felt like the universe was playing a tremendous prank on me, dumping riches in my lap while taking away my greatest treasure.

I kissed her and tasted her salty tears.

"Miller," she said brokenly, her hand in my hair, our foreheads pressed together. "It feels like the other half of my heart is being ripped away."

"I'll call you every day," I said. "We'll visit as much as we can, okay? Weekends, vacations, holidays." The words sounded hollow and inadequate, even in my own ears. I wanted her all the time, every minute, in my arms, in my bed, in my life.

The twinge of bitterness in my stomach grew and expanded. And I worried how big it would be a month from now. Or three, or six.

"Okay," she said, though I could read the doubt in her eyes too. The pain of enduring a long-distance relationship when we had only just begun to explore what we were to each other.

We kissed, and she cried, until I was in danger of missing my flight. But Violet would never let that happen. She pulled herself together and took me to the airport. At the curb, I held her close one last time.

"Call me when you get there."

"I will." I kissed her a final time, pouring myself into it, into her, trying desperately to seal a pact—the hope that we could make it.

Then the police officer was asking us to move it along.

I let her go, and she made her way back to her car.

"Violet," I called, my voice rough. "You're going to be an incredible doctor someday."

She stopped, alarmed; fresh tears came to her eyes at the strange tone in my voice and finality in my choice of words. I hardly understood them myself.

"I'll see you soon," she said firmly, as if trying to patch a hole I'd torn in our hope. She quickly got in her car and drove away.

I waited, watching her go, until the white SUV was lost in a sea of other cars. Until finally, I couldn't see her anymore.

PART IV

November—

It's been a while since I've written in this old thing, but desperate times and all... Okay, I'm not actually desperate. Just lonely. Desperately lonely.

Miller finished his EP and of course it shot straight to the top of every chart. Before he knew what was happening, they whisked him away on tour to open for Ed Sheeran. I saw the show in Austin two nights ago and I still get goosebumps thinking about it. Miller was just... I have no words. To see him on a real stage with a band behind him and thousands of fans was extraordinary. They were Ed's fans, but by the end of the first song, they were Miller's too. I must've looked like the crazed, obsessed groupie in the front row, crying her eyes out before he even sang a note. It was magic. It was where he belonged.

We hung out backstage with Ed Sheeran—he's lovely—and then we went to the hotel. I'm not going to lie; the sex was amazing. With Miller, not Ed Sheeran ;-) Miller was electric and humming and I could feel the energy still pulsing in him. He carried that sweaty, sexy aura he had on stage—pouring his heart out to the crowd—right into bed, pouring himself into me. That was a kind of magic too.

But the next morning he had to get on the bus to Dallas and I had to go back to Waco. We don't know when we'll see each other again. He'll be on tour with Ed for at least six months and then the label wants him back in the studio. I'm trying to stay positive, but I miss him so much. He calls as often as he can, but it's hard.

And as hard as we knew it was going to be, it's so much harder than that.

May—

Another plan made, another cancellation. This is the fifth time Miller and I have tried to carve out a little piece of time only to have the plans fall through due to his crazy schedule. Not that I'm counting or anything. Okay, so I totally am. Since we left Santa Cruz, Miller and I have spent a grand total of thirteen days together, scattered over eleven months.

He finished the tour with Ed Sheeran and I thought he'd have a little time off between it and recording his full-length album. But there are music videos to shoot, and publicity events, and if the album sells well, headlining his own tour will come next.

I'm really trying not to be the clingy, needy girlfriend waiting for her man by the phone. Not that Miller makes me feel that way. He never misses our nightly call unless he's on a plane. His schedule is grueling but then so is mine. Last January I couldn't be with him as he accepted his Best New Artist Grammy because I had a massive research paper due. I watched it on TV. He took his mom as his date and in his speech he thanked me. Not by name; we avoid that to keep from paparazzi showing up on my doorstep.

He called me the girl in his love songs.

I cried so hard my roommate, Veronica, thought I was having a stroke. Tears for missing him, tears for loving him so much that every second we were apart was starting to feel like we were going against the natural order of the universe.

Veronica comforted me with a quote she likes: Change is hard in the beginning, messy in the middle, and beautiful at the end. I don't know if this is the beginning or the middle. It's hard and messy. It's long stretches of not seeing each other punctuated by a stolen weekend here and there that ends with another heartbreaking goodbye.

I can only hope she's right, that all this heartache is worth it and that it'll be beautiful in the end.

October—

I haven't written much in here lately. I've been too busy; my studies get harder with every passing semester. But being that busy helps keep me occupied, so I don't spend every waking hours missing Miller.

Of course that's not true. I miss him always. Every minute is colored slightly by not having him. I probably sound dramatic, writing stuff like that, but this is my outlet. Miller's is his music. As everyone predicted, his first full-length album, Out of Reach, went triple platinum. It's beautiful and I can hear us in it. Our distance and our hard goodbyes.

He's in Europe now, headlining his own world tour. The last time I saw him was a month ago. The label set him free for an entire weekend before kickoff. We hid away in a cabin in Lake Tahoe to avoid the press, desperate to make the most of those forty-eight hours. He looked so tired. Exhausted. He loves his fans and playing live but the rest of it is overwhelming. I told him he was allowed to enjoy his success and take care of himself better, but he's determined to do this tour. He's negotiated that half of his profits will go to a charity that feeds the homeless and helps find them housing.

I do this and it all makes sense, he told me. Then I can look myself in the mirror every morning.

I loved him for that, even more than I thought possible. He asked me to wait for him and I promised him I would. Of course, I did. Because I'm the one who has to do the waiting. I can't jet off with him; I have my own work and my own goals to accomplish so I can be proud of myself.

We kissed and made love, and then he was gone again, and now there's nothing I can do but wait.

CHAPTER TWENTY-FIVE

VIOLET

March

"Violet, order up!"

Chef Benito—who everyone called 'Papa'—set two plates of eggs, bacon, and hash browns in the window. He banged on the bell, then disappeared again.

I wiped sweat from my brow with the back of my hand, finished taking a table's order, and hurried to the window to stick the ticket. Two other tables needed coffee refills, but nothing got cold faster than eggs. I'd learned that the hard way when I got hired at Mack's Diner two years ago.

I grabbed the plates Papa had set out, refilled coffee, dropped a check. When the breakfast rush ended, I had a moment to catch my breath.

"Hey, V." Dean, another server, sidled up and flashed me one of his trademark charming smiles. "There's an art exhibit opening downtown tonight. Want to check it out?"

"Can't," I said, marrying two ketchup bottles. "Have to study."

"How did I know you were going to say that?"

"Because for two years you've been asking me to go out with you, and for two years I've said no."

He grinned. "Make me sound pathetic, why don't you?"

I gave him a tired smile. "You know how it is."

"I know that all work and no fun is bad for your health." Dean leaned over the counter and whipped a lock of sandy blond hair off his brow. He nudged my arm softly, his fingers lingering on my skin. "I worry about you."

"Oh please," I said with a wry laugh, then dropped my glance to where he was touching me and back to him, brows arched.

He pulled his hand away and stood straight, grinning. "I don't understand how you can stay immune to my considerable charm. It's not like you have a boyfriend, right?"

I winced and busied myself with the ketchup. "Right." I gave him a look. "Have you ever stopped to consider that maybe I just don't like you?"

His eyes widened innocently. "Me? Nah."

Papa appeared in the kitchen window. "Violet! Order up." He banged the bell.

"I gotta get that."

Dean heaved a sigh and walked backward, hands up. "I'm not going to give up on you, V. Someday, I'm going to win you over and you're going to say, *why didn't I order the Dean Special sooner?*"

I rolled my eyes at him. He was so full of shit; most girls were *not* immune to his considerable charm. He only wanted me because I hadn't fallen into his bed immediately. He had no idea how impossible it was. How even the idea of it couldn't find a hand hold in my thoughts.

My shift ended, and I went to the backroom to take off my apron and unpin the silly cloth cap from my head. Other guys in the back and servers starting their shifts greeted me warmly or said goodbye for the day. The crew at Mack's had become like a second family to me, with grouchy Papa as head of household. It was one of the things I liked best about Texas—the southern mentality of warmth and familiarity that I'd have died of loneliness without.

I drove my Rav 4—which was getting old and needed some work—through Waco, Texas. Halfway between Dallas and Austin, the town was completely landlocked. Nothing but flat stretches of land as far as the eye could see. It had its own beauty, but I missed the ocean, forests, and mountains of Santa Cruz. The bonfires at the Shack were becoming a distant memory, replaced, instead, by scents of fried food at Mack's and the recycled air in the Baylor University Library.

Growing fainter still were the scents of Miller's skin and cologne. The way his shirt smelled when I wore it after he'd slept in it. The salt of his sweat in bed after he'd brought me from one delirious orgasm to another…

"Stop torturing yourself," I muttered as I pulled the car into the covered parking of the Desert Dune Apartments.

It was a cute complex about a mile from Baylor. Despite my roommate, Veronica's urging to make it my own, it had very little of me in it. Her tapestries and bizarre artistic knickknacks filled the cozy two-bedroom, one bath unit. My contribution had been to bring in a few houseplants for a bit of green, but I never quite felt settled there. Like wearing a sweater that was too tight.

Inside our apartment, I headed straight for the shower to wash the scent of bacon grease from my hair and skin. Afterward, I dressed in a tank top and sleep pants—my usual Friday night attire. Veronica's bedroom door was open, but she wasn't home. The apartment was thick with silence.

I had a report to write up for Physics Lab, but the couch called to me because suddenly, I was so tired. Tired of being sad. Tired of missing him. God, I missed Miller so much, my bones ached. Sometimes, in moments like that, I had the urge to throw it all away, quit school, and be with him on tour. But I knew it would wreck us. As hard as it was being apart, it would be harder still for me to do nothing and watch my own goals slip away, city by city, concert by concert. I would lose my sense of self. Miller and I were two halves of the same equation. If I faded away, we wouldn't work anymore.

Still, tears filled my eyes to look at the wreckage of my old life. I missed Mom and Dad. I missed my house in Santa Cruz and the family we'd once been in it. I missed Shiloh and River…all of us blasted apart and flung to all corners of the country.

As if she'd heard my silent plea, my phone lit up with Shiloh's number.

I swallowed my tears. "Hey, Shi."

"What's wrong?"

I sniffed a laugh. "Hello to you too."

"It's me, Vi," she said. "I know you."

"I'm so glad it's you," I said, curling up on the couch. "I miss your voice."

"Me too, girl. How are things? Though I think I already know."

"I've been better." I hesitated, then asked anyway. "How's Ronan?"

"Same." She bit off the word.

"And you? How are you, Shi?"

She exhaled softly into the phone, but when she spoke, her voice was hard again. "I'm fine. It's you I'm worried about. I read that Miller is going to be on the next cover of *Rolling Stone* and something told me to call."

"Is he?" I said, my heart soaring and cracking at the same time.

"He didn't tell you?"

"He never tells me stuff like that. He considers it bragging."

"Lord, that boy. He's the least-famous famous person I know. How are you holding up?"

"Okay. I had to take some time off from the diner to get a huge Biochem project completed. Now I have midterms coming up."

"You should be proud," Shiloh said. "You're working your ass off over there."

"Thank you. I'm sort of proud of me too." Tears filled my eyes. "This is hard."

Her tone grew soft. "I know it is."

I sniffed and wiped my eyes, trying to keep it together. "But we knew it would be. He's headlining a world tour. He has shows almost every night. There are time zone differences…" I heaved a sigh. "I'm trying to stay positive."

"I know. Long-distance relationships suck and you're over there without even a lifeline from your parents. Has Miller offered to help with your college? I'm sure he—"

"No, no. My tuition is paid for. I earned that scholarship on my own and I want to keep earning it."

"Okay, but how about rent? He's sent you money, right? He's making a fortune over there. There's no way he wouldn't help you."

"He wants to. And if I got in real trouble, he'd help but I don't want his money. All my life, I've been a pampered rich kid who never had to want for anything. Hell, I never even had a job until Mack's."

"Girl, you volunteered for every medical program under the sun."

"True, but ultimately that helped me get ahead in my career. I never had to earn a living. I think I need this. I can't see the whole thing yet, but I feel like my crappy job, my crazy school workload and even being apart from Miller are making me a better person. One who understands what it's like to struggle so I can appreciate what I have even more."

Like Miller has done is entire life.

"Well, dang, girl. I guess Snow White has left the building."

I laughed. "I hope so." I plucked a piece of lint off the couch. "Shi, you know you can talk to me, right? Like how I talk to you?"

A silence. Then, "I know."

"I mean, if it's too much to talk about, I get it. I don't want to make you relive anything over the phone with me. But I just want you to know that I'm here, okay?"

"Okay," she said, her voice breathy with tears. Then she cleared her throat, pulling her own protective walls around her. After all that happened, I couldn't blame her.

"Shi?"

"I'm okay. I promise."

"Okay. Call me if that ever changes. Hell, call me anyway."

"I will. Love you."

"Love you too."

I hung up with her and closed my eyes, allowing myself a rare moment of unscheduled rest, while shedding a few tears for my friend who'd suffered so much.

But only for a few minutes. I then sat up, dried my tears, and got back to work.

CHAPTER TWENTY-SIX

MILLER

A hard, sharp rapping came at the green room door. "Five minutes," Evelyn called.

"Coming," I called back.

I depressed the needle, emptying the little vial of insulin into my thigh. I'd already bolused to handle the carbs I'd eaten at dinner to get through tonight's concert, but my numbers had spiked again.

"Fucking hell," I muttered, pulling my pants up.

Other diabetics handled their shit well, but for me it was a constant battle. I followed plans, I counted carbs until my eyes crossed, and yet my numbers swung high and low no matter how careful I was. A few weeks ago, I'd passed out after a show in Lisbon, so the label assigned a doctor to babysit me for the duration of the tour, and even he was baffled. He wanted to get me in a hospital and run a bunch of tests and check my A1C which I was long overdue for, but that meant pausing the tour, and that couldn't happen.

I put away my insulin kit as the booming screams, stomps and applause of twenty-thousand fans in the T-Mobile Arena in Las Vegas rolled over me like thunder. Then the sound swelled louder—my band taking the stage ahead of me. They were good guys, all of them talented. We could've been close like brothers if I'd let them, but I burned that bridge early on. They all thought I was stuck-up and aloof. Fine by me. I'd already had friends who were like brothers and look how that turned out.

Pain tightened my chest for Ronan and Holden. For Violet.

I miss her so much, it's making me sick.

I gave myself a last glance in the mirror. My reflection glowered back in my usual jeans, T-shirt and boots. Except now the T-shirt cost $190, the jeans $450, and the boots, more than I wanted to think about.

"It's too much."

I went from having nothing to having everything, almost overnight. It reminded me of the urban legend that said if you took a person from the North Pole and dropped them in the middle of the equator, they'd die instantly from the sudden change in latitude.

I could relate.

The machine of the concert they'd built around me—a huge, lumbering apparatus that crawled from city to city, breaking down and reforming within days, was overwhelming to a former poor kid like me. I poured my focus into what I loved about music. The creation of a song and letting the harmony bend its way around the lyrics. The energy the fans gave to me and what I gave them. I worked to keep that connection with them, no matter how big the arenas got, because that's what mattered. The music and the listener. All the rest felt like something I hadn't earned.

I threw open the green room door. Evelyn was there in her headset with a clipboard in her hand. A badge hung from a lanyard around her neck and marked her as one of the two hundred or so other people who were making this tour happen.

I strode down the corridor, Evelyn's thigh-high black boots clacking along beside me. She wore a short black miniskirt and a fitted blazer that showed her cleavage. She looked more like an executive at a fashion magazine than a personal assistant.

"Do you have my phone?" I demanded.

She flinched at my harsh tone, then gave me a stern look. "You left it in the hotel. Again."

She handed it to me and I scrolled through. A text had come in from Violet earlier.

Miss you. Love you. Have a great show tonight. xoxo

My heart ached. "God, Vi."

She was still there, waiting for me. Even after months of separation, she was still on the other end of the line. Even when she had only two minutes of me before I was pulled away again.

The story of our life.

I bit off a curse and handed my phone back to Evelyn. "After the show tonight, I don't want anyone in the green room. No one. I don't care if fucking Elvis comes back from the dead, I need an hour alone."

Evelyn rolled her eyes. "Your nightly call with Vi. I know the drill."

"It's the only thing that keeps me sane."

"And here I thought that was my job." She cocked her head. "Have you told her?"

"Told her what?"

"About Lisbon. About how Dr. Brighton thinks you should quit the tour immediately."

"Why would I do that? It would only worry her. And I can't quit the tour. Not yet."

"I'm worried about you," she said as we resumed walking down the tunnel. "Not just because of what happened in Lisbon. You seemed a little bit out of it in San Diego. In fact, you *frequently* seem out of it. The tabloids think you're on drugs or a raging alcoholic."

"The tabloids can write whatever they want. I'm fucking tired, Evelyn," I said, striding toward the stage where the noise of the crowd was growing louder and louder, reverberating all around me. "We've done fifty-five shows in six months. Cut me some goddamn slack."

Guilt for snapping at her yanked me to a stop. I looked up at the ceiling, my hands on my hips. She didn't deserve my acid mood.

"I'm sorry."

She studied me, brown eyes softening. "Has Dr. Brighton checked on you recently?"

"Only every other minute. I'm fine."

"You don't look fine. I think he's right. You need to take a break, Miller. Run the tests he wants you to run."

"Can't. I have to push through."

"Even if it kills you?" She grabbed my arm and forced me to look at her. "I love this. Touring. Video shoots. The crowds and the paparazzi. All of it. But you don't. So why are you pushing yourself when it's making you sick?"

"You know why, Ev."

"That charity?"

"Yes, *that charity*. Helping Hands is going to save my ass."

"Save you? You're the one giving them half of your take of the tour."

She didn't get it. I'd been a kid who'd lived in a station wagon and plucked at a guitar, and now I was a guy headlining a sold-out global arena tour. The charity was my insurance so that guy wouldn't forget that kid. So I could keep hold of who I was and where I'd come from when everyone else I cared about was so far away.

"We only have one more leg left," I told Evelyn. "We get through that and Helping Hands International gets a very large check. Then I can feel like all this"—I waved my arms to encompass the arena"—is earned."

And be the kind of man who deserves a woman like Violet.

"*Only one more leg* of the tour is twenty-three more cities across the US," Evelyn said. "I worry about you, Miller. You leave so much on stage, night after night."

"Because the fans deserve it. If they're going to throw this much goddamn money at me, then I'd better give my best. Every night, every show, my absolute best."

Evelyn started to argue, but Simon, the equipment manager, came up and looped an electric guitar around my neck.

"Just…be careful," Evelyn said in a tone I didn't like. Soft and full of concern.

Two years ago, she'd been a brassy, flirty handful, and I'd had to remind her numerous times not to cross a line with me. But lately, she'd grown mellower, watched me when she thought I wasn't looking. Efficient, smart, good at handling people, she could've started her own PR company by now. She'd more than gotten her foot in the door, but she stuck around with me, fetching me shit and picking out clothes to wear for photo shoots.

One more reason to get through this tour.

My heart belonged to Violet. Only and forever. The attention of willing women was in ready supply on the road, but no matter how many after parties the band threw, I stayed away. I couldn't drink, and someone was sure to snap a photo that would put me in a compromising position and break Violet's heart.

I was doing a good enough job of that on my own, thanks.

I adjusted the strap around my neck and moved to the end of the corridor. The stage lay ahead, the crowd beyond. The lights went dark, and neon lights from thirty-thousand glow sticks swayed in an ocean of fans.

"Ten seconds," Evelyn murmured into her headset. She listened for the go ahead from the show director, then gave my arm a gentle nudge. "Go."

I closed my eyes for a moment, as I did before every show.

For you, Violet.

Everything was for her. When I stepped on stage, I could love her. I could throw it into the universe and hope it would find her, and she would feel it. I just had to get through this tour, do some good in the world, and then be with her. And doing good was how I could be the kind of guy Violet deserved.

There were a million ways to spend my life but only one that mattered.

I let the swelling thunder of the crowd fill me up. Their energy sustained me. Every night, I fed off of it and gave it back in my sweat and tears.

I strode onto the stage, followed the tape marking my path in the dark to my mic stand. And then one lone, green light fell over me. The stadium went crazy, an avalanche of sound. I closed my eyes and let it wash over me. Gratitude filled me up that so many people wanted to hear what I had to say. To let me bare my soul and tell my story every night on stage.

Every night, another step closer to Violet.

Wait for Me

A slow burn kiss caught fire
I tasted the sun, and you smiled
said let's try together alone
We've both cried our last goodbye
You're calling my name
I'm calling you home
Wait for me
Wait for me

When the noise gets loud
Put down the phone
I can't stand the sound no more
An empty bed and an endless road
drowning in the sea so cold

Please wait for me
Wait for me

People talk to me but I fade
they all look the same
Looking for you
in somebody's face
Hard to love and hard to chase
I felt so high, I crashed to earth
Please wait for me
While I search

When the noise gets loud
Put down the phone
I can't stand the sound no more
An empty bed and an endless road
drowning in the sea so cold
Please wait for me
Wait for me

Every night it's the same old thing
You're my best friend in my dreams
I go to sleep and I think of you
When I wake up it can't be true
Wait for me
Wait for me

I know that this can't be pretend
I'm here waiting till the end
One day I know it won't be hard
One day I know we'll feel so free
Baby please I'm asking you
To wait for me
Wait for me

I stepped off the stage, drenched in sweat. The other guys were high-fiving and congratulating each other. Dan, the bassist, fell in step beside me in the corridor, the echoes of music and twenty-thousand screaming fans still reverberating in my ears.

"Hey, man, great show," he said.

"Thanks, you too." My stock answer.

"Where did that last one come from?" Antonio, the keyboardist asked. "'Wait for Me'? Wasn't exactly on the set list."

"Yeah, sorry," I said. "It was something I wrote on the fly. Needed to get it out there."

"Beautiful shit, man."

"Thanks."

His brows furrowed as he looked me up and down. "You okay? You look a little white."

"I'm fine," I said, even as my watch started warning me that my numbers were dropping.

Fuck. Too high before the show. Too low, after.

"Hey, Miller—"

"I gotta handle this."

I forced my legs to move faster to my private dressing room. Evelyn was there with another assistant, Tina Edgerton, who was busy finishing setting up my post-show food and drinks.

Evelyn's eyes widened when she looked up from her phone. "Jesus, Miller…I'm calling Dr. Brighton."

"No," I said, slumping into a chair. My shirt was drenched in a cold sweat. "Just give me my med bag."

Evelyn hurried to do as I asked. I crammed a handful of glucose gummies in my mouth while Tina poured me a glass of orange juice. They both knew the drill.

"Thanks. You both can go. Can I have my phone, Ev?"

Evelyn slowly handed me my phone. "Are you sure? You still don't look—"

"I'm fine. Please." God, I was so tired. "I need to talk to her."

I need her. I need Violet. I can't do this anymore…

"Okay," Evelyn said reluctantly. "But I'll be right outside this door."

They both started to go and then Tina stopped, turned. "Oh, I nearly forgot. Your dad called. I guess he hasn't been able to reach you."

I froze. The world stopped. I sank deeper in my chair, as if the floor had dropped beneath it. "What did you say?"

Evelyn whirled on Tina. "What did you say?"

Tina recoiled under our scrutiny, her glance darting between us. "Your dad called about twenty minutes ago. Sharon got the message and gave me his number. He wants you to call him back..." She frowned at my deteriorating expression. "Is there a problem?"

Evelyn turned to stare at me, aghast. I'd told her my dad was dead. Because he was, as far as I was concerned. And now he was back, haunting me…

My jaw had gone numb. "You're sure it's him?"

"He said his name was Ray Stratton?" Tina bit her lip. "I'm sorry. Are you not close?

"No," I said. "No, we're not close."

Because he's dead. Dead to me.

"Do you want his number?"

I was aware I was breathing hard, my hands clutching the armrests of the chair. Emotions rampaged through my skull like an avalanche.

"No, I do not want his number. He's only calling because…he wants something. He saw the *Rolling Stone* article, maybe. He's seen my success, and now he wants a piece of it."

Evelyn recovered her poise and hustled Tina to the door. "Give me the number. I'll handle this."

The numbness was spreading, hollowing me out, making me tremble. My vision danced with black spots. Ray Stratton. The name like a baseball bat to my heart.

"Miller!"

Evelyn rushed toward me.

"No," I said, hardly able to make my lips move. My tongue weighed a thousand pounds. "Tell them…if he calls again, tell him to go to hell… Tell him…"

The black spots widened into a chasm, and then I fell in.

CHAPTER TWENTY-SEVEN

VIOLET

"Hey, V." Veronica came in the door of our place, her arms laden with groceries.

I looked up from my Physics text and started to uncurl from the couch. "Hey, V," I replied back with a smile, thinking—not for the first time—the universe had been kind enough to bestow Veronica Meyers on me, to make up for all the people I missed.

Two years older than me, Veronica took me in like an older sister and helped me get the job at Mack's. We had nothing in common. She was soft-spoken yet blasted old goth metal music with band names like *Type O Negative* and *Motionless in White* in our tiny apartment. She had a rotation of older boyfriends that I couldn't keep track of, while I was a recluse, studying in my room and hardly venturing out to socialize.

"Need some help?"

"I got it," she said, tossing her dyed-black hair over her shoulder. "I think you'd better stay sitting down. Your man is on the cover of this month's *Rolling Stone.*"

"I heard. Can I see?"

Veronica pulled out a magazine from one of the grocery bags and crossed over to me. "I haven't read it, but the headline is a little alarming."

She handed me the magazine and a rush of heat flooded me. Miller Stratton, the boy who'd had to pawn his guitar was now on the cover of the biggest rock and roll magazine of all time.

And he looked like he belonged there.

It was a candid photo taken at one of his sold-out concerts. He stood at the edge of the stage where a sea of adoring fans screamed for him, reaching arms clamored for him. An electric guitar hung off his slender frame that had filled out and grown more masculine and defined in the last two years. He wore torn jeans, boots, and a tight t-shirt that clung to his sweat-soaked body, revealing every line of his abs and the broad plains of his chest. His eyes shut, mouth open as he belted into a mic. Leather bands on his wrists highlighted the definition of his forearms, his longish hair falling in his eyes. The perfect image of a rock star.

For a few beautiful, shining moments, he'd been all mine. Now he belonged to the world.

Tears blurred my vision as I traced my finger along his jaw. "Hi, love."

"I'm sorry, hon." Veronica gave my hand a squeeze. "Should I not have bought it?"

"No, I'm glad you did. He looks sexy as hell, doesn't he?"

"No argument from me, there. I'm going to put away the groceries. I'll be two steps away if you need me."

I nodded absently and scanned the cover again. Miller looked on the verge of falling into the crowd, and the headline reflected it. *On The Edge: The Meteoric Rise (And Fall?) Of Miller Stratton, The New Demigod Of Alt Pop/Rock*

"He's falling?" I murmured.

A journalist had followed Miller on the European leg of his world tour. The first part of the article was beautiful, detailing how Miller visited shelters in each city, despite his tight schedule. How he gave away hundreds of tickets to his shows to underprivileged fans, donated money to fund diabetes research, and how he had pledged half of his tour earnings to a charity for homeless youth.

My eyes filled with tears at a photo of Miller sitting beside a homeless person in Dublin, Ireland. Miller's long legs were drawn up, hands tucked in the pocket of his jacket. The man wore a scraggly beard, and his face was streaked with grime. The two of them sat against the wall almost shoulder to shoulder, like two friends waiting for a bus.

Like how Miller and I had sat against the wall of my house that first night we met.

I read the text of the article, grabbing on to every word like a starving woman and savoring it.

They talked for more than twenty minutes. Stratton gave the man some money from his own pocket and then directed his team to get him somewhere safe for the night: a hot meal and a shower. That incident solidified him in the eyes of fans—especially women— as proof he was worthy of the rabid attention that followed him all over the globe. Others criticized it as a publicity stunt. To that Stratton's eyes roll.

"It was a thing that happened. The fact that the press was tailing me made it a 'stunt.' Which is bullshit. No one plans to be homeless. No one thinks they'll end up on the street. But I've been there and so I sat with the guy and was there again. He helped me much more than I helped him." When asked how, Stratton paused for a long moment. "Because, most days, I feel like an imposter, borrowing someone else's life. You can't go back to where you came from, but you can forget. Sitting with that man, he helped me remember who I am."

God, I wanted to crawl into the magazine and be with Miller. But he'd moved on. To another city. Another show. Long weeks of endless touring, and the tone of the article delved into the "fall" aspect of the headline. My lonely ache for him began to morph into fear.

The journalist wanted to know if what the tabloids had been blaring for months was true: that Miller had fallen prey to the vices of stardom, namely drugs and alcohol. Miller denied it all, but there were reports of him dozing off in the middle of interviews. Paparazzi photos accompanied the piece; Miller stumbling along Parisian streets with Evelyn hanging close. One image showed him with a cut on his forehead from having tripped and cracked his head on a cobblestone wall in Florence.

"He seems pretty out of it sometimes," noted an observer who wished to remain anonymous. "Off stage, it's like he's buzzed a lot. But he always seems to pull it together to put on a hell of a show."

Except that Miller didn't drink. He couldn't. Adding booze would only wreak havoc with his blood sugars.

The record company had sent a personal doctor on the tour for Miller. Dr. Brighton's statement was vague and optimistic, but I read between the lines. He was warning Miller—and Gold Line Records—that it would be in Miller's best interest to quit or postpone the tour and take some time off.

Because he's sick.

Since I was thirteen years old, I'd been researching every aspect of diabetes, so that I would never again be caught unprepared if something happened to Miller. I'd vowed to do my best to protect him, to tend to him through his highs and lows because his diabetes had always been hard to manage. Aggressive. I flipped through the article, scanning for telltale signs. Confusion, poor vision (the kind that led to bumping into walls), tiredness. It was all there, and the doctor knew it. But either the record company or Miller himself wasn't listening to him.

It's Miller. He won't quit. He's committed to the label, to the charity, to his fans.

I grabbed my phone and called his number. It immediately went to voicemail. I shot him a text: **Please call me as soon as you get this.**

But it remained unread. I paced the living room, my nerves lit up like a switchboard.

"V?" Veronica asked from the kitchen. "What's wrong?"

"It's Miller," I said. "I think...I mean, I don't know for sure, but I have a bad feeling."

"About what? Did something happen?"

"No, but I—"

I gave a little cry of surprise as my phone lit up with a call. Evelyn.

"Evelyn, talk to me. How is he? What's happening?"

"Violet," she said, her tone calm but tinged with fear. "I don't want to scare you but...how fast can you get here?"

CHAPTER TWENTY-EIGHT

VIOLET

It happened in a blur. One minute I was in my room throwing clothes into a bag, and the next, I was on a plane to Las Vegas, first class, courtesy of Gold Line Records. Evelyn picked me up at McCarran in a sleek black sedan with a driver. The Strip went by outside the tinted windows.

We were both only twenty years old, but Evelyn was dressed in an impeccable A-line skirt and blazer, while I looked like a pile of laundry in jeans and a sweatshirt, my hair in a messy ponytail.

"Tell me everything," I said after tense greetings. "The truth. Not the PR bullshit that he was hospitalized for 'exhaustion.'"

Evelyn scrolled her phone with long manicured nails. "I told you when I called that it was exhaustion because that's all the world needs to know. Now that you're here, I can tell you that, yes, Miller collapsed after the show two nights ago. His numbers were very low, but in the ER, they got him stable. Now he's at the hotel, resting."

"Collapsed?" My stomach felt as if it were made of stone. "How bad is it?"

"Bad enough that he needs to quit touring, and he won't," Evelyn said, finally setting her phone down to give me her full attention. "His doctor says Miller is pushing himself too hard. But he's determined to finish the tour to give that charity a bunch of money. He feels guilty about all this." She gestured at the elegant sedan. "And he's miserable without you. It's turned him into a bit of a bastard, to be honest. The long distance is too hard on him. You know how he is. He's all or nothing."

"I know. He's going to be just as dedicated to the charity. He won't want to quit."

"You have to make him quit. You're the only one who can convince him. He won't listen to me."

I glanced at her sideways, the old twinge of bitterness from our past still hovering between us. "I've seen the pictures of you two. You seem pretty close," I admitted.

"What you're seeing is a friendship." She smoothed her hair that was pulled in a tight elegant ponytail. "Despite my best efforts."

I whipped my head to her. "What does that mean?"

She shrugged. "It means I play to win, always." She smiled fondly to herself. "My dad likes to joke that ambition is my Gatorade. I would have gotten over our little rivalry, eventually. But then Miller wrote that song for you. So many songs for you. I wanted that too. What girl wouldn't?"

"So, you arranged to spend the next two and a half years with him to be that girl?"

"He's gorgeous. Talented. When he sings…" She bit off her words and shook her head. "I wanted that. I wanted to be the girl in the love song. I thought if I stuck around long enough, if I were there for him, I would be. That was my goal, and I *never lose*."

"Jesus, Evelyn."

"But I did lose. Hard. No, that's not true. To lose would mean he'd been playing the game, and he wasn't." She turned to face me. "There's no one else in his universe but you. Not me or a thousand other screaming girls could ever change that. God knows, I've seen women try and fail to get his attention, but he looks right through them. He wouldn't even entertain the possibility of sleeping with someone else. Which also contributed to him being an asshole, I'm sure."

"I know. It's been hard for me too. We promised to try to talk every night but—"

"He is talking to you. Every night." She scrolled her phone and then held the screen to me. "This was two nights ago. Right before he collapsed."

A video played, taken from someone just offstage. Miller sat on a stool alone in the center of the stage, a single light bathing him. He played his acoustic guitar solo and sang a song I'd never heard before. "Wait for Me," a thrumming song of desperation, his rich voice calling out into the dark void of the crowd, over and over again. He was saturated with emotion and longing in a way that only came out in his music. Every word sank into my heart.

"That's for you," Evelyn said quietly. "There is no one else."

The video ended, and she wordlessly handed me a tissue.

I dabbed my eyes. "Thank you for that."

"You shouldn't thank me," she said. "But you don't have to worry about me anymore, either. I'm going to offer him my resignation."

"What…why? In the middle of his tour?"

"I have my reasons." She turned to me. "But he's got to stop working himself to the bone. He needs you to convince him of that, especially now. His dad's been calling."

I stared, my eyes wide. "Holy shit," I breathed. "Really? Is it… Are you sure it's him?"

She nodded. "Since the *Rolling Stone* article came out, Ray Stratton calls almost every day. Miller won't talk to him. Won't even hear of it."

"Oh my God…" I felt pushed back in the seat, my heart aching for Miller. For how confused he must be. Or how much pain he must feel, old wounds torn open when they'd never fully healed in the first place. "He never told me."

"Because he doesn't want to worry you about any of it. But *I'm* worried, Vi. And so is Dr. Brighton."

The sedan turned into the Bellagio Hotel and Casino and rolled into the circular drive.

"He leaves for Seattle tomorrow," Evelyn said. "The show's a big one. The executives from the Helping Hands charity will be there, and they're bringing a bunch of kids backstage. Miller's invitation. I'll be gone by the end of the week."

She gathered her bag and phone and tossed on a pair of Gucci sunglasses to hide the tears in her eyes. "Make sure it's his last show."

Evelyn led me into the Bellagio casino, past the lobby where a thousand glass flowers covered the ceiling in a riot of color. Their beauty calmed the turbulent emotions coursing through me. I stared up as long as I could while Evelyn strode briskly, unimpressed. She looked like she belonged in the elegance of the hotel, while I felt unwashed and grubby.

"She's with me," she told the guard at a private elevator who let us on. The car went up and opened on a broad, quiet hallway.

"I feel like the paparazzi is going to jump out at any second," I said as we walked past door after door.

"We have the entire floor." Evelyn stopped at a suite where a big guy with a badge hanging from his beefy neck was standing. "Hey, Sam."

"What's up, G?" He gave me a nod as he opened the door for us.

I nodded back, amazed at how much the label had built around Miller: private elevators and security and entire floors of swanky hotels. Pride swelled in my chest, even as I felt more out of place and unsure that he'd want me here.

The suite Evelyn led me through was huge, twice as big as my and Veronica's apartment, with elegant furniture, like a royal sitting room in Italy. A tall man in a suit—a stethoscope looped around his neck—stood at the bay window. Miller sat on the ledge.

There he is.

I stopped in the middle of the room, watching him. Drinking him in. He looked tired, a little thinner than he did on the *Rolling Stone* cover. The doctor had a blood pressure cuff around Miller's upper arm, taking a reading.

Miller saw me, and his expression froze. He stood up, as if he were pulled by strings, and stepped toward me, yanked the pump from the doctor's hand.

"Vi…what are you doing here?"

His gruff voice went straight to my heart. It had been months since I'd heard him say my name in person.

"Evelyn called me," I said, tears filling my eyes. "It's so good to see you."

"God, baby…" He started toward me, then stopped, also realizing we had an audience. He tore the blood pressure cuff off his arm and handed it to the doctor. "Can you guys give us a minute?"

"I'll be back in one hour to finish the check-up," the doctor said sternly.

"I have an urgent matter to discuss with you, too," Evelyn said, giving me a parting glance, asking me to let her tell him the truth.

When they'd gone, Miller took me in his arms and I collapsed into them, my eyes falling shut with relief to feel the solidity of him and hear his heart beating against my cheek.

"Vi, you have midterms. Why did you leave Baylor?"

"You think I wouldn't? I love you, Miller. And you collapsed after the show. Evelyn says you need to quit the tour."

He stiffened and gently released me. "I see. She called you and got you all scared, so you dropped everything to be here. She shouldn't have done that."

"Your health is more important than my school or your concert."

"My *health* isn't going to change, Vi. It's always been this hard, and it's going to stay that way. Quitting the tour won't change that, but it will disappoint a shit-ton of people who have paid to hear me. The people who put me up in fancy hotels like this and let me take care of my mom. And you."

"You need to slow down, love. Before something happens."

"I can't," he said, dropping his head so that we were forehead to forehead. "There's too much at stake."

"Too much pressure on you," I corrected. I cupped his cheek, feeling the stubble under my hand, my eyes searching his. "Do you still think you haven't earned this?"

"You read that magazine article. I knew I said too much."

"It scared me, Miller. All that talk about confusion and falling asleep in interviews." My hand on his face moved up to touch a scar on his brow that wasn't there before. "You never told me."

"I didn't want to scare you, Vi. God knows I've done enough of that our entire lives. I figure if I can push through and finish this tour, then it'd be over. I'll have made enough money to take care of you. I could pay for your tuition anywhere you wanted. In Santa Cruz. I figured when it was done, we could go home."

"Home," I murmured, and then his arms tightening around me, holding me together when I felt I'd been falling apart.

"I love you, Violet. I am so completely in love with you that being away from you is making me fucking crazy."

Tears blurred my vision as my heart pulled toward him, the magnetic polarity of us realigning. "I know. I hate it, too. Every day is impossible. But I'm here now. No more goodbyes."

His eyes searched mine, hope and relief shining in them. Then his expression hardened, and this time with a desire that burned right through me. A possessive heat that flooded his eyes.

He stood up, towered over me. I felt the air between us tighten, pulling. His hands took my face, his thumb brushing my lower lip. My pulse was a drum in my chest, counting the seconds until he was mine again. But he took his time, soaking me in, savoring this moment when I only wanted him. We'd been apart long enough.

"Miller…"

And then his mouth descended, capturing mine in a heated, delving kiss. My eyes fell shut as I became saturated with everything that was him. The scent of expensive clothes and cologne suffused me, but beneath it, he was still there. His skin. The taste of him. So familiar and safe.

Like coming home.

His kisses erased the distance between us. His nipping teeth, his stubble grazing my chin, his tongue sliding and tangling with mine, a reacquaintance. A reunion of bodies and souls, hands pulling at clothes in an exchange of gasping breaths and moans. We kissed until we knew each other again, settled into each other's spaces after the long absence. We kissed until we fell back into place, where we belonged.

He lifted me and carried me to the bedroom, the window's shades drawn.

"I need a shower," I whispered against his lips.

I needed more time to reacclimate us. To be with him with nothing left between us. Naked together under a bright light, the distance between us washing away.

He nodded in understanding and pulled me to my feet. We kissed as our clothes came off, pieces at a time. In the cavernous bathroom, he turned on the shower and drew me under rainfall. I watched the water bead over his skin and slide in rivulets over the cut lines of his body. My eyes drank him in while my hands glided up and down the smooth, muscled perfection of his back.

"So beautiful," I murmured. "Magnificent."

"God, Vi… Never again. I'm not letting you go, ever again."

He wrapped his arms around me, pulling me into him. I planted open-mouthed kisses on his chest, over his heart, tasting the water and the salt of his skin. My exploring lips found one of his small nipples, and I sucked it between my teeth.

Miller hissed a breath, and his hands that had been tentative and soft on me, now roamed and grabbed, taking their fill. He reacquainted himself with my breasts, the curve of my hip, my stomach. Everywhere he touched left licks of fire while his hardness sought entry into the soft, wet heat of me.

"Vi…" he gritted out.

"Not yet."

I kissed him long and slow and then turned him around to take in the beauty of his back, the lines of his neck, the muscles moving under his smooth skin, tapering to his waist. I kissed him between his shoulder blades, tasted him with my tongue, then reached for the soap.

I lathered the broad plains of his back then moved around to his abdomen, skirting an insulin pump that had replaced his CGM implant—another change in his life I hadn't been aware of.

My exploration of his body grew more purposeful; I never wanted to not know him.

I slipped my hand down to his rock-hard erection, gripping its girth and stroking him. Anticipation lit my nerve-endings on fire, relearning what he liked. How to touch him in order to draw that sexy, masculine growl out of his chest. He had only been mine a handful of times, and now, I was taking him back, inch by inch.

Miller gripped my wrist that held him and looked at me over his shoulder. "I'm going to come if you keep doing that."

I let him go, and he turned to face me, his hair falling over his eyes that were blue, dark and hooded. My limbs weakened at the pure want I saw there, but I turned my back, before I surrendered to him completely. I wanted his hands on me, washing away the grit of time and distance, erasing our separation with every touch.

I lifted the long, wet mass of my hair off my neck and held it up, offering him my naked back and my breasts, exposed and defenseless in front. Miller's hands found them first, kneading them, making them slippery with soap, as his mouth clamped down on the slope of my neck. I gasped, arching into his touch while pressing my backside against his erection.

His hands skimmed down the curve of my spine, down to the rounded flesh of my ass, then back up my back. I felt the restraint in his every movement until his patience ran out, and my need had consumed me to the point of delirium. Quickly, we washed the soap away and then Miller lifted me again and carried me to the bed. My skin shivered in the cool air, but his body blanketed me with its perfect heaviness and heat. He kissed me until we were both breathless then lay his forehead to mine.

"I can't stop looking at you," he breathed.

"Neither can I."

"Tell me there's been no one else."

"Of course, not. No one but you. Ever," I said and swallowed. "You…?"

"No one," he replied, his voice gruff but his eyes soft and warm. "You're my first and my last."

His words and the intensity behind his eyes broke me open, erasing any lingering hesitation or doubt. Cold air swooped in as he withdrew to put on a condom from his wallet. Then he was back, beads of shower water pebbling his shoulders. He propped himself on his forearms, settling fully against me, his hands in my hair. Our eyes met in the dimness of the room's shaded windows, unblinking. I guided him to my entrance and slid his tip over my wet heat. His body coiled and tensed, using everything he had to hold back, as he kissed me. Softly. And then slid deep inside me with one smooth motion.

Every part of me tensed at the sudden, heavy fullness, then relaxed immediately under him, letting him in completely, as deep as he could get. He sank into me and held still a moment, head bowed.

"Jesus, Vi. So good. You feel so good."

I nuzzled his neck, kissing his ear, his jaw, and then his mouth as he raised his head and began to move in me. A few slow, deep, penetrating thrusts soon gave way to a hard, fast rhythm because it had been too long. Our bodies had been deprived, and now, we sought to make up for it.

His touch in the shower had already primed me. Our separation had my every nerve-ending clamoring for this moment. The perfect, heavy pressure of him hit that spot inside me again and again, driving me quickly to the edge.

"Miller…"

"Come, Vi," he said, his neck corded with tension, his body gloriously masculine and hard over my swaying breasts as he drove into me. He reached back and lifted one of my legs over the crook of his elbow, spreading me wider.

I gasped at the subtle change in angle that sent me over. I grabbed at Miller's shoulders, my nails scratching to hold on, as his body pistoned into me, pushing the orgasm higher and higher until a final cry tore out of me and I fell back, as if falling from a great height, incoherent in the pleasure that rolled through me in waves.

I let my legs fall open, reached my arms for the headboard and let him have me. Miller rose up to prop himself on his hands and thrust with abandon, driving into me again and again until at last, his orgasm gripped him, tensing in his body and then releasing into mine.

He shuddered, and a grunt escaped his locked teeth, a sound so purely masculine, it made me want him all over again. But we had time. Now, at last, we had time. No furtive weekends. No stolen hours.

Miller collapsed on top of me, wrapped himself around me, and we lay tangled that way, sweat-soaked and satiated, our hearts slowing their thundering beats together until finally, we slept.

CHAPTER TWENTY-NINE

MILLER

That night was mine and hers.

I told my team to leave us alone, and I ordered room service. I took my meds, we ate and laughed and talked, and I kept Violet in my bed all night. Naked and perfect, her black hair splayed out on the white pillow, her body smooth and pale in the glittering light of the Strip outside the window. My hands skimmed over her curves, molding her, creating her under me, after months of having only a fantasy. Erasing lonely nights spent with my hand wrapped around my cock, dragging myself toward something like relief.

Now she was here, her skin warm and silken, her arms reaching for me and pulling me into the soft heat of her, again and again.

Finally satiated in the late hour before dawn, we lay wrapped in each other, her head on my shoulder, my fingers twining lazily in her hair.

"As much as I hate to bring it up," I said, "what are you going to do about your school?"

"I said no more goodbyes, remember? If I bail on my midterms, my tuition will be in jeopardy, but—"

"I'll pay your tuition."

She sighed, her bare breasts pressing against my chest with a soft rise and fall. "I don't know, Miller. I've been struggling, but I was telling Shiloh that I don't think that's what's hurting me. It's making me stronger. More focused. I can handle hard work. But I wasn't prepared for how hard it is being apart from you."

"Neither was I. Is it asking too much for you to come with me on the tour?"

"Yes," she said firmly. "Because there shouldn't be any more tour, right? What does Dr. Brighton say?"

"That I need to rest more. Maybe he's right. I don't want to drag you around the country, Violet, and I don't want to give you up again. But the Helping Hands executive will be at the concert in Seattle tomorrow, and she's bringing a bunch of kids. I can't let them down. Hell, I'm already letting them down. If I cancel tour dates, that's less revenue for them, and for the label."

"There will be other tours, Miller. No one will begrudge you if you need to take care of yourself."

"I'm going to do this show. For them. One show and then we can plan our next step."

Violet was quiet for a moment, then she tilted her chin up to look at me. "Do you enjoy any of this? *Rolling Stone* made it sound like you didn't."

"I love being on stage. Being with the fans. But the rest of it is surreal."

"How?"

"Everywhere I go, people tell me how great I am, even if they don't know me. Even when I'm being a complete jackass. I haven't had a real conversation with anyone in six months. I only have to say 'I'm thirsty' to send ten different people scrambling to bring me a drink. I know it's the height of douchebaggery to complain about shit like that, but I think it would be really fucking easy to let it all go to my head. Giving to the charity makes me feel like I'm honoring my mom's struggle and not forgetting where I came from."

Violet smiled and kissed my chest over my heart. "I love that you said that." She cast her gaze down, her voice softening. "What about your dad?"

My stomach tightened into a knot, erasing the lazy heaviness. I sat up and reached for a glass of water from the nightstand. "What about him? I know why he's calling after seven years, and it's not to congratulate me. He wants a cut."

Violet moved to sit beside me and pulled the sheet up around her chest. "Maybe. But maybe not. Instead of wondering what he wants, ask yourself, instead, what you want. Do you want to talk to him?"

"Why would I want to talk to him? He ruined our lives. We had to live out of a fucking car. Mom had to do…horrible things to help us survive. He doesn't deserve for me to answer the phone."

She rested her cheek against me. “It’s not about what he deserves, Miller. It’s about what you deserve. If you talk to him, maybe it would bring you some peace.”

“Or it might just make everything worse.”

Violet’s hand slipped into mine, and she kissed my shoulder. “Only you know what feels right.”

“I’ll think about it,” I said. “He might not try back, anyway. I told the entire team I wasn’t taking his calls. Maybe I missed my chance.” I gritted my teeth against the ache in my heart at that thought.

“I think everything happens for a reason, but we can’t always see it at the time.”

I gave her a look. “Even us? It’s taken us years to get here. Except, now I’m not letting you go.”

“I’m not going anywhere.” She snuggled into me. “If you thought I was a nag about your numbers before…”

I laughed and kiss the top of her head. “I miss your nagging. The doctor irritates the hell out of me, but it always made me feel good that you were taking care of me.”

“Maybe that was meant to be too,” she said. “I’ve been thinking more and more about my path as a doctor. Being a surgeon was an idea that I got stuck on, like having a crush on River Whitmore. It was just always there, but I never examined it. But now I have been, and I don’t think that being a surgeon is right for me.”

“That’s been your dream since before I met you.”

She took my hand, traced the lines on my palm with her finger. “It may sound weird, but I’ve been feeling more and more that the key to knowing what is right is to get out of my own way. That’s how it was with you. I had to stop calling what I felt for you anything other than what it was. Real. Inevitable. Maybe it’s the same with my career.” She looked up at me, her smile brilliant in the soft light. “Maybe it was right in front of me, staring me in the face all along.”

My eyes widened. “What are you saying?”

“I don’t want to sound too weird or crazy, but maybe being an endocrinologist is part of how we just fit.”

I frowned. “I’m the guy you’ll have to take care of?”

“We take care of each other.”

“How? What do I give you in return?”

“You take care of my heart,” she said softly, then grinned. “You’ll be my on-call musician who writes me love songs when I need them.

Speaking of which, since this is your last concert for a while, do you think you could score me a ticket?"

"Hell, I can put you on the stage."

"No, no, no. I want to be like everyone else, watching you in your natural habitat while the entire world screams for you." She shook her head in mock annoyance. "I mean…who do you have to screw around here to get a ticket to a Miller Stratton show?"

I laughed and hauled her on top of me. "You're looking at him, baby."

Morning turned into late morning, and we hauled ourselves out of bed. Violet was in the adjacent room getting dressed for our flight to Seattle while I lingered over our room service breakfast at the table.

Dr. Brighton arrived to check my vitals and blood sugar levels.

"Looks good now," he said, "but it's the post-concert that concerns me, Miller. I'd hoped putting you on the insulin pump would have helped stabilize you, but that hasn't been the case. I suspect that your diabetes is of the rarer kind. Labile, we call it, or brittle. Meaning, it doesn't respond to treatment as effectively and brings higher risks."

"Meaning I'm fucked if I tour and I'm fucked if I don't," I said, bitterness flooding me. "I don't want to be reckless, Doc, but the numbers swing around whether I'm performing or not. Always have."

"That is a hallmark of lability, but stress can raise your blood sugar levels, and it's clear to me that you've been under a tremendous amount of pressure with this tour."

"True, but I feel fine now. Better than I've felt in a long time. What about tonight?"

"Are you asking me if you can do the show? Yes. Should you? I'd prefer you didn't until I can get a full endocrine and renal evaluation, and check your A1C, preferably in a hospital setting."

I grimaced. "I can't. Tonight is a big deal. We'll talk about it after."

He pursed his lips.

"*After.* Then I'll do whatever you want."

"Very well. I'll check in with you before the show, after, and first thing in the morning."

"Thanks, doc."

He packed up his tools, greeting Evelyn on his way out.

"Hey, Ev," I said. "Have you eaten? I can order you something…?

"No, thank you," she said, smoothing her skirt nervously. Evelyn was never nervous.

"What's up?"

"Tina has your schedule for today and will coordinate with you later about meeting Brenda Rosner, the Helping Hands CEO. In fact, Tina will be taking over all of my duties from now on." She squared her shoulders. "I'm here to offer you my resignation."

I blinked. "What…why?"

Evelyn glanced at the closed bedroom door. "Violet's here?"

"Yes. Is she why you're leaving?"

"Not exactly," Evelyn said stiffly. "I took a position with a public relations firm in Hollywood. Something I should've done a long time ago."

I got to my feet and gave her a hug. "Congratulations, Ev. That's great." She stiffened in my arms and I let her go.

"You've given me a lot, Miller."

"So have you. You held my shit together when I would've gone off the rails. Hell, I wouldn't even be here if it weren't for you. I bitch a lot, but when I'm on stage and it's just the music and me and the fans… You helped give that to me."

"Don't get all mushy on me now," she said and suddenly looked less confident than I'd ever seen her. "There's something I need to tell you. I…haven't been honest with you."

I leaned against the desk and crossed my arms. "Okay."

"This is harder than I thought." She huffed and put her hands on her hips. "And you know, I don't even have to tell you. I did get another offer, and I could just take it and be done. But I can't. I can't leave my lie hanging out there in the world."

"What lie?"

"About why I needed you to bring me with you to LA."

My arms dropped. "You told me you needed help."

"Because I knew you were a good guy who would do whatever he could." She delicately cleared her throat. "Especially if he thought someone was in danger."

"You were in danger. The same kind as me."

Evelyn turned her gaze to her heels. "Except I wasn't. I drove you to the airport and saw the bruises on your neck. When it looked like you wouldn't take me with you, I…improvised."

I stared, understanding starting to creep over me like cold fingers. "You're fucking kidding."

"Two days before, I'd banged my thigh on my brother's stupid air hockey table in the rec room and had a pretty good bruise. At the time, it felt like serendipity. The universe stamping my ticket out of town." She smiled wanly. "And it worked."

I gaped, slack-jawed. "What are you saying? That you saw where Chet fucking choked me and you said…?"

"That the same thing happened to me." She plucked a tissue from the Fendi bag and dabbed her eyes carefully. "Yes. I did."

"Evelyn, that's…despicable."

"I know it is. I'm not proud of myself, but I did what I had to do. Santa Cruz is too small and sleepy. I had to get out."

"So you lied about your dad—"

"I never said it was my dad," she said fiercely. "I would never… *He* would never."

"But you put it out there for me to believe."

"And now I'm taking it back. I have to take it back. I'm sorry, Miller." She squared her shoulders. "It was wrong, and I'm sorry."

"You didn't need to do that. Your vlog would have taken you wherever you wanted to be."

"Maybe. But I wanted to be with you."

I sagged against the desk, ran a hand through my hair as two years fell between us. Two years of her enduring my bullshit and moods and medical issues for something that would never happen. "I knew. I knew and I didn't want to know. I'm sorry, Ev."

"Don't feel sorry for me, Miller. I always knew what I was doing. You can ask Violet what I meant by that." She heaved a breath, then stuck out her hand, and I took it. "Thank you. For everything."

"Thank you, Ev. I'm going to miss you."

Surprise danced over her expression and then she regained her composure. "Of course, you will. Most days, Tina can barely remember her own name."

She pulled away quickly and went to the door. She opened it, turned, her expression unguarded and soft. "Tell Violet the best woman won."

Then she left.

Our plane touched down in Seattle late that afternoon. I introduced Violet to the guys in the band. She was an instant icebreaker, warming over the cold front I'd presented to them for so long. By the end of soundcheck, we felt more cohesive as a band then we had the entire tour, and I cursed myself for being such a dick. For holding myself back from giving a shit about anyone.

Holding myself back, I realized, had caused more problems for me than it had ever solved. My dad floated in on the tail of that thought, but I batted him away.

That's different. He wrecked us. He held himself back from us.

Even so, I pulled my new assistant aside. "Has my father called?"

Fear instantly washed over Tina's face. "I thought you said to tell him you're never available."

"I did," I said, irritated. "I was just…wondering."

"How come he doesn't have your cell number?"

I scrubbed my hands over my face, missing Evelyn already. "Never mind. If he calls again…"

"Yeah?"

I hung on the precipice of two possibilities. The way it'd been for seven years and some unknown future where I didn't hold myself back.

Tina was waiting.

"Nothing."

The executive from Helping Hands, Brenda Rosner, arrived pre-show with half a dozen young kids, most around eight or nine years old.

I took Violet with me. "I want you to see what it's all for."

We congregated in the green room with a slew of photographers and reporters. Pictures were taken for photo ops, and Violet hung out with the kids, talking and laughing with them and making them feel less intimidated by the surroundings.

Brenda shook my hand, thanking me for my contribution.

"I don't know how many shows I've got left in me," I told her. "My doctors," I said with a nod at Violet, "are saying I have to slow down."

Brenda smiled. "We're all so grateful. We don't need to ask anything more of you than what you've already given."

I believed her, but it still stung to have to quit on those kids. I signed autographs and took pictures with them. They thanked me, never knowing that I got more from them than I could ever give.

One kid stood apart from the others. Brenda told me he'd had it particularly rough and held himself aloof from the others. A boy, eight years old, he'd been shuffled around from shelter to shelter before being taken away from his parents and put in foster care. While everyone was partaking in the spread of food and drink, he leaned against the wall by himself. I moved to stand with him and leaned against the wall too, side by side.

"Your name is Sam, right?"

He nodded, his eyes on the commotion around us. "I've never seen that much food all in one place."

I swallowed hard at the sudden lump in my throat. "Yeah, I know what you mean."

He looked up at me with a depth in his brown eyes that should not have been there for an eight-year-old. "I heard you didn't have a home when you were a kid."

"That's right. My mom and I lived in our car for about six months."

"Was it hard?"

"Hell yeah, it was hard. I had to wash my hair in a gas station bathroom. That sucked."

"But now you're this world-famous rock star."

"True, but a lot of lucky shit had to happen for me to get here," I said. "What do you like to do, Sam? If you could do anything in the world, what would it be?"

"I want to be a photographer. I know that sounds lame…"

"Doesn't sound lame. You like taking pictures?"

"Yeah, I do. Annie, that's my foster mom right now, she says I'm pretty good at it."

"Do you have a camera?"

He shook his head. "Annie lets me take pictures on her phone sometimes. But it's not the same as a real camera."

I looked over at one of the press photographers snapping photos of the kids and gave a sharp whistle between my teeth to get his attention. He looked up, and I jerked my head to call him over.

"Sam, here, would like to be a photographer. Do you mind if he takes a few pictures with your camera?"

The photographer looked dubious about handing over his very expensive, professional camera to a kid.

"I got it covered if anything happens," I said. I didn't often use my status—whatever the fuck that was—to get favors, but this kid was worth it. I gave the guy a "Do you know who I am?" look that Violet would have rolled her eyes at, had she seen it.

"No, yeah, of course," the photographer said. "Do you know how to work one of these?" he asked, looping the strap around Sam's neck. "This is the aperture—"

"I know," Sam said. "This is the zoom and focus." He put the camera to his eye with me in the frame. I leaned against the wall, arms crossed, one knee bent. Sam took my picture, then showed me the image

"I've had my photo taken thousands of times, Sam," I said. "Too many. But this one is my favorite."

He beamed with pride, and my damn heart cracked. I jerked my chin. "Go. Take as many pictures as you want." I turned to the photographer, cranking up that *I'm famous* smile. "You don't mind, right?"

"Uh, no. Not at all."

"Thanks!" Sam said and wandered, photographing everything in the room, including close-ups of the food on that goddamn buffet table. The journalist trailed after him and his thousand-dollar camera.

I called Brenda over. "Can you do me a favor? Let me know what these kids need. Anything they want, just tell me."

She smiled. "I will, thank you."

"Sam needs a camera. Send me the bill, okay?"

Brenda looked about to gush more thanks, but she read my expression. "Very well, Mr. Stratton."

"Everything okay?" Violet asked, joining me as I blinked hard, watching Sam take his pictures and smile and laugh like a little kid's supposed to.

"Everything's perfect."

CHAPTER THIRTY

MILLER

Showtime arrived. That night, the air felt electric. The crowds were pouring into the Key Arena at the Seattle Center, and Violet listened to the thunder above and around us from the green room, her eyes shining.

"They're all here to see you," she said.

An assistant poked his head in. "Yo, Miller. Time to roll."

"You know how crazy it gets in the front row," I said as we headed for the door. "You sure you can handle it?"

She ringed her arms around my neck. "I'm going to drown in it and love every minute of it, watching my rock star."

I rolled my eyes. "I hate that word."

"But you wear it so well." She kissed me softly, then grinned. "It won't throw you off, will it? Me being out there?"

I hauled her to me. She wore a tight white T-shirt and short black skirt. My gaze swept over her, taking in every detail. "Every show I've ever done, you're out there." I brushed my thumb against her lip. "I told you, Vi. It's all for you."

I watched her delicate neck move as she swallowed. "I love you too, Miller." She closed her eyes and kissed me, then hurried out where another assistant waited to take her down to the front row.

I joined the band and we took the stage together as the lights went down. A thunderous roar from the crowd went up. We huddled in the dark around Chad's drum set.

"You guys have been really fucking great, every show," I said. "I don't say that enough."

"Or ever," Antonio said with a laugh. "We've only been on tour with you for about six months."

"Yeah, yeah, yeah. I got my head out of my ass. Better late than never."

"It's all good, man," Robert, the other guitarist said. "Let's give them a hell of a show."

And we did. Goddamn, I'd never felt so alive on stage before in my life. The music flowed through me, amplified by the guys in the band. And Violet was there in the front row, swaying in a sea of faces, so goddamn beautiful.

I poured my heart out onto that stage, into the microphone, laying it all out there, leaving nothing back. And when it came time to sing "Wait for Me," it was just me on the stool, my acoustic guitar, and Violet.

Everything I hadn't said to her in the last two years rushed out of me. The longing, loneliness, love. God, the endless well of love I had for that woman, as if I were born with it already inside me, in my marrow and cells. She was in every part of me that was whole and good, and what was broken in me, she had dedicated her life to healing.

When the last note of the last song dissipated, the applause and cheers rolled through me. I absorbed every single bit of that energy until I felt invincible. Sweat-soaked and powerful. I strode off stage after performing for fifteen-thousand screaming fans, and for the first time, I let my ego have a moment. My blood ran hot in my veins with the dire need to have Violet.

She was waiting for me in the green room, and in one glance, I felt the same need from her. A bunch of other people were hanging around, congratulating me as soon as I stepped in the door. I ignored them, striding to Violet with a single-minded purpose.

"Can I talk to you?" I said to her in a low voice, practically a growl.

Her lips parted with a breathy little gasp. "Yes," she whispered. "*Yes.*"

I took her by the hand and led her out, though I wanted to throw her over my shoulder like a goddamn caveman. Behind the green room, the venue had an executive suite set aside for me. I locked the door behind us, lifted Violet without a word, and set her on the long counter that ran along one wall.

Her skirt and T-shirt clung to her curves, hiding nothing. I moved between her legs, kissing her ferociously, mauling her, my hands in her hair, while her hands tore at the buttons on my jeans, her need as dire as mine.

"It was one thing to see you open for Ed, but you..." she breathed between kisses, lifting my T-shirt off. "All those people there for you. Now I know why rock stars have as much sex as they want. Why women throw their panties...flash their boobs. I get it now." Her hands were everywhere on my heated skin. "That was sexiest thing I've ever seen in my life."

I had no words but to kiss her hard, sucking at her luscious lips that were red and sweet. Something primal in me was coming awake. I needed to have her. To possess her. For years, I'd been singing to her since we were kids, cherishing her with every breath I took. When I finally had her, we'd been torn apart, leaving me wanting her from across so many miles and continents. My heart had pined and ached and loved. And now she was here for good, and my heart and soul could relax while my body took over. I wanted to fuck her hard and raw. No more poetry. No more music but for the banging of the furniture, her cries of pleasure singing out, the slapping of flesh on flesh and my own feral grunts as I took her.

My hands slid up her thighs and came back down with her silk panties, already damp. I grabbed a condom from the pocket of my jeans before they could drop to my ankles, put there for this exact moment.

I held her face in one hand, the other sliding under her ass, hauling her to the edge of the bar. She spread her legs wider to let me in and cried out as I thrust hard.

"*Yes*," she hissed, her hands dropping to my hips to pull me tight to her. Deeper.

I bent over her, holding her hip with one hand, the other planted on the cool marble. Vi's ecstatic cries rang out, adding to the delirium of this mindless, raw possession.

"Miller, I'm..." Her entire body tensed against mine, cutting off her words, her arms wrapping around me, her legs locked at the ankles, holding me tight to her. Her core clenched around me as her orgasm swelled.

I felt it build in her, and I wanted that too. Greedy for all of her after having gone without. I slowed my thrusting hips, pulled nearly all the way out, and then pushed back in, coaxing and drawing her orgasm to a crest. She clung to me, arms, legs, and teeth that bit down on the slope of my neck, screaming her pleasure into my skin as the wave tossed her.

My own release was crashing toward me. I gave in to it, driving inside her with a last, furious frenzy, until the knot of heat and electricity at the base of my spine exploded out and into her. I gritted my teeth, my fingers digging into her hips hard enough to leave bruises, but I didn't want to let go.

She's here. She's mine.

"Yes," she breathed, her hands in my hair. "Yes, come in me."

My body obeyed. I came in a final, shuddering thrust, emptying myself into her before sagging against her.

For a few moments, the only sounds were the rasping of our breaths and the muffled sounds of the after-party in the green room. Slowly, Violet released me, arms and legs falling loose and heavy.

"Jesus Christ, Miller…" Violet said with a tired laugh, both of us bathed in sweat and breathing hard. "I just lived every woman in that arena's fantasy." Her voice softened. "Except, I get to have all of you."

I gave a tired laugh into the crook of her neck. "Even the possessive part that would make our caveman ancestors proud."

"I like it," she said, pushing me back enough to kiss me and trail her finger along my jaw. "No, I love it. I love how you make love to me and how you fuck me and how I still feel safe with you no matter which. I feel how much you love me, even when you turn into a beast." Her fingers went to the small bruises forming on her thigh.

"I never want to hurt you…" I said, alarmed.

"I want them. I want to feel marked by you. Inside and out. Because there's no one else, Miller. There never was, and there never will be."

Her words sunk deep into my chest, and this time, they stayed. I trusted them. And her. "I've wanted this for so long, Vi. Years."

"Me too. It took us a long time to get here."

My thumb traced her lips made swollen by my kisses. "We're here now."

CHAPTER THIRTY-ONE

VIOLET

We pulled ourselves together and joined the rest of the band, a few VIP fans, and the press in the green room. I was sure everyone would know what we'd done, but the room was thick with post-show adrenaline and celebration. Miller hung around long enough to take a few photos, then we returned to our hotel room.

Dr. Brighton performed a check-up, and they went over his insulin dosages, loading the pump affixed to his abdomen to account for the exertion of the concert and the food he'd eaten post-show. The doctor gave us a stern look.

"We'll need to account for any other 'exertions' you might feel inclined to partake in tonight."

Miller shook his head. "I'm beat. And besides, Violet knows I'm saving myself until marriage."

I snorted a laugh, and Brighton smirked. "I'll be back first thing in the morning."

Miller and I showered—separately, to avoid tempting *exertions*—and then dressed in sleep clothes, he in flannel pants and a V-neck undershirt while I wore one of his T-shirts and my shorts. We climbed into bed and became entangled. Miller sank heavily into his pillow.

"You okay?" I asked.

"The concert took it out of me. Actually, the concert wasn't the only thing that took it out of me."

"Ugh, terrible," I laughed, curling into him. I reached over and took his arm to read his watch.

"How am I looking, Doc?"

"You look perfect," I said. "You were amazing tonight. It was as if everything I love about you that you keep inside came out. That's why they come to see you, Miller. You shine."

He toyed with a lock of my hair and then let his hand fall heavily down. "I'm done with the tour. I'm going to cancel the rest of the dates."

I lifted my head off his chest. "You are? And do what?"

"Be with you."

Swift tears sprang to my eyes at the simple declaration.

He touched my cheek, smiling tiredly. "You were right, Vi. We're done saying goodbye. But you can't give up your school and everything you've worked for. We'll get a place in Waco, and when you're finished with the year, you can transfer to UCSC. If that's what you want."

"I do, but my scholarship is with Baylor."

"Your *home* is in Santa Cruz. If you don't let me handle your tuition, I'll go fucking crazy. We'll get a place by the ocean. Maybe I'll write a new album, a smaller album, while you study and be brilliant." He smiled, his eyes heavy. "We'll take care of each other. Okay?"

I nodded and kissed him softly. "Okay. I love you. So much."

"Love you, Vi…" he said, and that was the last thing he said to me before he slept.

I drifted off more slowly, floating on the currents of a new life that was just on the horizon.

An alarm jolted me out of the warm, sleepy comfort, and I sat up, blinking, Miller's name falling from my lips automatically. He was still sleeping, though his alarm was beeping frantically.

"Miller? Wake up." I flipped on the nightstand light. A cry caught in my throat. He trembled as if an electric current were running through him, breathing in short, hiccupping gasps. His face was as pale as the pillow.

"Oh my God…" My gaze darted to the numbers on his watch. Forty-five. Then forty-four… "*Oh my God.*"

Instantly, my mouth went dry, and my blood thrashed in my ears. The words *catastrophic hypoglycemic event* streaked across my mind, called up from my years of researching diabetes as a kid. Research I'd done for him. So this wouldn't happen.

A sense of preternatural calm came over me. The terror balled itself into a stone, and I pushed it down deep where it sat in my stomach so I could do what I had to do. I threw off the covers, rushed for the minifridge where his medicine was stored. Insulin to bring his blood sugar down if the numbers were high, and emergency syringes of glucagon if the numbers were low.

"Miller! Miller, I'm here," I said, my voice jagged with fear. I tore the plastic packaging off a glucagon injection pen. "Stay with me, Miller. Stay *right here*."

I climbed back onto the bed and pushed up the short sleeve of his undershirt. I pinched the skin with trembling fingers and injected the needle, depressing it until the vial was empty.

"Wake up, Miller." I tossed the syringe and reached for my phone on the nightstand. "Come on, baby, wake up."

I dialed 911 and put my fingers to Miller's neck while I waited for an answer. His pulse thumped so fast, I could hardly distinguish one beat from another.

"911, what is your emergency?"

Calmly but quickly, I explained the situation, watching Miller's numbers rise but not fast enough.

"He won't wake up. Please hurry. He won't wake up."

An eternity crammed itself into the next fifteen minutes—the time it took for EMTs to bust in the door. I scrambled out of their way, the ball of terror in my stomach wanting to rise up into my throat.

Chaos ensued as Miller's security team poured into the room with Brighton and a handful of assistants and tour managers. I threw on jeans, shoes, and a sweatshirt as the EMTs lifted Miller onto a gurney. Faces swam in front of me, but I pushed past them to stay with Miller. He still hadn't woken up.

The EMTs asked questions about his medical history as Brighton and I hurried alongside the gurney through the hotel. Guests were peeking out of doors, gawking at the commotion. I told the EMTs about his past and Brighton explained his more current issues. Miller's numbers had always been hard to manage, but my heart cracked to hear how he'd been struggling recently.

I demanded to ride with him to the hospital, afraid to let him out of my sight, even for a moment. Afraid if I looked away, he'd disappear. In the chaos of the jouncing ambulance, with EMTs talking over the beeping of machines, I sat beside Miller, held his limp hand in mine, and leaned over close. My face was on fire, still too panicked for tears. There wasn't a drop of water in my body.

"Stay with me. I mean it. Stay right here," I told him, over the thrashing of blood in my ears. "Stay with me, baby, please."

Under an oxygen mask, Miller remained pale, eyes closed, mouth half open and slack.

At the hospital, they whisked him away, out of my sight and to the ICU. Someone led me to the waiting room, just outside the swinging doors. Someone else gave me a glass of water.

Dr. Brighton arrived. He touched my shoulder in a fatherly gesture. "You did good," he said, then pushed through the ICU doors. Because he was a doctor and I wasn't.

Assistants and managers arrived to crowd the room. I recognized one young woman, Tina, as his new assistant, a phone pressed to her ear.

"His mom," I said in a hollow voice. "Someone call his mom."

Helplessness pressed down on me now that Miller's care was taken out of my hands. I had nothing to do but wait. The terror had gripped my heart in an icy fist and wouldn't let go. Finally, a young doctor with a bald head but a full dark beard came out looking for Miller's family. His face was inscrutable, no way to tell if he had good news or…

A flash of memory streaked across my vision: Miller climbing up the trellis and through my bedroom window. Miller and me, thirteen years old, lying in bed face to face. Miller sitting across from me, his guitar in his lap, singing songs he wrote for me and I never knew…

"Me," I said hoarsely, mustering every ounce of courage I had. "Me. You can tell me."

I'll take it. I'll take whatever it is because he's mine and I'm his. Always.

The doctor sat across from me, a quiet smile under his beard. His nametag read Dr. Julian Monroe.

"Miller is in a diabetic coma."

My head bobbed in a nod. "Yes. Okay."

"We've given him fluids and glucose, and he's now flitting in and out of consciousness. A very good sign."

My eyes fell shut as relief washed over me. "He's…awake?"

"Not yet but he's trying. Were you the one who administered the glucagon?"

I nodded. "He had no symptoms," I said in a small voice. "The night before, he had no symptoms. He was fine. He was perfect. I missed something. I should have known—"

Dr. Monroe cut me off. "You could not have known. Miller's insulin pump malfunctioned and administered far more than he required. I also understand from Dr. Brighton that Miller has struggled to control his diabetes throughout his life. Prolonged fluctuation of blood sugars can lead to a dangerous suppression of symptoms called hypoglycemic unawareness."

That term floated out from my childhood research too.

"I had no idea it was this bad. I should have…done something. Done more."

"There's nothing you could have done but what you did. We have him stabilized, and we're running more tests. Brittle diabetes is not typical. It's unpredictable and baffles even the best kind of care, which he was under with Dr. Brighton. To be honest, the real concern right now are his kidneys. Miller managed his diabetes on his own for quite a while, but I suspect that his unstable levels over the years have taken their toll."

"In what way?" I asked, though I already knew.

"The nephrologist will confirm, but it's likely he's developed chronic kidney disease."

I fought the urge to bury my head in my hands, but the doctor read my face.

"The early stages of chronic kidney disease show few signs or symptoms. It's often not apparent until kidney function is significantly impaired."

The words battered me, but Miller needed me to keep it together. To stay clearheaded and take care of him like a doctor would. "What happens next?"

"The first step is to get him to regain consciousness. The tests will determine what his exact kidney impairment is, and then we go from there." He smiled kindly. "One of the nurses will tell you when you can see him."

He left, and Tina bent into my line of vision. "Miller's mom is on the way."

"Great, thank you," I said, trying not to sound as helpless as I felt.

After another agonizing stretch of time, they let me into the ICU room. Inside, Miller was hooked up to a dozen different machines. IVs trailed lines into his arm, and a bedside glucose monitoring system showed his levels. A nurse was bent over him, coaxing him to open his eyes. Underneath his eyelids, they roll back and forth, fluttering open and then closing again. I joined her at the bedside.

"He's almost there," the nurse said with a kind smile. "Are you the girlfriend?"

"Yes."

"Talk to him, honey. He'll listen to you better than me."

"Miller," I said softly. "Miller, wake up. Wake up and look at me. Please."

His eyes opened, closed, and then opened again, glazed and unfocused. Then they met mine.

Relief so profound, it nearly took my legs out from under me, swept through me. I took his hand. "Hi, baby."

His face was still so pale beneath the scruff of his beard. "Vi," he croaked.

"There he is," the nurse said. "Welcome back, honey. Let me take a look at you."

She worked her way around the room, making checks and taking readings, while I dragged a chair next to the bed and sank down into it, feeling a sense of déjà vu. Another hospital, seven years ago.

"What happened?" he asked, turning his head slightly on the pillow.

"The pump malfunctioned and dumped too much insulin into your system," I said. "Your numbers dropped."

"That's the long answer." The nurse came around to check his IV lines. "Short answer: she saved your life, is what happened."

Miller's lips pulled back as he tried for a smile. "She did. A long time ago."

His eyes fell shut, and I looked at the nurse fearfully.

"He's just resting, sweetheart. You look like you could use some sleep, too."

"I'm fine." I wasn't about to leave that chair for anything, my hand welded to his.

Hours passed, and Miller came awake for a few minutes at a time, then slipped back into sleep. They ran more tests, and I watched Dr.

Monroe huddle at the door with the nephrologist, both of them looking grim.

Miller's mother arrived close to nine pm. I'd only seen Lois Stratton a handful of times when I was in high school. She'd always looked tired and gray before her time. Miller had moved her to a bright apartment in Los Angeles, and now she seemed healthier and vibrant, though her face was painted with worry.

She rushed to Miller's side, her gaze inspecting him frantically. "I thought he'd woken up. They told me it was a coma but that he woke up."

"He did," I said. "He's sleeping now."

She sagged into a chair. "My sweet boy," she said, then looked at me tearfully. "Oh, Violet. Thank you, sweetheart. I'm so grateful you were there when he needed you most. Both times. The night in your backyard and now. The highest high and the lowest low."

"I should have been with him everywhere in between. The entire time. I could've taken care of him."

"That was my job first." She sniffed and wiped her eyes. "I left him, too, in a way. I left him to take care of himself. I brought bad things into his life because I was so tired. I needed help and didn't have any."

"You did the best you could," I said.

"And so did you."

A warm moment passed between us, the two people who loved Miller best.

A social worker entered, carrying a bouquet of flowers. "From someone named Brenda at Helping Hands. I'll just put them by the window."

She set the bright yellow daisies mixed with white roses on the windowsill, offered to bring us both coffee, and left.

"Helping Hands?" Lois asked, both of us talking in hushed voices. "Is that the charity Miller's going to give all that money to?"

I nodded. "For homeless families."

She smiled sadly. "Of course. He was adamant about doing something to give back. But even before he got famous, he had a compassionate streak in him. Injustice made him sad. And angry. Even as a child."

"There's nothing sadder than a birthday cake with only one piece cut out."

"I can think of a hundred things sadder," Miller said.

I smiled to myself. "He was like that when we met."

"He was born with it, I think. Certainly, Ray and I didn't teach it to him. We were so young when we had him. Hardly more than twenty years old, like you both are now."

With a soft smile, Lois brushed a lock of hair off Miller's brow, a reflexive action she'd probably done a thousand times when he was little.

"Once, he and another boy were playing in the sandbox," she said. "Miller must've been three years old; the other boy was a little bit older. This older boy reached out and snatched the plastic shovel out of Miller's hand and snapped it in two. I hurried over and scolded him, expecting to have to comfort Miller over his broken shovel. Instead, he just looked bewildered. It's hard to imagine such a look on the face of a three-year-old. He didn't cry. He only wanted to know why. 'Why did he do that, Mama?' He couldn't comprehend it, the cruelty of it."

Lois smiled fondly at her son.

"He was that way for a long time. Open. Curious about life. I think that's where he got his talent for writing songs. He had observations about life, and he wrote them down with music from that guitar Ray gave him. His most prized possession." She sighed heavily. "But everything changed when Ray left. Miller shut down. Turned guarded. He didn't want to love anything anymore. If he played music, I never heard it. That broke my heart."

Lois looked up at me over Miller's sleeping form.

"And then you came along. You opened his heart, Violet. I know that Evelyn woman gets a lot of credit for discovering Miller, but he sang for you first. You are the reason he has the career that he has. Because he loves you so much, he couldn't contain it. Even when he pushed you away, I knew. I always knew you were his girl."

His girl. I've always been his girl.

"I think I did, too," I said, smiling through tears. "Even when I didn't."

CHAPTER THIRTY-TWO

MILLER

I opened my eyes to see sunlight streaming in from the window at the end of the small room. My body felt welded to the bed, heavy and weak. Violet was there, her head pillowed on my mattress, her hand clasped in mine.

She hadn't left my side in the two days since I'd been moved out of the ICU. Two days in which Dr. Monroe and his team performed every test under the sun and gave me the solemn news that my kidneys, like my pancreas, had quit on me. A dialysis machine had been added to the bank of machines in the room, and my name had been added to the miles-long donor waitlist. And because my diabetes would only destroy whatever kidneys might become available, I could only be approved for a simultaneous pancreas-kidney transplantation.

"A whole do-over in my guts," I'd said to Violet to try to make her laugh when she'd wanted to cry. She'd held my hand through it all, and that old guilt found me, too, that I put her through this again.

That morning, she sensed my waking and raised her head and smiled tiredly at me. "Hey, you."

"Where's Mom?"

"She went down to the cafeteria to grab a coffee. How are you feeling?"

"Ready to get out of here."

"They said it could be soon. Tomorrow maybe."

Because there's no donor match.

She smiled wanly and wouldn't meet my eyes.

"Vi, what's wrong? Aside from…" I waved my hand. "All of this."

"Nothing. Just tired."

"You forget I have your every expression memorized. Something's wrong, and it's not just my shitty kidneys."

Violet pretended to think. "That's a punk band, isn't it? The Shitty Kidneys? I think they headlined Burning Man…"

"Tell me."

She plucked a thread on the sheet. "I had myself tested to see if I could be a donor for you. Your mom did, too. But we're not compatible."

I pulled her to me. "I disagree. I think we're really fucking compatible."

Violet sniffed a laugh and climbed on the bed, burrowing into me. She rested her head against my chest, and we lay in the relative quiet of beeping machines, me stroking her hair that was black against the white of my shirt.

"You're going to be okay, Miller," she said. "I'll make sure of it."

"Are you really going to give up being a surgeon?"

"I'm not giving it up; I'm moving it out of my way. I was meant to take care of you, and I will. There's hemodialysis that you can do at home. I'm going to learn everything I can about it while we wait for a donor."

I pressed my lips into her hair, kissing her and holding her tight to me. She was making it sound easier than it would be. There was a shortage of organ donors; I could be waiting for years, and we both knew it.

The next day, I was packing my shit to leave while Violet wrangled all the balloons, bouquets, and stacks of get-well cards from fans that covered every available surface of the window ledge.

"It looks like someone emptied the goddamn giftshop in here," I muttered.

"Your fans love you." Violet flipped around a card to show me the front. A photo of me in the green room at the Key Arena. "From Sam. Don't read what he wrote inside unless you're ready to cry for three days straight."

"What's this about crying?" Dr. Monroe entered the room, a tight, strange smile on his face. "No crying when I have good news. A match has been found."

The card fell out of Violet's hand. I dropped the shirt I'd been putting in a small travel bag. "What? Already?"

"We need to run a few more tests, but I feel confident we can schedule surgery for the day after tomorrow."

"That's amazing," Violet said, reluctant hope wanting to bloom over her features. "Oh my God…"

"But the Donor Network said the wait time could be years," I said. "They found a match already?"

"For one kidney and partial pancreas, yes."

Violet and I exchanged glances. "So, it's from a living donor," I said. Pancreases, it turned out, like livers and lungs, could be portioned out to give the recipient part of the organ without harm to the donor.

Dr. Monroe rocked on his heels. "This will change your life, Miller. No more insulin shots, no more highs and lows…"

"Who?" I asked, going cold all over. "Who's the donor?"

Dr. Monroe shifted. "I'm afraid I can't speak anymore to that. Confidentiality is of upmost importance in situations like this—"

"Tell me."

"Miller, I—"

"It's my dad. My dad's the donor. Isn't he?"

Dr. Monroe's expression shifted, a miniscule wince, and I knew I was right. I sank down on the bed. "Holy shit."

The doctor cleared his throat. "Protocol dictates that you'll need to speak to Alice, from the Donor Network before any—"

"No," I said, getting back to my feet. "Tell Alice—tell *Ray* that I don't want his fucking donation. Wait, you said we could do the surgery in two days?" My blood ran hot in my veins. "He's here, isn't he?"

Violet moved to put a soothing hand on my arm. "Miller, let's stay calm…"

Dr. Monroe wore a sympathetic expression. "I understand it's a complicated situation—"

"It's not fucking complicated," I snapped. "It's really damn easy. I don't want his help. Tell him to go back to wherever he's been for the past seven years and stay there."

"You have the right to consent or not for this procedure," Dr. Monroe said, trying for calm. "But I have to advise you that if you turn this down, you will spend whatever time it takes to find a suitable match with the same dangerous, wildly fluctuating glucose levels, compounded by chronic kidney failure. You'll need to set aside three days a week to spend four hours a day on a dialysis machine until that donor becomes available." His face softened. "He's a perfect match, Miller. One in a million. Please think very carefully before you make any decisions."

I gritted my teeth and waited until he was gone.

Violet slipped her hand in mine. "Miller…"

"No fucking way."

"Listen to what Dr. Monroe said."

"I heard what he said, and I'm not doing it, Vi. When Dad left, I vowed that no matter what happened, I would never need him again. Ever. And I did it. I took care of Mom and…" The emotions were rising in my throat, threatening to choke me. Stinging my eyes. "It's not right. It's not fucking right that he shows up after all this time. And when he does, it's for *this*? A fucking organ transplant that I'd be an idiot to refuse?"

I went past her to pace the small space in front of the window. A giant aluminum balloon with a yellow happy face drifted in front of me. I punched it out of my way.

"I know," Violet said gently. "It's a lot."

"It's too much. I can't say no, right? I'm a fucking idiot if I say no. If I say yes, I betray every fucking thing I worked so hard for."

She moved to stand beside me. "It only feels that way because you haven't reconciled with him. Or tried. Talk to him, please. Talk to him first before you decide anything."

I shook my head, wiping my eyes on the shoulder of my T-shirt. "What the hell do I say to him, Vi?"

"Everything, Miller, that you've ever wanted to say to him."

"That's too much." I shook my head, the armor I'd forged in the fire of abandonment reforming around me. "No, forget it. He doesn't get to do this. This is not how it happens."

"Miller," she said, pleading. "You need this. You need his help."

"Not like this."

"Miller…"

"I'm checking the hell out of here. I'll get through this the same way I have for the last seven years. Without his fucking help."

"And I'm supposed to be okay with this?" Violet said, her voice rising, tears standing out in her eyes. "You're sick, Miller. And your dad is trying to do what parents are supposed to do. Make it better."

I closed my eyes, willing her words not to seep in between the cracks in my wall. But I was so tired of fighting. Tired of carrying the pain around with me.

It's making me sick.

Violet took my hand again, her voice softer, soothing. The voice she would use with her own patients a decade from now.

"You have the right to be angry and hurt, but it's eating you up inside. Stop holding yourself back from him. Holding back to keep from being hurt never did either of us any good." She held the back of my hand to her lips. "Talk to him. Not for his sake, for yours. Give yourself some peace."

I stared at the ceiling, then at Violet's beautiful face. The anguish in her eyes, the same as it had been seven years ago. The same as it had been every time I pushed her away and hated myself for it later.

But God, how could I look my mom in the eye?

I shook my head. "I can't do it. Even if I wanted to…" I cleared my throat. "I can't do that to my mom. It'd be a betrayal."

"I already know," Mom said, stepping into the room. "About Ray? I'm sorry, I didn't mean to eavesdrop. He's been calling me too." She smiled kindly at Violet "Can you give us a minute, sweetheart?"

"Of course." She gave my hand a final squeeze and went out.

"You talked to him?" I asked Mom. "When?"

"Last week. He was asking about you. Worried."

"And you're okay, talking to him after so long? After what he did?"

"Not at first. But when you threw Chet out of the house in Santa Cruz, it was like coming out of a trance. I'd let that man hurt you and that was unforgiveable. But you forgave me."

I swallowed hard. "It's not the same thing."

"I wasn't there for you when I should've been," Mom said. "Chet was gone and it was a second chance. I vowed that I was done letting men dictate my life. When your dad called last week, I was afraid to pick up. But my God, I'm tired of being afraid. So I answered. And I'm so glad I did. We'll never be friends, but I don't have to carry him around with me anymore. I let him go."

"Is that why he's here now?"

"He's here for you. No other reason." She took my hand. "If you want to say no to him, that's up to you. But don't do it for my sake. I'm your mother. The only thing a mother wants is for her child to be healthy and happy." She smoothed a stray lock of hair off my brow. "It's not too much to hope you could be both."

The next morning, I dressed in jeans and a T-shirt. I'd agreed to meet with my dad but not in my goddamn hospital room with me looking pathetic and weak. Someone he felt sorry for. But a glance in the mirror showed I did look pathetic and weak. Pale and drawn and at least ten pounds lighter than when I checked in.

The hospital had a garden on the grounds with winding paths and a Celtic labyrinth painted on the cement. Under a bright sun, I walked the labyrinth, head down, hands in my pockets, following the path that curved in on itself, round and round.

"Miller."

The voice froze me in place. I hadn't heard it in seven years. Hadn't heard my name in that voice in seven years. Slowly, I turned. My own eyes stared back at me.

My dad stood next to a bench that fronted the labyrinth, hands in the pockets of his jeans too. I had a vision of myself in twenty years. His skin darker, from working outside maybe, but the resemblance was so stark, it was hard to look at him.

A thousand emotions battered my heart. A thousand thoughts swirled in my mind, none louder than *this was the man who'd abandoned Mom and me and left us homeless*. And yet, I nearly let myself soften to him.

"You look good," he said.

"No, I don't."

"Okay, maybe not like you usually do. But you look good to me. Seeing you right now…" He cleared his throat. "I've been calling."

"I know."

"I don't blame you for not wanting to talk. I don't know where to start."

"Neither do I," I admitted.

He sat down on the bench, rested his elbows on his long legs. Exactly the same way I did.

"I read the magazine article," he said. "How long have you had it?"

"Diabetes? Since I was thirteen. That's something, as my father, you probably should have been aware of."

"I know. I'm not here to ask for forgiveness. Or to take a piece of your fortune."

"What do you want?"

"To help. My wife, Sally, read the magazine article. Sounded like you were in trouble."

I winced, feeling like he'd punched me in the stomach with all the things about his life I didn't know. "My mother is your wife," I said acidly. "But I guess you forgot that."

He glanced down at his hands in his lap. "Sally is the woman I left your mom for."

"That's why you abandoned us? Another woman?" My emotions were bubbling to the surface, but I willed them back, buried them under the anger, spewing venom at my father. "Jesus, you're a fucking cliché. You couldn't keep it in your pants, so you decided to follow your dick, leaving us homeless. Mom couldn't pay the bills when you bailed, so we lived in the station wagon. Did you know that? Or did fucking Sally read it in *Rolling Stone*?"

"I'm sorry, Miller," his voice gruff but hard. "I was young and stupid, and I did the wrong thing. But I fell in love with her."

"You fell in love with her?" I barked a harsh laugh. "That's supposed to make it all better? Marriages fall to shit because people fall in love with other people, but they don't *fall out of love with their kids*."

"I never did," my dad said, his eyes shining. "I promise you I didn't. And I expect nothing from you. Not one thing. Not even your forgiveness. But I have nothing else to give you. You don't need my money anymore. You needed it a long time ago. I gave up my right to be your father a long time ago, too. But you're sick and I can help you get better."

I scrubbed my face with both hands. "Jesus, Violet said the exact same thing."

"Your girlfriend?"

I nodded.

"She pretty?"

"Beautiful."

"You in love with her?"

"She's the only reason we're talking right now. I was going to tell you to fuck off. Even if it killed me."

"Stubborn," he said with a proud smile, tears in his eyes. "Just like always. God, look at you. All grown."

"Dad…" I swallowed hard. "Don't."

"Let me do this for you, and then I'll go," he said hoarsely. "You don't have to talk to me or see me. You don't have to invite me into your life. I just want to make sure you have one."

"To make yourself feel better?" I asked, my voice cracking, tears threatening. I hated how his pain drew mine out, melting the hard armor of anger and leaving only the raw, naked wounds. "Is that the only reason?"

He got to his feet. "No. That's not why."

"Because it's a good one, Dad. Only a jackass would turn it down. Did you count on that? That I'd have no real choice? Well, I do." I felt cracked open, seven years of pain pouring out of me. "I can take your *donation* and still not forgive you. I won't forgive you. I won't…"

Wordlessly, he put his arms around me, and I was suddenly transported into a thousand childhood memories of my dad's embrace. They overwhelmed me, and I clung to them, clung to him. Real and solid, flesh and blood.

"I'm sorry," he said, his rough hands in my hair, grasping my shirt. "I'm so sorry."

Over and over he said it, and each time, the words sank deeper.

Until I finally let them in.

CHAPTER THIRTY-THREE

VIOLET

I walked the overly bright corridors, lit up like midday, despite it being near midnight. Night and day held no distinction in hospitals, which was fitting, I thought. Nor did it hold a distinction to the people who had loved ones lying in beds here. Hours melted together, punctuated by news—good or bad—that altered the entire course of the next handful of hours. Or a lifetime.

"You going to play something for us, Violet?" one of the nurses asked as I passed, Miller's guitar case secure in my grip.

"You deserve better than that, Eric," I teased.

He laughed, and I continued down to the end of the hallway, to Miller's room. Margarite, the duty nurse that night, greeted me with a warm smile.

"It's late," she said. "Big day tomorrow."

"I won't keep him up. But we have a guitar lesson scheduled. Can't miss it."

"I'm sure." She chuckled. "Have fun. But not *too* much fun."

I smiled, though my chest tightened. No, not too much fun the night before major surgery. But Miller had asked me to come back after visiting hours, and I wasn't about to leave, so long as he wanted me there.

He sat on the edge of the bed, on top of the covers; he hated the helpless feeling of lying down, and he absolutely hated the gown. Instead, he wore flannel pants and an undershirt, his eyes full of thoughts.

"Hey," I said, sitting down beside him, his guitar case resting on my knees. I kissed his cheek, his lips, brushed his hair back from his eyes. "Thinking about tomorrow?"

"Tomorrow and every day after," he said. "If I have them."

"You will," I said fiercely, a shiver skimming over my skin.

"I shouldn't talk like that to you, but…"

"It's okay," I said. "I'm scared too. But they're going to take care of you, and when it's over, you'll have a new life."

We'll have a new life.

Miller unlatched the case and retrieved his guitar. "We've been here before. Seven years ago. That was the day you saved my life. Feels like a lifetime."

"I think you saved mine that day too," I said. "That's when I knew I was in love with you. A pretty big revelation for a thirteen-year-old. I didn't know what to do with it all."

Miller turned to sit with his back against the mattress, raised all the way up.

"Come here." He made room for me as I climbed onto the bed, my back to his chest. He set the guitar in my lap, his arms reaching around me. "I don't know what to do with it all, either. Or mess it up with words. I want you to feel it, Vi."

I leaned back against him to give him room, his cheek brushing mine. I could feel his heart thump against me, a steady beat that kept time. The first notes of our song reverberated through me, joined by Miller's singing, low and rough, as he strummed the guitar gently.

"You know, you know I love you so…"

Miller's playing stopped abruptly, and he pushed the guitar away. He wrapped me up in him and pressed his face to my neck.

"I'm here." I held him, trying to be the anchor he'd so often been for me, when my world felt like it was coming apart. "Are you…scared?"

"Only of leaving you."

I closed my eyes. "You won't. I won't let you."

His chest rose and fell against my back in a heavy sigh. "I want to marry you, Vi. I want to grow old with you. I want to celebrate wedding anniversaries with you that make people stand up and applaud when they hear the number. I want to tell people that you're the love of my life and that I knew that was true because I met you when I was thirteen years old. And that was it. There was never going to be anyone else."

I turned in the circle of his arms, a tremulous smile on my lips. *What are you asking?*

He read my thoughts as he so often did. "I don't know what's going to happen tomorrow, so I'm just putting it out there to who or whatever's listening that if I get the chance, I'm not going to screw it up again."

"Neither will I," I said. "I'll just put that out there too. To who or whatever might be listening."

Happiness shone behind Miller's eyes. Elusive. He never trusted it to stay, and I vowed to do everything in my power to give it to him, every day.

He kissed me, and despite the fear, a lightness swelled in my chest. Hope. I fed it instead of the fear and smiled into our kiss. A pact that sealed the proposals and vows permeating that hospital room but waited for another day to be made real.

I knew that day would come. Miller and I ebbed and flowed, but we always came back. Inevitable as the tide and beautiful in the end.

EPILOGUE

MILLER

Three years later…

I see her the minute I take the stage. Even among a thousand faces in the festival crowd and wearing a floppy hat to protect her fair skin, I recognize Violet immediately. She's standing with Sam. He's getting taller, filling out more from the skinny boy we fostered six months ago. He has a camera up to his eye, snapping photos of the crowd, the festival tents, and me and my band on stage.

My family.

We didn't plan for this to happen so soon. Violet still has her residency to complete, but Brenda from Helping Hands International called me and said it was an emergency. The foster family that Sam had been staying with was moving and they weren't taking him with them.

I could only imagine how that felt. Like a family pet left behind, too inconvenient to take with. It wasn't the foster family's fault, necessarily. That's how the system works; people coming and going in Sam's life so that he knows not to get too attached. But Jesus, he's eleven years old. He shouldn't have to protect himself like that.

That's a parent's job.

It was supposed to be temporary, until the agency could find a permanent placement for Sam. But it became pretty obvious, pretty quick that Violet wasn't going to let him go.

I can't either, but God, I love how she loves him. We're young and she's busy as hell, working her ass off at UC San Francisco, but she made room for Sam in our home and in her heart immediately.

She's still on track to be an endocrinologist, even though the transplant I received from my dad essentially turned me into a former diabetic. But Vi didn't change her course solely for me, anyway. She just found her passion. I like to joke that she started med school when she was thirteen, taking care of me. I know she's going to be an incredible doctor, and I have been doing everything in my power to make sure that her runway is as free of obstacles as possible.

After the Seattle concert three years ago and my hospitalization, I took a lot of time off. The plan was to stay in Texas while Violet finished her studies at Baylor, but she missed Santa Cruz too much. Reluctantly, she allowed me to take over her tuition so that she could go to UCSC just like she'd always dreamed. She finished her undergrad and then began medical school in San Francisco. We got a place in the Marina district with views of the Bay and Alcatraz, and I wrote an album. If you can call lyrics scratched into a notebook an album. But that's how I started too. Thirteen years old, putting Violet in my music.

I quit touring to recuperate from surgery and my dad kept his promise. Once the surgery was over, he went back to Oregon to be with his wife. We email now and then; he likes to joke that he's checking in to see how his internal organs are doing and scold them if they're giving me a hard time. For the most part, they're not. I have to take immunosuppressant drugs, but he was a near perfect match. Thanks to him, my life has become vastly easier. A tremendous gift and a bridge toward the two of us maybe someday having a relationship outside of an email or two.

But there's no rush. I'm taking my time and letting it unfold as it should. Not holding back but not throwing myself forward either.

When I was well enough, and when the songs I'd been writing began to take real shape, I flew down to Los Angeles to record an album. But no touring. This festival in Mountain View, California is the first performance and the last performance I'll give for a while.

I can't just takeoff now. I have a family to think of.

The thought nearly makes me burst out laughing with crazy fucking happiness into the mic before I greet the crowd. I look down at Violet standing with Sam and a huge swell of love washes over me. Love mixed with fear, the kind that prompted my father to come out of hiding to help me. The love of a father for his son.

From under her big floppy hat, Violet gives me a knowing smile as her arm goes around Sam's shoulders. I wonder how I'm going to make it through the set.

Me and the guys, my band that had toured with me three years ago, play a set of songs off the new album mixed with some old standbys. I don't sing "Wait for Me" much anymore. I don't need to.

Our set ends, and it's clear three years of relative quiet didn't diminish the enthusiasm of my fans like I thought it would. They stuck with me through that quiet time of recovery and I'm so grateful for that. I'm finally able to appreciate everything that comes with this crazy job. I give them everything I have on stage, but they give it back to me, tenfold.

A bunch of the other guys are going to hang around and watch the other bands.

"Do you want to come?" Antonio asks. "There are some killer acts here."

"No doubt," I say, "but I have plans."

A ball of tingling excitement expands in my chest, completely different than anything I've ever experienced before, and more powerful than what I feel when I take the stage in front of twenty-thousand fans.

I slip out from behind the stage tent into a hot afternoon, and my security team and assistants hustle me into a waiting car to take me to the hotel.

"Who's got Vi and Sam?" I ask Franklin, my head of security.

"Morris is going to drive them over, ten minutes behind you."

"Awesome. Thanks, man."

At the hotel, Tina meets me in the lobby and she's already beaming. Tina became my indispensable right hand now that Evelyn is off working her way up in a PR company based out of Los Angeles. I have no doubt she'll will be a huge success. She has a way of bending the universe to conform to her will.

Inside the hotel room, a gift wrapped in blue paper with a green ribbon sits on the coffee table, a thick white envelope on top of it.

"It's the kind he wanted, right?" I ask Tina.

"Canon EF 24," she says.

I nod and rub my hands together to give them something to do.

Tina reads my nervousness and wordlessly hands me a bottle of water. "He's going to love it."

"Thanks, Tina. I hope so," I say, but it's not the camera lens that's making my stomach tie itself in knots.

I want Sam to have the best. He's only eleven but his talent is already apparent. Some people just know what they're meant to do early on. I did and so did Violet. But so many others have to toil at jobs they hate to make ends meet while their true passion stifles and withers for lack of use. So I started a foundation that helps fund arts programs for underprivileged kids. I would love to give the finger to the idea that one has to be lucky, or rich, or have the right set of circumstances align in order to make someone's passion their job.

Twenty minutes later, Violet and Sam arrive. I clear everybody out and Violet crosses to me immediately, taking off her hat and glasses. The same nervous excitement that's roiling in me lights up her eyes.

She kisses me. "Are you ready?"

"No." I laugh. "Are you?"

"I don't know," she says honestly. "But I'm going to do my absolute best. It's all we can do, right?"

"It's what you always do," I say. "It's what you've given to me."

"Same, love," she says. "We take care of each other." We both turn and look to where Sam is hovering around the coffee table, circling the gift uncertainly. "Now we're going to take care of him."

An ache grips my heart, watching the little boy study the present. The label has his name written clearly on it and he's still not sure it's for him.

"What is this?" he asks.

Violet and I join him at the table. "Why don't you open it and see?" she says.

Sam starts for the thick white envelope. "You're always supposed to start with the card before the gift," he says solemnly because he's a solemn little kid who's trained himself to be as polite as he can be in the hopes whoever is fostering him will keep him longer. Slow to laugh, cautious about letting in too much happiness. I could relate.

"Not this time, buddy," I say and take the envelope away from him, hoping he won't notice how my hands are trembling. "This time around, you start with the gift."

"Okay," he says and slowly, meticulously unwraps the present, careful not to tear the paper. To save it or maybe because he thinks he'll have to rewrap it when he's done and give it back.

I see Violet's thoughts are following the same train, her eyes shining, watching the little boy hesitantly open a present that he should already know is his.

"Oh, this is a very nice lens!" he says, almost formally, his eyes wide and a smile finally breaking over his face. "Just what I needed. It's the best one too. Thank you so much."

He hugs Violet and then me, quickly letting go. In the few months he's been with us, he treats us like the wrapping paper too; gently, careful not to tear anything, careful not to make us angry for fear we might send him back.

Violet and I spend every waking hour trying to show him that will never happen, but he's been let down too many times.

"Now can I open the card?" he asks. Violet and I sit down together on the couch, her hand clasped tightly in mine.

"Yeah," I say roughly. "You can open it."

"It's awfully thick for a card," Sam says.

I nod, not trusting my voice. Violet already has a tissue pressed to her mouth.

Sam opens the envelope and pulls out a sheaf of papers from the California Health and Human Services Department.

"What is this?" he asks and then reads the words at the top. The papers drop from his hands, and his chin drops to his chest.

"What do you think, Sam?" I ask, my voice fraying at the edges.

He manages to raise his chin, taking in both Violet and me. "Does this mean I get to stay?"

"Yes, baby," Vi says, tears streaming down her cheeks. "Would you like that? Would you like to stay with us?"

He doesn't answer, the disbelief is too strong. "You're adopting me?" Once the word leaves his mouth, his shoulders start to shake, and the tears fall. He covers his eyes with his hands.

Violet and I both shoot off the couch to either side of him, hugging him between us.

"We love you, buddy," I say. "We don't ever want you to go."

He nods, unable to speak and then he hugs Violet tight. She meets my eye over his little shoulders, smiling through tears in the most beautiful expression of pure joy I've ever seen her wear.

Then Sam turns and hugs me, but it's not like any hug he's ever given me before. He lets himself go, surrenders to the happiness. I hug him just as tightly, hoping that he can feel how permanent it is, this love I feel for him.

I look over at Violet, tears in her eyes as a thousand words pass between us. This is only the beginning of our happiness. Our future stretches out before us on parallel paths, never diverging, carrying us toward something beautiful.

And there's no holding back.

The End

AUTHOR'S NOTE

When I first set out to write this novel, I had no idea what would befall Miller in terms of his diabetes. I knew it would be something that he had but would not be defined by, but I actually had no idea how serious it was. When it became clear to me that he would need an organ transplant—a kidney transplant specifically—I suddenly knew where it had all been leading and why. Trigger warning: child loss. Izzy was an organ donor. Her kidneys saved the life of a woman in another state and over the course of that agonizing process, we found grace in knowing that she was saving another life. But for many people on transplant lists, the wait is very long. There are misconceptions about organ donation, and many grieving family members fail to honor a donor's wishes for various reasons, all of which lead to major shortages and long waits. I didn't set out to write about something that touched me this personally, but I know that that is unavoidable for as long as I write.

For more information on organ donation, please visit:
www.organdonor.gov

ACKNOWLEDGMENTS

This novel was written at such a tumultuous time in my life. I've never struggled so hard or put so many hours in to find the story that was trying to break free. I did, eventually, with the help of some amazing people.

Joanna Louise Weightman, you are an angel walking among us. Thank you for your honesty, time, and your generous, loving support that never wavered.

Nina Grinstead and your entire team at Valentine PR. I don't know how you fell into my life but I'm grateful every day that you did.

Rebecca Fairest Reviews, you did not sign up to support and nurture an emotional mess such as myself, but that's what you got, and you truly touched my heart with your sweet care and consideration of me. Thank you, always.

Colin Johnson and Katie Mielke, thank you for generously sharing with me your experiences with diabetes to help this poor romance author try to understand this complex disease and its equally complex day-to-day management. I know that I have only scratched the surface of it in this book. Any and all mistakes are mine, but thanks to you, I hope there are fewer of them. With love, and gratitude.

Lori Jackson, you are a genius! Thank you for bringing my Miller to life with your beautiful cover, and for being your wonderful self. Love you.

Angela Bonnie, someday I will give you a finished manuscript and you will have all the time in the world to work your formatting magic over it. This was not that day. Thank you for putting up with me and being so kind about it. Love you.

Thank you to Rich Trapp and Joshua Lopez of Future Ghost Brothers for stepping up HUGE and coming through for me with my crazy idea to turn my lyrics into actual songs. I am blown away by your artistry and cannot thank you enough for sharing it with me.

Joy Kriebel-Sadowski, thank you for slogging through the roughest of drafts and for being there for me for every book. You are a universe.

Melissa Panio-Petersen, you are the glue that holds me together, most days. Thank you keeping for everything afloat while I'm chained to my desk and continuing your billion-year streak of being the most thoughtful person I know. Love you.

My husband, Bill. Over the last few months of this quarantine, you have completely managed the entire household—even and especially as we prepare to move—while taking care of Talia, and solely handling her distance-learning schooling. You are the kind of man women write about in romance novels. Love you, always.

And to Robin Hill. This book would literally not exist without you and that's not hyperbole. No one can know how much time and effort and your own writerly artistry went into helping me, but I do. And I will never forget. Thank you doesn't feel like enough. Love you so much, I might even write some #RoHo4eva fanfic just to prove it. Thank you.

And thank you readers and bloggers. I will never run out of gratitude for your uplifting care and support of me and each other. This community, romancelandia, is my second family and I love you all. Thank you <3

Stay in Touch: Visit www.emmascottwrites.com to subscribe to my newsletter and never miss a release!

Listen to both tracks of original songs by Future Ghost Brothers and Emma Scott here: https://spoti.fi/36JGZdd

SNEAK PEEK

When You Come Back To Me, Lost Boys Book 2

Holden and River's story, coming this summer

Add to your Goodreads TBR: http://bit.ly/37BsCHh

ALSO BY EMMA SCOTT

A Five-Minute Life
Keep me wild, keep me safe...

"It's one of the best books I've ever read."—T.M. Frazier, *USA Today* Bestselling author of *King*

Bring Down the Stars (Beautiful Hearts Book 1)
For you, I would bring down the stars...

"I was not expecting to feel so lost. So emotional. So desperately in love with EVERYONE AND EVERYTHING about this novel."—***Angie & Jessica's Dreamy Reads***

Long Live the Beautiful Hearts (Beautiful Hearts Book 2)
Long live the beautiful hearts like yours...

"*INFINITE STARS* BEAUTIFUL. EXQUISITE. LITERARY PERFECTION!!"—
Patty Belongs to . . . Top Goodreads Reviewer

In Harmony
Never doubt I love...

"I am irrevocably in love with IN HARMONY."—**Katy Regnery, *New York Times* Bestselling Author**

"Told through Shakespeare's masterful Hamlet in the era of #metoo, In

Harmony is a deeply moving and brutally honest story of survival after shattering, of life after feeling dead inside. If you've ever been a victim of abuse or assault, this book speaks directly to you. This is a 6 star and LIFETIME READ!!!"—**Karen, Bookalicious Babes Blog**

Forever Right Now

You're a tornado, Darlene. I'm swept up.

"*Forever Right Now* is full of heart and soul—rarely does a book impact me like this one did. Emma Scott has a new forever fan in me."—***New York Times* bestselling author of *Archer's Voice,* Mia Sheridan**

How to Save a Life (Dreamcatcher #1)

Let's do something really crazy and trust each other.

"You're in for a roller coaster of emotions and a story that will grip you from the beginning to the very end. This is a MUST READ…"—**Book Boyfriend Blog**

Full Tilt

I would love you forever, if I only had the chance…

"Full of life, love and glorious feels."—***New York Daily News*, Top Ten Hottest Reads of 2016**

All In (Full Tilt #2)

Love has no limits…

"A masterpiece!"—**AC Book Blog**

Never miss a new release or sale!

Visit www.emmascottwrites.com to subscribe to Emma's super cute, non-spammy newsletter!

Made in the USA
Middletown, DE
22 August 2024

59028136R00210